SUSANNA GREGORY

Intrigue in Covent Garden

sphere

SPHERE

First published in Great Britain in 2018 by Sphere
This paperback edition published in 2019 by Sphere

1 3 5 7 9 10 8 6 4 2

A CIP catalogue record for this book
is available from the British Library.

ISBN 978-0-7515-6270-5

Typeset in New Baskerville by Palimpsest Book Production Limited,
Falkirk, Stirlingshire
Printed and bound in Great Britain by Clays Ltd, Elcograf S.p.A.

Papers used by Sphere are from well-managed forests
and other responsible sources.

MIX
Paper from
responsible sources
FSC® C104740

Sphere
An imprint of
Little, Brown Book Group
Carmelite House
50 Victoria Embankment
London
EC4Y 0DZ

An Hachette UK Company
www.hachette.co.uk

www.littlebrown.co.uk

For my dear Book Club friends from Wright's Food Emporium:
Caroline and Michael Daymond
Carwen and Stephen Earles
Veronika Hurbis and Paul Cleghorn
Rob Gittins

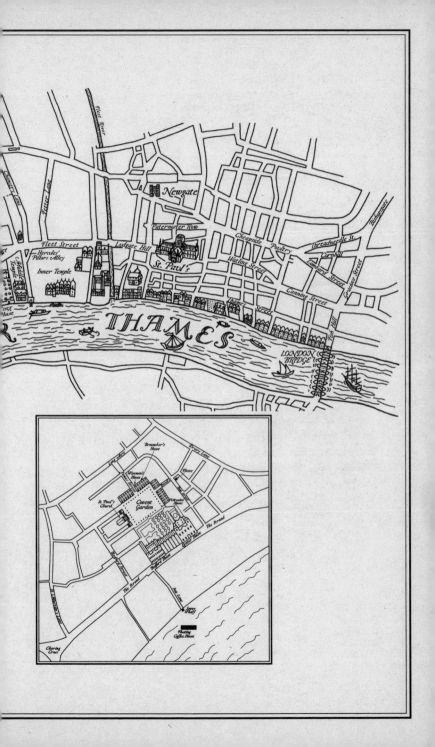

Prologue

13 June, 1665; aboard HMS Royal Charles, near Lowestoft

Captain John Harman peered through the gathering dusk, to where the tattered remnants of the Dutch flotilla was struggling to escape. They would not get far. *Royal Charles* would give chase, and the enemy would surrender or be blasted into oblivion. By noon the following day, the proud navy of the United Provinces would be no more.

The Duke of York stood nearby, drinking a toast to the victory with his jubilant entourage. He was the King's brother – and his heir, given that the Queen had yet to conceive – as well as Lord High Admiral. He had commanded the fleet well that day, although Harman was glad he had not tried to interfere with the actual handling of the ship – for all his warlike mettle, the Duke was still a landsman, and it took a man born to the sea, like Harman himself, to coax the best out of a big, powerful vessel like *Royal Charles*.

However, while Harman was honoured to have the Duke aboard, the same could not be said about the rest of the Court popinjays. Early in the skirmish, three had

1

been decapitated by a chain-shot, and the severed head of one had bowled the Duke over like a skittle. Their cronies had promptly become a dreadful liability: a few had set a dismal example by fleeing below decks in a blind panic, but most had milled about in terror, getting underfoot and unsettling the crew with their petrified whimpering.

Harman turned to the man who stood next to him – his friend and sailing master John Cox. Life at sea had turned Cox's face to the texture of old leather, although this was barely visible under the film of smoke and sweat that now streaked it.

'I wish the Duke would stop congratulating himself and give the order to pursue,' Harman muttered tersely. 'It will be dark soon, and we will lose them.'

Cox nodded agreement, but his reply was drowned out by the booming voice of the Duke's leading admiral, Sir William Penn, a crusty old sea-dog with years of active service. Unlike the courtiers, Penn had thoroughly enjoyed himself that day.

'I am looking forward to tomorrow, by God!' he declared, rubbing his hands together gleefully. 'We shall begin the process of finishing them off at first light. Of course, Hollanders always fight hardest when they are cornered, so we can expect some ferocious resistance.'

'You mean they will fight harder than they did today?' gulped one of the Duke's sycophants in alarm. 'Is that possible?'

Penn laughed. 'Just you wait and see, laddie! They will come at us like ravening beasts, knowing the very survival of their country depends on it, and today's business will look like a lovers' tiff by comparison. Harman! Set a course: west by south-west.'

The Duke yawned. 'I am going down to my quarters. If I should sleep, wake me before dawn. Then we will show the rogues, eh, Penn?'

Harman began to issue the stream of instructions that would prepare *Royal Charles* for the chase. It was not a moment too soon, as the enemy was now no more than pale dots on the horizon. The Duke and his chattering train trooped below, leaving the sea-officers to see that every scrap of canvas was spread. Away to the stern, Harman saw the rest of the fleet preparing to follow him, and his heart swelled with pride.

'Will we catch them?'

The question came from one of the ship's medics, Dr Merrett, who had come to snatch a breath of fresh air, away from the hot stench of blood. His gentle face was anxious.

'Easily,' replied Harman. 'But do not listen to Admiral Penn – the enemy will surrender without another shot being fired. To do anything else would be suicide, and they know it.'

He forced the horrors of the battle to the back of his mind as *Royal Charles* flew across the waves, concentrating instead on the thrill of commanding a good, weatherly ship and a well-disciplined crew. He did not permit himself to consider the hundreds who had died that day: there would be time for grief later, when they had won not just a battle, but the war. Yet within the hour, an order came to shorten sail and heave-to. He, Cox and Merrett gaped their disbelief at the man who had brought the message.

'Do not be ridiculous!' he snapped, once he had found his voice. 'You misheard the Duke – go below and find out what he really wants us to do.'

The man disappeared, but it was not long before he

3

was back. 'I did not mishear: you are to shorten sail at once. We shall resume the chase in the morning.'

Harman stared incredulously at him. 'How? Once we lose sight of the enemy, they will change course under cover of darkness, and we shall have no idea where they went. The Duke knows this perfectly well.'

The courtier shrugged. 'He says he is exhausted and needs to sleep – which he cannot do while the ship tosses and pitches like a cork in a barrel.'

Even Dr Merrett, no mariner, gasped his astonishment at this claim. 'I hardly think a little movement should determine the outcome of—' he began.

'And we are to rescue survivors,' interrupted the courtier curtly. 'He does not want the death toll to be higher than it is, even if those we save are only Dutchmen.'

Harman thought fast. 'In that case, we shall lower our water-boats. They can stay to fish out enemy sailors, while we pursue—'

'The Duke has spoken,' snapped the courtier, growing irked with the discussion. 'And we must obey. Unless *you* want to go downstairs and tell him he is wrong?'

Cox lurched forward to grab Harman's shoulder, preventing his old friend from storming below to do just that. 'Of course we will obey,' he said quickly. 'But even so, you must admit that the order is mystifying.'

The courtier glanced around to make sure no one else was listening. 'Personally, I think that the vicious duel we fought with *Eendracht* has addled his wits. And when she exploded in front of our eyes, so suddenly and unexpectedly . . . well, it shocked him.'

'It shocked us all,' said Harman tightly. 'But we must harden our hearts to such weakness and do our patriotic duty – which is to press on and end this war tonight.'

'Then *you* go and tell him so,' retorted the courtier. 'Because I am not doing it.'

He waited to see if Harman would accept the challenge, but Cox's restraining grip tightened, and although he was fit to explode with incredulity and frustration, Harman knew his sailing master was right – he would likely find himself on a charge of treason if he informed the Duke that he was making a massive mistake. Even so, he could not bring himself to give the order to his crew, obliging Cox to step up to the mark.

'Reduce sail!' the sailing master bellowed. 'Reef the mainsail!'

Cox had to repeat himself twice before the astonished sailors did what they were told, leaving Harman thinking that even the rawest recruit had more sense and understanding than their asinine Lord High Admiral.

'Perhaps the Duke *is* out of his wits,' whispered Cox a short while later, when *Royal Charles* had slowed to a crawl, and the Dutch fleet had vanished over the horizon. 'Because no sane leader would have made this decision. It is utter madness!'

'The government will demand an explanation when we return home,' said Harman between gritted teeth. 'And I shall not speak in support of this foolery. Heads *will* roll.'

'Only figuratively, I hope,' said Cox nervously.

30 October 1665, The Hague,
United Provinces of the Netherlands
Thomas Chaloner was in his element. He had been sent to deliver letters from his employer, the Earl of Clarendon, to the English ambassador in The Hague. He knew the city well. He also understood its politics and spoke Dutch,

5

although perhaps less fluently than when he had actually lived there, and was enjoying every moment.

After the civil wars that had turned England upside down, Cromwell's government had been desperate for good intelligence from hostile foreign countries, and Chaloner had been one of the resourceful young men recruited to supply it. He had completed tours all over the continent, but the United Provinces had always been his favourite, and he liked to think he had played a role, albeit a minor one, in keeping the two nations from each other's throats. Then Cromwell had died, the monarchy had been restored, and Chaloner had been dismissed from the intelligence services. Relations between England and Holland had deteriorated fast, and war had been declared within five years.

Chaloner knew the Earl had chosen him to deliver the letters because the task was a dangerous one and he was considered to be expendable, but he did not care. As far as he was concerned, it was a perfect opportunity to gather information that might help England win the current conflict. He had already contrived to examine the sea-defences at Rotterdam, Groningen, Middelburg and Flushing, and had eavesdropped on several conversations between Dutch admirals. He had also learned which enemy ships were at sea and which were in port, and how much ammunition each vessel carried.

However, that evening would put the real icing on the cake – assuming he was not caught, of course. He had learned from a reliable source that a meeting had been scheduled between Grand Pensionary de Witt, de facto head of the United Provinces, and his leading admiral, Michiel de Ruyter.

Such encounters were traditionally held deep inside

the Binnenhof – the Gothic palace that was the seat of government – a place impossible for foreign spies to infiltrate. However, de Witt was having trouble with the royal House of Orange, which aimed to undermine his authority by contesting every detail of his naval campaign. He had quickly learned that the best way to circumvent them was by giving his admirals their orders in secret. He used a number of places for the purpose, and that day's venue was Rosee's Coffee House in Korte Voorhout, a street in the heart of the old city.

Chaloner was ready for him. Rosee was trussed up on the kitchen floor, and most of the customers had fled when Chaloner had started to complain about a bubo in his groin – London was not the only city to have suffered an outbreak of the plague that summer. A few diehards had declined to be frightened away, but that was fine – all Chaloner wanted was for the room to be quiet enough for him to eavesdrop.

De Witt and de Ruyter arrived separately, both in disguise. They chose the secluded table at the back of the room, exactly as Chaloner had predicted they would. He bustled forward in Rosee's apron, bearing two dishes and a long-spouted jug, but retreated obediently when de Witt waved him away. He returned to the kitchen, and put his ear to the hole he had drilled in the wall earlier.

The pair began by discussing finances, and Chaloner was sure his own government would be delighted to learn that the war had all but drained de Witt's gold reserves. However, that did not stop the Grand Pensionary from promising de Ruyter twenty-five new battleships. These were to be funded by a tax that would hit particularly hard at the House of Orange, so Chaloner was not surprised that de Witt did not want his political opponents to get wind of it before it could be put into law and enforced.

'And what of the other matter?' de Witt asked eventually, after Chaloner had gathered a veritable wealth of sensitive information to take home with him. 'Did our scheme work?'

'Like a charm,' the admiral replied gleefully. 'As you predicted, the English attacked our merchant fleet without provocation, prompting Norway and Denmark to declare an alliance with us, and to sever all ties with them.'

'That is excellent news! So what happened precisely?'

'The moment an English cannonball landed in Bergen, the outraged Norwegians joined their firepower to ours. The English were driven back in disarray, and although they lost no ships, we still killed a hundred or so of their sailors and wounded three times as many more. It shocked them, and they no longer see themselves as invincible.'

'Whereas our own navy is heartened by the victory,' said de Witt approvingly. 'It has given morale a massive boost, which we needed after the disaster at Lowestoft.'

'Officially, we lost thirty sailors,' de Ruyter went on. 'Although between you and me, it was actually nearer ninety. I am astonished, de Witt. I did not think the enemy would fall for such a transparent ruse.'

De Witt laughed. 'A convoy of fat Dutch merchantmen in a neutral harbour, the king of which had promised to turn a blind eye to any efforts to seize them? Of course the English would snap at such juicy bait! Naturally, the King of Denmark and Norway now claims that they

8

misunderstood what he said, and is all outraged indignation at the assault on his shores.'

'The English skulked home with their tails between their legs,' grinned de Ruyter. 'The carnage of Lowestoft is avenged at last.'

Chapter 1

Visiting a mortuary was not Thomas Chaloner's idea of fun. Unfortunately, his employer, the Earl of Clarendon, had ordered him to guard two other members of his household, so when they had decided to join a Court excursion to a house of the dead that bitter winter morning, he had had no choice but to accompany them.

The Westminster charnel house did not look like much from the outside. It was sandwiched between an old granary and a coal warehouse, and stood at the end of a mean, smelly little lane. Inside, however, was a revelation. At the front were two very finely appointed rooms. One was an office, and the other a comfortable parlour where its keeper, Mr Kersey, comforted grieving families. Behind these was the large, low-ceilinged, windowless chamber that contained the corpses, each one lying on a table draped with a clean blanket.

Kersey was a neat, dapper little man, who made a good living from his trade. His success was evident in his fine clothes and expensive wig – not items taken from

11

dead bodies, as Chaloner had originally assumed, but bespoke garments designed to show off his trim figure. His wealth came not just from selling goods salvaged from those 'guests' who were never formally identified, but from tips pressed on him by grateful kin, who appreciated the quietly respectful way in which he tended their loved ones.

Another source of income was his museum, where he displayed some of the more unusual artefacts that had come his way. For a modest fee, visitors could inspect all manner of curiosities, including jewellery, items of clothing, an array of false teeth and eyes, hairpieces of all shapes and sizes, and a display of objects retrieved from his customers' innards, most of which beggared belief.

The recent plague might have terrified most people, but it had been very lucrative for Kersey, who had grown richer still from acquiring goods that no one else had dared to touch. It had allowed him to buy the granary next door, and his treasures were now displayed there in custom-built cases. In pride of place was a vast pair of drawers, so large that three men could have fitted inside them and still had room to spare.

'Friends enter for free,' he murmured, smiling when he saw Chaloner bringing up the rear of the party. He indicated that the spy should put his purse away, although everyone else had been charged full price. The gesture was intended as a compliment, although Chaloner would not have regarded the charnel-house keeper as a *friend* exactly – more a colleague with whom he shared several delicate secrets. Feeling obliged to make polite small talk in return, Chaloner nodded to a wiry little man who was showing the other visitors around.

'You have a new assistant, I see.'

'James Deakin.' Kersey glanced around quickly, then lowered his voice. 'He was hanged a few weeks ago, and brought here prior to being shipped to Chyrurgeons' Hall for dissection. But before I could let the surgeons know he was available, he sat up and asked for a cup of ale.'

'Goodness!' muttered Chaloner, amazed the authorities had not demanded that Deakin be returned to them immediately, so the executioner could try again.

'I was terribly busy at the time, so he offered to help me out in exchange for free bed and board – and a blind eye turned to his predicament for a short while. But as days turned to weeks . . . well, it seemed unfair to turn him in. He may look like a rogue, but he has some very useful talents.'

Chaloner started to ask what they were, but then decided that he did not want to know, given that they were evidently ones that made him useful in a charnel house. 'What was his crime?'

'He tried to blow up a tavern that had cheated him of his wages, although he did set the fuse for a time when no one would be in it.'

'Well, that is something in his favour, I suppose,' said Chaloner, hoping the encounter with the hangman would deter Deakin from solving future grievances with gunpowder.

Kersey turned to watch the rest of Chaloner's party coo over the exhibits. 'How can you bear to be with them?' he asked wonderingly. 'Courtiers lost any respect *I* might have held for them when they fled London, leaving us to cope with the plague alone.'

Personally, Chaloner thought that most courtiers would

13

have been of scant use anyway, and that the city had been better off without them.

'Two work for my Earl,' he explained. 'And he wants to keep them in his service, so my orders are to repel anyone who approaches them with a better offer.'

It was a demeaning task for someone with his talents, but beggars could not be choosers, and he was lucky to have a job at all, given that he had supported the 'wrong' side during the civil wars and the interregnum that had followed. Now that the Royalists were back in power, old Parliamentarians were *persona non grata*, so Chaloner never dared refuse the petty, degrading or dangerous assignments his Earl set him, lest he was dismissed.

'I have no idea how they dare show their faces,' declared Kersey, becoming indignant. 'That goes for the King, too. It was selfish of him to skulk away to Oxford without a backward glance at the subjects he claims to love.'

'Easy!' breathed Chaloner, alarmed. This was treasonous talk, and surprising from a man who had always been moderate in his opinions. 'Someone might hear you.'

'I expected more of him,' Kersey continued bitterly, albeit more softly. 'We did not invite him to reclaim his throne, only to have him abandon us at the first hurdle. He should have stayed in White Hall, to comfort and aid us in our hour of need.'

Privately, Chaloner agreed, although he understood why the King had cut and run. With no legitimate heir, his brother the Duke of York would inherit the crown, at which point the monarchy was likely to be overthrown once and for all – the Duke might be a fearless admiral who won sea-battles, but he was also stupid, vain, arrogant and dictatorial. Yet Chaloner would never say so to anyone else, and especially not in a place where so many sly and self-serving courtiers were within earshot. He changed the subject hastily.

'You are very full today,' he remarked, nodding through the open door that led to the mortuary, where nearly every table was occupied by a blanket-covered form.

'*Assurance*,' explained Kersey. 'The thirty-two-gun warship that sank off the Savoy Wharf a week last Saturday, leaving twenty sailors dead. Surely you heard about it?'

Chaloner had. 'They are not buried yet?'

'There is a dispute about who should pay for the funerals – their families or the government. Their kin cannot and the government will not, so they remain with me.'

'Their captain did not offer to shoulder the bill? Look – he is here now, admiring your display of false teeth.'

Chaloner nodded to a red-faced, bearded man in a blue coat, whom he knew because the fellow was married to Olivia Stoakes, one of the two people Chaloner had been instructed to mind that day. John Stoakes was a belligerent drunk, who had not been sober since his ship had gone down.

'Common decency would dictate so,' replied Kersey, eyeing Stoakes in distaste. 'But he declines, on the grounds that he lost a lot of personal possessions in the disaster, and he feels it should not cost him any more than it has already.'

'Perhaps he—' began Chaloner, then noticed what was happening by the vast pair of drawers. 'Damn it! Harry Brouncker has just cornered George Thompson. Excuse me – duty calls.'

15

Usually known simply as 'George', to distinguish him from several others at Court with the same surname, George Thompson was the second retainer whom the Earl had charged Chaloner to watch. And as Brouncker was one the Earl's most fervent enemies – one among many he had accumulated by being inflexible, moralistic and hypercritical – Chaloner knew he should hasten to make sure no sly offers of employment were being made. He nodded a brisk farewell to Kersey and strode towards them.

The Earl did not treat his staff well, as Chaloner could personally attest, so it was no surprise that he was worried about losing them. However, he had no cause to be concerned about George, as *he* earned a salary far in excess of what he was worth, so was unlikely to be seduced away by other offers. This arose not from generosity on the Earl's part, but because George was a wealthy man with two wealthy brothers, and the Earl thought that by wooing one, he could win all three. Rich and influential friends often meant the difference between life and death to those embroiled in the turbulent world of White Hall politics, so acquiring some was a precaution all sensible courtiers took.

George was an imposing figure, who wore a false leg to replace the one he had lost in the civil wars. It was no mere peg, but an object that had been lovingly crafted to match the limb that had gone, right down to skin-coloured paint, real hairs and some very authentic-looking toenails. Chaloner understood the need for it better than most – he had suffered a serious leg injury during the wars himself, caused by an exploding cannon during the Battle of Naseby. It had healed, but not perfectly, and made him limp when he was cold or tired.

He approached George and Brouncker discreetly, and pretended to inspect a nearby exhibit while he eaves-dropped – there was no point barging in on their discussion if Brouncker was innocently passing the time of day. And, if Chaloner was honest with himself, he disliked Brouncker, and would just as soon avoid his company if he could.

Brouncker was Gentleman of the Bedchamber to the Duke of York, and a typical courtier – debauched, haughty and sly. He aped the King's penchant for large black wigs and thin moustaches, and his clothes were ridiculously ornate. He had a reputation for licentiousness and corruption, and ran a bawdy house to keep his master supplied with prostitutes. He was one of the men who gave the Court its bad name, and the best anyone could say about him was that he played a good game of chess.

'. . . talking to Lady Castlemaine about your Earl's *medicus*,' he was saying spitefully.

'You mean Dr Quartermain?' asked George, laughing. 'What did you tell her, exactly?'

'That I do not blame Quartermain for refusing the Earl's summons, because *I* would not touch Clarendon's gouty old legs for a kingdom. The Lady said she would not either.'

The Earl had been upset when his physician had failed to answer an urgent call the previous day. Indeed, it was why Chaloner had been told to watch Olivia Stoakes and George – to make sure they did not abandon him, too. Chaloner felt his dislike for Brouncker intensify. Was nothing sacred? Did the man really have to gossip about the Earl's medical problems?

'Clarendon is not so bad,' shrugged George, which

was hardly a resounding defence of the man who paid him a fortune each week. 'And I do not like Quartermain anyway. I hired him once, and he stank of garlic.'

'Probably from his plague medicine,' surmised Brouncker. 'He calls it King's Gold.'

'Well, it was nasty, and while the Earl might miss his malodorous presence, I shall not. He had the audacity to allege that my leg is anatomically incorrect.' George hoisted up his petticoat breeches. 'Does that look anatomically incorrect to you?'

Brouncker gushed a polite denial, and eventually George shambled away. Chaloner was about to return to Kersey when Brouncker hailed him.

'Chaloner! Are you recovered from your recent visit to The Hague? It cannot have been pleasant for you, dwelling among all those butter-eaters.'

Chaloner went to considerable trouble to make himself unobtrusive. He had mid-brown hair, grey eyes, and was of medium height and build. His clothes were smart without being showy, and would look as natural in a tavern or a coffee house as at Court or in church. Thus it was irksome that Brouncker should have noticed him. Fortunately, Brouncker was more interested in talking about himself than hearing a reply to his question, and promptly launched into a monologue about his importance to the smooth running of his Duke's household. Eventually, he turned the conversation to the Battle of Lowestoft and the vital role he had played in it.

'I was at the Duke's side throughout,' he bragged. 'On *Royal Charles*. I enjoyed it immensely, and the fight itself was great fun.'

Chaloner had also been there – representing the Earl on HMS *Swiftsure* – but he would never have described the encounter as fun. It had been bloody, noisy and terrifying, and he would never forget the horror of *Eendracht* exploding, killing all but five of her complement of four hundred.

'It was a day to remember,' he acknowledged cautiously. 'But too many sailors died.'

'True,' agreed Brouncker. 'Although the toll would have been higher still if we had hared off after the Dutch fleet. Thank God the Duke ordered us to fish out survivors instead.'

It was generally held that not giving chase had been a serious error of judgement, but of course Brouncker would feel obliged to support the Duke's decision. Chaloner was not, though.

'We could have done both,' he pointed out. 'The damaged ships could have stayed behind to rescue drowning seamen, while the rest of us set off in pursuit.'

Brouncker raised his eyebrows. 'You would have inflicted another terrible skirmish on our brave sailors? After all they had done for their country that day?'

'The Dutch were outnumbered and had lost their ranking admiral,' shrugged Chaloner. 'I doubt there would have been another fight – they would have surrendered.'

'Nonsense! I clearly heard Sir William Penn remark that the Dutch never fight so hard as when they are in a corner. He thought Lowestoft would be nothing compared to what would have followed if we had raced after the surviving ships and caught them.'

'The Dutch are not stupid – they would not have thrown away their lives on a hopeless cause. By letting them escape, we guaranteed that the war will continue, and the next time our fleet meets theirs, we may not be so lucky.'

'Luck had nothing to do with it! Our victory was down to the skill and courage of the Duke of York. But you were not on *Royal Charles*, so you cannot expect to have an informed opinion. Let us talk of something else – such as what you think of *her*. Is she not lovely?'

Brouncker's eyes were fixed on a woman who stood with her back to them. She was slightly built, and wore clothes that showed her figure to its best advantage. Her hair was a mass of gold curls, pinned up at the sides but allowed to tumble freely down her back. Chaloner supposed she was one of Brouncker's teenaged prostitutes, taken on a courtly jaunt as a perk of the job.

'How long has she been working for you?' he asked politely.

'She is not one of my girls, more is the pity! She is my brother's mistress.'

It was clear from his lustfully glittering eyes that Brouncker aimed to steal her away from his hapless sibling. Chaloner was sorry. He had met the older Brouncker and liked him, mostly because he was everything his younger kinsman was not – honest, hard-working and intelligent. Unfortunately, decent, staid Sir William would pale in comparison to lively, handsome Harry.

'Why her?' asked Chaloner reproachfully. 'Surely there are other fish in the sea?'

'Plenty,' smirked Brouncker. 'But none like Abigail Williams. She is unique.'

Chaloner saw what he meant when she turned and revealed herself as not a young girl in her teens, but a woman well past fifty. There were wrinkles around her eyes, although a sterling effort had been made to disguise them with face-paints, and her neck was scraggy. Her mouth had begun the inevitable downward sag, which she had attempted to circumvent by drawing in lines of her choosing instead. The result was vaguely surreal.

'As Navy Commissioner, my brother is obliged to be in Portsmouth a lot,' Brouncker went on. 'And he charged me to look after Abigail while he is away.'

'I doubt seducing her was what he had in mind,' said Chaloner, feeling his opinion of the younger Brouncker sink lower with every word that fell from the man's lips.

Before Brouncker could reply, Abigail saw she was the subject of attention, and flounced towards them.

'There you are, Harry,' she simpered. 'Will you accompany me to see the glass eyes? I may need your strong arms to hold me up, if they make me feel faint.'

She batted her eyelashes, so Brouncker led her away, although not before Chaloner had seen the predatory gleam in her eyes. It left him wondering exactly who was hunting whom.

When Brouncker had gone, Chaloner went in search of Olivia Stoakes, to make sure none of the Earl's other enemies were queuing up to poach her services – he could safely forget George for a while, as he was busy showing off his false leg to a politely interested Kersey.

Ever since he had met them, Chaloner had been amazed that Olivia and John Stoakes should be married. He could only assume their families had arranged the match, as he was sure neither would willingly have chosen the other. Stoakes was brash, loud and stupid, while Olivia was poised, diffident and scholarly. She had astonished everyone during the Christmas revels by parodying several leading courtiers with uncanny precision, demonstrating a lively and mischievous wit. Chaloner suspected this was partly why the Earl was so determined to keep

21

her – he did not want her including *him* in her scurrilous repertoire, and being in his employ meant she already had a wealth of mortifying anecdotes at her disposal.

He found the couple by the display of items retrieved from the innards of the dead. Olivia was scratching her neck, and he saw an ugly rash beneath the shining auburn curls. She stopped clawing it when he approached, although the stiff way she held her shoulder suggested it continued to itch. Stoakes was sipping from a silver pocket flask, his eyes glazed and bloodshot.

'Medicinal,' he slurred, when he saw Chaloner's disparaging expression – it was very early in the day for strong drink. 'To help me recover from being dragged out of bed to go to church. I know we are obliged to put in an appearance if we do not want to be seen as nonconformists, but Sunday worship is a damned nuisance.'

Usually, Chaloner would agree, but he had enjoyed the ceremony that morning. The Earl had taken his household to St Paul's in Covent Garden, the congregation of which he had joined after falling out with his own. St Paul's had an excellent choir, and Chaloner had not minded at all listening to them sing anthems by Gibbons and Lawes.

Olivia gave her neck a quick, furtive rub while her husband held forth about nothing, and when the mindless prattle eventually petered out, she pointed at one of the items in the display.

'What is that, do you think? Mr Brouncker says it is a soap dish, but I cannot agree.'

The object in question was a round metal disc about the circumference of an apple, with a handle on one side and spikes on the other. Chaloner had no idea how

22

it could have ended up inside someone's stomach. Not easily, certainly.

'You are right to be sceptical, my dear,' slurred Stoakes, peering at it. 'Because if it were a soap dish, the points would be on the same side as the handle.' Then he reconsidered. 'Unless the object is to *impale* the soap, to ensure it does not slither away. That would be useful at sea – it is almost impossible to keep hold of soap when one is on a bucking ship.'

Ablutions afloat had never presented a problem for Chaloner, and he considered remarking that Stoakes might have more success if he tried doing it when he was sober. He held his tongue out of deference to Olivia, who was looking embarrassed.

'I understand condolences are in order,' he said instead, and when Stoakes looked blank, he added with asperity, 'Your ship, *Assurance*.'

'Oh, yes,' sighed Stoakes. 'Thank God it happened when I was at the gentleman's club in Hercules' Pillars Alley, or I might have drowned, too.'

That particular 'club' was a brothel, which catered to an exclusive clientele. Chaloner glanced at Olivia, but there was no discernible reaction, so he could only assume she had no idea her husband had been enjoying the company of prostitutes while his crew had drowned.

'The Navy Board says the disaster is my fault,' Stoakes went on mournfully. 'For not tying *Assurance* securely to the quay. How dare they blame me! I was not even there.'

Chaloner opened his mouth to point out that captains were responsible for their vessels no matter where they happened to be, and if Stoakes disagreed, then perhaps he should consider a different career. But Olivia spoke first.

'Mr Kersey says your sailors are still not buried,' she

23

told her husband. 'The Navy Board quibbles over technicalities, and the families cannot do it as they have no money – no seaman has been paid in months. So I told him that *we* will pay for the funerals.'

'Did you?' said Stoakes crossly. 'You should not have done. It is not our concern.'

Olivia shot him a cool glance. 'We will also give each family a few shillings, to tide them over until the navy pays them what they are rightfully owed.'

'No, we will not,' countered Stoakes firmly. 'The navy cannot dispense what it does not have, and its coffers are empty. Ergo, the sooner the families get used to the idea that they will never have a penny from the government, the better off they will be. No sailor will be paid, whether he is dead or still in service.'

'But that is outrageous!' exclaimed Olivia indignantly. 'You cannot expect them to work for free – they have families to provide for.'

'Their parishes will have to oblige,' shrugged Stoakes. 'But the navy's money is needed for building and victualling ships. It cannot afford wages as well.'

'Then perhaps we should invite the Dutch to take up residence in White Hall right now,' declared Olivia hotly. 'Because our sailors will not defend us if we let their loved ones starve.'

'Dear Olivia,' said Stoakes sarcastically. 'Always the champion of the weak and helpless. But never mind them. How much do you think Kersey will accept for this nautical soap dish? It will be very useful for when I return to sea.'

'It is a biscuit pricker,' said Chaloner, struggling to mask his dislike of the man. 'For punching holes in dough to prevent it from over-rising. My mother had one.'

'It must have been attached to the biscuit when its previous owner swallowed it,' said Olivia, and shot her husband an unpleasant glance. 'It is the kind of thing drunks do, which is why so many of them meet sudden and unexpected ends.'

And with that, she stomped away.

There was a great deal to see in the museum, and its ghoulish nature kept the courtiers entertained far longer than most of their excursions did – they had short attention spans and grew bored very quickly. Chaloner had no desire to inspect the displays, though, and leaned against a wall, arms folded, wishing someone would suggest going home.

'I am glad Stoakes has agreed to bury his crew at last,' said Kersey, coming to stand next to him. 'Or rather Olivia has. She is much nicer than him.'

'It is a curious business. How did *Assurance* come to sink while she was in port?'

'A chance gust of wind, apparently, but we shall find out for certain when she is weighed in a few days' time. But you look as though you need a cup of wine. I certainly do. It galls me to see my domain filled with these arrogant monkeys.'

Chaloner was sure he did not look as though he needed wine, as he was currently in excellent health. After spending several pleasant weeks spying in The Hague, he had joined the Earl in Oxford, where there had been very little for him to do, allowing him the luxury of unlimited riding, walking and reading. He had been sorry when the Earl had announced that it was time to return to London, where they had arrived five days ago.

'You must be shocked to see the city in such a state,'

25

said Kersey, leading the way to his parlour. Chaloner followed, confident that no one aimed to poach Olivia or George from the Earl that day – if they did, they would have tried already. 'Weeds growing in the streets for want of use, cemeteries overflowing, hundreds of houses empty . . . And you lost your wife.'

Chaloner nodded, but even now, months later, it was not a subject he was comfortable discussing. Hannah was the second spouse he had lost to the disease – the first had died during an outbreak in Holland – and he was surprised by how much he missed her, especially as theirs had been a stormy marriage, which would not have survived the test of time.

'Come,' said Kersey kindly. 'Sit and drink this.'

His parlour was a handsome room. Its chairs were Venetian, its walls papered – a recent, expensive and not very practical innovation from France – and its desk German. Kersey served the wine from a crystal decanter, and it was Malaga, a costly import from Spain. Despite having condemned Stoakes for enjoying strong drink so early in the day, the quality of Kersey's was such that Chaloner decided there was nothing wrong with hypocrisy just this once.

'The plague was good to me,' said Kersey, sitting back with a contented sigh, and casting a happy eye around him as he lit his pipe.

'Were you not afraid of catching it?' Chaloner did not like to imagine what the charnel house must have been like at the height of the epidemic, when more than seven thousand people had died in a single week.

'Not as long as I had a good store of tobacco. It kills all pestilential vapours.'

'Wiseman claims otherwise.'

Richard Wiseman was a mutual friend. He was the King's surgeon, and his practice was lucrative enough to allow him to buy a fine house in Covent Garden, in which Chaloner was currently renting rooms. He often visited Kersey in the hope of securing specimens to dissect at Chyrurgeons' Hall.

'Then he is wrong,' declared Kersey. 'I would be dead if I had not smoked a pound of tobacco a day. Of course, now the plague is over, I find myself reluctant to give up the pleasure it provides . . .'

'Then you must be glad of the revenue from your museum,' remarked Chaloner, aware of how costly the leaf had become.

'Yes, but I wish courtiers would not visit. They are universally despised, and I do not want to be associated with them. They think we are pleased to have them back in the city, but they delude themselves. Not only was their flight bad for morale, but they left us with no provision for helping the sick and no plan for dealing with the dead.'

He was right, and the fact that London had survived at all was down to a few brave individuals who had stepped into the breach. Worse yet, the Court had caroused wildly wherever it had fetched up, and tales of merry – and expensive – parties had added insult to injury. The King was preparing to return now the danger was over, although Chaloner suspected that the damage done by his hasty departure would take a long time to mend.

He was spared from having to reply by a scream, which came from the museum. He was on his feet in an instant, running towards it, although he suspected it would be nothing more serious than someone spotting a rat. There

27

were plenty of them in the charnel house, especially during winter, when cold weather drove them indoors.

He arrived to find the courtiers milling about in alarm. The screech had come from Abigail, who sat, white-faced, by a case marked *Latest Acquisitions*. Olivia knelt next to her, holding her hand, while Brouncker had loosened her bodice to allow her to breathe – although Chaloner was sure it should not have been necessary to undo quite so many laces.

'It was the pen,' explained George, in answer to Chaloner's unspoken question. 'I think she recognised it as belonging to someone she knows.'

'The fountain-pen?' asked Kersey, unlocking the case and withdrawing the item in question. Fountain-pens were new-fangled devices currently popular at Court because the King had one; they were writing implements with an internal supply of ink. 'It came in last week, on a guest with nothing else to identify him. Are you saying that you know him, madam?'

Abigail nodded tearfully. 'It belongs to a very dear friend – poor Willy.'

'Poor Willy who?' asked Brouncker in alarm. 'Not my brother?'

'No – Willy Quartermain. You must know him, Harry. He is the King's physician, and tends many wealthy courtiers.'

'Lord!' murmured Chaloner to Kersey. 'I overheard a conversation about Quartermain not half an hour ago, in which Brouncker claimed that Quartermain had deserted my Earl in favour of nicer patients. And all the while, the poor man was dead!'

'I am astonished to learn my guest was a courtier,' Kersey muttered back. 'He reeked of garlic, whereas the

28

King's monkeys tend to smell of other things – usually wine, but sometimes perfume or expensive cloth.'

'His plague remedy,' surmised Chaloner, recalling what Brouncker had said. 'Yet I am surprised you never met Quartermain.'

'Why would I? First, he was a courtier, and I try to minimise my association with those as much as possible. And second, physicians rarely come here – unlike surgeons, who pester me relentlessly in their quest for corpses to dissect the Anatomy Theatre.'

'You did not identify him as a man of substance from his clothes?'

'They were respectable, but not exceptional, so no.'

'I have been hearing all week about how Willy has offended his rich patients by failing to answer their summonses,' Abigail was mournfully informing her audience. 'But he was in here the whole time. He could hardly be expected to physick customers from a mortuary slab, could he?'

'Some *medici* manage to do it very well,' quipped Brouncker.

Chapter 2

The courtiers twittered in excitement at the news that the King's physician was not only dead, but had been buried in a pauper's grave because no one had identified his body. But none of them had known Quartermain well, and they soon lost interest in the affair, especially once the sobbing Abigail Williams had been escorted to Kersey's parlour, away from prurient eyes. Then George suggested an excursion to the Fleece tavern in Covent Garden, where a troupe of entertainers called Urban's Men were scheduled to perform.

'They are very talented,' he declared. 'Jugglers, acrobats, actors, fire-eaters . . . I was spellbound, especially when one contrived to remove my leg without me seeing. I only noticed it was missing when I tried to stand up.'

Chaloner could only assume that the occasion must have involved a great deal of alcohol, because false limbs were attached with a vast array of straps and buckles, and George must have been drunk indeed not have spotted someone unfastening them.

The courtiers disappeared in a noisy hubbub, leaving

Chaloner to ponder whether the Earl would prefer him to continue minding George and Olivia, or find out what had happened to his physician. The Earl, being a difficult man to please, would find fault with either decision, so Chaloner opted for the one that sounded more interesting – exploring how and why Quartermain had ended up in the charnel house.

Tears had made a terrible mess of Abigail's face-paints, exposing the wrinkled skin beneath, while the ungloved hand that dabbed at her eyes was peppered in age-spots. Chaloner wondered what induced her to persist with the pretence of youth when she was old enough to be his mother. Her advanced years did not seem to bother Brouncker, though: he was clearly relishing the opportunity to worm himself deeper into her affections with a display of kindly concern, which he expressed by resting one hand on her shoulder and the other on her thigh.

'I had no idea that you and Willy were friends,' he was saying solicitously. 'It must be a terrible shock to learn that he is with our Lord in heaven.'

'I was his patient,' explained Abigail, although the sly flash in her eyes betrayed the lie. 'He had a rare talent with hips.'

'Well, do not worry about that,' leered Brouncker, 'because I do, too.'

Chaloner could not bear to watch as Abigail gave a brave little smile and Brouncker responded by squeezing her leg encouragingly. Instead he turned his attention to the fountain-pen, which lay on Kersey's desk. He owned one himself and hated it. It ran out of ink at critical junctures, and refilling the reservoir was complicated and messy. Worse, it leaked, and he had stopped using it in disgust after it ruined his favourite coat.

Quartermain's was silver and engraved with: *For WQ with love from AW.* Chaloner stared at it, thinking Abigail Williams must have been fond of Quartermain indeed to furnish him with such a costly gift. Her high little-girl voice intruded on his reflections.

'He used it to write instructions for the apothecary – his recipe for King's Gold.'

'Ah, yes,' recalled Brouncker. 'King's Gold was his plague remedy. It earned him a fortune, although Surgeon Wiseman declared it no more effective than all the other so-called cures – Goddard's Drops, Dragon Water, *sal mirabilis*, Venice Treacle . . .'

'It kept *me* safe,' flashed Abigail, obviously irked by the criticism.

But Brouncker had taken the pen from Chaloner and was not listening. '*AW*. Is that—'

'His sister,' interrupted Abigail, looking directly into his eyes. 'They were very close, although she died last year, so you cannot ask her about it.'

'Was Quartermain's a natural death?' asked Chaloner of Kersey, at the same time wondering if Brouncker would be so credulous as to believe such an obvious lie.

'Well, there was no blood,' replied Kersey. 'So he was not shot, beaten or stabbed.'

'What else can you tell us?'

Kersey went to the ledger on his desk, and ran his finger down the page until he found the correct entry. 'He came to us last Sunday morning, after being discovered by a fellow named Laurens van Heemskerch in the grounds of Bedford House. Ah, yes! I remember now. Bedford House is in Covent Garden, and is currently leased to the Dutch ambassador.'

'You mean Quartermain died while making a professional call to the embassy?' asked Chaloner, his curiosity piqued.

'They denied it,' recalled Kersey, 'and insisted that they had just stumbled across him in their garden. To be honest, Deakin and I assumed that he had died elsewhere and the body was deposited in Bedford House to unsettle the enemy. An act of intimidation, if you will. But it is only our opinion. If you want the truth, you will have to speak to Heemskerch himself.'

'I will,' determined Chaloner, his interest deepening.

'I live in Covent Garden,' put in Brouncker. 'Quite close to Bedford House, in fact. I reside with my brother, although he is rarely in the city these days, being so busy with the war.'

He shot Abigail a look that suggested the two of them should take advantage of his sibling's convenient absence.

'Were you at home last Sunday morning?' asked Chaloner, wondering if Brouncker had found out that Abigail entertained Quartermain as well as his brother, and had taken steps to eliminate some of the competition. If he lived nearby, it would not be difficult to deposit an inconvenient corpse in a neighbour's backyard.

Brouncker gave a thin smile, guessing exactly why the question had been put. 'I was in White Hall, working with the Duke. I did not leave the palace all day. Ask him, if you want.'

Abigail also hastened to answer. She had recovered suspiciously fast from her distress, and there was a hard, calculating gleam in her eye.

'I was at home in Southwark. I rarely go out these days, unless someone kind comes along to offer an entertaining excursion with courtiers.' She simpered at Brouncker.

'What about Quartermain's house?' Chaloner asked her. 'Did you visit that?'

'No, because he lived in Axe Yard – a place I dislike.'

And Chaloner knew why: Axe Yard was near the Treasury, where Brouncker's brother would go in his capacity as Navy Commissioner. She could hardly expect to keep Sir William if he caught her with another lover. Sensing his distaste, she quickly changed the subject.

'Was there anything else with Willy's body? I shall keep the pen, of course, as I was his closest friend and he had no living kin. But was there a purse?'

'Not that I recall,' replied Kersey smoothly.

'What about his clothes?' persisted Abigail.

'He was buried in those,' said Kersey, 'so if you want them, you will have to dig him up. Would you like the location of his grave?'

'No, thank you,' said Abigail stiffly, and turned back to Brouncker. 'Will you escort me home now, Harry? I am quite worn out with all the distress.'

She gave a girlish giggle when, in helping her to stand, Brouncker's hand contrived to brush her rump. Behind their backs, Kersey rolled his eyes, and Chaloner knew that their antics would convince him more than ever that courtiers were useless rogues.

'Quartermain *did* have a purse,' the charnel-house keeper confided when the flirting pair had gone. 'It contained five shillings and three coffee-house tokens. We also retained his coat, which I sold for two pounds. However, I do not see why *she* should have it – we only have her word that the deceased's sister is dead.'

'There will be no sister,' predicted Chaloner. 'So keep what is lawfully yours.'

*

Chaloner's first task after leaving the charnel house was to follow Olivia Stoakes and George to the Fleece. This was a large, rambling tavern on the corner of Bow and Russell streets. It was in the vicinity of some very handsome properties, including Bedford and Exeter houses, and the beautiful new homes that fringed Covent Garden's Piazza, which were popular with wealthy merchants and courtiers, Chaloner and Wiseman included.

Like most coaching inns, the Fleece boasted a huge courtyard where riders could dismount and carriages could set down their passengers. The yard had a range of two-storeyed buildings on each of its four sides. The largest wing held the public rooms, while the others had bedchambers that could be hired by travellers. The upper floors had wooden balconies that overlooked the yard, which meant that guests could stay under cover as they walked from bedrooms to taproom to stables.

The inn had once been an upmarket establishment, but the wealthy elite now favoured the Strand, for no reason other than fashion. The Fleece had fallen into decline, and the plague had been the final nail in its coffin. It had not hosted an important guest in years, and its owner was reputed to be drowning in debt. In an effort to make some much-needed money, he had put his courtyard to another use – as a venue for entertainment. A makeshift stage had been built at one end, while the overhanging galleries were convenient for those who were willing to pay sixpence for a seat with a good view of it.

The tavern was busy when Chaloner arrived, crammed with folk from all walks of life. It was a colourful spectacle, as almost everyone had contrived to don something bright – a scarlet ribbon, a yellow feather, a blue hat. There was also laughter, which was a welcome change after the misery of the plague. Vendors were there to sell oranges, roasted chestnuts, pastries and pies, while pickpockets weaved among the standing masses like eels.

Most attention was on the stage, where a dwarf wearing a lion mask performed a series of tumbles and tricks. He was assisted by a fire-eater, and the two executed an intricate ballet that had the audience gasping its admiration. Such precise choreography must have taken weeks to perfect, and Chaloner was not surprised that the audience appreciated the result.

When the dwarf and the fire-eater had finished, a rope-dancer took their place. Chaloner recognised him, as he had been hired to perform at Court. His name was Jacob Hall, and he was a wiry, muscular man in almost indecently tight clothes. He not only did impossible things on two ropes slung between opposing galleries, but 'painted' pictures in the air by flinging cords around. His performance drew delighted applause from the spectators.

Eventually, Hall yielded the stage to a sword-swallower, and retreated to one side of the dais to catch his breath. Immediately, someone in the audience slithered forward and wrapped her arms around him in a very possessive manner. The movement caused her hood to fall back, revealing the beautiful but spiteful features of Lady Castlemaine, the King's mistress. She was currently out of royal favour again, although Chaloner could not recall why – perhaps something to do with her latest child and the rumours that the King was not its father.

He was surprised she dared visit a rough place like the Fleece on her own, but then he saw that a number of her Court cronies were with her. He had to sidle through them to reach his own party, and was uneasy when he saw that their part of the yard was receiving a good deal of hostile attention from the rest of the audience.

'Damned cowards,' muttered a butcher venomously. 'They scuttle off to the country to save their own miserable skins, and expect us to be glad when they come back again.'

'They cared nothing for what their flight meant for us,' whispered a baker. 'So I shall sell them my cakes, but I will spit in them first.'

Chaloner moved away, lest the grumbling tradesmen should notice him listening to their discussion and take offence – he was perfectly capable of defending himself in a brawl, but he had no wish to be the cause of one. He reached his own band of courtiers, and saw that they were blithely unaware of the enmity that crackled around them.

George was standing with his brothers, guffawing loudly enough to attract attention, none of it friendly. Chaloner suspected they would be safe from attack, though, as he and his siblings carried a veritable arsenal of guns, swords and knives. All three had fought in the wars, and although George's missing leg would make fancy footwork difficult, he was still reputed to be a deadly warrior.

Chaloner had a moment of panic when he could not see Olivia, but then he spotted her near the stage. She was scratching the rash on her neck, while talking animatedly to one of the performers – a burly actor in multicoloured hose. When other members of the troupe joined them, she earned their instant affection by handing out coins. They made themselves scarce when Stoakes stormed up, though, his scowl revealing that he disapproved of both her generosity and her fraternising with commoners. Perhaps he was afraid she would follow Lady Castlemaine's shining example and take one as a lover, thought Chaloner caustically.

Stoakes grabbed his wife's arm and towed her back to the rest of their party. She went meekly enough, although she did not stay with him for long. Within minutes, she had slipped away to chat to the Thompson brothers instead.

Chaloner watched her and George for a while, but when it became clear that they intended to enjoy the entertainment in its entirety – and the programme he retrieved from the floor told him there were three short plays, dulcimer music and a magician to come – he decided to begin his enquiries into Quartermain's death instead.

Just the previous year, the Dutch ambassador had been sumptuously housed in the Savoy Palace, along with a staff of several hundred. Most of these had been recalled to the United Provinces when war was declared, obliging Michiel van Goch to rent somewhere more modest. He had chosen Bedford House for four reasons: it was still smart enough to impress; it was in the prestigious Covent Garden area; it was convenient for White Hall; and its owner let him have it cheap.

The house was an unremarkable E-plan building with Tudor chimneys. Its main entrance was on the Strand, but its crowning glory was at the back – grounds that ran all the way to the Piazza, separated from it by a tall wall. They were vast, and included not only formal gardens, but woodland, an orchard and vegetable plots.

The house had a sorry appearance from the front.

Londoners knew who lived there, so its walls were pitted with dents and smeared with excrement. The window shutters were always closed, and a grille had been inserted into the door, to allow the armed guards within to size up any would-be visitors before letting them in.

'Heemskerch not here,' declared one in faltering English, when Chaloner knocked and stated his business. 'He disappear after corpse in garden.'

Chaloner switched to Dutch. 'He has gone home to the United Provinces?'

The guard was relieved to revert to his mother tongue. 'No, I mean we have not seen him since last Sunday, when he stumbled over that body. Why do you want him?'

'The Earl of Clarendon has asked me to investigate what happened to the victim, lest the incident represents a danger to the ambassador.'

It was a lie, but as the Earl was one of few members of government who thought war with the Dutch was a bad idea, he and his staff were always greeted very civilly at Bedford House. The door opened and Chaloner was ushered politely inside.

'What is it?' came an unsteady voice from the far end of the hall. 'More trouble?'

The speaker was van Goch himself, a man wholly unequal to handling the situation in which he found himself. He looked the part, with patrician features and a distinguished air, but his diplomatic skills were mediocre, and he was no match for England's boisterous politicians.

'Are you leaving?' asked Chaloner, noting that the hall was full of trunks and boxes; a clerk moved among them with an inventory.

'I have been recalled to The Hague,' explained van Goch, and could not prevent a relieved grin. 'We shall be home by the end of the month, thank God!'

'Who will take your place?'

'No one. At least, not until the war is over.'

Chaloner was sorry. It was only a matter of time before both sides realised that nothing could be gained from the conflict, but peace would take longer to negotiate once the embassy in London was abandoned. Not for the first time, he pondered the Duke of York's curious decision not to chase the surviving Dutch ships after Lowestoft, thus ending the war there and then.

At that moment, another man appeared. He was plump and pale, and moved with restless energy. There was a peculiar scar on the tip of his nose, as if someone had once tried to slice it off. Van Goch introduced him as Coenraad van Beuningen, so Chaloner regarded him with interest – Beuningen was famous as the United Provinces' most talented emissary.

'I wish we could stay longer in London,' Beuningen sighed ruefully, gazing around at the packed crates. 'There are one or two diplomatic avenues that might still be explored, even now. But our Grand Pensionary has spoken . . .'

'He has,' said van Goch, a warning in his voice lest Beuningen took it into his head to encourage de Witt to change his mind. 'Besides, we should not forget the outrage at Vågen.'

He referred to an incident that had occurred the previous August, when the English fleet had attacked a convoy of Dutch merchant ships in Norway, thinking an agreement had been made with the ruling Danes to share the resulting plunder. It had been an unmitigated disaster.

The Norwegians had opened fire on the English, inflicting a humiliating defeat, while the King of Denmark promptly began to deny any such complicity. Worse yet, the debacle had led to Denmark siding with the United Provinces, so England now faced two enemies instead of one. Chaloner recalled the last time he had heard Vågen mentioned – in Rosee's Coffee House in The Hague, when Grand Pensionary de Witt and Admiral de Ruyter had discussed it so gloatingly. Prudently, he changed the subject.

'I would like to speak to Laurens van Heemskerch about the body he found last Sunday.'

'Heemskerch is no longer with us,' said van Goch flatly. 'He has gone.'

'Gone where?' asked Chaloner.

'If we knew that, we would order him to come back,' replied van Goch tersely. 'He has no right to wander off alone, especially when we are so busy preparing for our departure. There is a lot for him to do.'

'Mundane tasks, of course,' put in Beuningen quickly. 'He is a lowly cog, entrusted with nothing important.'

It was not difficult for Chaloner to read between the lines. 'You suspect him of betraying you,' he surmised. 'Giving your secrets to English paymasters.'

Beuningen started to deny it, but the truth was in van Goch's face, so it was not long before the diplomat abandoned his efforts to convince.

'Yes, Heemskerch is a traitor,' he admitted. 'Fortunately, he knows nothing to harm us. However, any intelligence he provides may well hurt *you*. For example, you might want to remember that your defeat at Vågen was largely due to the information that *he* provided.'

'I see,' said Chaloner, wondering if Quartermain's

might not be the only body to be discovered lying in the garden of Bedford House – that Heemskerch's would turn up once the ambassador and his staff had left. Regardless, if the United Provinces' top diplomat was telling him that Heemskerch knew nothing of import, the chances were that the exact opposite was true.

'Perhaps *we* can answer your questions about the corpse,' offered van Goch helpfully. 'What do you want to know? I am afraid we cannot tell you his name. None of us recognised him – he was a stranger to us.'

'Oh, we know his name,' said Chaloner, watching them both intently for a reaction. 'It was William Quartermain – the King's physician.'

Van Goch's eyebrows shot up in apparent astonishment. 'What was *he* doing in our orchard? We assumed it was someone who came to cause us harm, but who dropped dead before he could put his evil plan into action. It would not be the first time.'

Chaloner blinked. 'Other men have dropped dead in your orchard for no obvious reason?'

'Of course not,' snapped van Goch. 'You deliberately misunderstand me. What I meant was that other rogues have broken in with mischief in their hearts – they smear excrement on our walls, shove nasty messages under our doors, or try to set us alight.'

'We knew the body was no commoner, because of the nice clothes,' mused Beuningen. 'But it never occurred to us that it was a courtier. God save us! Is this the depth to which your government sinks? Sending Court physicians against us?'

'It was not the government,' averred Chaloner, hoping he was right. 'Besides, Quartermain may have died elsewhere, and his body left here to unsettle you.'

42

'Then it worked,' said van Goch sourly. 'Because I *was* unsettled, and I have forbidden my staff to venture out there for a morning stroll again. It is a pity, as it is the only place we could exercise without being pelted with rotten vegetables.'

'Is that what Heemskerch was doing when he found Quartermain? Taking a stroll?'

Beuningen nodded. 'We all went out together, for security, and the clerks took it in turns to scout ahead and make sure the way was safe for the rest of us. Heemskerch shot off obligingly, but raced back moments later, braying about a cadaver. A short while later, when we were still in an uproar over it, he packed his bags and slunk away.'

'And that is all we can tell you, I am afraid,' said van Goch with finality.

Chaloner left Bedford House in a thoughtful frame of mind. He may not have questioned Heemskerch, but he had learned three useful facts. First, that Quartermain's body must have appeared in the orchard *after* the diplomats' Saturday walk, if it was discovered on their Sunday one, which narrowed down the time frame for it being dumped there, if not for his death. Second, that Heemskerch had fled suspiciously soon afterwards and was suspected of being a spy. And third, that Heemskerch was not as lowly a cog as van Goch and Beuningen wanted him to believe.

Outside, he hesitated, wondering whether to go to the Fleece and check on his charges again, or report Quartermain's death to the Earl. He opted for the latter, thinking his employer would rather hear it from him than a gossiping courtier. So he set off towards the rural lane called Piccadilly, where his employer had built himself a glorious mansion.

He could have taken a hackney carriage, but he felt like stretching his legs. However, he had not gone far before he began to doubt the wisdom of his decision. It was bitterly cold, sleet slanted into his face, and the winter-bare branches of trees flailed in the wind. He glanced up at the scudding clouds, and wondered if the sleet would turn to snow.

Clarendon House was a handsome building, with enormous windows that flooded its interior with light. Unfortunately, they also flooded it with cold, and to make it remotely habitable, the shutters had to be kept closed all day, rendering it a gloomy place to live. The fact that there was so much marble and stone did not help either, and it was not unknown for the Earl and his family to abandon their dark, chilly splendour to join the retainers in the plainer but cosier attics upstairs.

The mansion was unpopular with Londoners, too, who believed the Earl had built it using bribe money won from selling the port of Dunkirk to the French at an absurdly low price. Because of this, they scathingly called it Dunkirk House. Soldiers patrolled its grounds and guarded its gates, repelling those who wanted to smash windows, hurl muck, and uproot the saplings along the drive.

Chaloner trotted up the steps and hurried through the front door, glad to be out of the wind. He removed his coat and shook off the worst of the wet, noting from the puddles and smears on the floor that others had done the same before him.

He glanced around. The Earl had crammed his home with priceless works of art, all designed to show how far he had risen in the world. There was barely a scrap of wall that did not have a painting, while sculptures of all shapes and sizes lined up like armies preparing for battle. The time was evidently three in the afternoon, because the house exploded into sound as fifty clocks began to sound the hour. The cacophony lasted for some time, as most were not very accurate, and one kept striking until Chaloner lost count at thirty-four.

While at home, the Earl spent most of his time in the chamber called My Lord's Lobby. It was a wintry, unwelcoming space, even with an enormous fire blazing in the hearth and thick Turkey carpets on the floor. Chaloner turned towards it, stopping en route to exchange greetings with the new secretary, Matthew Wren, who sat shivering at a desk by the door.

Wren was a quietly modest man, the son of a bishop and cousin to the city's most celebrated architect. He had dark hair and eyes, a delicate, almost pretty face, and an elfin physique. He had the happy knack of always saying or doing the right thing, and the Earl had taken to him at once. So had Chaloner, although there were times when he wondered if the secretary was not a little *too* good to be true.

'It is bitter today,' remarked Wren pleasantly. 'My friends at the Royal Society say we shall have a gale before too long.'

'We have a gale now,' averred Chaloner. 'The trees are bent double with the force of the wind, and the sleet was like needles in my face.'

'No, a *real* gale,' said Wren earnestly. 'One that will do far worse than bend a few trees. They predict a blow that will bring down houses.'

Chaloner regarded him curiously. 'How can they tell?'

'Science.' Wren smiled beatifically. 'It is all to do with

the displacement of mercury and the theory of *horror vacui* – nature abhorring a vacuum. I can explain further if you like.'

'Later, perhaps,' said Chaloner. Listening to Wren explain some new scientific principle was infinitely preferable to telling the Earl that his favourite physician was dead, but nothing would be gained by delaying the inevitable.

Wren gestured towards the door. 'Watch yourself in there today, Tom. George arrived a few minutes ago, and reported something that made him very angry. Our master will be looking for someone to lash out at, and as he does not like you very much . . .'

Moments later, Chaloner stood in front of the Earl. His employer was sitting almost on top of the fire in an effort to keep warm, and had opted for a nightcap in place of a wig, which looked peculiar with his ceremonial robes of office. Most ministers only donned their official finery for special occasions, but the Earl loved his, and wore it all the time. The garb for Lord Chancellor of England was especially glorious, and included a handsome gown with thick gold stripes and plenty of tassels.

'Chaloner,' he said crossly. 'I understand you disobeyed me, and wandered off in pursuit of your own pleasures this morning. I told you to watch Olivia Stoakes and George.'

'Quartermain is dead, sir,' explained Chaloner. 'And as his body was found in the Dutch embassy, I thought you would want me to start investigating.'

'The Dutch embassy?' squawked the Earl, horror replacing ire. 'What was it doing in there? That will do nothing for the cause of peace!'

46

'The cause of peace is dead, too,' said Chaloner soberly. 'Van Goch and his people are preparing to leave as we speak.'

The Earl put his head in his hands. 'Well, history cannot blame *me* for this stupid war. I did all I could to prevent it, even though it made me unpopular in many quarters – including with the King. But tell me about Quartermain. Are you sure he is dead?'

'Yes – he was identified by his fountain-pen.'

'The silver one with the inscription?' asked the Earl, who loved expensive things, and always noticed other people's. Chaloner nodded, so he added, 'How did he die?'

'Natural causes, apparently.'

The Earl regarded him askance. 'So he went to Bedford House and promptly breathed his last? That does not sound very likely.'

'No,' agreed Chaloner. 'Was I right in assuming that you want me to look into it?'

'I suppose you had better, given that he was the King's physician, as well as my own. However, first you must find Olivia Stoakes. She failed to return from today's jaunt – which I was in the process of telling you when you interrupted with the news about Quartermain.'

'Is that why George came to see you?'

The Earl nodded. 'He and Olivia are related by marriage, so he is naturally concerned for her welfare. When they left the Fleece, George assumed she was with Stoakes, and Stoakes assumed she was with George, so no one missed her. Then my wife called for her services, and it was discovered that Olivia was nowhere to be found.'

'They left her behind in the Fleece?' asked Chaloner in alarm, recalling that not everyone there had been happy to see courtiers in their midst. 'All alone?'

'She is not there now – George went back to look. I would be less perturbed if her husband was not the master of *Assurance* – the unlucky ship that went down while fastened to a pier. God only knows how *that* happened.'

'Shall I try to find out, sir?'

The Earl pondered for a moment, then nodded. 'Yes, because I dislike the coincidence of Stoakes losing his ship and his wife within such a short period of time. Perhaps it is happenstance, but I should like to be sure. However, there is another matter I want you to explore as well. Do you know Simon Beale, the royal trumpeter? I imagine you do, as he was one of you.'

Chaloner frowned. 'One of me, sir?'

'A Parliamentarian. He played music for Cromwell.'

Blowing a few fanfares for the Lord Protector hardly made Beale a Parliamentarian, although Chaloner had the sense not to say so, especially as the Earl was regarding him rather beadily, as if to remind him that his own past had not been forgotten either.

'Presumably, he has renounced his former allegiances,' he said, keen to discuss the trumpeter rather than himself. 'He must have done, or the King would not have reappointed him.'

'Yes, yes – I am not concerned about *his* loyalty,' said the Earl, in such a way that Chaloner wondered if he was really saying that the same could not be said of present company, which would be grossly unfair, given all Chaloner had done for him since entering his employ. 'He is a staunch Royalist now.'

'Right,' said Chaloner. 'But what about him, sir? Do you want him monitored?'

'No, I want you to find his trumpet, which he has

mislaid. Not only is it solid silver, but I want it played at the ceremony next week.'

'The ceremony in White Hall, to celebrate the King's return to the city?'

The King was currently at Hampton Court, and word was that he would return to his capital at the end of the month. The average Londoner might not be thrilled by the prospect of having him home, but his sycophants were busily preparing a suitable welcome. Several events had been organised, including a night of revels in the Banqueting House.

'Of course not,' said the Earl indignantly. 'I refuse to have anything to do with that – it will be debauched. I refer to the one where we shall all observe the late King's murder. He was beheaded on the thirtieth day of January, and we have marked the occasion ever since with a national day of mourning. There will be church services all over the country, and I am organising the ceremony in Covent Garden.'

'Oh, yes. You have been generous with funds to improve the place.'

'Because the King will be there,' explained the Earl, 'which means that my service *must* be the best in the city. And Beale's silver trumpet is an essential part of it.'

'The King will not attend the commemoration in St Paul's Cathedral or Westminster Abbey?'

'No, he will come to mine,' stated the Earl firmly, but then winced. 'Although my enemies are trying their hardest to lure him away. I *cannot* let them succeed, Chaloner – if they do, it will be a public snub, which would be disastrous for my standing at Court. It is imperative that all goes according to plan, so you must do your utmost to locate the trumpet.'

'As well as finding Olivia, learning what happened to *Assurance*, and investigating how Quartermain came to be dead in the grounds of Bedford House?' asked Chaloner, a little pointedly. It was a heavy workload by any standard.

'If you would not mind.'

At the back of Clarendon House was a suite of rooms for the Earl's senior staff. It comprised not only beds for those obliged to work late, but a place to store ceremonial livery and accoutrements. There was also an informal parlour where they could relax between duties.

The parlour was rarely used, as most retainers preferred to spend their spare time somewhere other than a large, cold, inhospitable room with uncomfortable furniture, meagre victuals and no fire. It was busy that day, however, because George had invited the courtiers who had been at the Fleece to join him there for a glass of wine – which he had supplied himself, as the Earl considered such perks a waste of money. Chaloner was pleased. It would make asking about Olivia much more convenient. Unfortunately most of the party were already drunk, so unlikely to be helpful.

George was with his brothers, and Chaloner reviewed what he knew about them before going to ask about the missing woman. All three had been staunch Parliamentarians, who had grown rich during the interregnum by selling property confiscated from bishops. They had declared themselves to be Royalists at the Restoration, and the government had chosen to believe them, purely because they had also expressed a desire to be generous to 'worthy politicians' if past 'errors of judgement' were overlooked. No money had come the government's way so far, but its ministers continued to live in hope.

The Thompsons were unmistakably siblings – tall, striking, confident men in their forties with fine yellow hair. The wars had cost each one something that had changed his appearance for ever: George had sacrificed a leg, Robert his teeth and Maurice his eyebrows.

George was the eldest, most elegant and wealthiest, and had been a major in Cromwell's army. Next came Robert, reputed to have been a Commonwealth spy, although Chaloner did not believe it – whispering was essential for such an occupation and Robert never spoke in anything less than a bellow. He had replaced his missing teeth with false ones, but the clips holding them in place were unreliable, so they often fell out, most famously when he was taking Holy Communion in St Paul's Cathedral, obliging him to retrieve them from the chalice when the rite was over. The youngest was Maurice, who resolutely painted in new eyebrows each morning, although they had always been rubbed off by the time he retired to bed.

'We should forget the old King's execution,' Robert was bawling, rather imprudently given that he was in the home of a very passionate monarchist. 'Most of the regicides are dead, imprisoned or exiled, so it is time to put the sordid past behind us and look to the future.'

'Hear, hear,' agreed Maurice. 'I shall not attend one of those dismal church services, where we recount every grisly detail of the day he lost his head. I would rather spend the time in my new coffee house.'

'Did you hear that Maurice has bought the Floating Coffee House?' asked George of his guests. 'You should visit – it is a splendid place. Very smart.'

Chaloner had been, although not since it had changed ownership. It was a converted barge, moored in the middle of the Thames, which meant it could only be reached by boat. It was a pleasant jaunt on a fine day, less so when the weather was inclement.

The courtiers began to relate tales of their experiences with the place. As the brothers were clearly delighted with the chance to indulge in a little impromptu advertising, and would probably resent being interrupted, Chaloner went instead to where Stoakes was helping himself to wine. Unfortunately, the captain was struggling to stay upright, and his flushed face, unsteady hands and glazed eyes suggested that asking him about Olivia was likely to be a waste of time.

'When did you last see your wife?' Chaloner asked, deciding to try anyway.

'In the Fleece,' slurred Stoakes. 'Hours ago. I told the blasted woman to stay by my side, but she does love a church. She must have wandered off to look at one and . . .'

Chaloner caught him as he pitched forward, and was grateful when someone came to help manoeuvre him to a bench, where he promptly began to snore, still clutching a goblet. As it was glass, Chaloner tried to prise it away from him, lest he injured himself, but the fingers tightened like small vices.

'Do not bother,' advised the good Samaritan. 'He is the sort who cannot rest easy without some sort of drinking vessel in his hand.'

Chaloner had met Dr Christopher Merrett several times. He was a navy physician, which meant he was acquainted with Wiseman, and also a member of the Royal Society. He had an open, honest face, and was famous for his work with the wounded after the Battle of Lowestoft, saving dozens of lives with his skill and care.

'Are you one of George's guests?' asked Chaloner, unable to recall him among the party that had gone to the charnel house.

Merrett regarded him askance. 'Certainly not! I came to tend the Earl's gout, given that his own physician failed to answer the summons. Of course, I have just learned from this horde that poor Quartermain has been dead for God knows how long . . .'

'I have been charged to find out exactly what happened to him. Do you know anything that might help me understand how he came to die in the grounds of Bedford House?'

Merrett shook his head. 'All I can tell you is that he had an enormous medical practice – everyone wants to be tended by the physician who looks after the King. But he was surly and unfriendly, and I am afraid I found him difficult to like.'

'Abigail Williams did not have that problem.'

A smile twitched Merrett's lips. 'She would find something to admire even in the most sullen of rogues, as long as he was rich. So she seduced Quartermain, did she? I am not surprised: her regular beau, Sir William Brouncker, is in Portsmouth, and she is not a lady for chaste solitude.'

'I do not suppose you have seen his wife, have you?' Chaloner nodded towards Stoakes.

'Olivia? I met her this morning, and she told me that she planned to spend her day visiting churches – we both share a love of ecclesiastical architecture, you see. I imagine she was vexed when Stoakes insisted on going

53

to a mortuary instead, and she is making up for lost time.'

'Which churches?'

'She did not say. Do not worry about her, Chaloner. She will return when she has had her fill of clerestories and piscinas. After all, where would you rather be – here among this rabble or discovering the delights of medieval architecture?'

Neither option sounded greatly appealing to Chaloner, so he avoided a reply by asking more questions about Olivia, although he learned nothing new. Eventually, he saw the Thompsons had exhausted the subject of coffee houses, so he excused himself from Merrett and went to talk to them instead. The brothers also advised him not to be unduly concerned about Olivia, while the courtiers who were with them added that she had a reputation for unorthodox behaviour.

'She is peculiar,' confided Lady Muskerry, who was famous for her paucity of wits. 'In Oxford, she turned down an invitation to the King's masque in order to attend a lecture on crypt-building. It beggared belief!'

'And she *reads*,' added Sir Alan Brodrick, the Earl's favourite cousin, with a fastidious shudder. 'Books and the like. She is a queer old duck.'

Eventually, Chaloner decided there was nothing more he could do, other than wait until Olivia elected to return of her own volition – when he would beg her not to disappear without telling anyone again. He stopped at the Fleece on his way home, just in case she had decided to stay on after the others had left. She had not, and the rope-dancer Jacob Hall informed him that the performance that evening was not open to courtiers anyway.

'It is for *normal* people,' he explained curtly. 'With the

54

kind of jokes *they* like. We exclude your type, lest your delicate ears are offended.'

If Hall meant the show would be lewd, Chaloner could only assume that he had not yet spent much time with Lady Castlemaine, as she and her cronies could give the most ribald of acts a run for its money. Or did Hall mean that the jests would be directed against the King and his Court – that the performance would be danger-ously subversive? Chaloner shrugged inwardly. If so, His Majesty and his asinine friends only had themselves to blame.

Chapter 3

It was seven o'clock before Chaloner woke the following morning, roused from sleep by a racket from the Piazza, where the market was just getting under way. The stalls had no licences, so were technically illegal, but residents turned a blind eye, because it was convenient to have fresh produce available right on their doorsteps.

He went to look out of the window. Wiseman's house stood on the corner of James and King streets, affording splendid views over the spacious square with its fringe of elegantly arcaded mansions and the barn-like St Paul's church opposite. It was still dark, so the stallholders were working by lamplight. Sadly, he noted that there were far fewer of them than there had been before the plague.

He washed in the bowl of lukewarm water left for him by Wiseman's servants, and dressed in blue jacket and breeches, white shirt with just enough lace on the collar and cuffs to be respectable, and black riding boots. Over them went a dark-brown long-coat that had been oiled against the rain, and a hat with a wide brim. They were neither showy nor plain, and would allow him to move comfortably in the variety of places he would need to visit that day – Clarendon House to check that Olivia had returned, the Fleece again if she had not, White Hall to ask after the trumpet and Quartermain, and the Savoy Wharf to see about *Assurance*.

When he was ready, he walked down the stairs, but met Wiseman coming up them to see him. The King's Surgeon was an impressive man, tall with the physique of a wrestler, which he maintained by lifting heavy stones before breakfast every morning. He never wore any colour except red, which his detractors said was to disguise the blood he spilled. Chaloner thought it was just because he liked to be noticed. At first, Chaloner had rejected Wiseman's overtures of friendship, as the surgeon was arrogant, rude and opinionated, but he had gradually come to appreciate his finer qualities: loyalty to friends and a keen intelligence.

'Do you fancy an excursion to the Floating Coffee House?' Wiseman asked. 'It has recently been purchased by Maurice Thompson, and my colleague Merrett tells me it is now an excellent place for a brew.'

Chaloner tried to avoid going to coffee houses with Wiseman, as the surgeon's bombastic presence invariably led to trouble, and while such establishments encouraged freedom of speech, Wiseman's tended to annoy rather than inspire. He flailed around for an excuse.

'I have a lot to do today and—'

Wiseman made a dismissive sound in his throat. 'You can spare an hour for a jaunt with me. Besides, I do not want to go alone, as I am tired of everyone making snide remarks about me having no friends. I have lots of them: you, Temperance . . .'

He trailed off, the list complete, and Chaloner reconsidered the invitation. The Floating Coffee House was moored near the wharf where *Assurance* had gone down, and as it was still too early to go to Clarendon House to see about Olivia, it would be a good opportunity to ask questions about the lost ship. He nodded assent and received a grin of pleasure that made him slightly ashamed of his motives for acquiescing.

Outside, they huddled into their coats as they were buffeted by an angry breeze, and were glad of the shelter afforded by the wall at the back of Bedford House. Before they turned south, Chaloner waved to a hunched figure hobbling through the churchyard. It was Widow Fisher, a woman of indeterminate years who lived in the vicinity, although no one knew precisely where; she earned a meagre living as a seller of vegetables and second-hand newsbooks. She waved back, then staggered in a particularly fierce gust.

'I heard Olivia Stoakes gave you the slip yesterday,' said Wiseman as they went. 'Of course, you could not have stopped her once she had made up her mind to go a-wandering. She is a very determined person. Dangerously so, in fact, and does not know what is good for her.'

Chaloner smiled wryly, knowing exactly what had precipitated the remark. 'In other words, she is your patient, but refuses to follow some advice you have dispensed.'

Wiseman regarded him in surprise. 'How did you guess?' When Chaloner did not answer, he went on, 'She has a skin rash, but declines to let me drain the evil humours with leeches, electing instead to use hot poultices. It is working, more is the pity – I wanted it to get worse.'

It was Chaloner's turn to be startled. 'You do not like her?'

'I do not like anyone who thinks they know better than me,' declared Wiseman, then softened. 'Yet despite her arrogance, she does have a fine mind, and often asks my opinion. I gave her a lengthy lecture on drowning the other day, and she sat spellbound the entire time.'

Chaloner smothered a smirk, knowing the surgeon often interpreted glazed eyes and blank stares as proof of appreciation. 'I don't suppose you know where she might have gone?'

'The general consensus is that she went to admire churches, although she had not returned when I left Clarendon House at ten o'clock last night. I hope she has come to no harm.'

Chaloner was alarmed: after everyone's assurances, he had expected her to wander in during the evening, bemused as to why her disappearance should have caused such concern.

'Do you have any reason to think she might be in trouble?' he asked worriedly.

'Not specifically, but London is less friendly to courtiers than it was before the plague. For example, Harry Brouncker's brothel was attacked without provocation the other day. Of course, I cannot abide that man, so I was rather gratified by the incident.'

'What has Brouncker done to earn your ire?'

'He cheats at chess,' replied Wiseman, which Chaloner took to mean that they had played a game and the surgeon had lost.

Wiseman changed the subject then, unwilling to be quizzed about his defeat, and began to talk about the entertainers at the Fleece – the troupe called Urban's Men – from an anatomical point of view. Several had skeletal or muscular anomalies that intrigued him, and he was itching to look down the throat of the sword-swallower.

'There is a dwarf, too, and I have never dissected one of those,' he enthused. 'I told Landlord Clifton to let me know if there are any accidents. I pay well for unusual specimens.'

'Are you sure it is wise to make that sort of offer?' asked Chaloner. 'It is begging for someone to provide you with a body before its owner has finished with it.'

'Perhaps, but just think of the benefits to medical science,' shrugged Wiseman, unrepentant. 'Besides, these people should be flattered that I am interested in them.'

The Savoy Wharf was reached via a narrow, tunnel-like alley off the Strand called Ivie Lane, which tended to be used as a latrine during the night, so was never a pleasant place to linger. Chaloner and Wiseman hurried down it, trying not to breathe too deeply, and emerged into the open cobbled square that provided a working space for carts with goods to collect or deliver. Leading from it was a long, wide wooden pier that was large enough to accommodate several ships simultaneously. It was studded with bollards, and reeked of seaweed and sewage.

Moored a short distance away was the Floating Coffee House, sometimes called the Folly. This was a sturdy barge with a wooden superstructure, which comprised one long room with plenty of large oblong windows. It had been elegant when it had first been built, but had suffered from sitting in the middle of the Thames for six years – its timbers were stained an unattractive blackish green, and its glass was opaque with grime. Chaloner regarded it critically, thinking that the improvements

Maurice claimed to have made must all be inside, as its exterior was, if anything, shabbier than ever.

'This is where *Assurance* went down nine days ago,' remarked Wiseman, breaking into his thoughts by pointing to a spot halfway along the pier. 'Look – you can just see the top of her mast sticking out of the water.'

Chaloner peered down at it, pondering the disaster. The fact that twenty men had drowned suggested it had happened very quickly, or the alarm would have been raised and they would have managed to jump ashore. He wondered if the Navy Board had a theory as to what had occurred there, and decided to visit their headquarters later to ask.

He and Wiseman walked to the end of the pier, where a small flotilla of boats was waiting to ferry patrons over to the Folly. He expected a noisy ruckus as the watermen vied for their custom, so was pleasantly surprised to discover that someone had introduced a system – the skiffs queued up in the order they arrived, and so did those wanting a ride.

'The Folly is currently popular with sea-officers,' explained Wiseman, 'and you know how they love neatness and discipline. To provide it, Maurice hired some wounded sailors to oversee business shore-side: Judd and his shipmates not only prevent unseemly scuffles, but the work allows them to earn an honest living – the captains are generous with tips.'

He nodded to a wooden booth, where several men lounged. The one called Judd had pride of place on a high chair that allowed him to survey his domain without moving. He was missing both legs below the knee, while his friends had lost arms, eyes, feet and wits. When he saw Chaloner and Wiseman, he gave a piercing whistle, and a waterman immediately began to row towards the pier steps. He watched the manoeuvre critically, simultaneously holding forth to two captains, who had just arrived back from the Floating Coffee House and had stopped to exchange pleasantries with him.

'Do not talk to *me* about the Sick and Hurt Fund,' he was declaring, all righteous indignation. 'The money is gone – spent on the veterans of Lowestoft. There is nothing left for those of us maimed at Vågen.'

'I am not surprised,' sighed the first of the two sea-officers, a tall, handsome man with a confident demeanour. 'The government would rather forget that Vågen ever happened.'

'But it *did* happen,' growled Judd, indicating his legs. 'These remind me of it every day.'

'What about your back pay?' asked the second officer, who was shorter, plumper and older than his companion. 'Have you had it yet?'

Judd scowled. 'No, and some of us are owed for *two years'* service! We beg and beg for what is ours, but the government claims its coffers are empty. Of course, it can still find the money to let His bloody Majesty drink himself senseless with expensive whores every night.'

'Hush, Judd!' gulped the tall captain uneasily. 'It is treason to disparage the King, and I do not want to end my days in the Tower.'

The ferry arrived at that point, so Chaloner heard no more of the discussion as sailors came to hand him and Wiseman down the steps and into the bobbing craft. There followed a wet and choppy ride to their destination, leaving him hoping that the Folly would be worth the discomfort of a sodden rump and several facefuls of drenching spray, or he was going to be irked with

Wiseman for suggesting it. More sailors were waiting to help them up the steps when they arrived, and another had been allocated the task of opening the door.

Inside, Chaloner saw that Maurice had given the walls a lick of paint, but had not done much else to beautify his new domain. Perhaps he had decided that no further investment was needed, as his coffee house was already popular – it was packed to the gills. It smelled of burned beans and pipe-smoke, all overlain with mould, wet clothes and seaweed. Yet the atmosphere was convivial, and Maurice himself was there to greet newcomers with the traditional coffee-house greeting.

'What news?'

'Just the usual,' replied Wiseman. 'The plague continues to decrease, London is its customary troubled self, and the King will soon return to White Hall.'

Maurice waved a hand to indicate he knew all that. He had applied fresh eyebrows that morning, although with more enthusiasm than care, so the result was a single dark slash across his forehead.

'Well, you are both welcome anyway,' he said. 'Sit down and try my lovely brew.'

He placed two dishes on the long table that ran the length of the room, and filled them with a black, viscous liquid from his long-spouted pot. Then he waited expectantly for compliments. Chaloner was impressed and said so, although he suspected that the coffee was palatable mostly because it had been pre-sweetened with sugar, which he usually declined to use as a silent and useless crusade against the deplorable treatment of plantation workers. Wiseman, never gracious, responded only with an ambiguous sniff.

'Tom!' came a cheerful voice from the far end of the

63

room, and Chaloner smiled when he saw Captain Salathiel Lester, master of HMS *Swiftsure*. Lester was a burly, genial man with a ready grin, and he and Chaloner had become friends when they had been shipwrecked together in the Baltic. 'I heard you were back. Indeed, I planned to call on you today.'

He came to sit with them. There was not really enough room, and resulted in some serious elbowing on Wiseman's part, all of which Lester amiably ignored.

'I thought you would be at sea by now,' said Chaloner, grabbing the table to prevent himself from being jostled off the end of the bench. 'Do not tell me *Swiftsure* is still being repaired from the mauling she suffered at Lowestoft?'

Lester grimaced. 'She should have been ready months ago. Our dockyards are a disgrace, Tom! Even bribery does not encourage them to hurry.'

'Good gracious!' murmured Chaloner.

'John Harman offered a colossal sum to expedite matters on *Royal Charles*,' Lester went on in disgust, 'but it made no difference. He was supposed to get her back in December, but they keep on dallying. Still, they promised to have her ready by Monday, so perhaps the end is in sight. For him, at least.'

'And *Swiftsure*?'

'God knows,' sighed Lester. 'Weeks, probably.'

'*Assurance*,' said Chaloner, seizing the opportunity to talk to a man whose nautical opinions he trusted. 'Do you know how she came to sink?'

Lester shook his head. 'But we will when she is weighed. I wish *you* would investigate what happened to her, Tom. It is altogether a peculiar affair.'

'Christopher Merrett agrees,' put in Wiseman. 'Do

you know him, Lester? He was one of the physicians at Lowestoft.'

'A good man,' averred Lester. 'Our death toll would have been much higher if he had not been on hand to help the wounded.'

'Why do you think *Assurance* is a "peculiar affair"?' probed Chaloner.

'Several reasons,' replied Lester. 'First, she was moored when she went down. Second, twenty crew were supposedly keeping watch on board. Third, it was not a rough night. And fourth, she is a young ship, barely two decades old. Have you spoken to Stoakes about it? He must have a view – although he is a courtier, and thus an incompetent, so bear that in mind when you corner him.'

'I will do it today,' promised Chaloner. 'When I ask after his wife.'

Whom he sincerely hoped would now have returned safely to hearth and home.

Not long after, Wiseman began informing the other Folly patrons about the forthcoming day of Fast and Humiliation for the executed King – Londoners generally referred to it simply as 'the Fast'. He planned to attend the ceremony in Westminster Abbey, because it was the one that the King would favour.

'His Majesty will be coming from Hampton Court, so will pass the abbey en route,' he explained. 'Stopping off there will mean he will not have to get up so early.'

'No, he will go to the service in the cathedral,' argued Lester. 'The royal pew has high sides, so he can sit inside and take a nap with no one any the wiser.'

'Nonsense,' declared Maurice. 'He has pledged to grace the church in Covent Garden. My brother George told me, and he is a member of Clarendon's household.'

There was general laughter at the notion that the King's word should be considered binding, which was the point when Chaloner stood to leave. Of course no one could believe anything the duplicitous monarch promised, but only fools said so in public.

He had a soggy journey back across the river, and was glad that Judd's men were there to catch his arm when his foot skidded on the slick steps of the pier. He tipped them generously, because he had been appalled to learn that they had given years of loyal service to the navy, which had then decided it was not going to pay them for it.

It was less than a mile from Ivie Lane to Clarendon House, but he took a hackney carriage anyway. The weather was too cold for needless heroics. He alighted at the front door, and hurried inside, where he learned that Olivia was still missing.

'And I am now very worried,' said the Earl tersely. 'I wish you had not abandoned her.'

'I assumed she would be safe with her husband and a score of other courtiers,' objected Chaloner defensively. 'She was—'

'Just find her,' snapped the Earl. 'Now what about Beale's trumpet? How is the search for that going?'

It was not going at all, given that Chaloner considered it less important than Olivia, a courtier's body in the Dutch embassy, and the loss of one of His Majesty's warships.

'No progress as yet, sir, but—'

'It is imperative that you locate it before the Fast,' interrupted the Earl sternly. 'If you fail, His Majesty might attend another ceremony instead.'

66

Chaloner was sure the King would not base his decision on whether a trumpet was present or not, but suspected there was no point saying so. 'I will do my best, sir.'

The Earl glared. 'I am not sure you understand the gravity of the situation, Chaloner. I invited the King to my Fast and he agreed to come. If he then chooses to go elsewhere, it will tell the world that I have lost his favour, and my enemies will race in to destroy me. I *must* have the trumpet. *Everything* depends on it.'

Chaloner was sorry that the Earl felt his future was so precarious. He was alarmed, too, that the livelihoods of everyone who worked in Clarendon House should be contingent on whether a trumpet was produced. Moreover, if able ministers could rise and fall on such an issue, it made him wonder if a monarchy was really such a good system of government. Not for the first time, he wished Cromwell had not died and England was still a republic.

'So go and find it,' the Earl continued testily. 'And bring it to me as soon as possible. You may hunt for Olivia, look into Quartermain and investigate *Assurance* at the same time.'

Chaloner bowed and took his leave, wondering how easy it was to buy a trumpet. No one would ever know – except Beale, and Chaloner was sure he could be paid for his silence.

As he was hungry, Chaloner went to the retainers' parlour on the top floor before resuming his enquiries. The cook usually sent up a batch of freshly baked knot biscuits at that time in the morning, which would suffice until he could buy something more substantial.

He was not very pleased to discover that the plate

contained nothing but crumbs. This was because the courtiers George had invited the previous evening were still there, having enjoyed a night of serious gambling. The air was hazy with smoke, and smelled of stale sweat and wine. Stoakes was sound asleep, but everyone else stood around Brouncker and Wren, who were playing a game of chess. As everyone was betting on Brouncker to win, Chaloner put two shillings on Wren. Touched by the expression of support, the secretary came to talk to him while Brouncker considered his next move.

'Are you sure it is wise to turn your back on him?' asked Chaloner. 'I am told he cheats.'

Wren winced. 'He has no need to cheat – he can win honestly, as you are about to learn to your cost. Have you come to ask after Olivia again?'

'Yes. Have you seen her?'

'Not since yesterday morning, when she was dismayed to learn that Stoakes wanted her to accompany him to the charnel house – she had planned to spend her day visiting churches. However, I went to the Fleece myself yesterday, and I was not very impressed with those entertainers. I would not be surprised if one of them has done away with her.'

Chaloner blinked in surprise. 'Urban's Men? But I saw her giving them money. Why would they hurt someone who was generous to them?'

Wren sniffed. 'Because they are rebels. Once the fire-eating, acrobatics and sword-swallowing acts were finished, they put on a series of nasty little satires. It had the mob baying for blood – *our* blood.'

'Did you see Olivia there while this was going on?'

'No – her party slipped out during the first burlesque, once the audience began to scowl at them. Any remaining courtiers, including me, beat a retreat during the second, when it became clear that trouble was in the air. I can only assume that Olivia was left behind in the scramble, although I did not notice her obviously, or I would have done something about it.'

'But equally, she may have taken her leave *before* the mood turned ugly?'

'She might,' conceded Wren. 'I hope she did – she is a nice lady. A little quick to express her opinions, perhaps, but I admire that in a person. Damn! Brouncker has just moved his Queen. I was hoping to trap her.'

While the secretary went to assess if the game could be salvaged, Brouncker sauntered to a table, where he poured himself some wine. Then he came to talk to Chaloner.

'Wren says you are good at solving mysteries,' he said keenly. 'Is it true?'

'Why?' asked Chaloner warily. 'Do you have one that needs exploring?'

'Of course not! I merely wondered if you were looking into any naval matters. I have an interest in them, you see, because *I* am a veteran of Lowestoft.'

Chaloner was not in the habit of discussing his work with the Earl's enemies, so was unwilling to mention his interest in *Assurance*. 'Yes, but I am not at liberty to discuss it.'

A sly expression suffused Brouncker's face. 'Are you sure? The Duke of York is very generous to those who provide him with pertinent information.'

'I shall bear it in mind,' replied Chaloner, although with no intention of accepting the offer. The Duke could commission his own investigations if he was worried about what went on in the fleet he commanded.

Wren moved a pawn at that point, so Brouncker returned to his game. Chaloner went to rouse Stoakes, which was far from easy. When the captain's eyes eventually flickered open, they were red and glazed, and the first thing he did was demand wine. Chaloner gave him a beaker of breakfast ale instead, a weak brew that might help wash the poisons from his system.

'I take it my wife is still missing,' he slurred, sitting up and draining the cup in a single swallow. 'I wonder where she can be.'

'Where have you looked so far?' asked Chaloner.

Stoakes frowned his puzzlement at the notion that he should have taken action himself. 'Nowhere. I stayed here, ready to greet her if she came back. I left others to do the hunting.'

'So when did you last see her?'

Stoakes struggled to remember. 'She was at my side when the fire-eater performed in the Fleece, then she wandered off to chat to the Thompson brothers. I assumed she was with them when we decided to leave. It transpires she was not.'

'Why would you assume such a thing?'

'Because they are kin – Maurice's wife, twenty years in her grave now, was Olivia's cousin. She has always enjoyed his company more than mine.'

Chaloner gazed at the dissolute specimen slumped in front of him, and did not blame her. 'Have you spoken to them about her disappearance?'

'Not today, but I shall amble along to their house later. They live in James Street, just off the Covent Garden Piazza.' Stoakes sighed gloomily. 'January has not been good to me. I lose my ship one week, and my wife the next.'

70

'Ah, yes,' said Chaloner. '*Assurance*. Do you know why she sank?'

'Weather,' replied Stoakes promptly. 'There was a wind that night, so water slopped through her gunports, flooding her lower decks.'

That did not sound very likely to Chaloner, as he knew for a fact that it was standard practice to seal gunports when a ship was in enclosed waters. 'Why was she moored at the Savoy Wharf? It is not the usual haunt of warships.'

'I put her there because I had planned to host a banquet for selected sea-officers – I thought the Savoy would be more convenient for them than Chatham, because most have lodgings in the city. Obviously, I cannot offer on-board entertainment with no ship, so I have had to abandon the scheme, which is a wretched shame.'

Chaloner continued to ply him with questions, but by the time he was forced to concede defeat, he had no idea if the captain was just a bumbling drunk who should not have been given command of a rowing boat, or a man adept at keeping secrets who knew exactly what had happened to his wife and his ship.

Wren had just lost the chess, so Chaloner went to hand over his two shillings. Grinning victoriously, Brouncker began calling for another opponent. Suddenly, everyone found other things to do. Brodrick, the Earl's favourite cousin, came to chat to Chaloner, aiming to look busy so that Brouncker would not challenge him.

'Do not bother looking for Beale's trumpet,' he advised. 'It is solid silver, so whoever took it will have melted it down by now. You will be wasting your time.'

Brodrick was one of the Court's most infamous rakes, although the Earl would hear no bad word spoken against him. Thus it was entirely possible that *he* had made off with the instrument during some drunken jape, and was now afraid to admit it.

'No thief would risk selling such a distinctive item,' he went on. 'And it *is* distinctive, as you would know if you had ever heard the thing – a truly vile instrument. So what other option would he have, other than turning it into ingots? If I were you, I would buy another. No one will ever know, least of all my cloth-eared cousin.'

It was advice Chaloner fully intended to act upon.

As it happened, there was an instrument-maker in Covent Garden. His name was William Bull, and he was delighted by the prospect of a sale. Unfortunately, it transpired that producing trumpets was a lengthy process, and could not be managed in time for the Fast. Disappointed, Chaloner asked him to keep an eye out for a second-hand one. Then he walked to the Stoakes house on Long Acre, hoping to find Olivia there, all astonishment to learn that she was the subject of a hunt.

Long Acre had once been an elegant street, boasting such residents as Oliver Cromwell, the poet John Dryden and the sculptor Nicholas Stone. It had fallen into disrepute after the Restoration, when its wealthy elite had moved to newer, more fashionable developments in Hatton Gardens, Clerkenwell and St James's Square. Tradesmen and prostitutes had taken their places, and Long Acre was now famous for coach-makers and brothels. Chaloner had lived there himself not long ago, although his former landlord had died of the plague and the house was now converted into tenements. It was already suffering under the new regime: its windows were filthy, its door was battered and moss grew on its roof. He could not bear to look at it, and hurried past with his head bowed.

Stoakes and Olivia occupied a large residence at the Drury Lane end. Chaloner knocked on the door, which was opened by a maid with enormous teeth, freckles and a bonnet under which every strand of hair had been scraped. There was a running sore on her left cheek, which she fingered continually, and was the reason why Chaloner declined her offer of a freshly baked cake, even though he was hungry. She introduced herself as Emily the cook-maid, and said she had not seen her mistress since the previous morning.

'You must be concerned,' said Chaloner.

'Not at all, sir,' replied Emily, looking startled by the notion. 'She is always disappearing to visit some church or other, and will return when it suits her. You should not worry.'

'The Earl of Clarendon disagrees, and has charged me to find her. Stoakes has given me permission to explore the house and look for clues as to her whereabouts. May I begin?'

It was a lie, but Chaloner doubted Stoakes would remember what he had or had not said in Piccadilly. Emily looked sceptical, but stood aside, albeit reluctantly. She then proceeded to accompany Chaloner to every room, clearly of the opinion that he was not to be trusted. All the while, she regaled him with a non-stop stream of information, none of it helpful.

'I feel sorry for the mistress,' she confided at one point. They were in an uninviting parlour – it had furniture, but none of the effects that made a house a home, like cushions, paintings and ornaments. 'He is a dimwit, whereas she is clever. She reads all the time, and loves music, the theatre and witty conversation.'

'You denigrate the man who pays your wages?'

Chaloner started up the stairs, noting marks on the walls where other artwork had been removed.

'*He* does not pay me – she does,' replied Emily. 'So it is she who has my loyalty.'

Chaloner entered a room that contained a number of manly accoutrements – a blade for shaving, a pot of wig powder and some coffee-house tokens. He did not need Emily to tell him it was Stoakes' domain, and that the couple slept apart.

'I went to the Fleece this morning,' Emily chattered, 'which is where the captain thinks he lost the mistress. No one there remembers her staying on after the other courtiers left, so she must have slipped out before the trouble started.'

'What trouble?' asked Chaloner sharply.

'Oh, nothing to worry about,' Emily assured him hastily. 'Just a disagreement over the satires that Urban's Men performed. Not everyone likes them, see. Mrs Stoakes would have done, though, if she had stayed on to watch. She *loves* entertainment that makes people think.'

Chaloner entered a second bedchamber, where there was an array of hairbrushes, pots of face-paints, writing paraphernalia and some slippers. As many were items that Olivia would have slipped into a reticule if she was going to spend a night away, he was forced to conclude that she had not planned to be gone, which did not bode well for a happy ending.

'Do you know which churches she wanted to see?' he asked, supposing he would have to search them all before making his concerns public.

'No, but I can tell you that she has been to one hundred and twenty-nine to date,' replied Emily proudly. 'She adores old buildings.'

'Please think about it, and let me know if anything comes to mind. Incidentally, I cannot help but notice that the house is oddly devoid of frills – the furniture is here, but there are no paintings, clocks, cushions, ornaments and the like. Where are they all?'

'The captain took some to *Assurance*, as he likes his creature comforts when he goes to sea. But most are still in storage, because we have only just returned from Oxford, and I have not yet had time to unpack them.'

Chaloner sent her to fetch him a cake, just to grab a few minutes on his own. The moment she had gone, he conducted a rather more invasive search of Stoakes' room, which paid off, because under the mattress was a letter. It was a very long one, and at first glance appeared to be a meaningless ramble. However, Chaloner was a spy, and knew a coded missive when he saw one. And as most people did not communicate so without a good reason, it told him that Stoakes was involved in something questionable.

He sat on the bed and studied the missive, but there was no pattern that he could see, so he supposed he would have to work on it later. Or better yet, ask his friend John Thurloe to do it for him. Thurloe had been Cromwell's Secretary of State and Spymaster General, and now lived quietly in Lincoln's Inn or at his Oxfordshire estates. Chaloner had not seen him since September, although they had exchanged several letters.

'What is that?' demanded Emily, and Chaloner glanced up to see she was standing at the door, watching him suspiciously. She had a very stealthy tread. Or perhaps she had just learned to creep about, so as not to wake the belligerent Stoakes from his drunken stupors.

Chaloner showed her the message. 'Have you seen it before?'

'No, but it looks like a lot of nonsense to me.' She glared at him. 'Shall we put it back where we found it? I do not think the captain will appreciate you prying into his private papers.'

'He might,' replied Chaloner, putting it in his pocket, 'if it helps me to find his wife.'

'And what if she does not want to be found?' asked Emily rather sulkily. 'What if she has taken herself off for a bit of peace and quiet? I would not blame her. *I* would not want to spend time at White Hall – it is very noisy and horribly debauched.'

'Then she can tell me so herself,' said Chaloner firmly, 'when I track her down.'

Chaloner's next port of call was around the corner, to the Thompsons' house on James Street. There was no reply to his knock, so he climbed over the wall at the back and picked the lock on the scullery door. He did it not because he suspected them of anything remiss, but because they were Olivia's kin, so if she had decided to escape her bullying sot of a husband, then where better to hide than with family?

He knew the brothers were rich, but he had not appreciated how much until he stepped inside their home. Its décor was sumptuous, and all in exquisite taste. It made Clarendon House look cheap and vulgar by comparison. He recognised any number of original paintings by Holbein and Caracci, and the rugs on the floor were made of imported silk. What it did not contain, however, was Olivia.

He let himself out the way he had come, and took a

hackney carriage to the Navy Office. This was a handsome building in the shadow of the Tower, where an army of officials and their staff oversaw the construction and repair of ships, along with the management of the dockyards. One was a man with whom Chaloner was slightly acquainted: Samuel Pepys, the ambitious Clerk of the Acts. Pepys occupied a very lavish office, which made Chaloner wonder how the navy had the gall to claim there was no money to pay its sailors.

Pepys was in a hurry, as he had a boat waiting to carry him to Greenwich, but he spared a moment to tell Chaloner that engineers had conducted a preliminary survey of *Assurance*. Unfortunately, it had not revealed why she had gone down, although answers were expected the following Saturday, when plans were afoot to weigh her.

'The theory is that she was by a gust of wind sunk down to the bottom,' he confided. 'She was designed for Guinea, manned and victualled. Twenty men drowned. Poor ship! I was twice merry on her in Captain Holland's time.'

Pepys could tell him no more, so Chaloner took another hackney to Lincoln's Inn, only to be told that Thurloe was out. He went to the nearest coffee house and faithfully duplicated the message he had found in Stoakes' room. He then sent the original to Thurloe, along with a note saying he would visit the following morning. When he had finished, he returned to Clarendon House, to corner Stoakes and demand an explanation of the coded missive.

The captain was still in the retainers' parlour, but Chaloner had made a tactical mistake by sending the original document to Thurloe, because it allowed Stoakes to swear with perfect honesty that he had never seen the copy before. Chaloner tried every ruse he knew to make him talk, but to no avail.

'It was in your bedchamber,' he said, frustrated enough to lay himself open to accusations of burglary. 'Hidden under the mattress.'

'Not by me,' declared Stoakes stubbornly. 'And remember, Olivia and I were in Oxford until recently, and our house was shut up. Anyone might have put it there while we were gone.'

Eventually, Chaloner gave up, contenting himself with the thought that he would not need Stoakes' cooperation if Thurloe broke the code. He stayed a while longer in Clarendon House, asking questions of anyone who would talk to him about Olivia, the trumpet, *Assurance* or Quartermain, then walked to White Hall, to do the same there.

He persisted until evening, then gave up. He knew he should go to the Floating Coffee House to ask Maurice if Olivia had confided any plans to leave her husband or visit churches outside London, but he was tired, cold and very hungry. He decided to go home instead. He pulled up his coat collar and huddled into it. The wind was back, making him stagger, and the ground was strewn with broken twigs and wet litter. It was raining, too, needles of sleet that slanted into his face.

Then he saw three distinctive figures ahead: the Thompson brothers. They were being conducted over Charing Cross by a linksman – a boy with a torch, who helped pedestrians along streets that were uneven and covered in things that were not very nice to tread in.

Chaloner could have run to catch up with them, but he lacked the energy. Nor did he have a linksman to prevent him from stumbling over unseen obstacles in the dark. He hurried after them as best he could, but lost them at the corner of Piccadilly and the Haymarket. Then his eye lit on an establishment called the Gaming House. As there was nowhere else the Thompsons could have gone, he aimed for it.

The Gaming House had once been a fashionable resort, but like many such places, it had fallen into decline under Cromwell's Puritans. It was reputed never to close, and was certainly lively that evening, as music could be heard thumping from within long before Chaloner reached the door.

He entered and immediately wrinkled his nose at the reek of stale tobacco smoke, spilled wine and sweat, along with the cheap perfume that had been sprayed around in an effort to disguise them. The décor was black and red, as if it could not make up its mind whether to be sinister or sultry, and the lighting was low. Several card games were in progress, some players showing the strain of heavy losses, others impassive. There were laws against excessively high wagers, but the Gaming House ignored them, as many reckless gamblers had learned to their cost.

George, Maurice and Robert had found a table, and several serving girls had descended on them, perching on their laps, giggling and flirting. Although it was not officially a brothel, the lines were very finely drawn, and the Gaming House prided itself on its versatility. The brothers were obviously enjoying themselves, and as Chaloner knew it would be counterproductive to alienate them by driving the women away, he decided to wait until they were alone. To pass the time, he would order some dinner.

As if she had read his mind, a woman with provocatively swinging hips came to recite a list of what was on offer from the kitchen that evening, although it was difficult to concentrate on what she was saying while she undulated so. Chaloner chose dressed cod's head, as it was the only item he could remember when she had finished. He accepted a glass of hot wine, too, but declined the offer of a romp upstairs while the cook prepared his food. Pouting her disappointment, the woman swayed away.

While he waited for his cod, he opened the latest government newsbook. It was *The Oxford Gazette*, which had supplanted *The Newes* and *The Intelligencer* when the Court had fled London the previous summer. Although the title page proudly declared it was 'Published with Authority', Chaloner thought it was a waste of good paper, because, like its predecessors, it contained little of substance. Overseas intelligence revolved around the marriage of the Pope's 'nephew' and a 'tragedy in Vienna' involving a pair of sparring eagles. Chaloner liked birds, but even he failed to understand why this particular item should have made international headlines.

Home news was even less inspiring. There was a snippet from Berwick telling of privateers cruising off the coast – Dutch, no doubt, hoping to catch British merchantmen; and a note from Falmouth reporting the arrival of a ship from New England carrying masts for the navy.

Inevitably, his eye was drawn to the back page, which carried the latest Mortality Bill: two hundred and seventy-one deaths in the city, only seventy-nine of which were the plague. It represented another drop from the terrible figures of August and September. Of course, seventy-nine was no small number, and he wondered if the disease would rage again when winter broke.

His meal arrived, an alarming dish with eyes and teeth. He ate the onions that surrounded it, and mopped up the juice with bread, but did not feel equal to tackling a severed head. He pushed it away, but too vigorously – it skittered off the plate and on to the floor, leaving an oily trail across the open newsbook. He objected on principle to paying threepence for the damage – which was how much *The Oxford Gazette* cost – so he stuffed it in his pocket, hoping he would remember to remove it when he got home, or his coat was going to stink of fish.

Feeling more energised with the food inside him, he went to tackle the Thompsons. The women had gone and the brothers were huddled over their table, looking for all the world like conspirators about to bring down the government – a notion that was reinforced when they sprang apart guiltily when they realised he was standing over them. Fortunately for them, he knew they had only been talking about Olivia, as Robert had been speaking, and his idea of a discreet whisper was a bellow that could have been heard in White Hall.

'George and Robert looked for her today,' said Maurice, once Chaloner had sat down and explained why he was there. All that remained of the single slash of eyebrow applied that morning was a bluish smudge that looked like dirt. 'I would have done it myself, given that she is my kin by marriage, but I was busy at the Folly.'

'Unfortunately, we have nothing to report,' bawled Robert, speaking around his false teeth with difficulty. 'We visited all her favourite churches, plus the New Exchange. Personally, I suspect she has had enough of her dimwit husband, and has gone back to Oxford.'

'I would not blame her,' growled George. 'The man is a disgrace.'

'She *loved* Oxford,' averred Maurice. 'With all those books. I imagine she *has* gone there, and is happily ensconced in a library as we speak, reading to her heart's content.'

'Tell me what happened in the Fleece,' said Chaloner, recalling the personal effects in Olivia's bedchamber, and sure she would have packed a few if she had jaunted off to another city. 'Stoakes thought she was with you when everyone left.'

'And we assumed she was with him,' said Maurice, rubbing his eyes tiredly. 'He is her husband, after all. I was wed once, and I always looked to *my* wife's personal safety.'

'When did you last see Olivia exactly?'

'After the fire-eater,' replied Maurice. 'She was all admiration for his skill. As were we.'

'George and I went back to the Fleece this afternoon,' shouted Robert. 'But no one there remembers her. It is no surprise, I suppose, as the place was packed last night – for the satires, which was why we had to leave, of course. They poked fun at White Hall.'

'That should not worry *you*,' Chaloner told him. 'You are not a courtier.'

'But George is, and we Thompsons always stick together,' bawled Robert. 'Of course, no Londoner can accuse *us* of cowardice, as we did not flee during the pestilence – we stayed, attending to business and helping the Lord Mayor to implement his plague measures.'

'Will you tell me if you hear from Olivia?' asked Chaloner, standing to leave. 'Or if you remember anything that might help me to find her?'

'Of course,' replied Maurice. 'Although I do not think we need be unduly concerned. She is a resourceful lady, and will reappear when it suits her to do so.'

As it was on his way home, Chaloner decided to stop off at the Fleece. The Stoakes' cook-maid and the Thompsons claimed that no one there remembered Olivia, which might well be true, as most folk thought all courtiers looked the same in their frilly clothes and silly wigs. But the entertainers would recall her, because she had given them money.

The tavern was emptier than it had been the previous night. The atmosphere was different, too. Then, it had been full of noisy revelry; now it was quiet and rather sullen. Chaloner attracted no attention in his anonymous brown long-coat, but Lady Castlemaine and her friends were the recipients of some very hostile glares when they sailed in asking for Jacob Hall.

'He is not here,' snarled the landlord, William Clifton, a tall, thin man with angry eyes.

'Then where is he?' she demanded petulantly. 'I want to see him.'

'Performing in another tavern,' replied Clifton shortly. 'I cannot recall which one.'

'Of course you can,' coaxed Will Chiffinch, one of the Court's least likeable debauchees. He took a coin from his purse and waved it tantalisingly. 'I imagine this will jog your memory.'

'Then you imagine wrong,' retorted Clifton, so offended that the rage in his eyes burned brighter than ever. 'They live here, but they do not tell me their business, and I do not ask. Now bugger off.'

Realising at last that she was not welcome, and might

even be in danger, the Lady took her leave, dragging the bemused Chiffinch with her. The moment the door closed behind them, a growl of resentment rose about the arrogance of the Court. Chaloner had heard it all before, although not from quite so many people all at the same time. He hoped the King would contrive to worm his way back into his subjects' affections fast, or there was going to be some serious trouble.

He ordered a flagon of ale, and mentioned Olivia's disappearance to one or two patrons who claimed to have been watching Urban's Men the previous night, but it soon became clear that he was wasting his time. People remembered being 'infested' by courtiers, but no one recalled individuals – they were all just wealthy people in impractical clothes.

After a while, he went to the courtyard, trying to recall where Olivia had been standing. The night was dark, wet and very windy, with noisy deluges of water splattering from roofs and balconies. The yard looked vast now that it was empty, lit by two feeble lamps, the beams of which did not penetrate very far into the blackness.

So what had happened to Olivia? Had she gone to explore churches, or to enjoy herself in Oxford, and would return at her own convenience? If she had, she would be dismissed from Clarendon House, as the Earl hated unreliable staff. Or had she inadvertently strayed into the wrong company, and had suffered the consequences? Would her body be found floating in the Thames in a few days' time? Or had she been kidnapped, and would be held prisoner until a ransom was paid? But surely a demand would have been made by now if that were the case?

The more Chaloner considered, the more he became

certain that Olivia would not have vanished without telling anyone – if not Stoakes, then her cook-maid or her Thompson kin. She also would have taken some of the accoutrements from her bedchamber. Logic told him that she was dead, no matter how much he might wish it were otherwise.

He was so engrossed in his reflections that he almost did not hear the sound of attack until it was too late. He whipped around, drawing his sword even while his brain was still registering that all was not well. He ducked in time to avoid the cudgel that was aimed at his head, and heard a grunt as the weapon cracked into the wall, jarring its wielder's arm.

'Stop,' he ordered. 'I am—'

He faltered, aware of several shadows converging on him, although the darkness made it impossible to tell exactly how many. Alarmed, he went on a wild offensive in the hope of thwarting the ambush before it began in earnest, and heard any number of hisses, howls and yelps as he laid about him, sword in one hand and dagger in the other. Then a blow knocked him to his knees, and he knew he had to do something fast, or he would be overwhelmed by sheer force of numbers.

He lurched upright and launched another furious attack, driving his assailants towards the stage. There was a large canopy above it, designed to protect the entertainers from the elements. It should have been flapping in the wind, but it hung still and heavy-bellied because of the amount of rainwater that had pooled in it.

He hopped on to the dais, and backed away until he was sure his attackers had followed. Then he reached up and slashed the canvas with his sword. Freezing water cascaded down, and although he was also drenched by the deluge, he had been braced for it, and was able to dart away while everyone else was still spluttering in shock.

Outside the Fleece, he ducked into a nearby doorway, to see whether anyone would give chase. No one did, perhaps because they were wet through and the wind was picking up again. His teeth began to chatter, and eventually he could stand it no longer. He abandoned his hiding place and hurried home, glad it was not very far.

Chapter 4

There followed one of the windiest nights that Chaloner could ever remember. He heard tiles ripped from the roof, and there was such an unnerving rattling from the chimney that he wondered if it might crash through the ceiling on top of him. He drowsed fitfully, then leapt up clutching a knife when he heard someone open his bedroom door. It was an apparition in a billowing scarlet gown, and for one terrifying instant, he thought it was the devil, come to snatch his soul.

'A blade will not save you from a collapsing roof,' remarked Wiseman drily, 'which is why I am here – to urge you to sleep in my laboratory instead.'

'No, thank you,' gulped Chaloner. That particular chamber was full of horrors in glass jars, none of which would be conducive to a good night's rest.

'My parlour, then,' said Wiseman impatiently. 'Hurry, man! The chimney is unstable. I should have seen to it last summer, but as I was away with the Court . . .'

Chaloner followed him down the stairs to the room where the surgeon liked to relax. It was decked out in red, and looked more like a harlot's boudoir than the haunt of a successful *medicus*. Chaloner slumped into a cushion-filled chair, and accepted a cup of wine.

'I am beginning to wish I had stayed in Oxford,' the surgeon muttered, sitting opposite and drinking his claret straight from the jug. 'Not only are Londoners annoyingly reproving of those of us who had the sense to flee the plague, but the city is not the place it used to be – too many of my favourite places have closed, never to reopen.'

'You cannot blame people for being bitter about being left to fend for themselves,' said Chaloner quietly. 'Their loved ones might still be alive if the government had done its duty.'

'Nonsense,' declared Wiseman. 'It would have made no difference.

Chaloner knew better than to argue. 'How was Hampton Court today?' he asked instead.

'Dull – there is hardly anyone left. The King plans to leave it in eight days, timing his arrival here to coincide with the Fast. Most of his courtiers are already home, preparing a suitable welcome for him.'

'The Fast,' sighed Chaloner, suspecting that a good part of the city would like to see His Majesty suffer the same fate as his 'martyred' father. 'People do not want to mourn the old King, and it is unwise to force them to do it. There will be trouble.'

'Excellent! Trouble means wounds, which is always good news for a man in my profession.'

'Speaking of medical men, how well did you know William Quartermain?'

'Not very, although we both held royal appointments, so our paths often crossed at White Hall. I heard his body was identified from a fountain-pen, which is hardly scientific, so I have arranged for him to be exhumed. *I* will recognise his person, regardless of its state of decay.'

'That will not be necessary,' said Chaloner hastily. 'There are—'

'It is no bother,' interrupted the surgeon, eyes gleaming. 'Indeed, I shall enjoy it. There is nothing quite like dissecting a person one knows. It helps no end.'

'Helps with what?' asked Chaloner, but then decided he did not want to know. 'If *I* die, please stay away from me. I want to go into the ground intact, with everything where it is meant to be. I do not want parts of me pickled and kept for posterity.'

'Quartermain said the same thing,' confided Wiseman, 'but I doubt he meant it.'

Chaloner was sure he had, but before he could say so, there was an almighty gust of wind that made him and Wiseman start up in alarm. The windows groaned in their frames, and the fire guttered furiously. There followed a nerve-racking series of thumps and scrapes, as lumps of masonry were either dashed against the house or torn off it.

'Was Quartermain the kind of man to drop dead from natural causes?' Chaloner asked a few minutes later, when the racket had subsided somewhat.

'Any of us could drop dead from natural causes, at any time,' replied Wiseman darkly. 'However, he had no underlying medical problem that I know of, which is even more reason to dig him up and have a rummage through his innards.'

Chaloner could not suppress a shudder. 'Let me try one of two other lines of enquiry before you resort to that. Such as looking at the place where his body was found.'

'Bedford House's garden. Well, you know what you

are doing, I suppose, but I doubt you will find any clues there. Not after ten days.'

Chaloner imagined he was right, but dared not say so, lest it prompted Wiseman to dash off in search of a spade. 'What else can you tell me about Quartermain?'

'He invented a remedy for the plague, which he called King's Gold. Yellow is my wife's favourite colour, and I considered buying some for her – until I discovered what was in it.'

Wiseman's wife was a resident of Bedlam, the victim of an insidious brain-rot that had stripped her of all rational thought. Despite the fact that she had been lost to him for many years, he still took considerable care over her well-being. He had whisked her away to safety while the plague had raged, despite the burden she imposed on him socially and financially. Chaloner liked him the better for it.

'Which was what, exactly?' he asked.

'A compound known in the trade as *poxbane*, because we surgeons use it – in a very diluted form – to treat sufferers of the French pox. It reeks of garlic, which is why I knew at once what Quartermain had added to his so-called remedy.'

Many medical men were of the opinion that the best way to combat a virulent infection like the plague was by deploying a similarly powerful cure, and Quartermain would not have been the first to devise a tonic that was more dangerous than the disease.

'Did he sell a lot of it?'

'No, because I challenged him shortly after he had manufactured his first batch, and we had a full and frank discussion about how much poxbane is safe. He was reluctant to listen at first, so I told him that I would report him for murder if he sold another pot.'

It sounded more like a vicious quarrel than a 'discussion', and Chaloner could well imagine the scene: Quartermain's outrage that a mere surgeon should attempt to interfere with a physician's business, and Wiseman's arrogant conviction that he was in the right.

'So what did he do?' he asked.

'What I told him,' shrugged Wiseman. 'He reduced the amount of poxbane to what I consider to be a safe level – enough to be beneficial without being toxic.'

'And what happened to the first batch? Did he destroy it?'

'Unfortunately, some had already been sold, although we shall never know if it killed anyone, as any fatalities will have been blamed on the plague. Incidentally, I saw Kersey last night. I told him to be on the lookout for corpses with rashes on their necks. Olivia was my patient, and I would know those pustules anywhere, even if the rest of her is missing.'

'You think she is dead?' Chaloner hoped that if she were, they would recover more of her than just a neck.

'Of course she is dead! She was not the sort to quit the city without telling anyone, and if she had been abducted, you would have heard from those responsible by now. I imagine she became separated from her cronies in the Fleece and fell victim to thieves. Or vicious cowards who saw a lone courtier and decided to vent their spleen on an unarmed lady.'

'I hope you are wrong.'

'So do I, but we both know I am not. Lord! Listen to that wind! Let us pray we still have a roof over our heads in the morning.'

*

The gale made sleeping all but impossible, and Chaloner jumped every time something was hurled against the window shutters or ominous creaks came from above. Wiseman nodded off, though, worn out from his excursion to Hampton Court, leaving Chaloner to ponder his investigations alone. He feared too much time had passed to solve the mysteries surrounding Quartermain and *Assurance*, while he was not sure how to proceed with Olivia. And the trumpet? He would hunt for it when he had time, but it was not as important as the other matters, no matter what the Earl thought.

Shortly before dawn, there was another violent gust, this time accompanied by the roar of falling masonry. It came from the attic, so Chaloner followed Wiseman gingerly up the stairs to see what had happened. They were greeted by the sight of Chaloner's bed heaped in broken chimney, and the roof open to the sky.

'That will be expensive to repair,' grumbled Wiseman. 'Although at least I shall not have the added cost of a lodger's funeral to bear.'

Chaloner clambered across the rubble to rescue his viols, the only items he owned that were important to him. He tutted at a scratch on one, but they were otherwise unscathed, which was little short of miraculous. More practically, Wiseman excavated some of Chaloner's clothes, and when he had collected a big enough armful, led the way back down the stairs. He opened the door to his laboratory.

'You may use this as a sitting room until the attic is rebuilt,' he said generously. 'I shall clear a space for two chairs, so you can entertain. And you may sleep in my parlour.'

'Thank you,' said Chaloner, although he could not

imagine subjecting any guest of his to the laboratory. It contained, among other grisly items, the brain of Wiseman's brother-in-law, which Chaloner considered a downright peculiar thing to hoard.

It was well past seven o'clock by the time they had salvaged all they could from the attic, although it was still dark outside. Wiseman hurried away to start his morning stone-lifting routine, while Chaloner went to the kitchen in search of something to eat.

The servants were there, sitting comfortably around the table. Wryly, Chaloner noted that although they must have known about the fallen chimney, none had come to help. There were three of them, all minus various body parts, and although he had never asked, Chaloner had a nasty suspicion that the missing pieces were preserved in the laboratory.

They smiled a friendly welcome, and gave him a bowl of cold oatmeal flavoured with salt. There was also a cup of the surgeon's best wine, which Chaloner declined, partly because he disliked strong drink quite so early in the day, but mostly because he doubted they had Wiseman's permission to raid it, and was loath to be accused of complicity in their crime.

'You want to be careful,' said the footman, who was missing a leg. Unlike George, he had refused a wooden replacement and used crutches. 'You should not go out looking like that.'

'Like what?' asked Chaloner, glancing down at his black breeches, blue coat and white shirt. None of it should have raised eyebrows.

'Fashionable,' explained the cook. He had been relieved of an arm, which he used as an excuse to explain away his mediocre culinary skills. 'People despise courtiers for disappearing during the plague, and there is talk of reprisals.'

'What sort of talk?' asked Chaloner uneasily.

'Talk by Adam Urban,' supplied the groom, who claimed his left eye had been bitten out by a horse, although Chaloner had always failed to see how this was possible, given the shape of human faces and equine teeth. 'Have you heard of him? He has a fine way with words, and makes us understand how seriously we have been wronged.'

'You mean he is a rabble-rouser,' said Chaloner coolly. 'Is he associated with Urban's Men – the troupe that performs in the Fleece?'

Wryly it occurred to him that Adam Urban was almost certainly an alias, as it roughly translated as *defender of men in the city*. It was a clever name for someone who performed political satires that turned his audiences against White Hall.

The groom nodded. 'He is not afraid to speak the truth. And I agree with him – no one should have been allowed to abandon London without a backward glance.'

'You did,' Chaloner pointed out. 'You went to Oxford with Wiseman.'

'Yes,' acknowledged the groom. 'But that was different.'

Chaloner could not see how.

'Urban is right to tell people to rise up against cowardly courtiers,' declared the cook, deftly moving away from an argument he knew they would not win. 'And when they do, we shall stand shoulder to shoulder with them.'

'Wiseman is a courtier,' Chaloner reminded them. 'Will you denounce him, too? Think very carefully before you reply – you might find yourselves homeless.'

The trio exchanged alarmed glances. 'But Urban wants

us to fight tyranny and oppression,' objected the cook, dismayed. 'We cannot refuse! It will look as though we think the King was right to leave London at the first sign of a bubo.'

'Where did you hear this treasonous call to arms?' asked Chaloner curiously. 'In the Fleece on Sunday evening?'

When they nodded, he reflected that it was small wonder that his fellow courtiers had been encouraged to leave with hostile glares – the rest of the audience had known what was coming and wanted them gone before the troupe got down to the real business of the night. And yet, Olivia had given the actors money, and earlier, had pressed her husband to pay for his dead crew's funerals. Did this mean she considered herself a woman of the people, and had lingered in the Fleece in the mistaken belief that she would be spared the fury of a mob whipped into a frenzy by Urban's radical homilies?

'He is scheduled to speak at our church in an hour,' put in the groom. 'Why not go and hear him for yourself? Then you will see that everything he says makes sense.'

Chaloner decided that he had better do just that, because if Urban and his cronies *were* preaching insurrection, they needed to be stopped. Such speeches delivered to a city that already seethed with resentment and privation were likely to see it in flames.

When Chaloner stepped outside the house, he was almost blown off his feet by the force of the wind. His hat was torn from his head, and would have been lost permanently if it had not snagged on a bush. He did not attempt to don it again, but shoved it in his pocket.

Smashed tiles and debris littered the street, and Wiseman was not the only one to lose a chimney.

Everywhere was a chaos of dead leaves, sodden paper, branches and sundry other rubbish, all blown into untidy piles or churned into damp eddies in porches and corners.

A few doors down, someone else was emerging into the gale. It was Brouncker, who was promptly deprived of his hat and wig. They blew towards Chaloner, who managed to snatch them from the air before they sailed off towards Kensington. He went to hand them back.

'Thank God it was not gusting like this at Lowestoft,' gasped Brouncker. 'Or our cannonballs would have been hurled straight back at us.'

The remark revealed that Brouncker knew little about naval warfare, as any ship opening gunports in the middle of a storm was likely to sink. But Chaloner let it pass.

'I see you suffered some damage, too,' he said, nodding at the heap of tiles that had been ripped from Brouncker's roof and deposited in the street below.

'My brother did,' replied Brouncker. 'It is his house, not mine, so he can see to it when he gets back from Portsmouth. Although that will not be too soon, I hope, as I prefer living here alone.'

'Will you move out when he returns?'

'Give up free bed and board?' asked Brouncker archly. 'Not on your life! However, his presence does cramp my style. I dislike a straitlaced older brother pursing his lips every time I bring home a whore.'

Especially if the whore was Abigail, thought Chaloner drily. Both men staggered as another gust struck them, and Brouncker tightened his grip on the papers he was carrying.

'I hope our navy has not lost any more boats,' he said worriedly. 'It was not blowing nearly so hard when *Assurance* went down, but go down she did.'

'What do you know about her?' probed Chaloner.

'Going to sea with the fleet has made me an expert in matters maritime,' boasted Brouncker, 'so I can tell you lots. For example, I know the *precise* contents of her wine cellar, where the cheese was stored, and how many courtiers can fit around her captain's table.'

Chaloner saw he was wasting his time. He started to nod a farewell, but Brouncker was going in the same direction and kept pace with him.

'I shall be busy today,' he chatted. 'The Duke wants my advice on a new kind of sea-warfare, after which I must choose him a new lady from my bordello. The last one has a cold, and no man likes to be sneezed at while he is about his business.'

Chaloner hoped the Duke would have more sense than to solicit Brouncker's opinion about anything remotely nautical, but would not bet on it. However, he had every confidence that Brouncker's selection of prostitutes would be exemplary.

At that moment, the wind plucked several pages from Brouncker's hand. Wailing in alarm, he scurried after them, and Chaloner started to help until the first one he caught transpired to be a filthy poem by one of the Court wits. He was no prude, but he was not about to waste his time haring after that sort of thing. He left Brouncker to manage alone and resumed his walk across the Piazza.

The only vendor at the market that morning was old Widow Fisher, struggling to stay upright as she clutched the basket that held her wares. She opened her mouth to hail Chaloner, but one of Brouncker's pages landed square on her face. She peeled it away, leaving a trail of dirty finger marks on the clean white paper, then stuffed it inside her hat as extra insulation against the cold.

'Got any *Gazettes*?' she asked, when the grubby head-piece was back in place.

She begged all the residents of Covent Garden for newsbooks, which she then sold cheap to those who could not afford the full three pennies. She did not read them herself, because, as she had mentioned rather proudly several times, she was illiterate. She grinned when Chaloner handed over the one he had stolen from the Gaming House the night before, either uncaring of or oblivious to the powerful reek of fish that went with it.

'Buy a carrot from me, sir,' she begged plaintively. 'I got some nice ones.'

As it was a foul day for an elderly person to be out, Chaloner gave her a shilling, and told her to deliver them all to Wiseman's house. She snatched the coin before he could change his mind, then regarded him with beady black eyes.

'I saw you last night, coming home late. Got a sweet-heart, have you?'

'I am done with those,' he replied, not without rancour, given that he invariably fell for the wrong kind of woman entirely. 'They are more trouble than they are worth.'

'Ach – you will change your tune when the right lass comes along. Now, give me a penny and I will tell you something worth knowing. One good turn deserves another, after all.'

Chaloner thought he had done her a good turn already, but she was shivering from the cold so he obliged, glad no one was there to see him as a soft touch.

'No one approves,' she said, jerking a gnarled thumb over her shoulder to the church. 'Good folk being kept out while it is prettified to remember that vile old tyrant. I was *glad* when they chopped off his head. He was a monster, who considered himself equal to God. Well, we are well rid of him, and if his sons do not watch themselves, they will follow him to the scaffold. And good riddance.'

'Lord!' breathed Chaloner, stunned to hear such opinions so brazenly expressed. 'I hope you do not say this to anyone else.'

'I say it to anyone who will listen,' she declared haughtily. 'And I shall say it to His so-called Majesty, if he dares pollute my nice church with his debauched presence next Tuesday. It is shameful – all that money squandered on it, just because *he* might deign to come. And all the while, his subjects suffer from lack of food and warmth.'

Chaloner started to back away, but she gripped his arm with a claw-like hand. He could have broken free, but not without hurting her.

'And I will *not* be solemn on the anniversary of the beheading,' she went on defiantly. 'It should be a day of celebration, not "fasting and humiliation". Things were much better under Cromwell, and we should never have invited another pleasure-loving wastrel to rule over us.'

'Please,' begged Chaloner. 'You really should not—'

'Lots of people agree with me. There have been rumblings in taverns and coffee houses for weeks, and Mr Urban says nothing new. Have you heard him yet? He has been preaching all over the city, and will talk here today. Look – hordes of folk are going to listen.'

Chaloner glanced to where she pointed, and saw that dozens of people were trooping into the church. Tuesday mornings – especially windy ones – never usually attracted those sorts of crowds.

'The vicar is rash,' he said, 'allowing a fanatic to use his pulpit.'

Widow Fisher chortled. 'He is still abed and knows nothing about it. And it serves him right! How dare he say that we, his faithful flock, can only use *our* church for one hour each morning, while the rest of the day is for courtiers and their workmen only!'

Chaloner sincerely hoped she was exaggerating, as if not, it would be yet another grievance Londoners could add to what was already a lengthy list.

'Urban will be arrested soon,' he predicted. 'So will anyone caught listening to him.'

'They will not catch him – he is too clever. But this is not the information your penny bought. I thought you should know that I was not the only one who watched you walk across the Piazza last night. So did someone else.'

'Who?'

'The acrobat dwarf who lodges in the Fleece.'

Chaloner was fairly sure that a dwarf had not been among those who had attacked him the previous night, but decided a visit to the entertainer was in order anyway. Why else would the man be watching him, unless he had been involved in the assault?

'You are very well informed,' he said. 'I do not suppose you know anything about the courtier who disappeared from the Fleece on Sunday evening, do you?'

Widow Fisher shook her head. 'I see everything that happens here in the Piazza, but the Fleece is too far away to interest me. Although I do enjoy an ale there on occasion . . .'

Chaloner nodded toward Bedford House. 'Then what about the body that was found in the garden there last week?'

Her eyes lit in triumph. 'Now *that* I can answer. I saw the Court physician sneak in alive, and I saw him carried out dead the next day.'

'*Sneak* in?' echoed Chaloner.

'Yes – he crept along like a thief until he reached the back gate. Then he looked around to make sure no one was watching, opened the gate with a key, and stepped inside.'

Chaloner regarded her intently. 'He had a key? Are you sure?'

'There is nothing wrong with my eyesight.'

'So he died in there? No one dumped his corpse in the garden later, in the hope of frightening the Dutch ambassador?'

'No – he walked in hale and hearty enough. I can tell you something else, too: he went in just before midnight, because I heard the bellman call the hour.'

'Why were you out at such a time?'

She lowered her voice. 'No one knows, but I live inside the Brouncker family vault. It is nice down there – dry and clean. It is also as silent as only graves can be, so the only way I get to know the time is by coming out and listening for the bellman. Which is what I was doing when I spotted you and the dwarf last night.'

'You have taken up residence in a tomb?' blurted Chaloner.

She nodded. 'The coffins were inconveniently placed, but I have them arranged to my liking now. It is very comfortable, and much nicer than a shack with a leaky roof.'

'I hope none of its inhabitants died of the plague.' Chaloner stepped away smartly.

'One did, so I dragged him out and put him in the

common pit. I do not mind sharing with the ancient dead, but fresh ones smell.'

Chaloner was sure they did. 'No one has noticed you down there?'

'Why would they? The Brouncker brothers have never visited, and nor will they now they think a plague victim is within. They will not bother me. But it is cold standing here and I have your carrots to deliver. We shall chat again another time.'

Mention of the plague made Chaloner look at the graves as he walked through the Covent Garden churchyard, particularly the common pit, which was a sinister mound at the back. The wind had scoured off a layer of its topsoil and exposed something pale – a bone perhaps, or a sliver of dead, white flesh. He shivered, and began to plan his day to avoid thinking about it.

Now added to his list of things to do was visiting the Fleece, to ask the dwarf why he had been watching him. Perhaps the man would know something about Olivia's disappearance, too, and could be persuaded to talk. He also had to see if Thurloe had decoded the message from Stoakes' house, and find a way forward with Quartermain. He could not forget *Assurance* either, although the trumpet would have to wait. However, none of it was as important as assessing the danger posed by Urban, because taking steps to prevent civil unrest had to be his first priority. After all, nothing else would matter if the country descended into the chaos of another civil war.

He entered the church, glad to be out of the wind. Over the last month, a remarkable transformation had taken place within. Thirty years of smoking candles had dulled its walls and ceiling, but the Earl had ordered –

and paid for – a coat of creamy white paint and the plasterwork to be touched up with gilt. He had also arranged for any broken windows to be repaired and scrubbed until they shone, while new pews had been purchased to replace the ones that left splinters in their users' thighs.

Although it was still the hour when the church officially belonged to locals, several craftsmen had already arrived, doubtless under pressure to finish their work on schedule. Three were on the scaffolding around the altar, while others were buffing the marble steps. All studiously ignored the glowers of those who resented the infraction.

'Urban will kick them out,' Chaloner heard one man whisper to his wife. 'He will not overlook this outrage – this brazen breaking of what was agreed.'

Nearly everyone in the congregation that day hailed from London's underclasses – those with the meanest of jobs or no jobs at all, for whom life was a desperate daily struggle. They had come from the rookeries in St Giles and the Savoy, eager to hear what Urban had to say about the injustices inflicted upon them by the ruling elite. Chaloner moved among them, listening to conversations. Most revolved around being abandoned to the plague, or the money squandered on revels while the poor starved. Resentment also focused on the Earl – for living in Dunkirk House, for spending a fortune on 'unnecessary' improvements to the church, and for closing it during the day, when it was a convenient place for the homeless to sit.

There was a sudden murmur of anticipation as a man with thick white hair and matching whiskers stepped up to the pulpit. There was a marked similarity between Adam Urban and the painting of St Paul over the altar, and when he spoke, his voice was full of fatherly kindness. He seemed to have some deformity of his ears, leading Chaloner to wonder if he had lost them as a punishment for preaching sedition.

Chaloner had expected a fiery oration, but Urban confined himself to facts. His speech was impassioned, but eminently reasonable, and the authorities would have been hard-pressed to find fault with any of it. It was a masterpiece of political obfuscation – assuring his listeners that they had cause for discontent without actually telling them to do anything about it. When he had finished, Urban paused by the altar, to make sure everyone noticed the resemblance between him and the apostle in the window, then took his leave to tumultuous applause.

'He is a saint,' one woman informed her friends. 'So sweet and calm – not like those rampaging wastrels at White Hall.'

It was a sentiment repeated many times by the people who filed past Chaloner on their way out. Urban was doubly clever, he thought grudgingly, because if he was arrested now, there would be a riot. People loved him for his gentleness and compassion, and he was obviously a lot more popular – and likeable – than the King.

Chaloner was about to leave himself when he spotted Jacob Hall, looking drab in a brown coat and a tatty felt hat. He was standing with a dark-featured man who reminded Chaloner of a painting he had once seen of the scheming Renaissance politician Niccolo Machiavelli. There was no sign of the dwarf.

'Are you sure it is wise to stir up discontent so fragrantly?' he asked, watching them jump at the sound of a voice so close behind.

Hall recovered quickly. 'And are *you* sure it is wise for

a courtier to be in a place that is full of people who hate them? I know you hail from White Hall – I have seen you there.'

'You might be considered a courtier yourself by some,' retorted Chaloner, 'given your friendship with Lady Castlemaine.'

The dark man laughed. 'He has a point, Hall. There are many who would not understand how you can service her by night, yet claim to be one of us by day.'

Hall declined to answer, so Chaloner introduced himself, and told them that he was investigating Olivia Stoakes' disappearance.

'We do not know her,' said the dark man, who had given his name as Pietri Gimonde from Bologna. 'Although we did hear that a lady has gone missing. Her husband is said to be so worried that he has not stopped drinking ever since he was told the news.'

'Poor man,' said Hall flatly. 'The wealthy lead such difficult lives.'

'She vanished during your performance in the Fleece,' pressed Chaloner.

'Perhaps she did,' shrugged Gimonde, 'but we can tell you nothing about it, because we were concentrating on our art. We are professionals: we do not allow our attention to wander while we are working.'

'You allowed it to wander long enough to accept the money she gave you,' Chaloner flashed back. 'And do not deny it, because I saw her handing out coins myself.'

'*She* is the missing lady?' asked Gimonde, and shook his head. 'Then I am sorry – I did not know. She gave us each sixpence, which was more than any of her cronies did. Perhaps one resented her generosity, and dispatched her for putting the rest of them in a miserly light.'

'You think she is dead?' fished Chaloner.

'I have no idea,' replied Gimonde. 'I was merely musing aloud.'

'Where were you last night?' asked Chaloner, aiming to find out if they were among those who had attacked him.

'Performing at the Beare Garden in Southwark,' replied Hall promptly. 'Ask anyone – our show was very well attended. It was late by the time we finished, so we decided to sleep there.'

They had no more to add, so Chaloner followed them outside, where the wind seemed fiercer than ever. He was just crossing the Piazza when he saw a familiar figure battling through the gale in front of him. He smiled. It was Salathiel Lester.

A short while later, Chaloner was in a hackney carriage rattling towards Ivie Lane – Lester had insisted on buying him breakfast, but refused to go anywhere except the Folly. Chaloner knew he should be working, but felt like spending an hour with an old friend first.

'If I cannot be at sea, then I must find other ways to feel water moving beneath me,' Lester said, to explain his liking for a place that was inconveniently located and not particularly nice. He grinned. 'It will be a fine old ride over the river today, with this wind.'

When Chaloner saw the state of the Thames, he had serious reservations about venturing across it. It was a raging torrent, full of debris scoured from the banks upstream. The watermen waiting for fares were struggling to keep their craft from being dashed against the pier.

'Do not worry,' said Judd, when Chaloner voiced his misgivings. 'You will be perfectly safe. I shall send you over with Scull, who knows the river like the back of his hand.'

'Good,' said Chaloner acidly. 'He will know exactly where we are when we capsize.'

Judd and Lester laughed uproariously, although Chaloner had not meant to be amusing. He approached the ladder cautiously, fighting against a wind that threatened to tear him off it. Lester followed much more confidently, jumping into the waiting craft as nimbly as a gazelle, despite his bulk. Then they were away, Chaloner clinging on for dear life in the middle, and Lester standing in the prow, whooping with the sheer joy of the spray dashing into his face.

'Next time, we are going to the Rainbow,' grumbled Chaloner, when they arrived at the Folly and he was assisted aboard by a pair of sailors. He tipped them generously, sure he would have fallen in without their steadying hands.

He was surprised to find the Folly busy, having assumed that its regulars would have more sense than to attempt such a journey. Then he saw that most were sea-officers, for whom such a trip was more a delight than a trial. Even so, none had escaped a drenching, and so many wet clothes in a confined space had turned the atmosphere steamy. The windows dripped with moisture, and the floor was slick with mud and dirty water.

'What news?' called Maurice, and when he recognised Chaloner, added, 'Any word of Olivia? Poor Stoakes is here, distraught.'

Chaloner went to speak to Stoakes, but quickly deduced that the captain was not so much distraught as drunk. He had added tots of this and that to his coffee, and his rumpled appearance suggested that he had probably spent most of the previous night drinking as well.

'You still have had no word from your wife?' Chaloner asked him. 'No demands of money in exchange for her safe return?'

'Nothing,' slurred Stoakes. 'And I am now resigned to the fact that I shall never see her again. Alive, at least. You should have watched her more closely, and so should I.'

'Why? What do you think has happened to her?'

Stoakes raised his hands in a shrug. 'She fell foul of thieves. The Fleece is not the place it was before Landlord Clifton took over, and we should never have gone there. Still, we have learned our lesson. No courtier will ever set foot in it again.'

'Have you thought any more about the coded message I found in your house? I shall have the translation today, so if you do know what it says, now is the time to tell me.'

Stoakes scowled at him. 'I have thought no more about it, because I knew nothing in the first place. It is not mine, and I cannot be held responsible for whatever nasty secret it holds.'

'How do you know it holds a nasty secret?' pounced Chaloner.

Stoakes eyed him with dislike. 'Do not twist my words, Chaloner. I repeat: the letter is not mine and I have no idea what it contains.'

'Then what about *Assurance*?' pressed Chaloner. 'Have you thought any more about why she sank for no apparent cause?'

'There *was* a cause,' snapped Stoakes, nettled. 'She was broached by a gust of wind. And she is in my thoughts constantly. I lost a lot of property when she sank.'

'You mean the paintings and ornaments that are missing from your home?'

'Yes – I like nice things around me while I am at sea. Now they are all on the bottom of the Thames. I doubt I shall want them back after she is weighed – they will be ruined.'

Chaloner questioned him a while longer, but learned nothing else, and was about to rejoin Lester when he was intercepted by Harry Brouncker, who had been in the process of informing anyone who would listen that the current gale was nothing compared to the ones he had experienced aboard *Royal Charles*.

'I lost some of the Duke's private correspondence this morning,' he told Chaloner worriedly. 'It was plucked away by the wind while I was talking to you. I do not suppose you happened to pick any up, did you?'

'Just one of Buckingham's bawdy poems, which I am sure the Duke can survive without.'

'Damn!' sighed Brouncker, but then brightened. 'How about a game of chess? And while we play you can tell me about your enquiries – Quartermain, Olivia, the navy and so forth. I am interested in it all.'

It was such a brazen effort to get information for his employer that Chaloner regarded him askance. He was spared from the awkwardness of a refusal by Lester coming to drag him away.

'My friends Harman and Cox are eager to meet you – you will like them,' said Lester, then glanced disapprovingly at Brouncker, and muttered, 'Better than him, I warrant.'

He introduced two sea-officers, who transpired to be the pair Chaloner had noticed when he had last visited the Floating Coffee House – the men who had listened sympathetically to Judd's complaints about the navy not paying its mariners. Harman was the handsome, charismatic captain of *Royal Charles*, while John Cox was his plump, weather-beaten sailing master. Dr Merrett was with them, his amiable face troubled.

'Do not fraternise with Brouncker,' he advised Chaloner in a low voice. 'At least, not when there are sea-officers in the vicinity. You will damage your reputation.'

'Why?' asked Chaloner curiously. 'Because he is one of the worst of the Court debauchees and runs a brothel into the bargain?'

'Well, that certainly,' said Merrett. 'And because he is a liar and a fraud. Good manners prevent me from adding more, but suffice to say he is not the bold sailor he claims to be.'

'He is a disgrace,' said Cox bluntly, overhearing. 'Did you know he was seasick while we were still in port, so could not write the Duke's official dispatches?'

'No, but it does not surprise me,' growled Lester. 'Someone should end this nonsense of giving courtiers duties on warships.'

'They should,' agreed Harman. 'Let them fight on land, when all they have to do is point two armies at each other and tell them to charge. The sea is different – amateurs there are a menace to themselves and everyone else.'

'I was lumbered with several courtiers on *Swiftsure*,' recalled Lester. 'They were aboard for Lowestoft, where they were a wretched nuisance. At the height of the battle, one ordered me to sail backwards. Do you remember, Tom?'

Chaloner laughed. 'I remember the language you used to tell him it was impossible.'

'It was not funny! It was disgraceful that I had to tear my attention away from the ship in order to explain the basics of sailing to them. But let us not discuss it any longer – it makes me too irate. Harman, tell Tom what happened to you, Merrett and Cox as you travelled home from the Deptford yards last night.'

'We were assaulted,' replied Harman, and pulled up his sleeve to reveal a bandage. 'Although they did not cut my sword arm, thank the good Lord. I suppose we were mistaken for courtiers – my crew tell me that Londoners hate those at the moment.'

'One made a grab for my purse,' added Merrett, 'but I lashed out with my walking stick and landed him a colossal blow on the shoulder. He will have a nasty bruise this morning.'

'And I stabbed another with my cutlass,' put in Cox. 'I suspect they were astonished to discover that we could fight back, and I am only sorry that I did not kill one of the bastards. Speaking of killing, have you heard that Stoakes' wife is missing? It is a pity – she was kind to my sister when she had the French disease.'

'The French disease is syphilis, Cox,' put in Merrett mildly. 'I imagine you mean *la grippe*, which is a winter ague.'

Over a peculiar breakfast of boiled fish and pickled quinces, Chaloner discussed *Assurance* with the three seamen, and Quartermain with Merrett, but learned nothing of any relevance. Then, with considerable trepidation, he summoned a boat to carry him back to dry land.

Chapter 5

If anything, the gale was fiercer than ever when Chaloner reached the Strand, and the trees in the Savoy Palace garden made a tremendous racket as they whipped back and forth. The air was full of flying debris, and as his hackney carriage had no windows, he had to fend off all manner of windborne missiles as he was transported to Chancery Lane. His driver wore an old helmet and breastplate from the wars, which was a very sensible precaution.

He arrived at Lincoln's Inn to find the gates wide open, something he had not seen since June, when it had become clear that a deadly and insidious disease was about to ravage the city. He stopped at the porter's lodge on the way in, although the lad who came to greet him was unfamiliar, as were the gardeners who were busily sweeping leaves and broken tiles from the paths – new staff, hired to replace the ones who had died of the plague.

'Mr Thurloe,' the unsettlingly young porter mused, running a grubby finger down the book that told him who was in and who was out. 'Is he the short, fat, fanatical one with no ears? Or the one who looks like a donkey?'

'Neither,' replied Chaloner, thinking that the boy's predecessor would sooner have cut out his tongue than pose such disrespectful questions. 'He is the one who lives in Dial Court.'

'Lots of them do,' sighed the boy. 'What is your name? I must put it in my ledger.'

'Julius Caesar,' replied Chaloner flippantly, then watched in disbelief as the lad wrote *Jew le Ussezer* in a large, childish hand. Reading upside down, he saw that King Leer, Robbing Hoode and Gay Fawks had also passed through the Inn's portals that day.

'Watch how you go now, sir,' the youth said, looking up with such a sweet smile that Chaloner was ashamed of his mean-spirited deception. 'The paths are very slippery today, and we do not want you to have a fall.'

Chaloner nodded his thanks and stepped inside, trying to recall if *he* had ever considered anyone of thirty-five to be in his dotage. He did not like to imagine what the child thought of most of the Inn's benchers, who were not a youthful body of men.

He walked to Dial Court, named for the complex astrological device that had pride of place in the centre, although not even the combined intellect of the lawyers who lived there had worked out how to read it. It had blown over and lay on its side amid a raft of broken twigs. Parts were buckled beyond repair, but Chaloner doubted it would matter – the benchers would just set it upright and let it go on being a piece of pretty but unfathomable garden furniture.

He climbed the stairs to where Thurloe occupied a pleasant suite overlooking Chancery Lane. It comprised a bedchamber and a parlour, with an attic above for his manservant, although this was currently empty, as the fellow had been unwell when Thurloe had returned to London, and had been left in Oxfordshire to recuperate.

'Tom!' said Thurloe warmly as Chaloner knocked and entered. 'I suppose you have come for a translation of the message you sent?'

He was a slightly built man with shoulder-length hair swept back from his face. His clothes were plain, but of good quality, and everything about him was tastefully understated. He had run the entire country while he had been Cromwell's Secretary of State, and his intelligence network had terrified his enemies. Even now, when he had vowed to play no further role in politics, he was a figure who commanded respect, despite his unassuming appearance.

He and Chaloner exchanged news of family and mutual friends for a while, before Chaloner felt compelled to turn to business.

'Have you decoded Stoakes' letter yet?'

'I am afraid not,' replied Thurloe. 'And nor will I, because it requires a cipher key.'

He referred to a piece of paper with holes punched out of it. When a page of writing was placed beneath the key, only specific letters or words would show through – the ones comprising the secret message. It was one of the more secure ways of sending communiqués, as usually only the intended recipient had the means to interpret them.

'Damn,' muttered Chaloner. 'Are you sure?'

Thurloe nodded as he handed back the original. 'Just look at it. The clue is in the way the text is written – each word carefully separated so as to prevent misunderstandings. I am sorry I could not help. Is it important?'

Chaloner gave a brief account of Olivia's disappearance, then told Thurloe about the other matters the Earl had told him to explore. When he had finished, he went to stoke up the fire. It was already stiflingly hot in Thurloe's parlour, as the ex-Spymaster was of the opinion that he had a delicate constitution that needed to be cosseted, but the wet journey from the Folly had chilled Chaloner to the bone.

'I would also like to know why Quartermain was dead in Bedford House,' said Thurloe, watching him. 'Indeed, I had planned to ask you to look into the matter for me.'

'You knew him?'

'I met him once or twice. But that is not my reason for wanting answers. Laurens van Heemskerch is – the man who found the body.'

Understanding flashed suddenly in Chaloner's mind, so he knew *exactly* why a man suspected of betraying his embassy's secrets should be of concern to an ex-Spymaster.

'Heemskerch is an intelligencer? One of yours?'

Thurloe inclined his head. 'I recruited him years ago, and he supplied me with information that was very helpful the last time we were at war with the Dutch. He has continued to feed me embassy gossip ever since, as he prefers to deal with someone he knows, rather than the current Spymaster General. I then pass his reports to the relevant bodies.'

'Unfortunately, the Dutch now know all about him. I suspect it was Beuningen who guessed – he is cleverer than poor, plodding van Goch. So where is Heemskerch now?'

Thurloe lowered his voice. 'Upstairs in my attic. He came to me in terror nine days ago, and I agreed to hide him here, because he claims to have intelligence that might help us win the current outbreak of hostilities with the United Provinces.'

Chaloner regarded him sceptically. 'You do not consider it odd that he should flee the same day that he stumbled over a corpse in his embassy's garden? Kersey thinks Quartermain's death was natural, but he is not a *medicus*. Perhaps Heemskerch killed him, and ran away because he does not want to hang for murder.'

'Heemskerch did not kill Quartermain, Tom – it was Quartermain who was sent to kill *him*. But we should not discuss it here. Heemskerch is adept at eavesdropping, and while I believe he is asleep at the moment, there is no harm in being careful. Walk with me in the garden.'

'Now?' asked Chaloner, startled. 'In all this wind?'

'Why not? Fresh air will sharpen our minds.'

'Or send an uprooted tree through them,' muttered Chaloner.

It did not take long for Thurloe to realise that the blustery gardens were no place for a man in fragile health, so he and Chaloner went to the undercroft below the chapel instead, doing circuits over the slabs that formed the tombstones of fellow benchers.

'I shall lie here one day,' he said, 'with the chapel above and my colleagues all around.'

'But not yet,' said Chaloner firmly. He hated it when Thurloe talked of death.

'No,' conceded Thurloe, 'although my zeal for life in London wanes. There are so many factions, all clamouring and plotting against each other, that nothing ever gets done. Their antics convince me more than ever that a military dictatorship is the only way to rule.'

'I am sure the King would agree,' said Chaloner drily. 'So thank God he has no standing army. *He* would like nothing more than to govern without listening to public opinion.'

Thurloe shot him a sour look. 'I mean a *proper* military dictatorship, with an ethical general at its helm – not a weakling who abandons his people to the plague. But you want to hear about Heemskerch, not my political musings. What would you like to know?'

'For a start, why Quartermain – a physician, whose patients included the King and my Earl – was trying to kill Heemskerch. Was he a spy, too?'

'It is possible. Heemskerch believes that Quartermain's orders were to dispatch him quickly and without evidence of foul play.'

Chaloner frowned. 'His *orders*? Quartermain was some-one's hired assassin? Whose?'

'Now that I cannot tell you. Nor can Heemskerch. However, there are three possibilities. First, someone in the embassy; they are naturally vexed by Heemskerch's betrayal. Second, our own side – we do not want Heemskerch to fall into Dutch hands, as it is in our interests to keep them wondering exactly what he has told us. And third, people who hold his intelligence responsible for the disaster at Vågen.'

Beuningen had also hinted that Heemskerch was to blame for that particular defeat, although Chaloner had assumed he was doing what any canny diplomat would do in his position: planting the seeds of distrust, so his opponents would question the validity of *all* the infor-mation acquired from that particular source. He told Thurloe about the discussion he had overheard in The Hague between Grand Pensionary de Witt and his admiral, which had led him to surmise that the whole debacle had indeed been orchestrated by the Dutch government.

'I presumed as much,' said Thurloe, when he had finished. 'However, all Heemskerch did was hand the information on – it was our responsibility to decide whether to act on it.'

'Yes and no,' argued Chaloner. 'It exposes Heemskerch as a poor spy, who cannot distinguish between good intelligence and bad. If he suspected the latter, he should have included a caveat in his report.'

'Years of easy success did turn him complacent,' acknowledged Thurloe, 'and Beuningen is a formidable adversary. But regardless of the rights and wrongs of the affair, Heemskerch's flight is inconvenient: it has deprived us of our only eyes and ears inside the embassy.'

'It will not matter much longer anyway,' said Chaloner, feeling that a spy of Heemskerch's calibre represented no great loss. 'Van Goch has been recalled to The Hague.'

'Yes, much to Williamson's dismay. As you well know, it is easier to spy on the Dutch here in London, than it is to acquire reliable intelligence from within the United Provinces.'

Joseph Williamson was England's current Spymaster General, a man who was not nearly as good at the job as Thurloe had been.

'So the Quartermain enquiry is now much more complex,' mused Chaloner. 'I must learn who hired him to kill our agent in Bedford House, as well as finding out how he came to breathe his last in the ambassador's garden. I cannot imagine the Dutch are behind it – they will have their own assassins.'

'Not necessarily. Most of van Goch's staff left once

war was declared – their usual killer may have been among them. We can assume nothing, Tom.'

'What will you do with Heemskerch? You cannot keep him here.'

'No,' agreed Thurloe. 'My colleagues are already wondering why I have suddenly started to eat like a horse, and it is only a matter of time before they guess that I have secret company. I must get him out of the city as quickly as possible.'

'Why not send him to your family in Oxfordshire?'

Thurloe regarded him balefully. 'I do not want him with them, thank you very much.'

The response was telling: Heemskerch had been useful, but he was not a friend.

'Well, he certainly should not be here with you,' determined Chaloner. 'It is too dangerous for a man in your position. Let me hide him until he can be spirited away.'

'I have already suggested that, but he refuses to leave me.'

'I could make him,' offered Chaloner determinedly.

Thurloe gave a brief smile. 'I am sure you could. However, before he left the embassy, he managed to steal a number of documents, which Williamson says are vital to national security. Heemskerch will give them to us, but only on two conditions: that we arrange safe passage for him out of the country, and that he resides with me in the interim.'

'How long will that be?'

Thurloe grimaced. 'And there lies the crux of my problem. Heemskerch does not trust Williamson to organise his flight – he believes there is a mole in the Spymaster's office. He is probably right, as vipers always emerge in times of crisis, and Williamson does not treat his staff well enough to keep them loyal. Unfortunately, I dare not look for a ship myself, lest someone puts two and two together . . .'

'Then I will do it,' said Chaloner, aware of Thurloe's immediate relief. 'But only if you promise to leave London the moment he is away. Then, if there are repercussions, you will not be here to stand accused.'

'I suppose there is nothing pressing to keep me in the city at the moment,' conceded Thurloe. 'And I do have a hankering to see Ann and the children again.'

Chaloner held out his hand to seal the agreement. 'Be ready to move at short notice. Meanwhile, may I speak to Heemskerch myself?'

When they returned to Thurloe's rooms, a man was standing by the ex-Spymaster's desk, and Chaloner was sure he had been rummaging through the papers that were scattered across it. He was a small, plump, mean-faced person with a thin moustache. Chaloner disliked him on sight, and determined to rid Thurloe of him at the earliest opportunity.

'Who is he?' demanded Heemskerch, eyeing Chaloner in alarm.

'A trusted friend,' replied Thurloe soothingly, 'who will help you escape. However, it will be dangerous, not to mention costly, so will you show a little good faith by making a down payment in the form of some of your documents? It may serve to expedite matters.'

'No,' snarled Heemskerch. 'You get nothing from me until I am on a boat heading for freedom. I have no preferences as to where – Spain, France, Portugal, Greece. Anywhere nice.'

'How about Vågen?' asked Chaloner acidly.

Heemskerch glared at him. 'I supply intelligence. How it is interpreted is not my responsibility – it is Williamson's. It is *he* who should be blamed for any . . . embarrassing consequences.' A sly expression stole across the portly features. 'Perhaps he was led astray by the traitor.'

'What traitor?'

'The one who is almost certainly responsible for *my* current predicament – forced to hide like a rat in a hole until strangers arrange my escape. You must know that Grand Pensionary de Witt has spies here, just as you had me in his embassy. Now, when will I be leaving?'

'Soon,' promised Chaloner sincerely. 'However, to keep you truly safe, I need to know more about the circumstances that caused you to leave Bedford House in the first place.'

Heemskerch sighed wearily, as if he considered talking to Chaloner a bore. 'I had a fever, which I thought was the plague, so I summoned a physician. Dr Quartermain came, and prescribed a pot of his King's Gold. I took the tiniest sip, but it tasted so strongly of garlic that I poured the rest away. Later, I vomited violently – it had been poisoned.'

'How do you know it was the medicine that made you ill?' asked Chaloner, although he had not forgotten Wiseman railing about the dangerous levels of a garlic-scented toxin – poxbane – in the physician's first attempt to produce an effective plague remedy.

'I did not – not then. However, a letter arrived a couple of hours later, warning me that Quartermain meant me harm. It was unsigned, and I have no idea who sent it, so do not ask.'

'Then what?'

'Quartermain came the next morning with a second phial of his stinking King's Gold. I promised to take it with my eleven o'clock coffee, but fed some to a mouse instead. The creature died within moments.'

'Did you confront Quartermain about it?'

Heemskerch nodded. 'On his third visit, which was two Fridays ago. He denied it hotly, and left a different potion for me to take. Needless to say, when I smelled garlic, I tossed that away as well. And that was the last I saw of him – alive, at least. Later that day, I noticed my keys were missing. I am sure *he* stole them, aiming to come back and murder me in my sleep.'

Given that Widow Fisher had seen Quartermain open Bedford House's back gate with a key, Chaloner suspected that Heemskerch was right. 'But two days later – on the Sunday – you found him dead in the embassy garden. Did you dispatch him before he could kill you?'

'No, of course not!' cried Heemskerch, genuinely appalled by the notion. 'I was as shocked by the discovery as anyone. Moreover, no one "dispatched" him – the charnel-house keeper thought he died of natural causes.'

'Then what an uncanny coincidence that it should be you who found the body,' mused Chaloner. 'The corpse of your would-be assassin.'

Heemskerch shot him an unpleasant look. 'It *was* uncanny – and not very nice – if you want the truth. I was out walking with the rest of the staff, and I stumbled across him when it was my turn to scout ahead for danger. I have no idea how he came to be there.'

'Is there a regular gardener at Bedford House?'

'Not now. Van Goch sent him home with the other non-essential staff weeks ago.'

'Why did you not identify Quartermain when you found him? He went to the charnel house without a name, and is buried in a common pit.'

Heemskerch regarded him pityingly. 'You mean publicly admit that my physician – a man who had tried three times to poison me – had dropped dead in the house where I was living? Do not be an ass! It was then that I decided it was too dangerous for me to stay at the embassy, so I fled.'

'Van Goch and Beuningen knew there was a traitor in Bedford House. Were you aware of their suspicions?'

'If I had been, I would have left a lot sooner, believe me! Yet I am not surprised Beuningen guessed – he is clever, and deceiving him was hard, not like poor gullible van Goch. But I have indulged your curiosity quite long enough. I am going upstairs now. When we next meet, you had better bring news of my escape, or I shall start destroying the documents I stole.'

'Then perhaps I should take them now,' said Chaloner, aiming for the attic stairs.

'They are not here,' said Heemskerch smugly. 'I put them in a safe place, where they will remain until I am sure that Williamson and Thurloe have kept their end of the bargain.'

And on that note, he turned and sailed out. Chaloner watched him go unhappily.

'Are you sure these documents are worth the risk of harbouring him?' he asked. 'I imagine his enemies – whoever they are – will not hesitate to kill you in order to get at him.'

'You are doubtless right,' said Thurloe tiredly. 'So perhaps you will see about arranging passage on a suitable ship at your earliest convenience.'

When Chaloner left Lincoln's Inn, he went straight to Lester's house on Wych Street. The captain would know which ships were due to sail soon – and which masters could be trusted to provide a berth with no questions asked.

'He is out, sir,' said the sailor who answered the door. His name was Naylor, and he was *Swiftsure*'s steward, a prim, fussy man who always acted as housekeeper for his captain when they were ashore. 'Will you come in to wait?'

Chaloner did step inside, but only so he could speak out of the wind. Then he gazed around in astonishment. Every available surface of Lester's parlour was covered by flags of all shapes, colours and sizes.

Naylor grinned at his surprise. 'They are the captain's and I am airing them out for him. They are worth a fortune, and include ones flown at all manner of great events. Take this one, for example. It witnessed the defeat of—'

'Lester,' interrupted Chaloner urgently. 'Did he say where he was going?'

'No, sir, but have you tried the Floating Coffee House? He always goes there for his morning brew, and I have not seen him since he headed off in that direction earlier.'

Chaloner hurried to the Savoy Wharf, where Judd informed him that Lester had ridden away a full hour before, on navy business with Captain Harman.

'So he might be anywhere,' said Judd apologetically. 'Greenwich, the Victualing Office, the Deptford yards – where both *Royal Charles* and *Swiftsure* are being refitted. But if he comes back here, I will let him know you are looking for him.'

Chaloner considered locating a suitable ship for Heemskerch himself, but then decided against it. It would be safer for the spy – and more importantly, for Thurloe

– if he consulted Lester first. And he had plenty to do in the interim, the most pressing being Olivia. He trotted briskly to Long Acre, where the door was answered not by Emily the cook-maid, but by Stoakes himself.

'No, she is not back,' Stoakes snapped, returning to his parlour and his wine, leaving Chaloner to follow him inside as he would. 'She has disappeared off the face of the Earth. And that damned Emily has abandoned me for greener pastures, too. How am I supposed to manage with no womenfolk to cook and clean?'

Chaloner spent the rest of the day and much of the evening in White Hall, questioning again those courtiers who had been with Olivia when she had gone missing. But he had never encountered a less observant group, and he suspected that they would not have noticed if Olivia had been dragged away screaming by robbers right in front of their bleary eyes.

He gave up eventually and trudged through the dark, windy streets to the Fleece, to ask its landlord and his patrons the same questions – and about the attack on him the previous night. Hopefully, the evening regulars would have arrived by now and would be willing to talk in exchange for a jug of ale.

The Fleece was busy, and smelled pleasantly of roasted meat and sweet tobacco. It was warm, too, after the chill of the storm outside, and Chaloner was glad to shake the rain from his coat and find a seat near the fire. He ordered a slice of venison pastry, and informed the pot-boy that he wanted a word with Landlord Clifton. While he waited for the man to appear, he plied two garrulously indiscreet customers with wine and questions.

'Clifton has debts,' confided one. 'Massive ones, which

meant he could not leave London while the plague raged – he had to stay here, and keep this place open.'

'But it cost him his entire family,' put in the other. 'Wife, parents, children and servants – all dead within a week. Now he hates the King, his government and anyone else who was not here during the crisis. You will see what I mean when he comes.'

Chaloner did see. Clifton burned with white-hot rage, just as angry with Chaloner as he had been with Lady Castlemaine when she had come asking after Jacob Hall earlier.

'How many more times do you need to be told?' he snarled. 'There were upwards of three hundred people here on Sunday, all demanding ale and meat. I never saw your missing woman. Besides, she vanished from the yard, by all accounts, and I was in here.'

'I explored your yard last night, hoping to find clues as to what happened to her, but I was attacked and driven off. What can you tell me about that?'

'That you had no right to go poking around,' spat Clifton. 'It is *private* property.'

'Yes,' acknowledged Chaloner. 'I should have asked your permission. However, I assumed you would not object, given that you must be concerned for the lady's safety.'

'Well, I am not. Courtiers are unwelcome here, and this Stoakes woman had no business coming. Urban's Men do not perform for the likes of her and her cronies, but for decent, hardworking Londoners who need to be informed of their rights.'

'You play a dangerous game, Clifton,' warned Chaloner. 'If Urban's Men are caught preaching insurrection, you will join them on the scaffold.'

'What do I care? My family is dead and this place . . . well, I am tempted to let my creditors have it, because it no longer brings me joy.' Then Clifton smiled, although it was a cruel expression, entirely devoid of humour. 'Urban's Men do, though. Gimonde plays a character called Pulcinella, who made me laugh for the first time in months.'

Chaloner knew 'Pulcinella' from his travels in Italy. He was a subversive maverick in a long-nosed mask, who dealt with his problems – usually the political, religious or legal authorities – by hitting them over the head with a pretend cudgel called a slap-stick. Superficially, it was harmless fun, but Pulcinella's antics often carried a very real and seditious message, and his appearances were invariably followed by civil unrest.

'You think rebellion is amusing?' asked Chaloner coldly.

'No,' replied Clifton unconvincingly. 'But ridiculing those in power is. They deserve it, because they are a useless rabble.'

'Is that why Olivia was abducted from your domain? Because she is part of that "useless rabble"? After all, she is only a courtier, and who cares what happens to those?'

'I know nothing of any abduction. However, the woman *chose* to come here – I did not invite her. Or you, for that matter, so if someone did attack you last night, you only have yourself to blame. You should not have trespassed.'

'So you have no objection to your tavern being the haunt of kidnappers and rebels?'

Clifton shrugged. 'Even if you are right, it is still a better place than White Hall – *that* is full of thieves, lechers, bawds and idlers. At least everyone here works for a living.'

Chaloner glanced at the patrons around him and was not so sure, unless crime could be considered a valid occupation. 'You might want to warn Gimonde—'

'There is nothing wrong with healthy mockery,' interrupted Clifton shortly. 'And if our so-called leaders cannot tolerate humour, they should piss off back to Oxford. We Londoners have always laughed away our troubles, and no one can stop us. No one *should* stop us.'

'Then you had better hope the government agrees,' said Chaloner, 'because the penalties for insurrection are severe. Now, I would like to speak to Urban's Men. Are they here this evening, or fomenting dissent somewhere else?'

Clifton sneered. 'They *did* perform here earlier, but do you see a rampaging mob, whipped into a frenzy by what it saw? No, you see a room full of people who have enjoyed an evening of innocent entertainment. If you want examples of riotous behaviour, then go to White Hall. That is where you will find a disorderly rabble.'

It was difficult to argue with that.

Itinerant players led hard lives. They owned only what could be packed on a cart, and although their performances were full of glitter and shine, they tended to be a disreputable horde in the cold light of day. They often stole, knowing they would be gone before any losses were discovered, and some troupes even hired professional pickpockets, who plied their trade while the audience was engrossed in the action on stage.

Urban's Men were different. His rope-dancers, sword-swallowers, actors, fire-eaters and acrobats were respectable and famous, having performed all across

Europe. Each one usually worked alone, but Urban had invited them to join forces when they had happened across each other in Oxford. As their show was so successful, they aimed to tour the whole country.

'Sowing discord wherever they go,' muttered Chaloner, as he followed Clifton's grudgingly given directions to their quarters.

They had rented a dozen or so rooms in one wing of the Fleece, along with a sizable chamber in which they could relax after performances. Chaloner entered it to see roughly two dozen people there. Gimonde was mending a tear in his costume, Hall was practising a rope trick, while others played cards, chatted or read.

'Where is Urban?' asked Chaloner, looking around and not seeing him.

'He is giving a *private* performance elsewhere,' replied the dwarf, who was lounging on a bench with his arms around two buxom lasses. He wore clothes that would not have looked out of place in White Hall, and his yellow hair was rich and thick. He had delicate, almost pretty features, although there was something cold, hard and bitter in his dark brown eyes. 'You may speak to me instead. I am Jeffrey Hudson, his deputy.'

Chaloner had vague recollections of being told about a dwarf named Jeffrey Hudson some years earlier. He scoured his memory and then it came to him: the King's mother had employed a man of that name, whose entertainment value had faded when he had grown from a compliant child into an intelligent and ambitious adult. He had been exiled for killing another courtier in a duel, after which nothing more had been heard of him.

'The Queen's Dwarf,' he said, recalling Hudson's official

title. 'You were banished from the country – promised execution if you ever dared return.'

Hudson spread his hands in an expansive shrug. 'No one cares about that silly old squabble now, and I have been away quite long enough. It was time to come home.'

Chaloner was not sure the King would agree, especially if Hudson was celebrating his return by performing seditious burlesques.

Hall stepped forward, jerked a thumb in Chaloner's direction, and addressed his cronies. 'Earlier, this fellow told Gimonde and me that the woman who disappeared is the one who handed us each sixpence. Sadly, I remember the coin, but the giver – whom I understand was Olivia Stoakes, wife of the captain of *Assurance* – is less clear in my mind. The only courtier I noticed that night was Lady Castlemaine.'

'You demean yourself by cavorting with her,' said Hudson, sniffing to indicate that *he* would not stoop so low. 'She is nothing but the King's cast-off.'

Hall grinned impishly. 'Yes, but a very generous cast-off. You should see all the gifts – money, clothes and jewels – that she presses on me.'

'I saw Olivia talk to you all,' said Chaloner, looking around to include every member of the listening troupe. 'What was she saying?'

'She spoke to me the longest,' declared a portly man with a booming voice. 'I am Walter Clun, and she was keen to compliment me on my acting.'

The name jarred another memory, and Chaloner experienced a sudden, sharp pang of loss when he recalled why: he had seen Clun perform in the King's Theatre the previous year, playing Falstaff in *Henry V*. He had been with Hannah, and vividly recollected peeling an orange for her during a scene-change.

'But then her husband came and pulled her away,' said Gimonde, dragging Chaloner's thoughts back to the present. As he spoke, he shook out his jester's motley to examine the rip he had repaired. 'It was rude, so I think Pulcinella will knock *him* over the head with his slap-stick when he next takes to the stage.'

Hudson crowed his delight. 'People will *love* it, given that Captain Stoakes is the rogue whose ship sank while in port, killing twenty hapless sailors. But all he mourns is the furniture he lost.'

'I heard he still refuses to pay for them to be buried,' said Gimonde soberly, 'even though his wife told him that it was the decent thing to do.'

'Because he is a drunkard,' explained Hall sourly. 'He probably does not even remember her, let alone what she asked him to do in the name of propriety.'

Chaloner regarded Hall and Gimonde thoughtfully, thinking they knew a lot about Stoakes, considering that they had denied knowing him when he had spoken to them earlier.

'Your questions this morning piqued our interest,' explained Gimonde, evidently reading his mind. 'So we asked around.'

'You come *here* for answers,' said Clun, 'but you should look to your own kind instead – to unscrupulous courtiers, who probably killed this Olivia Stoakes because her generosity and kindness made the rest of them look mean.'

'Or to her husband,' put in Gimonde. 'A miserly sot with half a brain.'

'Or the King,' added Hall. 'I have seen him prowling White Hall in search of new conquests. Perhaps he abducted Olivia when she refused to yield her favours willingly.'

131

They all laughed, and Chaloner saw he would waste his time by pressing them further. He took his leave, but Hudson followed him outside.

'Do not even think of accusing us of arranging her disappearance,' the acrobat said warningly, once they were alone. 'We are not common itinerants, who can be made scapegoats when you fail to find the real culprits – we are players of international renown. Touch us, and governments all over the civilised world will rush to punish you for it.'

'The *real culprits*?' echoed Chaloner, treating the threat with the contempt it deserved by ignoring it – no country would put itself out for a few roving entertainers, no matter how special they considered themselves. 'So you *do* suspect foul play!'

Hudson nodded. 'Yes, I do – because of the way those courtiers left the Fleece that night. It was when Pulcinella directed his wit against them, obliging them to make a hasty departure. You see, some of the audience were more inflamed than amused by what he was saying.'

'You mean there was violence?'

'No, because the King's toadies departed with prudent speed, so there was no time for trouncing. However, it is possible that your lady was left behind in the scramble to escape, and found herself the centre of hostile attention . . .'

Chaloner moved to another subject. 'Are you sure it is wise to let Gimonde say whatever he likes? Word is sure to reach the Spymaster, who will arrest you all for fomenting rebellion.'

Hudson sneered. 'Rebellion? All we do is tell the truth – White Hall *is* full of cowards who abandoned the city in her hour of need, and most Londoners are *not* happy to see them crawling back. Let Williamson put us on trial. Not a jury in the land would convict us.'

'What makes you think there would be a trial?' asked Chaloner, amazed that Hudson should believe that the government would handle the matter publicly. 'So unless you want to end up in the Tower, tell Gimonde to stop—'

'No one tells Pulcinella what to do,' interrupted Hudson defiantly. 'His bold tongue is what makes him – and ergo our troupe – so popular. If we muzzle him, there will be nothing to distinguish us from any other band of tumblers and jugglers.'

'I saw Pulcinella in Italy,' said Chaloner, growing exasperated. 'He was popular there, too, but it did not save him from being hounded by the authorities until he was forced to flee for his life. Was that Gimonde or someone else in a mask and jester's motley?'

'Probably Gimonde – he did invent the character and Bologna is his home.'

'Then he will know what will happen – not just to him, but to all of you – if he continues along this path. I urge you to desist before it is too late.'

'The government's monkeys will never catch us,' stated Hudson confidently. 'They are too slow and too stupid, and we will outwit them at every turn.'

'Then what about the people you inflame with your wild ideas?' demanded Chaloner. 'You may escape, but what happens to those you leave behind? Will you abandon them to take the consequences alone, like Gimonde did in Italy?'

Hudson regarded him icily. 'We merely point out injustice and corruption. What people choose to do with that information is not our concern. Our audiences have minds of their own – they are capable of choosing for themselves which path they wish to follow.'

Chaloner could see he was wasting his time. Hudson and his cronies were malicious mischief-makers, who aimed to start a rebellion, but did not care what happened to the folk who would be in the firing line. Fighting down his dislike of the man, he turned to another subject.

'I was attacked here last night. Not long after you watched me cross the Piazza.'

'I did see you scurry across the square,' acknowledged Hudson. 'I had just stepped outside for a breath of fresh air. However, I witnessed no assault.'

'Yet you do not seem surprised to hear it happened.'

'You pose impertinent questions, dispense unwanted advice, and make unfounded allegations, so no, I am not surprised. Indeed, I am astonished it does not happen more often.'

'Why were you here?' asked Chaloner. 'I understand the rest of your troupe were performing at the Beare Garden in Southwark.'

Hudson shrugged. 'We are a large company, so no one is needed for every performance. The occasional night off allows us to replenish our energies for—'

He broke off at a sudden shout from the tavern's main room, and went with Chaloner to find out what was happening. A cluster of patrons stood around the trapdoor that led to the cellar. Clifton had opened it to fetch a new barrel, and discovered someone lying on the steps. Chaloner felt his stomach give an unpleasant lurch of dismay as he recognised the sorry bundle.

It was Widow Fisher and she was dead.

Chapter 6

No surgeon was needed to explain how the old woman had died – there was a savage dent in the top of her head, inflicted by a blunt instrument. Chaloner carried her up the stairs and laid her on the floor, where a quick search of the body revealed the coins he had given her. Thus the motive for her murder was not robbery – although it would have had to have been a very desperate thief to tackle a victim who was so patently poor.

He glanced at Hudson, who was sighing his boredom, as if seeing murder victims was something he did every day. Was the dwarf the culprit – he had killed Mother Fisher because she had blabbed about him watching Chaloner after the attack? Or had she witnessed something else she should not have done? After all, she *had* proudly declared that nothing happened on the Piazza without her knowledge. Or had Brouncker discovered that she had made a home for herself in his family tomb, and brained her in a fit of outrage?

Clifton was polishing tankards. He also seemed indifferent to the fact that such a nasty, cowardly crime had been committed in his domain, which made Chaloner wonder if he had turned a blind eye to whatever had happened to Olivia, too. The landlord only shrugged when Chaloner demanded an explanation as to what had happened.

'Widow Fisher was forever in here trying to steal ale, and those stairs are slippery – she was old and she lost her footing.' His expression grew harsher. 'All her kin died when the King abandoned us to the pestilence – just like mine – so the state will have to bury her, because I am not doing it. Amey, send word to the charnel house.'

The lass who loitered nearby nodded, but made no effort to do as she was told. She had evidently survived the plague, as her neck boasted some savage scars, presumably inflicted when a surgeon had lanced her buboes. She wore a scarf wrapped around her head, which was a curious fashion choice, as loose hair would have gone some way to concealing the disfigurement, whereas the turban ensured that it was ruthlessly exposed.

'Poor old lady,' she said softly. 'She was a thief and a gossip, but she did not deserve to die in such a stupid accident.'

'It was not an accident,' stated Chaloner tightly, anger vying with grief in his mind. 'She was bludgeoned to death. Then the killer shoved her down the steps, probably to hide the body until he could find a more permanent place for it.'

'What nonsense!' spat Clifton. 'You cannot know the difference between a wound caused by a fall and one inflicted by an assailant. No one can.'

'I know it is unlikely that she tripped and suffered no injury except one to the top of her skull,' retorted Chaloner. '*And* I know that corpses do not close trapdoors behind them.'

Clifton's expression was contemptuous. 'Who would bother killing a lowly beggar that meant nothing to anyone?'

'She meant something to me,' said Chaloner shortly. 'And I *will* find out who hurt her.'

'Good luck with that,' drawled Hudson, and turned to shoulder his way outside.

The excitement over, most onlookers also began to drift away, Clifton still telling anyone who would listen that the thief had got what she deserved. It made Chaloner even more determined to bring her killer to justice, and he found himself hoping the culprit would be the surly landlord.

Unfortunately, although he lingered in the Fleece until very late, eavesdropping and asking questions, Chaloner learned nothing to help him identify the murderer, and it was with a sense of bitter defeat that he eventually gave up and left. Acutely aware that he might be in danger once outside, he took a circuitous route home, but his journey was uneventful.

He had climbed up to the attic before remembering that there was a chimney on his bed. Wearily, he retraced his steps to the parlour, glad that a fire still burned in the hearth. He curled up in front of it, covered by his coat and with one of Wiseman's medical tomes for a pillow, and fell into an uneasy sleep.

The next day seemed windier than ever, and Chaloner was beginning to think there would be no tree left standing in the entire city by the time the gale blew itself out. He lay for a moment, staring at the dead embers of the fire while he reflected on his enquiries. He now had a murder to explore, as well as finding out what had happened to

Olivia, *Assurance*, the trumpet and Quartermain, not to mention arranging Heemskerch's escape.

Olivia had disappeared on Sunday, and it was now Wednesday, but he was no nearer to finding her than he had been when he had started. He was sure answers lay in the Fleece, but three visits had failed to shake them loose, and he knew there was no point in persisting alone. He needed help, and although he disliked working with anyone else, he saw he had no choice: he would have to ask Spymaster Williamson to lend him some soldiers, in the hope that their menacing presence would persuade witnesses that it was time to cooperate.

He began to plan his day. He would go to Williamson first, to beg for men *and* ask what the Spymaster knew about Heemskerch. While the soldiers were being assembled, he would speak to Lester, so they could organise Heemskerch's escape; Lester might have ideas about how to proceed with *Assurance* as well. When the soldiers were ready, he would descend on the Fleece and demand answers about Olivia, Widow Fisher and the unrest that was bubbling there. And the trumpet? That would have to wait until he had some spare time.

He rose and went to look out of the window. It was still dark, but he could see what the wind had done to the Piazza, which was illuminated by lamps outside the wealthier houses. Several more trees in the churchyard were down, and the square itself was strewn with branches, soggy litter and smashed tiles. No one had come to open the market stalls, so the whole area was unusually empty and still.

He dressed for foul weather: an oiled cloak in place of his more usual long-coat, waterproof riding boots, thick woollen jacket and breeches, and a felted hat that was less likely to be torn off by the wind than one with a brim.

The servants were still abed, so he helped himself to a carrot from the basket on the window sill – the one Widow Fisher must have delivered before she was murdered. He thought about her as he stepped into the blustery darkness, sorry that she would never again regale him with gossip and demands for used newsbooks.

Head bowed against the wind, he trudged towards Charing Cross, wondering if he had ever seen it so deserted. True, the storm would keep some people safely indoors, but a few would normally have ventured out, and its vast emptiness was a stark reminder of the devastation the plague had wrought on the city.

He reached King Street and battled down it to Westminster, where Williamson worked. The Spymaster had also fled the disease, and had not long returned to his lair, so some of the windows of the building that he and his staff occupied in New Palace Yard were still boarded over. A sentry was on guard outside, one hand gripping his musket and the other clutching the door, which he was struggling to hold open for Robert Thompson, who was just coming out.

'What a wind!' Robert bawled, as Chaloner staggered towards him. 'I have never seen its like. Indeed, I dare not wear my teeth today, lest they are sucked out and carried away.'

'Very wise,' said Chaloner, thinking he looked ten years older without them. 'What brings you to such a place?'

'Joe,' yelled Robert, jerking his thumb over his shoulder. 'I came to bring him a freshly baked meat pie from my brother's coffee house. Joe does so love a pie.'

'Joe?' Chaloner regarded him blankly before realisation

dawned. When it did, it came with a hefty dose of disbelief. 'You mean *Joseph Williamson*?'

It was not just that Chaloner was astounded to learn such a disagreeable and devious character should have friends who liked him enough to take him early-morning treats, but that the relationship was affectionate enough to warrant nicknames. He could – just about – see the humourless, arrogant Spymaster being 'Joseph' to a few select intimates, but he was not, and never would be, 'Joe'.

'He and I share an interest in *blattae*,' bellowed Robert. 'That is moths to you.'

Williamson did like moths, and spent much of his spare time pinning their dead little bodies into specially crafted cases. Chaloner had always considered it a particularly apt pastime for him. It did not seem like something the bluff, noisy Robert would enjoy, though, but before Chaloner could ask him about it, Robert nodded across to Westminster Hall, the oldest and most solemn of the palace buildings, and the venue for many state ceremonies.

'Just look at that,' he hollered. 'Can you believe it?'

Chaloner grabbed the doorframe for balance and glanced behind him. The yard was piled with broken roof tiles, and he did not like to imagine what it would cost the public purse to replace them all. A ginger cat tottered diagonally across it, aiming for one direction, but being propelled in another, and the black-robed clerks who worked in the Treasury and the Houses of Commons and Lords were balls of furiously flailing sleeves and coattails.

'The birds?' he asked, aware that the kites who liked to range themselves along the roof, ready to swoop down on tasty bits of rubbish, had relocated to the more sheltered façade of St Margaret's Church, where they preened and surveyed with dispassionate interest the antics of humans far below.

'The heads,' shouted Robert. 'They have gone – puffed clean away.'

One of the more ghoulish things that had happened at the Restoration was taking revenge on the regicides. Some were already dead, but that had not satisfied the unforgiving Royalists. Oliver Cromwell, Henry Ireton and John Bradshaw were just three who had been dug up and 'executed' at Tyburn. Their heads had then been stuck on pikes and displayed outside Westminster Hall as a deterrent to anyone else who was contemplating killing a monarch. That day, the poles had snapped and the skulls were gone.

'Lord!' muttered Chaloner, making a mental note to tell Thurloe. It was true that loyal Parliamentarians had rescued Cromwell's sorry remains years ago, and someone else's head had been on display ever since, but the ex-Spymaster would still want to know.

'I had a scout around, but God only knows where they rolled,' said Robert in a confidential roar. 'I suppose they will come to light when the street-sweepers clean up.'

'I suppose,' said Chaloner, glad it was not his responsibility to hunt for them, and sincerely hoping that the Earl would not include that on his list of things to do as well.

Despite the early hour, Williamson's clerks were busy. Chaloner weaved through them, then ran up to the Spymaster's sumptuous suite on the next floor. He knocked and entered, noting that it had been refurnished since he had last been there. As the selection of paintings was eclectic, and the rugs were of excellent quality but did not match, he could only conclude that they were items appropriated from those deemed to be enemies of the state.

Unfortunately, the sculptures comprised busts of Roman despots and a bas relief depicting the grislier exploits of Ivan the Terrible. Although Chaloner was sure it was not deliberate, they simply begged the visitor to draw uncomplimentary parallels between the room's occupant and other vicious tyrants.

Williamson himself sat behind a desk piled so high with papers that he was almost invisible behind them. He was a tall, aloof man who had been an academic before deciding to turn to politics. Chaloner thought him ambitious, sly, treacherous and petty, and a bumbling amateur compared to Thurloe. His failings were particularly unfortunate now the country was at war, when the difference between good intelligence and bad cost lives. He looked tired and strained that day, and although Chaloner disliked him, he was sorry to see him in such a state.

'Busy?' he asked sympathetically.

'I am expected to do twice the amount of work with half the budget I had a year ago,' grumbled Williamson peevishly. 'I have not paid my Dutch spies in months, so they begin to desert me, while I am forced to make do with some very inferior specimens at home – mercenaries and cut-throats.'

'Like Robert Thompson?' fished Chaloner.

Williamson glared at him. 'He is a friend, not a spy. I suppose your paths crossed as he was leaving. Well, if you must know, he was kind enough to bring me a pie.'

It sat on his desk, several bites already taken out of it. It smelled delicious, a much more appetising breakfast than a bendy carrot.

'Have you heard about the resentment brewing over the Court's return?' asked Chaloner, aware that he needed to state his business quickly – Williamson could not afford to waste time with idle chatter and nor could he. 'Londoners do not want them back.'

'I hear whispers, but they are very faint.'

'They are not,' warned Chaloner. 'There may be trouble.'

Williamson groaned. 'But we *had* to go! When the order was given to run, we all believed the move might be permanent – that London would never recover from the devastation the plague was wreaking. And can you imagine what would have happened if the King had died? We would have been plunged into another civil war, because no one likes the Duke of York.'

'He is all right,' hedged Chaloner, unwilling to voice his real opinion of the Duke to a man whose remit was to arrest traitors.

Williamson sighed wearily. 'So I am expected to quell insurrection here, as well as amassing intelligence on the Dutch? *And* the French and the Danes, who plan to declare war on us officially this week because of what we did at Vågen?'

'Do not worry about the French and Danes,' said Chaloner confidently. 'They will bluster and rattle their swords, but they will not fight us at sea, and nor will they invade.'

Williamson regarded him askance. 'You sound very sure.'

'I *am* sure. Neither has large enough warships to risk

143

tackling ours – I saw the reports they sent to the Grand Pensionary about it. I wrote you a full account. Did you not read it?'

Williamson indicated the mounds of paper on his desk. 'Did you mark it as urgent?'

Chaloner had not, assuming the clerks would understand that a letter containing information directly from the office of Grand Pensionary de Witt should be presented to their employer at once. But Williamson looked disheartened and tired, and Chaloner did not have the heart to tell him that his staff were a lot of dangerously incompetent imbeciles. Instead, he summarised what he had learned, pulling his report from the middle of one pile as he did so.

'You learned far more than my other spies,' said Williamson grudgingly, taking it from him. 'Including Heemskerch in Bedford House. I assume Thurloe told you about him?'

Chaloner nodded. 'Although he passed you some significant misinformation, so perhaps it is just as well he is no longer in business. The Vågen affair not only proved to de Witt that there was indeed a traitor in his embassy, but it inflicted an embarrassing defeat on our navy.'

Williamson winced. 'I urged caution, but all the government saw was a fat Dutch convoy, ripe for the taking. Greed overcame prudence, and we paid the price. Still, before he abandoned Bedford House, Heemskerch laid hold of some secrets that will allow us to even the score.'

'Are you sure he is not overstating their importance, just so you will help him escape?'

'But he does not want me to help him escape,' said Williamson sourly. 'He only trusts Thurloe. He will not even accept Swaddell's assistance, although I cannot imagine why.'

Chaloner could. Swaddell was Williamson's favourite clerk, although everyone knew he was really an assassin. He was one of the most dangerous men in the city, and Chaloner was not surprised that Heemskerch shied away from having anything to do with him.

'Of course, Swaddell is not the man he was,' Williamson went on bitterly. 'He has acquired an annoying habit of itemising all his expenses, because he thinks it will combat corruption. That kind of honesty has no place in my service.'

Chaloner struggled to keep a straight face, sure Williamson had not meant to be amusing. And yet the Spymaster was right to discourage the practice to a degree: de Witt had agents in London, so it was reckless of Swaddell to record his every transaction when the wrong eyes might learn from them.

'Did Heemskerch tell you that Quartermain was hired to kill him?' he asked.

'Yes, but I have no idea by whom. However, Thurloe and I agree that there are three possibilities: someone from the Dutch embassy; someone from our government; or someone angry about Vågen. I would order an investigation, but I do not have any spare agents.'

'Then do you know why Quartermain died in Bedford House's garden?'

'No, and nor do I know why Olivia Stoakes disappeared, why *Assurance* sank or who took Beale's trumpet.' Williamson smiled slyly. 'I met your Earl last night in White Hall.'

Then the Earl should have kept his mouth shut, thought Chaloner irritably. It was unwise to gossip about ongoing investigations, especially to a spymaster.

'Poor Olivia,' Williamson went on; he sounded sincere. 'I imagine she is dead, poor soul, or we would have had news of her by now. It is a pity. She was kind to moths – she always set them free, whereas most people swat them. You included, I expect.'

On that note, Chaloner decided he had better ask his favour before they fell out. 'Will you lend me a dozen soldiers? I will not have answers from witnesses at the Fleece unless they feel threatened, and no one is afraid of me.'

'They should be,' muttered Williamson. 'I certainly am.'

Chaloner was sure he had misheard. 'A dozen soldiers,' he repeated. 'For the rest of the day. In return, I will tell you all I learn about Quartermain and Heemskerch.'

Williamson considered the offer carefully, searching for loopholes, and seeing none, inclined his head to accept the deal. 'But I need them back by eight o'clock tonight, because that is when I shall mount a raid on Chatelaine's Coffee House.'

'The one in Covent Garden? Why?'

'Because a band of dangerous fanatics is due to meet there – rebels, who aim to spread dissention and unrest. I shall catch them in the act, and imprison them before they set the whole city alight with their poisonous ideas.'

Idly, Chaloner wondered if they would include any members of Urban's Men.

As Williamson needed time to pull so many soldiers from their other duties, Chaloner went to the Savoy Wharf to ask after Lester. He was in luck: Judd told him that the captain had gone over to the Floating Coffee House not ten minutes before.

'He braved *that?*' asked Chaloner, eyeing the river in disbelief. It was a raging brown torrent, made even more deadly by its bobbing cargo of uprooted trees, planks of wood and smashed boats. There were bodies, too, of animals that had been swept away and drowned.

Judd laughed at his landsman's timidity. 'Do not worry, sir. I shall send you over with Scull again. He will keep you safe.'

Under other circumstances, Chaloner would have waited for Lester to come back, feeling such a journey was a needless risk, but time was short and he wanted Heemskerch away from Thurloe. He nodded reluctantly.

'Then give us a minute,' said Judd. 'You see that great oak lodged against the bow of the Folly? Well, the lads need to prise it loose before it does any damage. The moment it floats away, you can go.'

Chaloner's reservations intensified, but he told himself that Lester would not have attempted the crossing if it had been unduly dangerous; he ignored the part of his brain which warned him that Lester's idea of 'unduly' and his own were likely to be rather different. He glanced around while he waited, noting the quay was unusually busy. Most of the milling throng were navy officials, who congregated near the spot where *Assurance* had gone down.

'They will weigh her on Saturday,' explained Judd, seeing where he was looking. He nodded at the two sailors who stood next to him. '*Assurance* is their ship – Knapp here is her boatswain, while Fowler is Captain Stoakes' steward.'

Fowler did not look like a steward. He was a great hulking brute of a man with brawny arms and massive fists, and Chaloner could not imagine him serving food

147

or powdering wigs. He wondered what had induced Stoakes to appoint such a man. Or was it Fowler's strength that had been the attraction – that Stoakes was an unpopular leader who needed a beefy bodyguard? Knapp was smaller, and sported an impressive pigtail that swung well below his waist.

'I saw *Assurance* at the Battle of Lowestoft,' said Chaloner. 'In the centre, under the Admiral of the White. She was a proud ship, and a fine sight with all her canvas spread.'

He had no idea if the last bit was true, and was only repeating what he had heard Lester say about her, but it was compliment enough to win him smiles from Knapp and Fowler.

'We had another master then,' said Fowler. 'Captain Jefferies, a hero among men.'

'Yes, *he* would not have allowed her to sink at a pier,' said Knapp in disgust.

Fowler nodded fervent agreement, which told Chaloner all he needed to know about Stoakes' nautical abilities and his crew's opinion of him.

'Captain Jefferies would not have let the government cheat us either,' growled Fowler. 'I am owed two years' wages, but the navy says I can only have three months, because that is all it can afford. Captain Jefferies would have argued my case, but Stoakes does not care.'

'The navy refuses to pay the sick and hurt as well,' put in Judd angrily, and indicated his missing legs. 'The Lord High Admiral *promised* we would be looked after if we were maimed serving our country, but now he bleats that there is no money. If it was not for the sea-officers who visit the Folly, I would be starving in a ditch, and my shipmates with me.'

'Captains Lester and Harman fight for *their* crews,' put in Knapp. 'But Stoakes? Oh, no! He sits in White Hall, quaffing wine all day. He is nothing but a damned courtier!'

'*And* a landsman,' said Judd, with utter contempt. 'We could have crushed the Dutch once and for all after Lowestoft, but *landsmen* let them escape. Stupid bastards!'

'Did you know that Stoakes' wife is missing?' asked Chaloner, wondering if *Assurance*'s crew had kidnapped her, in the hope of blackmailing their master into doing what was right.

Fowler's fierce expression softened. 'She tried to help me get my wages, and it is a pity she is gone, because Stoakes is less of a man without her.'

'Personally, I think he is glad to be rid of her,' confided Knapp. 'She was always trying to get him to do the decent thing, and he hated her for it. If she was alive, our dead mates would be buried by now. Instead, they lie rotting in a charnel house.'

So the sailors had not taken Olivia, surmised Chaloner – they would rather have her alive, petitioning Stoakes on their behalf. He nodded to where *Assurance* had gone down.

'What happened to her? I do not believe she sank from a rogue gust of wind.'

Fowler and Knapp exchanged a glance, and there was a moment when Chaloner thought they would refuse to answer, but then the steward spoke, the anger back in his eyes.

'Someone sank her on purpose, to get rid of . . . evidence. You know what I mean?'

'Not really,' said Chaloner.

'Stoakes is a courtier,' elaborated Knapp, pursing his

lips. 'What more needs to be said? Everyone knows that White Hall is a pit of treachery, filth and intrigue.'

'Too right,' agreed Judd. 'After all, look at what they did to poor Cromwell's corpse. If digging him up and chopping him into pieces wasn't despicable, then I don't know what is.'

'Right,' said Chaloner. 'But what "evidence" necessitated the sinking of a ship?'

'Something to do with White Hall,' replied Knapp shortly, so that Chaloner saw, with a pang of disappointment, that their claims were based on nothing but frustration, rage and supposition. 'Because everything vile, sinful and cunning comes from that place. Is that not so, Judd?'

'It is indeed,' replied Judd with conviction.

Moments later, Knapp and Fowler were handing Chaloner down stairs that were even more slippery than last time, with the wind threatening to pluck him off and deposit him in the churning river below. Then he was subjected to a hair-raising passage during which the little craft was battered by all manner of flotsam, and Scull grunted and gasped with the effort of keeping his boat on course. By the time he arrived, Chaloner was wet, cold and acutely aware that he would soon have to do it all over again in order to return to shore.

The only customers on the Folly that morning were sea-officers, who were used to water and its deadly power. They were being served by Maurice, whose charcoal eyebrows were lopsided, perhaps from being applied on board – the barge was prone to random judders as it was struck by objects tearing past outside. Robert was also there, drenched to the skin and bellowing angrily about money wasted on beautifying churches for the Fast. There was no sign of George.

'I was going to close today,' said Maurice, bustling forward to take Chaloner's sodden cloak. 'But my patrons would not hear of it.'

'They are used to choppy water,' explained Robert in a voice that would be audible back on the pier. As he spoke his teeth popped out and skittered across the table. They landed in someone else's lap, where they were retrieved and politely handed back.

'When *I* saw the state of the river last night,' Maurice went on, pouring Chaloner a dish of scalding hot coffee that was a pleasure to hold in cold-numbed hands, 'I decided to sleep aboard, and what a rough time I had of it! Pitching and tossing, creaking and thumping. Still, better that than the journey poor Robert had just now.'

'All the day's pies were washed overboard,' yelled Robert. 'And I nearly joined them!'

Chaloner was sorry. He would willingly have bought one, given how delicious Williamson's had smelled.

I shall be glad when this bad weather ends,' sighed Maurice. 'I long to stand somewhere stable. George refuses to come over at all, afraid that water will stain the finish on his false leg.'

'He loves that limb more than the original,' confided Robert. 'Well, it was expensive.'

'Now go and sit with Lester,' said Maurice convivially, shooing Chaloner in the right direction. 'And I shall bring you some buttered eggs. They are not the most exciting of fare served cold, but it is the best I can do now the pies have gone.'

'Yes, join us, Tom,' called Lester, who was with Harman and Cox. 'We do not bite.'

'Unless you plan to swing at us with a cudgel,' growled Cox. 'Then we might.'

'He and Harman were attacked again last night,' explained Lester, as Chaloner sat reluctantly; he could not waste time chatting when there was so much to be done.

'As we were coming home from Deptford,' elaborated Harman angrily. 'Is nothing sacred? To assault men who strive to defend our country from the Dutch?'

'How many of them were there this time?' asked Lester sympathetically.

'It was difficult to tell in the dark,' replied Cox. 'Five, perhaps.'

'I wish I had killed a couple,' said Harman savagely, revealing himself to be very much the warrior, despite his elegant appearance. 'Then we could have used their corpses to identify their confederates and hang the lot of them.'

'They were probably hungry,' said Lester, a kinder, gentler man than his colleagues. 'Life is hard for the poor in winter.'

'Then they should join the navy,' declared Cox. 'We offer free bed and board.'

'But no wages, alas,' sighed Lester. 'Perhaps *that* was the reason behind the attack – they were desperate seamen, forced to steal what they should have been given.'

'No sailor blames us for his predicament,' countered Cox irritably. 'These were *landsmen*, Lester. I could tell by the sloppy way they fought.'

'I hope they try again,' said Harman, and patted the cutlass in his belt. 'I will show them what happens to those who ambush senior members of His Majesty's navy.'

152

'Speaking of the navy,' interposed Chaloner, the moment he could fit a word in edgeways, 'some of *Assurance*'s crew think she was deliberately scuppered. Have you heard rumours to that effect?'

'Every day,' replied Harman. 'Lester believes them, but I do not. Her master was Stoakes, for God's sake – a courtier! He probably tied her up with a bit of twine from his pocket, and his people were so demoralised that they did not rectify the matter. Then when the wind blew . . .'

'Twenty of their shipmates died,' argued Lester. 'They would not have ignored his incompetence if it put friends' lives in danger. But we shall have answers when she is weighed on Saturday. Then you will see that a saboteur *was* at work.'

'Why would anyone sink a vessel that will protect them against the Dutch?' demanded Harman impatiently. 'It makes no sense.'

'It does if her captain is involved in something untoward,' Chaloner pointed out. 'Something treasonous, perhaps.'

'*Stoakes?*' sneered Harman. 'He does not have the wits! What do you think, Cox?'

'I agree with Lester,' said Cox soberly. 'There *is* something odd about what happened to *Assurance*, and Stoakes is a crony of Harry Brouncker. We all know—'

'We all know what?' asked Lester, when Cox stopped mid-sentence, apparently having been kicked by Harman under the table.

'We all know that Brouncker runs a brothel,' finished Harman, although it was clear from Cox's chagrin that this was not what he had been going to say. 'Which is hardly genteel.'

153

'Quite,' agreed Cox. 'The Duke should find his own whores, like the rest of us do.'

It was not easy to pull Lester away from his companions, although Chaloner had done no more than draw breath to explain what he wanted when Maurice arrived with the food. It comprised hard-boiled eggs on toasted bread, each one encased in a sarcophagus of solid fat.

'I use a pound of butter for each egg,' confided Maurice proudly, as he set it down.

'Crikey!' breathed Chaloner. 'How many eggs are here, exactly?'

'Half a dozen. Eat up.'

Chaloner was saved from having to oblige by the arrival of more guests. The moment Maurice had gone to welcome them, Chaloner lobbed most of the fatty mass through a broken window, where it bobbed away, too oily to sink. He and Lester shared the six greasy eggs.

'I need to get someone out of the country fast,' he said in a low voice. 'Can you help? Anywhere but the United Provinces.'

'Are you in trouble with your Earl again?' asked Lester sympathetically. 'You should resign and join the navy instead. You meet a better class of person on a ship than you do on land, as you can tell from this place. We are—'

'It is not for me. It is for a spy, who has been providing us with information about the Dutch.'

'Not the spy who was responsible for urging us to attack the Dutch at Vågen, I hope,' said Lester coolly. 'Because the answer would be no. My conscience would not allow it.'

Chaloner considered a fib, but it would be unfortunate if Lester then learned the truth and withdrew his help at the last minute. Besides, he was a friend, and deserved honesty.

'It is, I am afraid. His name is Laurens van Heemskerch, and he claims that he still has vital intelligence to share – which he will divulge as soon as he is safely away. He may be lying, but Spymaster Williamson seems to think he is worth the risk.'

'Why not make him divulge it now?' asked Lester coolly. 'Then we can shoot the rogue, and save ourselves the bother of sorting out his future.'

'If we coerce him, he will likely mix real intelligence with rubbish, which means we would not be able to trust any of it. We have no choice but to accede to his demands.'

'A lot of people want him dead,' warned Lester, and nodded to his fellow captains. 'Them, for a start. Plus those sailors who lost shipmates at Vågen. Moreover, the government cannot be pleased with him either – he made them look like asses.'

'No, he is not popular,' acknowledged Chaloner with a sigh. 'So, will you help? Or shall I try to manage by myself? It is important, Sal. We really do need the secrets he has.'

Lester scowled. 'He should be grateful that you and I are friends, because I would not do this for anyone else. Good men died at Vågen, while poor Judd is maimed for life. Your Heemskerch is either incompetent or treacherous – either way, the world would be a better place without him in it.'

'Yes, it would,' agreed Chaloner. 'Will you take him on *Swiftsure*?'

'Only if you do not mind delaying his departure until spring. He will have to go on another ship if you want him away quickly. A merchantman would be best. I shall ask Harman and Cox, as their connections in that quarter are much better than my own.'

'No! You cannot tell anyone else.'

'We must, Tom. Harman and Cox will know not only which cargo vessels are suitable, but which of their masters can be trusted. Do not worry – they can keep their mouths shut.'

'I hope you are right,' said Chaloner unhappily. 'Or the next Vågen will be *our* fault.'

'I *am* right. Meet me here at dusk, by which time I shall have the basis of a plan.'

'Not here,' said Chaloner, unwilling to risk two return journeys across the turbulent Thames that day. 'The church in Covent Garden.'

'As you wish,' said Lester. 'Although I shall feel like a spy myself, passing you information in such a place.'

A few minutes later, Chaloner scrambled up the Savoy Wharf steps. He had suffered another soaking, although that was neither here nor there, given that he had not dried out from the first one. He declined Judd's offer of a sailor to find him a hackney, and began to trot towards the Strand, hoping that exercise would restore some warmth to his frozen limbs. He turned west, to tell Thurloe that he had taken the first step in getting Heemskerch away.

The same boy was on duty at Lincoln's Inn's main gate, where Chaloner was unimpressed to be addressed as 'Mr Hoode' – the lad could not even remember the right false name. He nodded curtly, then swore under his breath when he was intercepted by a plump, bustling individual who wore an ugly woollen cap.

William Prynne was one of the least likeable men in the city, a religious fanatic who regaled the world with his rabid opinions by means of pamphlets, all published at his own expense. He had written a scurrilous one about the King's mother, for which he had been deprived of his ears – he wore the vile old cap to hide the mutilation. His punishment made Chaloner think suddenly of Urban, who had also suffered some aural disfigurement. As a deterrent against future infractions, ear-mangling had not worked at all – Urban was still making seditious speeches, while Prynne was more vitriolic than ever.

'Come to see Mr Thurloe, have you?' Prynne asked nosily.

'No, to borrow a book from the library,' lied Chaloner.

'On ecclesiastical law, no doubt,' growled Prynne, thus revealing which subject he had chosen to rant about that day. 'All bishops are vainglorious, corrupt, wanton, scandalous—'

'Yes,' interrupted Chaloner hastily, aware that Prynne had a vast number of adjectives at his disposal to describe things he did not like, and that allowing him to continue would see him listening for some time to come. 'Quite right.'

'You will see them at the Fast,' the old man went on venomously. 'All decked out in their heathenish vestments. I shall attend the service in Covent Garden, and when they walk in, I shall leave – as noisily as I can. After all, there is no point in taking a moral stand if no one notices.'

'Clarendon will not appreciate you using his ceremony to score political points.'

'*He* is doing it,' Prynne pointed out tartly. 'He thinks that if the King goes to Covent Garden, it will tell

157

everyone that His Majesty still loves him. But the King will break his word because he loves his dissolute cronies more.' He winced. 'I wish he did not – some of them visited the Fleece on Monday, where they sank so low as to watch *dancers and actors.*'

The last three words were delivered in a sibilant hiss, as Prynne held an especially vehement dislike for the stage. Chaloner tried to walk away, but Prynne grabbed his arm and held it tight. He could have broken free, but he had no wish to knock an old man to the ground, even one as objectionable as Prynne. The pamphleteer took a deep breath and let rip.

'Dancing is ever attended with amorous smiles, wanton compliments, unchaste kisses, scurrilous songs, effeminate music, lust-provoking attire and foolish love-pranks, all of which promote sensuality and raging fleshly lust. Therefore it must be abandoned by all good Christians. It serves no profitable, laudable or pious end, and is derived from the vanity, wantonness, incontinency, pride, profaneness and madness of men's depraved nature.'

'How do *you* know there were dancers at the Fleece?' asked Chaloner, the moment he could insert a word into the tirade. 'Did you go there yourself?'

Prynne sniffed. 'I cannot condemn these vices if I do not witness them personally – it would be hypocritical.' He reflected briefly. 'Yet I enjoyed parts of the show – the fire-eater and Adam Urban, who made a pretty speech condemning debauchery and vice. Incidentally, if you see Mr Thurloe, tell him to be on his guard – Cromwell's head has disappeared.'

Prynne liked Thurloe, and was always trying to win his approval, even though they were at opposite ends of the political spectrum.

'What does that have to do with him?' asked Chaloner coolly. 'Or do you think it might roll here, for an evening of reminiscing and gossip?'

Prynne glared at him. 'No, but there are those who might accuse him of stealing it, in order to give it a decent burial. After all, men have been asking questions about him of late.'

'What men?' asked Chaloner, trying to hide his alarm.

'I think they were sailors. Maybe they want him to intercede with the government on their behalf, in the hope that *he* can get them the pay they are owed.'

Or perhaps they had learned that the person responsible for Vågen was in Thurloe's attic, thought Chaloner worriedly. Time was short indeed.

'Of course, Cromwell would have defeated the Dutch by now,' declared Prynne. 'He would have finished them after Lowestoft, not let them sail off to fight another day.'

'Everyone is wise with hindsight,' shrugged Chaloner, unwilling to tell him he was right.

'Mr Thurloe is worried about the war,' confided Prynne. 'He is eating twice as much as he normally does. I always eat more when I am anxious, too.'

'So do I,' agreed Chaloner, keen for him to believe it. 'It helps.'

'Go,' said Prynne, releasing his arm abruptly. 'And wage war on sin, vice and wickedness. And on the United Provinces, should the opportunity arise.'

It took but moments for Chaloner to report that Lester had agreed to help Heemskerch, that Prynne had noticed how much Thurloe ate, and that 'sailors' had been asking questions in Lincoln's Inn. Thurloe nodded his thanks for the first piece of information, but said he was already aware of the second two and had taken appropriate measures.

'Then have you heard that Cromwell's head blew away in the storm?' asked Chaloner.

Thurloe smiled serenely. 'The authorities will have to find a replacement yet again. It will be at least the fifth time it has happened. Loyal Parliamentarians are always rescuing heads from Westminster Hall, each one convinced that he is saving the genuine article.'

Chaloner shrugged. 'Skulls will be ten a penny these days, given how many were dug up to make room for the plague pits. And all look the same once they have been boiled in tar.'

Thurloe made a moue of distaste. 'That would be disrespectful to the anonymous victim. However, wonderful things can be done with wax nowadays, and while Surgeon Wiseman may be able to tell the difference, to everyone else . . . Speaking of Wiseman, I confess I find him ghoulish. He told me the other day that he keeps his brother-in-law's brain in a bottle.'

'And his liver,' said Chaloner glumly, thinking that he would be compelled to keep company with both until the roof was mended.

Messages delivered, he took a hackney back to Westminster. He glanced at the clock as he passed White Hall, and saw there was still a full half hour before Williamson had told him the soldiers would be ready. He asked the driver to stop at Axe Yard, thinking that exploring Quartermain's house for clues was as good a way as any to use the few spare minutes.

Axe Yard was mostly inhabited by people who worked in the nearby palaces – clerks, Treasury officials, minor courtiers and men of law. Quartermain had occupied one of the larger houses, indicating that he had made a respectable living from being a royal physician. Chaloner knocked on the front door, and when there was no answer, went to the back, picked the lock and let himself inside.

There was an elegantly appointed parlour for entertaining on the ground floor, and a small, functional bedchamber upstairs, but the rest of the house was completely bare – the physician had bought a large property for appearances' sake, but most of it had been superfluous to his needs, so had been left empty. Thus it took no time at all for Chaloner to search, and to learn that it held nothing to help his enquiries. He left the way he had come, careful to secure the door behind him.

'Who are you?' came a voice from over the garden wall. The speaker was a large woman with rouged lips and inquisitive eyes.

'The Earl of Clarendon's envoy,' replied Chaloner. 'I am looking into William Quartermain's death. Who are you?'

'His neighbour, Mrs Vaughan. Do you want to hear about him?' She began to hold forth before he could reply. 'He was a surly devil, although it pains me to speak ill of the dead. Indeed, I was astonished when he won a royal appointment, as he was not a very good doctor.'

'How do you know?' fished Chaloner, willing to listen to her spiteful gossip if it provided him with useful information.

'Well, for a start, his manner at the bedside was discourteous. He had the audacity to tell me that I was malingering! And his plague remedy stank so badly of garlic that I was unable to swallow mine. I had to pour it away.'

Luckily for her, thought Chaloner, or she might not

161

now be standing in her garden, denigrating its inventor. 'Did he have many visitors?'

'None recently, except for the man who started coming just before Christmas. I cannot tell you his name, and nor can I describe his face, because he never arrived without a hood pulled over it. However, I can tell you that his shoes were always clean.'

'So he came by coach or on horseback?'

'Or he did not have very far to walk.'

Which meant he might have hailed from White Hall or the Palace of Westminster, thought Chaloner unhappily. 'How many times did he visit?'

'Four,' she replied promptly. 'And Dr Quartermain always peered around very furtively before letting him in, as if he did not want anyone else to see. But my windows overlook his front door and I rarely go out, so I noticed every time. The doctor was never pleased to see him, though. The last time was the Friday before his death, and I heard him crying afterwards.'

She was a spy's dream – observant and nosy – and Chaloner was sure the mysterious visitor was significant, particularly given the timing of the final visit. Now all he had to do was find someone with clean shoes and the ability to make grown men weep.

He met someone with the ability to make grown men weep when he returned to Westminster Palace, although Williamson's expensive shoes were filthy. Moreover, the mud on them had dried, and there was a nasty stain on the toe of one, suggesting that they had not been polished in weeks. It was possible that Williamson owned a second pair, but Chaloner could not see him donning clean ones just to plough through the filth of Westminster.

Therefore, he was able to conclude that it had not been the Spymaster who had visited Quartermain in Axe Yard.

Chaloner was pleasantly surprised to discover that Williamson had chosen some of his best men for the assault on the Fleece – the prospect of trouble brewing there had evidently alarmed him. However, he was less pleased to learn that he was to have company: John Swaddell was waiting with them, clearly with the intention of joining the expedition.

Swaddell was a deeply sinister individual who always dressed in black, other than a spotlessly white 'falling band' that lay in a neat square across his chest, like a bib. He was ruthless, cold and unpredictable, and although he tried to be amenable, Chaloner was always uneasy in his company.

'There is no need for you to come,' Chaloner said hastily. 'I can manage alone.'

'I do not doubt it,' said Swaddell and smiled; it was not a very nice expression. 'But life has been all gruellingly hard work of late, and I need some light relief. Just look on me as another hired hand.'

'Very well,' said Chaloner reluctantly. 'But no throat-slitting. People cannot give us information if they are dead.'

An expression of hurt suffused Swaddell's face. 'What a low opinion you have of me, Tom! I see I shall have to redeem myself – *again*.'

Aware that time was short, Chaloner briefed the soldiers, then led them at a rapid clip to the Fleece. Swaddell trotted at his side, chatting so cordially that anyone watching might be forgiven for thinking they were old friends. The notion made Chaloner deeply uncomfortable. Suddenly, without warning, the assassin's reptilian grin faded, and a darker, more unsettling expression took its place.

'Williamson made a new acquaintance in Oxford,' he said, and there was no mistaking the venom in his voice. 'A wealthy merchant named Robert Thompson. I cannot *abide* the man. He has no control over his false teeth, and he cannot whisper to save his life.'

'He does have a penetrating voice,' acknowledged Chaloner cautiously.

'But worse yet,' Swaddell went on tightly, 'he thinks that being one of Williamson's acquaintances gives him the right to waste our time. Take last night, for example. He sailed into the office at nine o'clock, and squandered a whole hour chatting about some kind of moth.'

So Swaddell was jealous of Robert, surmised Chaloner, while Williamson disapproved of his assassin's recently acquired honesty. Was this the beginning of a rift between the two?

'The respite probably did Williamson good,' said Chaloner, who liked to play his viol when he was tense and overworked. It helped to clear his thoughts, which was something all those in the intelligence business needed to do if they were to function efficiently.

Swaddell shot him a malevolent glance. 'Not as much good as if he had spent it with me. I know a lot about *mattae*, too.'

'*Blattae*,' corrected Chaloner automatically. '*Mattae* are reed mats.'

Swaddell gave him another icy glare, and they walked in silence for a short distance. Then Swaddell shrugged off his sour temper and forced a smile.

'The Royal Society met for the first time since the

plague last night,' he reported conversationally. 'And Dr Goddard explained why he and his fellow physicians chose to abandon London.'

'What was their excuse?'

'That their patients had gone, so what would be the use of staying when they were needed elsewhere? He had a point: all those who can afford their exorbitant prices *had* left the city.'

'And who cares about the poor?' muttered Chaloner acidly.

Swaddell chuckled. 'You sound like a republican. Next you will be wanting free elections and claiming that democracy is the most effective form of government.'

'Oh, no,' quipped Chaloner facetiously. 'Give me a military dictatorship any day.'

'I could not agree more!' exclaimed Swaddell. 'You and I have much in common.'

While the assassin outlined his own proposals for a government that had the power to crush anyone with the audacity to disagree with it, Chaloner found himself staring at Swaddell's shoes. They were spotless, and Swaddell could certainly reduce someone to tears. Yet the assassin was neither stupid nor careless, and would never enter a house by a front door when a nosy neighbour was at large.

'Did you ever meet Quartermain?' Chaloner asked anyway, when the subject of repressive regimes had been exhausted.

'I summoned him once when I had a fever. He prescribed a pot of his King's Gold, which tasted of honey and made me sleep like a baby. I woke the next day feeling much better.'

'So you thought him a good physician?' pressed

Chaloner, thinking Swaddell was lucky he had not called Quartermain when the King's Gold contained dangerous levels of poxbane.

'Well, he cured me. And the King must have admired his talents, or he would not have appointed him to serve the Court. Yet I did not like him as a man – he was more arrogant than Wiseman, more expensive than Goddard, and about as friendly as one of Williamson's moths.'

'Abigail Williams found something in him to love.'

'Yes – his purse,' said Swaddell acidly. 'He showered her with gifts, and she is a greedy whore. Now he is no longer available, she has shifted her affections to Harry Brouncker, the brother of the fool who thinks that *he* is her only amour.'

'What about Heemskerch the spy? Did you ever meet him?'

Swaddell shook his head. 'We did not even know his true identity until he was forced to flee Bedford House. All the information he provided came to us via Thurloe.'

They reached Charing Cross, where Swaddell began to confide his reservations about the planned raid on Chatelaine's Coffee House that evening.

'It is popular with courtiers, and I do not see *them* conspiring to rebel. We should be aiming to suppress organisations like Urban's Men, which represent a genuine danger.'

'Have you seen them perform?'

'Just Urban – at the Rose on Cheapside. He is the most accomplished orator I have ever heard, because he can *read* an audience – he senses when they need to laugh or cry, and gives them what they want. It is what makes him so deadly.'

'Then why did you not arrest him?'

'Because three hundred people would have torn me to shreds if I had tried. But here is the Fleece. We shall station two armed guards at each door, and take the rest inside with us. We shall draw our weapons, too. That will show these rogues we mean business.'

Their arrival in the tavern resulted in a tremendous kerfuffle, especially when people discovered the exits were blocked, although it was Swaddell who caused the most consternation. All he did was stand in the shadows and finger his dagger, but it was enough to strike terror into the hearts of all those who saw him.

Chaloner questioned staff, patrons and entertainers, using every trick and bluff he knew, but to no avail. He learned nothing new about Olivia, Widow Fisher or anything else on his list. However, as the hours ticked by, he became increasingly certain that something *was* brewing at the Fleece. For a start, there was a general, smug conviction that Urban and his followers would not rest until the King had made amends for all the wrongs he had inflicted on his subjects.

'Hurry up,' ordered Gimonde, when it was his turn to be grilled. It was at a point when Swaddell had grown tired of being menacing, and had taken himself off for something to eat, which meant the Bolognese was rather more curt with his interrogator than he might otherwise have been. 'We have a special performance tonight, and we need to rehearse.'

'What manner of special performance?' demanded Chaloner.

'A new satire.' Gimonde's expression was contemptuous and challenging at the same time. 'Which is an ancient and perfectly legitimate form of drama, developed by the Romans.'

'Williamson will not see it as legitimate,' warned Chaloner. 'You will be arrested for preaching sedition.'

'He would not dare,' said Gimonde smugly. 'Not unless he wants an instant riot. People adore us, and will not stand by while we are illegally silenced.'

'Not true,' countered Chaloner. 'He will consider it better to provoke a small disturbance now, than crush a serious uprising later.'

'But all we do is say what most people think,' argued Gimonde irritably. 'Including you, if you are honest with yourself. Or are you fool enough to believe that the King is a just and kindly ruler? That his Court is worth the money it costs? That his government is efficient, and worthy of our trust? Or that White Hall was right to abandon us during the plague?'

'What I think is not important. You should be more concerned about—'

'But your opinion *is* important,' Gimonde assured him earnestly. 'As is mine, the landlord's, the people's you have terrorised today, and even Swaddell's. That is the point. We *all* matter.'

Chaloner did not want to discuss it, sure he would never prevail over such passionately held beliefs. 'Where is Urban? I would like to speak to him next.'

'He went to visit some friends this morning, and has not yet returned. Do not ask me which ones, because I do not know.'

He could be persuaded to say no more, so Chaloner indicated that he could go. He quizzed the rest of the troupe, but although they were less combative than Gimonde, it was clear that they also believed they were doing London a favour by pointing out the deficiencies of its ruling elite. Then Swaddell reappeared and indicated that Chaloner's loan of the henchmen was about to end.

'This tavern is not as great a threat as you led me to believe,' the assassin said, once they were outside. 'Oh, people *want* the King overthrown, but wanting is not doing.'

'No,' acknowledged Chaloner tiredly. 'But I still think—'

'How about helping us with the raid on Chatelaine's tonight?' interrupted Swaddell. 'I should appreciate a man I trust at my back.'

'I cannot,' said Chaloner, trying to disguise his surprise at the last remark, as the feeling was certainly not reciprocated. Indeed, the more Chaloner came to know the assassin, the less he understood him. 'I have a meeting to attend.'

'Then watch yourself. You made no friends here today – and you did mention earlier that there has been one attempt on your life already.'

Chapter 7

The wind had picked up again while Chaloner had been in the Fleece, and had blown down so many lanterns that it was impossible to see where he was putting his feet. He usually liked the dark, a time when all spies felt more comfortable, but he longed for some light that evening. He could not hear whether he was being followed over the noise of the gale, while whirling rubbish flashed and flicked at the corners of his vision. He was relieved when he reached the Covent Garden church, where he had agreed to meet Lester.

Work had continued apace with the beautification, and the decorative gilt shone richly in the candlelight. The floor was scrubbed to a creamy whiteness, and all the windows had new glass. Chaloner marvelled at the transformation, especially given that it had been done in such a short space of time. As he walked through it, he saw several craftsmen only just packing up their tools for the day, explaining to several resentful onlookers that they had *had* to work late, because they were behind schedule. And if the congregation had a problem with that, they should take it up with the Earl.

'We have,' grumbled an elderly parishioner named Mrs Price. 'But he never listens. What time will you start tomorrow? It had better not be when the church is supposed to be ours.'

'It will be, I am afraid,' replied a carpenter apologetically. 'We have to start work on that wobbly old gallery at first light, see. The royal trumpeter will stand up there, ready to play the fanfare before we all shout "God save the King". We do not want it collapsing under his weight, do we.'

'No,' growled Mrs Price, although the tone of her voice suggested the opposite. 'But we *need* our church back! It is good for sitting out of the wind. And for praying, of course.'

'We are doing our best to finish fast,' said the carpenter defensively. 'But Clarendon keeps making ever more demands of us. He says everything must be perfect, although I have heard rumours that His Majesty will go to Westminster Abbey instead, so it might all be for nothing in the end.'

'Good,' hissed Mrs Price venomously. 'Mr Urban says that the King and Clarendon should be treated with compassion because they cannot help being selfish. But I think we should lop off their heads and bring back the republic.'

Unwilling to listen to that sort of talk, Chaloner hurried to the chancel, where Lester was passing the time of day with two of Mrs Price's equally ancient cronies. As he went, he wondered how much the renovation was costing his employer. Certainly enough to pay the defrauded sailors, so it was small wonder that the brazen extravagance was causing so much resentment.

'I told them we are in for a storm,' said Lester, watching

the two old ladies hobble away, clearly having had the wits scared out of them. 'So they should batten down the hatches.'

'*In* for a storm?' echoed Chaloner. 'What do you call these last three days?'

'A stiff breeze. But what we shall have over the next twenty-four hours is a *hyrricano*, which is a tempestuous kind of whirlwind, much feared by mariners. We know it is coming, because of the new predictive instruments invented by the Royal Society.'

Chaloner nodded. 'Wren told me about those. So there will be yet more damage?'

'Tonight will see houses falling down, not just roofs. Unfortunately, it means that Heemskerch is going nowhere, as ships are now looking for safe havens, not heading out to sea. Hah! Here come Harman and Cox. Let us see what they have to tell us about this escape.'

Chaloner looked to where the two officers were carefully wiping their feet to avoid staining the pristine floor. He hoped yet again that Lester was right to say they could be trusted.

'We found a sloop sailing for Guinea on Saturday,' reported Harman, once polite greetings had been exchanged. 'Hyrricano permitting, of course. I hope you can keep your spy safe until then, Chaloner. We would not want him to die in the interim, would we?'

'We would not,' said Chaloner coolly. 'Because he has information that Williamson believes will help us win the war. If we lose him, we lose the intelligence.'

'Then let us pray that it is more accurate than his assessment of Vågen,' said Cox, equally cold. 'I should not like to think that we have spent an entire afternoon planning something that might bring harm to His Majesty's navy.'

'You can believe Tom,' Lester assured them earnestly. 'If *he* thinks Heemskerch is worth saving, then Heemskerch is worth saving. And we must do all we can to help.'

'If you say so,' muttered Harman, clearly unconvinced.

Lester was right about the wind. When he and Chaloner stepped outside the church, they narrowly missed being crushed by the weather vane as it plummeted down from the roof. The gale had also flattened three of the market stalls and blown over the decorative cross in the middle of the Piazza.

Despite Swaddell's dismissive remarks about the Fleece, Chaloner was still sure the inn lay at the heart of something deadly, and if he could not find out what it was by asking direct questions, then he would have to see what might be learned by stealth. So, although he would much rather have spent his evening huddled by the fire, duty obliged him to don a disguise and spend a few hours eavesdropping.

Lester walked with him to his lodgings, where they arrived at the same time as Wiseman. The surgeon was just rolling up in a coach that was emblazoned with the royal coat-of-arms – he had been in Hampton Court all day, and the King had insisted on providing one of his own carriages for the journey home. Uncharitably, Chaloner wondered if the 'kindness' had been to make sure Wiseman actually left – the Court usually began its frolics once darkness fell, and *medici* tended to frown upon of the kinds of bodily abuses the King and his rambunctious followers enjoyed.

'Come in, Captain,' Wiseman ordered. 'You will want

to hear my clever diagnosis of an imbalance in the humours surrounding His Majesty's bowels.'

'That is a tempting proposition,' said Lester, backing away. 'But I—'

'I have a new cask of claret,' coaxed Wiseman, who was used to his invitations being rejected, and had learned that he needed to make them more enticing. 'And cake.'

When these did not tempt either, he reached out and hauled Lester inside by force. Lester was a burly man, but the surgeon was stronger and Lester was too gentlemanly to engage in a tussle. Chaloner left them to it, and went to turn himself from an employee of Clarendon House to a ruffian from the rookeries – a jacket stuffed with straw to make him fatter, a greasy old long-coat, a cheap horsehair wig, and soot from the chimney on his face and hands.

By the time he was ready, Wiseman had finished with the King's digestive tract, and was regaling Lester with his opinions about *Assurance*, which he insisted on calling a boat, despite Lester's pedantic insistence that she was a ship.

'You are right to be suspicious about her sinking,' the surgeon declared, returning to his rant after he and Lester had declared themselves impressed by Chaloner's disguise. 'Because I had a look at those twenty corpses, and all of them had drowned.'

'Of course they did,' said Lester, frowning his bemusement. 'How else would they die?'

Wiseman looked smug. 'Well, just *think* about it for a moment. This boat was tied to a pier, and all sailors can jump. Why did they not do so when it started to go down?'

'Because they were asleep,' explained Lester. 'It happened at night.'

'And none of them were on watch?' demanded Wiseman archly. 'Not one woke to sound the alarm when icy water lapped around his hammock? All twenty were so weary that the sounds of a foundering boat did not penetrate their senses?'

'That is a good point,' breathed Lester, while Chaloner stared at the surgeon and wondered why *he* had not thought to pose those questions. Wiseman was right: it was indeed unlikely that twenty men should notice nothing amiss until it was too late.

Wiseman preened at their reactions. 'So do you want to hear what *I* think happened?'

'I do,' Lester assured him, winning himself a new friend by nodding so eagerly.

'They were dosed with a potion that rendered them insensible or immobile,' announced Wiseman, 'and as the cause of death was *drowning*, it means they were alive when the boat sank, but were not in a position to save themselves. If you want more evidence, think about the fact that all twenty corpses were very quickly recovered.'

'Whereas if they had been sleeping below, their bodies would still be down there,' acknowledged Lester. 'But they were all found, suggesting they were probably on deck.'

'Quite! I suspect they were provided with free wine or ale, which they imbibed eagerly, as most sailors will. Once they were helpless, someone crept aboard and . . . did whatever it is one does to sink a boat.'

'I knew it!' exclaimed Lester, thumping one hand into the other. 'I *knew* there was something odd about this business. But I shall get to the bottom of it, and Tom will help.'

'I will,' promised Chaloner. 'But let me do it alone.'

'No,' said Lester firmly. 'This is important to me. If you want my help with Heemskerch, then we must explore *Assurance* together.'

'Heemskerch?' asked Wiseman. 'Who is he?'

'No one,' said Chaloner, glaring at Lester, who had the grace to blush. 'But we need proof if we are to pursue this line of enquiry with *Assurance*. In other words, we must be able to state with certainty that her crew was deliberately incapacitated.'

'Leave that to me,' said Wiseman. 'They are still with Kersey, because Stoakes reneged on his offer to bury them the moment his wife was not here to shame him into it.'

'That man is not fit to call himself a sea-officer,' spat Lester in distaste. 'Will you look at them tonight, Wiseman? Now, in fact? Then *I* shall pay for them to be buried tomorrow.'

'No – anatomy is best conducted in daylight,' averred Wiseman, although Chaloner knew the surgeon indulged in nocturnal dissections when it suited him, 'otherwise people suspect bad things. Meet me in the charnel house at two o'clock. You may watch me work.'

'Lord!' gulped Lester. 'Can you not just do your worst and tell us your conclusions?'

'I could, but I perform better with an appreciative audience. And while we are on the subject of that hapless boat, would you like to hear another of my insightful opinions? It is that Stoakes knows more about the tragedy than he is prepared to admit – I can tell by his demeanour, which is suspiciously unconcerned.'

176

'It *is* unconcerned,' agreed Lester. 'He does not care about his missing wife either. I asked him today what he had done to find her, and the answer was nothing. He would rather sit and drink.'

'Perhaps he has not looked for her because he knows she is already dead,' suggested Wiseman darkly. 'I would not put it past the rogue to have dispatched her himself, either by design or in some drunken haze. But now you must excuse me, as my presence is required at Hercules' Pillars Alley.'

Once the surgeon had gone to pay his nightly visit to his mistress's brothel, Chaloner turned to Lester.

'I am going to the Fleece, where I will listen for rumours about *Assurance*, as well as Olivia and Widow Fisher. You concentrate on Heemskerch – devise another plan to get him away, should this hyrricano persist.'

'There *is* no other way, so I shall help you in the tavern instead,' determined Lester. 'Four ears are better than two. Now, what about a disguise? I happen to be very good at dressing up, and my crew loved my Christmas performance as Helen of Troy.'

Chaloner tried, and failed, to see Lester as the most beautiful woman in the world, and could only surmise that sailors must have very vivid imaginations.

A short while later, Lester wore a rough old cloak belonging to the footman, and his cheerful red face had been rendered disreputable with a mixture of grease and soot. It was not perfect, but it was the best Chaloner could do without taking all night. Then they struggled across the Piazza, keeping to the middle, so they would not be hit by the roof tiles that were still being torn from the surrounding houses by the screaming wind.

'Stay by my side,' instructed Chaloner as they neared the Fleece, 'and do not speak – your voice will betray you as a gentleman in an instant. If you see anyone looking too hard at us, leave immediately. Do not wait for me. I can look after myself.'

The tavern was in darkness when they arrived, and the stage was draped in the tarpaulin that Chaloner had slit when he had been attacked. The place was far from deserted, though, as people were converging on the main room, most glancing around furtively before they went inside. Landlord Clifton had posted servants at each door, not only to collect the entrance fee, but to vet those who wanted to enter. As far as Chaloner could tell, the decision to admit or exclude was based solely on clothes – anyone too well-dressed was assumed to be a spy and was roughly repelled. He raised no eyebrows himself, but the doorkeepers regarded Lester with open suspicion. Chaloner was tempted to let them oust him, but was afraid the captain might try to sneak in another way and thus put himself in danger.

'Look at his hands,' he growled instead. 'They belong to a *working* man.'

Lester held out his weather-roughened palms for inspection, and grinned when he was waved past. Then he and Chaloner stepped into a room that had been cleared of furniture, other than a platform at the far end, around which curtains had been hung. The place was packed, and more people crammed in with every passing moment. However, unlike the last performance, when the atmosphere had been cheerfully boisterous, that night it felt sullen and dangerous.

'I hope no one will need the latrine,' Lester muttered, disliking the way he was hemmed in so tightly that it was a struggle even to pull out his handkerchief and mop his sweaty brow. 'Because leaving will be impossible. They will have to wait until the show is over.'

Chaloner shot him a warning look – to listen, not talk, then proceeded to eavesdrop on his nearest neighbours. They were embroiled in a hissing debate about the Covent Garden church, and how *they* would not attend a Fast for the old tyrant. Moreover, they suspected the current King would not bother either, as the ceremonies were in the morning, a time when he would still be in bed with his latest whore.

'A lass provided by Brouncker,' growled one, 'from his brothel.'

'No, Brouncker supplies the Duke of York,' corrected his crony. 'It is Chiffinch who finds them for the King. Did you hear that a courtier vanished from here last Sunday, by the way? A woman? She was abducted by thieves, apparently.'

'She should not have been here in the first place. It is our tavern, not theirs.'

'Yet I would not mind seeing their faces if they did come tonight,' chuckled the first. 'They *should* know that their days are numbered. Thank God for Urban! He will put matters right.'

'Aye. Things will be different this time next week.'

When they began to discuss the price of fish, Chaloner broke his own rule about keeping quiet to bring the conversation back to the bubbling rebellion.

'I heard Urban preach in the church earlier,' he told them. 'He was an inspiration.'

Both men regarded him askance. 'Did you think so?' asked the first. 'We thought he was dull and overly cautious – on his best behaviour, because he was in a holy place. But I have a good feeling about tonight – I am expecting it to be his best performance yet.'

Before Chaloner could ask more, the lamps in the room were doused, drawing a murmur of eager anticipation from the audience. A single torch flared, and the curtains were pulled back to reveal a man on the stage. It was Urban, his white hair and whiskers forming a halo around his head, something that was not lost on his audience, as several people called out for him to bless them. Even from a distance, Chaloner could see his disfigured ears, which were thick and puffy. The old man waited for absolute silence before speaking.

'Good evening, friends,' he began. 'Smile and be happy, for a very dear comrade has agreed to join us this wild and windy evening. It is Pulcinella!'

He stepped aside, and 'Pulcinella' exploded from behind the curtain. Gimonde wore a mask with a long nose, pointed chin and diabolical features, and his costume comprised an Elizabethan-style ruff and jester's motley – harlequin hose and a jerkin with huge buttons. He carried his trademark slap-stick, and when he spoke, it was in his characteristic squeaky voice.

'I am an exiled monarch,' he declared, 'and here is the tale of how I reclaimed my throne, which was stolen from me by vile and common men.'

Lest anyone was in doubt as to who Pulcinella represented, Urban drew a pencil-thin moustache on the mask, and placed a crown on Gimonde's head. After this, the show took off at an astonishing rate. Clun dashed on and off the stage as the King's various mistresses, including a lecherous Lady Castlemaine with a train of royal brats; and Hall took the role of noble but abused Londoner,

180

frequently beaten with the slap-stick to boos from the audience.

But the star of the show was Urban, who transformed himself into a host of unpopular public figures: Williamson, slinking along while a cheese-obsessed Dutchman – played by Hudson – ran circles around him; the Duke of York, losing sea-battles through incompetence; the Earl of Clarendon, selling English territories to anyone who would bribe him; the lascivious Chiffinch, keeping the King exhausted with prostitutes; and Brouncker, aping His Majesty in dress and manners, then cheating at chess to win money for his brothel.

'Goodness!' murmured Chaloner, astonished that Clifton should have allowed such a performance in his tavern. 'When Williamson hears about this, he will close the place down and execute every person here as a traitor.'

'Then let us hope his raid on Chatelaine's will keep him busy until it is finished,' Lester murmured back. 'I do not want to witness a bloodbath.'

'Of course!' breathed Chaloner in understanding. 'An informant recommended that he visits Chatelaine tonight, but he will find nothing there, because it is a diversion – a ruse to distract him while Urban's Men foment unrest in here.'

At that moment, 'King' Pulcinella segued from a plan to tax paupers on the number of toes and fingers they owned, to the navy. Urban was the Duke of York, and together the pair of them hatched a plot to use the sailors' wages as a means of subsidising Brouncker's brothel. The audience jeered so loudly that the clamour hurt Chaloner's ears.

'And if they disagree, we shall send them to the bottom

of the river,' Pulcinella declared. 'Just like we did with *Assurance*.'

'*You* sank her, Your Majesty?' blurted someone at the front, so caught up in the drama that he forgot none of it was real. 'It was not an accident?'

'Nothing in London happens by accident, my son,' squeaked Pulcinella. 'Not even the plague. After all, how else would I have got you to pay for me to enjoy Oxford all summer?'

The tavern erupted into bellows of rage, and Chaloner recalled that much the same had happened when he had seen Pulcinella perform in Bologna, where Gimonde had stirred up resentment over a new tax levied by the Vatican.

'*Do* they know the truth about *Assurance*?' whispered Lester in confusion. 'Or are they just using her to score political points?'

'I do not know,' replied Chaloner. 'But we should speak to the cast and find out.'

The satire did not last long after that, because Urban's Men knew the best performances were those that left an audience clamouring for more. They retired from the stage to tumultuous applause, having exploited any number of popular grievances, ranging from the unsavoury antics of the Court to the ultimate crime of abandoning the city to the plague. Urban was the last to step off the dais, but before he went, he paused for a final word.

'Friends,' he called, holding up his hand for silence. He did not get it, and his voice cracked as he struggled to make himself heard over a crowd that had become a mob. 'Go home, and remember that Pulcinella is not the

King and I am not the Duke of York, Brouncker or Clarendon. We are actors, whose aim is to entertain. So we wish you goodnight and—'

The rest of his speech was inaudible.

'Sly old dog,' muttered Lester. 'Now he can claim with perfect honesty that he did not incite anyone to violence, although the flame has been lit and he knows it.'

Outside, people gathered in angry clots, although the storm caused most to hurry home soon after. The weather did not deter one gang of spirited apprentices from marching on the Covent Garden church though, where they lobbed stones through its newly repaired windows.

Lester watched worriedly. 'They are in high dudgeon now, but can you imagine what they will be like on Tuesday, when the King returns and they are forced to mourn his unloved father? Urban will needle these crowds bit by bit, timing his speeches so that they reach boiling point just when they can do the most harm.'

Chaloner was sure he was right. 'So stay here and listen for rumours about *Assurance*, while I ask Urban what he thinks he is doing.'

Lester shook his head. 'No, it should be me who speaks to him. You are a courtier – he will take umbrage at an interrogation from such a quarter.'

Chaloner indicated his disguise. 'He will not know who I am.'

Lester was deeply unhappy with the arrangement, but eventually nodded agreement, and Chaloner left him lurking by the stables. He knocked on the door to the players' parlour, which was answered by a jubilant Clifton, whose normally sullen face wore a savage grin. He gave Chaloner a perfunctory glance, but there was no recognition in it.

'We are not accepting congratulations today,' he said. 'Come back tomorrow.'

'No, let him in,' called Hudson. He waved a goblet, slopping red wine down his tunic. 'Adulation never goes amiss, and we excelled ourselves tonight. Why not bask in our success?'

Clifton stood aside to reveal the players peeling off their stage clothes and packing them away. All were drenched in sweat, revealing how much effort had been expended on the performance. The room was oddly bare, and Chaloner immediately guessed why: the troupe was leaving the Fleece before they could be arrested.

'Where is your next show?' he asked, thinking that it would be better for all concerned if it never happened. 'I should like to see you again.'

'We have not decided yet,' replied Hudson slyly. 'So you enjoyed us, did you? Which part did you like best? My portrayal of de Witt making an ass of Spymaster Williamson?'

'Oh, all of it,' replied Chaloner glibly. 'Unfortunately, some of your followers then went out and smashed the church windows, which I am sure is not what you intended.'

'No,' smirked Hudson. 'I hoped they would march on White Hall and set it ablaze – with the King and all his merry friends inside it.'

He laughed, to show he was in jest, although Chaloner knew he meant every word.

'Is this why you came here?' asked Gimonde, hoarse from squeaking. 'To berate us for what some silly hotheads did to a church?'

'No,' lied Chaloner, realising he had been naive to think any of them could be persuaded to see reason,

184

especially after the delighted reception they had been given that night. 'I came to ask what you know about *Assurance*. I had a brother on her, you see, and—'

'Then join us in our fight against injustice,' urged Clifton keenly. 'Because it was the *King's* fault that she went down – just like Vågen and the plague were his fault. He calls himself God's Anointed, but all he is good for is drinking and lying with whores.'

'Unfortunately, we do not know what really happened to *Assurance*, friend,' came a soft voice from the corner. 'If we did, we would make it public.'

It was Urban, sitting quietly with a cup of wine. It was the first time Chaloner had seen him close up, and he was surprised to note that he was younger than he appeared on stage – a father, rather than a grandfather, with smooth skin and intelligent eyes. Moreover, his ears had not been mutilated as Chaloner had supposed, but fitted with a line of rings that looked odd on so paternal a character. There was a different design on each, and Chaloner found himself trying to identify them. One had a ship, another a bird . . .

'But you claimed her sinking was deliberate,' he pressed, dragging his attention back to the matter in hand.

'Pulcinella says many things in the heat of the moment,' declared Hudson with a smirk. 'You cannot believe it all.'

'I am glad you enjoyed tonight,' said Clun, with a rascally grin that reminded Chaloner of when the actor had so skilfully portrayed Falstaff, 'as it will be our last in London. Soon we shall head north, to entertain the good people of Ripon, Sheffield and Leeds.'

'They will like us up there,' predicted Gimonde smugly. 'Yorkshiremen do not sit back and allow tyrants and wastrels to trample them.'

There had been several serious uprisings in the north since the Restoration, so Gimonde was right: Yorkshire *was* an excellent place to promote seditious ideas.

'You will leave us Londoners?' asked Chaloner, feigning dismay. 'After filling us with hope of a new order?'

'We said nothing about a new order,' countered Hudson slyly. 'We merely point out the inequities of the current one. What you do with the knowledge is up to you. Eh, Urban?'

The older actor nodded slowly. 'It is always better to have one's eyes open than closed. Yours are open now, friend. Keep them that way.'

The conversation was over, so Chaloner left. He put his ear to the door after it closed behind him, and listened to the conversation that followed. Disappointingly, all he heard was Clifton holding forth about his unscrupulous creditors. Then the door opened, and Chaloner only just managed to duck out of sight before Gimonde and Hall emerged, lugging a chest. He trailed them to the yard, where a cart was waiting.

'They are leaving, Tom,' came Lester's low voice from the shadows. 'Which is probably wise after what they did tonight. I imagine Williamson will be all over this place tomorrow.'

Chaloner agreed. 'So follow the cart, and find out where they plan to stay next. It will not be Yorkshire just yet – not when they are doing so well at fomenting rebellion here.'

'What will you be doing?'

'Searching their rooms. Be careful – do not let them see you.'

It was not long before the wagon was loaded up, and

Hudson clambered into the driver's seat. His colleagues, all cloaked and hooded against the hyrricano – and recognition – walked behind it, making for an eerie procession. Chaloner almost laughed when Lester set off in pursuit, scuttling from shadow to shadow like Urban's portrayal of Williamson chasing Dutch spies.

When they had gone, he spent a long time carefully combing through the abandoned lodgings, but they had left nothing of relevance to his enquiries, although he discovered plenty of evidence that Gimonde in particular had incited rebellion in other countries. Disappointed and frustrated in equal measure, he gave up and went outside, where Lester was just coming to meet him. The captain's shoulders were slumped in defeat.

'One minute I was following them, and the next they had gone,' he said helplessly. 'Cart and all. Of course, the hyrricano did not help. It blew dust in my eyes, so I could not see . . .'

'It is my fault,' said Chaloner, struggling to conceal his disappointment. 'I should have known a trick was in the offing when they seemed not to care if they were seen walking away.'

'Well, it *is* what they do – sleights of hand to make things vanish. Shall we see what Clifton has to say about guests who flit off in the middle of the night? He may know where they have gone.'

If he did, thought Chaloner glumly, he would not be sharing the information with them. He followed Lester to the main room, where they found not the landlord, but Amey the maid, sitting on the floor and weeping disconsolately. The only other people present were a gaggle of scruffy, hollow-eyed paupers, who looked as though they had nowhere else to go.

'What is wrong?' asked Lester, going to comfort her. He recoiled when he saw the livid scars on her neck, but manfully patted her shoulder in an awkward expression of sympathy.

'He has gone!' she sobbed. 'Mr Clifton, I mean. He has taken his family Bible with him, which means he is never coming back.'

'Gone where?' demanded Chaloner.

'With Urban's Men. It explains why he let them loose tonight – he knew he could not be arrested for it, because he would not be here. He often said he wished he could run away from his sorrows. Well, now he has. But what will happen to me?'

Lester gestured around him. 'You could take over this place yourself.'

'It is crippled with debt, and there is not so much as a dribble of ale left – the last was sold tonight. How can I run a tavern with no ale? I shall starve!'

No wonder the paupers had lingered, thought Chaloner, glancing at them. They knew there was no landlord to pitch them out into the storm outside, and they aimed to take advantage of the fact. More were arriving by the minute.

He and Lester gave Amey all the money they had, both wishing it was more. Then they explored the tavern, where it took but a moment to see that Clifton's flight had been no spur of the moment decision but a carefully planned escape. Nothing of value remained, and a pile of receipts showed that he had sold all he owned. Amey was right: Clifton had abandoned his sad old life and was embarking on an exciting new one.

'What now?' asked Lester, once they were outside, staggering in the wind. 'Shall we look for the cart? I can show you where it disappeared, and you may find clues that I missed.'

Chaloner shook his head. 'They are too clever to make stupid mistakes.'

'Then come to my house and rest until morning. It has a roof – unlike yours.'

Chapter 8

Although Lester snored contentedly for what remained of the night, Chaloner barely slept a wink. It was partly because he was angry with himself for letting Urban's Men escape, but mostly because he was startled awake every few moments by the hyrricano. He was amazed that Lester could slumber through it, and could only assume that a life at sea had made the captain oblivious to the racket made by foul weather. He rose when the bellman called five o'clock, and sat by the fire, wrapped in one of Lester's flags for warmth. He thought about his investigations and the conclusions he had been able to draw.

First, he was sure that Olivia was dead, because something would have been heard of her by now if she was alive – a ransom demand or a rumour about a wealthy prisoner. For suspects, he had a whole city that hated courtiers.

Second, he was certain that *Assurance* had been deliberately sunk – in part because he trusted Lester and Wiseman's opinions, but also because Stoakes was her captain, a landsman who should never have been given a naval command. And Stoakes was married to Olivia, of course. Perhaps she had learned the truth about what had happened, and had been silenced for it. Chaloner decided to question Stoakes again that day, using force if necessary.

Third, he was positive that Quartermain's death was suspicious, given that the physician had been trying to kill Heemskerch when he had died himself. Had he been dispatched by whoever had employed him to end Heemskerch's life, because he kept failing? His neighbour had heard him weeping after one encounter with a mysterious clean-shod visitor, so perhaps Quartermain had not been hired but *blackmailed* into becoming a murderer. Not that the distinction mattered much from Heemskerch's point of view, of course.

And what about Widow Fisher? Had she been brained by one of Urban's Men, because she had watched Hudson spy on him after the attack in the Fleece – and had then been seen telling him about it the following day? Or for something else she had witnessed? Was Clifton the culprit, and he had fled not to join Urban's men, but to avoid a charge of murder? Chaloner decided he would have the truth from the landlord if their paths ever crossed again.

He leaned forward, elbows on knees, planning the day that lay ahead. He would go home first, to change before reporting to the Earl – his employer liked to be kept informed and suspected shirking unless provided with regular updates. While there, Chaloner would tell him there might be trouble at the Fast, and suggest he opt for a ceremony with less inflammatory pomp.

Then he would go to Bedford House, and see what more could be learned about Quartermain and the secrets Heemskerch was alleged to have stolen. After that, he would find the Brouncker tomb, and assess whether Widow Fisher could be quietly interred there, sure it was what she would have wanted. And finally, he would go to the charnel house, where Wiseman would tell him if *Assurance*'s sailors had been drugged before they had drowned.

He lit a lamp and scribbled a coded message to Thurloe, warning him that the hyrricano would delay the departure of his unwanted guest for a few days. He also wrote to Williamson, telling him again that rebellion was brewing. When Lester's steward, Naylor, arrived with an early breakfast of bread and dried meat, Chaloner asked him to deliver the letters as soon as possible. Their voices woke Lester, who appeared rubbing sleep from his eyes. He gave a strangled cry and snatched the flag from Chaloner's shoulders.

'This is a royal standard, man! The only one that still exists from a skirmish won by the King during the wars – Cropredy Bridge.'

'And he did not win many of them,' put in Naylor sagely, 'on account of him being such an awful general. Cromwell was much better. *He* would not have lost at Vågen.'

'Easy, Naylor,' said Lester mildly. 'You do not want Tom thinking that you are the kind of rogue who attends political rallies in the Fleece.'

'How did you know—' began Naylor. Then he shook his head in a belated attempt to bluster. 'That wasn't us, sir. It was just men who *looked* like me, Judd, Knapp, Fowler, Shackleton, Owen—'

'Yes, yes,' interrupted Lester, before the steward could betray every sailor in his acquaintance. 'But the next time you are tempted, you might want to remember that those sorts of events are usually monitored by government spies.'

'I will, sir,' promised Naylor, and then shuffled his feet awkwardly, a gesture that made Lester regard him with suddenly narrowed eyes.

'What is the matter? I have seen that shifty expression before, and it never bodes well.'

'I have bad news, sir,' replied the steward unhappily. 'Mr Cox came in the small hours. He urges you to be on your guard, because poor Dr Merrett has been brutally murdered.'

'Merrett dead?' gasped Lester, shocked. 'No! Why did you not come to tell me at once?'

'Because Mr Cox ordered me not to disturb you,' explained Naylor wretchedly. 'Although Dr Merrett's body was found last night, Mr Cox said all the evidence points to him being killed on Tuesday, not long after meeting you and his other friends at the Folly. In other words, too much time has passed to warrant any urgent racing around.'

'Where was he found?' asked Chaloner. 'At his home?'

'In Covent Garden. Apparently, he was walking across it when he was killed by a single blow to the head. It was a damned cowardly attack!'

Chaloner was sceptical. 'But Covent Garden is a public space. It is impossible that a body should lie undiscovered there for a day and a half.'

Naylor nodded. 'That is what I said, but Mr Cox told me that it had been slyly covered with branches and leaves. Indeed, it might still be there if some children had not happened across it while they were playing.'

'But who would do such a terrible thing?' asked Lester

in a strangled voice. 'He was the gentlest and kindest of men – a healer.'

'His purse was stolen,' explained Naylor, 'which Mr Cox says is clear evidence that robbers are responsible. He thinks they are the same rogues who keep attacking him and Captain Harman.'

Lester grabbed his sea-cloak. 'I shall go to the Folly at once. Cox will be there – he can tell me this sorry tale himself.'

'Dr Merrett died because of the government,' said Naylor softly, watching Lester fasten the clasp. 'It paid its captains on Tuesday, but then claimed there was nothing left for the rest of us. I am lucky, because you pay me from your own pocket, sir, but other lads . . .'

'Is this true, Sal?' asked Chaloner, thinking that if so, Londoners would have yet another grievance to add to their list. 'Officers were paid but the men were not?'

Lester nodded. 'Those of us born to the sea will divide the money among our crews, but the courtier-officers . . . well, I do not see landsmen like Stoakes and Brouncker sharing.'

'Dr Merrett would have tried to persuade them,' said Naylor.

'I must find a suitable flag to fly at his funeral,' said Lester, still shocked. 'The one *Swiftsure* had at Lowestoft, perhaps. He saved many lives that day. Yes, a flag will be a fitting tribute to that kind and godly man.'

'You have a lot to choose from,' remarked Chaloner, aware that there were at least a hundred draped around the room. 'How did you acquire them all?'

'I buy them when they come up for sale,' explained Lester, absently fingering an ominous stain on the one from Cropredy Bridge. 'This belonged to the old King himself, and I am sure he would be pleased to know it is in appreciative hands.'

Chaloner suspected he would not have cared one way or another, being a man who was notoriously uninterested in the doings of his lesser subjects.

'I hate to impose on you while you are grieving, Sal, but will you press Harman and Cox for more details about Heemskerch's escape when you see them? You can tell me what they say when we meet in the charnel house later. If I am late, ask Wiseman to start without me.'

'You mean you aim to arrive when the worst is over,' surmised Lester. 'Well, I cannot say I blame you – I am tempted to do the same myself.'

Although nearly eight o'clock, it was still not fully light as Chaloner hurried to Covent Garden through streets that looked like a battlefield. Smashed masonry lay everywhere, and there was barely a tree or a bush left standing. It was windy still, although not as bad as it had been during the night.

Once home, he divested himself of his disguise and donned the kind of clothes that were suitable for Clarendon House – dark-green long-coat and breeches, clean shirt, and boots that would protect his feet from fallen rubble. When he was ready, he went to the kitchen, where he had left his favourite hat drying by the fire.

The servants, also unable to sleep through the hyrricano, had been at their employer's wine again. The footman lay in a drunken stupor, but the groom and cook were alert and feisty.

'If you want food, take these,' said the cook, presenting

Chaloner with a dish of cold boiled carrots. 'Your crone brought them – so many that we shall be eating them for months.'

'And one carrot a week is more than ample for good health,' declared the groom. 'Any more brings a risk of stomach gripes.'

Out of deference to Widow Fisher, Chaloner took several, despite the bread and dried meat he had devoured in Lester's house. While he ate, the servants regaled him with gossip, and he was concerned to learn that they had also been in the Fleece the previous evening.

'You should not have gone,' he admonished. 'Wiseman is a Royalist – he will dismiss you if he learns you attend republican rallies.'

'He cannot help being misguided, poor soul,' said the groom sadly. 'But *we* will protect him when next week's revolution comes to pass. The rebels will get nowhere near him, I promise. Even if he is a courtier.'

'There will be trouble at the Fast, see,' elaborated the cook. 'Which no honest man will observe. You might want to tell your Earl to stay at home, because *he* will be one of the first to die if we Londoners do decide to rid ourselves of the stinking nobility.'

'The stinking nobility have armed men at their disposal,' warned Chaloner. 'They are ruthless, dangerous and powerful, and you should play no part in whatever happens.'

'We shall decide on the day,' said the cook loftily, which Chaloner took to mean that they would assess which side would win before committing themselves. It was a sensible strategy, and wryly he wondered if he should do the same himself.

'Mr Wiseman told us that you are trying to find Mrs

Stoakes,' said the groom. 'I am glad. She was good to me before I got this job – gave me bread when I was hungry.'

'And she is always ready with a smile,' added the cook. 'Although not as much in the last month or so. I think she was troubled by something. She still waved and gave coins to those who needed them, but you could see that her heart was not in it.'

'Do you know why?'

'Her husband, probably – he is a pig, who would drive a saint mad. He does not care about her, and has made no effort to see about a rescue. If you ask me, he is glad she has gone.'

As it happened, Chaloner was spared a trek to Clarendon House, because the Earl's carriage was just pulling up outside the Covent Garden church. The Earl had also slept badly, and was frantic to know if the hyrricano had damaged the place where he hoped to prove to the world that the King still loved him.

At that hour, it was supposed to belong to its parishioners, but the Earl sailed inside anyway, not caring that he was breaking the terms of the agreement. He was not the only one to flout the rules: two carpenters were busy with the gallery, repairing the parts that could be salvaged and replacing those that could not, while a glazier was working on the shattered windows. They were watched by a group of furious but impotent locals.

'The storm did not do this,' cried the Earl, regarding the smashed panes in dismay. 'A mob did! I want the leaders caught and punished. How dare they assault a house of God!'

'Trouble is brewing all over the city, sir,' said Chaloner

quietly. 'So perhaps you should consider holding your Fast in White Hall instead.'

'It will be *here*,' hissed the Earl between gritted teeth. 'I have spent a fortune on this place, and I will *not* run away with my tail between my legs. I shall stand firm, like the old King did at the Battle of Naseby.'

The old King had lost the Battle of Naseby, Chaloner thought, but decided not to point out. 'But it represents an unnecessary risk, sir. It will be safer to—'

'Rubbish! Now what about the trumpet? Have you tracked it down?'

'Not yet,' replied Chaloner, hoping the Earl would never learn how little he had done to locate the thing. He returned to the Fast. 'Are you *sure* His Majesty will come here? Only I have heard rumours that he plans to go elsewhere.'

'You mean one arranged by someone he loves more than me?' asked the Earl acidly. 'Such as Arlington, Buckingham or Ormonde?'

Chaloner did mean that, but again, decided it was safer to keep his real thoughts to himself. 'One that will not be so far to travel,' he hedged. 'So he can spend longer in bed.'

'I hardly think *that* will influence the way he mourns his father,' said the Earl, a remark that showed he did not know his monarch as well as he thought he did. 'Besides, he made me a promise, and he is a man of his word.' His eyes met Chaloner's briefly, then both men looked away. 'So what of your other enquiries – Olivia, *Assurance* and Quartermain?'

'*Assurance* was almost certainly sunk deliberately, and Olivia is probably dead. I will speak to Stoakes again today, to see if he can shed more light on either matter.

198

I am sure he knows more than he has been willing to say so far.'

'Olivia dead?' breathed the Earl, shocked. 'That will upset my wife. And me. I liked the lady – she was always sympathetic about my gout. I hope you are wrong.'

'So do I,' said Chaloner sincerely.

Next, Chaloner walked to the Strand. He did not really expect to find clues in Bedford House's garden after so many days, but felt compelled to look anyway. He decided against knocking at the front door when he saw several sailors standing outside it, drunk and swearing revenge for Vågen. He went to the back gate instead.

When he was sure no one was watching, he climbed over it, a feat that was ridiculously easy for a place that was meant to be secure. He straddled the top for a moment, and looked down over one of the largest private arbours in the city. It had grown unkempt during the ambassador's occupancy; fountains and statues were covered in lichen, while weeds had encroached paths. The storm had left its mark there, too, and so many trees were down that the place looked like an enormous, sprawling bonfire.

He jumped down the other side, landing lightly, but aware of a twinge in the leg that had been injured at Naseby. Limping slightly, he aimed for the orchard, taking care to stay out of sight of the house. It was a hazardous trek, as branches flailed in the continuing wind, posing a serious risk to face and eyes, while the ground underfoot was treacherous with frozen ruts.

It was not difficult to identify the spot where Quartermain had been found. It lay to the right of the main path, recognisable by the number of feet that had trampled around it. Within moments, Chaloner had found a wig of the type worn by physicians, and a phial marked 'King's Gold'. The pot was empty, and he regarded it thoughtfully. Had its contents spilled accidentally, after Quartermain had died from the stress of trying – unsuccessfully – to kill a patient? Or was there a more sinister explanation – that he had swallowed it on purpose, to escape the clutches of the man in clean shoes who made him weep? Or had someone from the embassy caught him prowling, and forced him to drink the poison intended for his victim?

Chaloner tucked wig and pot inside his coat and looked at the house. He wanted to search Heemskerch's quarters, but doubted van Goch would allow it. However, early morning was an excellent time to enter the place unseen – the few remaining servants would be busy with their chores, and he knew from his own service in embassies that the rest of the staff would be at their daily briefing.

He padded to a side door and picked the lock. He found himself in a kitchen, which stank of old grease and food past its best. He soon learned why. Rather than buy fresh supplies, the cook was using up what was stored, so as to avoid venturing out. There was a dying fire in the hearth, and the remains of a meagre breakfast served to a much-reduced retinue.

The rest of the ground floor comprised the formal rooms used for entertaining, all full of boxes ready to be shipped out when the embassy closed. A murmur of voices came from one chamber – van Goch and his people discussing the day's programme of work.

A sweeping staircase led to the first floor, where the suites allocated to the ambassador and his senior staff were located. The attic had smaller, meaner chambers for less important officials. Chaloner soon found Heemskerch's. First, it was the only one where the door stood open. And second, there was a large pile of unpaid bills on a table with the traitor's name on them – his abrupt departure would leave a lot of tailors, cobblers, milliners and grocers seriously out of pocket.

Chaloner looked around, trying to gauge the character of the man who had lived there. From the items that remained, he deduced that Heemskerch had made a respectable living as an envoy, but betraying his country had been more lucrative still – the furniture and décor were modest, but smears in the dust on the mantelpiece and spaces on the wall showed where more costly items had stood or hung, while scratches on the floor under the bed indicated that a sizeable trunk had recently been there, no doubt stuffed with other portable valuables.

He was about to leave – empty-handed – when he saw a shadow in the doorway. He whipped around fast, and found himself face-to-face with Beuningen. The diplomat was watching him with an expression that was impossible to read, and he was carrying a sword.

Chaloner was in serious trouble. Embassies were sacrosanct, and although spies could and did invade them, they only did it when they were sure they would not be caught. The repercussions of being apprehended were severe, not only for the spy himself, but for his embarrassed government. He glanced around wildly, looking for a way out of his predicament, but there was none: he had been caught red-handed in a place he had no right to be.

'Thomas Chaloner,' said Beuningen softly, swishing the rapier back and forth as if to test its balance. Chaloner considered drawing his own weapon, but the sound of clashing steel would not only alert the guards to his presence, but fighting a diplomat would see him in even deeper water. 'Why are you here?'

Chaloner decided his best option was honesty. He replied in Dutch, aiming to prevent misunderstandings; Beuningen's English was good, but Chaloner's Dutch was better.

'I am still trying to solve the mystery surrounding Quartermain's death, and Heemskerch found his body. I thought there might be something here to help.'

'It is a pity Heemskerch is missing,' sighed Beuningen. 'We have questions to ask him ourselves. Do you know where he is? And before you deny it, let me tell you that working with us could prove *very* lucrative.'

It was not a sensible time for Chaloner to declare that he was not for sale, so he answered with a query of his own.

'You mean questions about the information Heemskerch stole from you?' he asked bluntly, although he had a bad feeling that learning the truth now would do scant good, given that he was unlikely to be in a position to pass it on. 'What do you want to know, exactly?'

'We cannot discuss it here,' replied Beuningen. 'It reeks of pilchards.'

Chaloner regarded him warily. '*Pilchards?*'

'It is quite foul, so I suggest we continue our conversation in my quarters, where the aroma is far more pleasant. Come, come. I do not bite.'

When Chaloner hesitated, Beuningen grabbed his arm and propelled him down the stairs to the floor below, gripping the sword in his other hand. The diplomat opened a door and ushered Chaloner into a sumptuous chamber, exquisitely furnished and with a fire blazing in the hearth. A bowl on the table was loaded with fresh fruit, doubtless imported at considerable expense from the warmer lands around the Mediterranean Sea. Three clerks were there, folding clothes and placing them in chests.

'The Mongolian horde is coming,' Beuningen whispered in Chaloner's ear. 'So we must be ready to flee at a moment's notice.' He glared at the clerks, who had stopped their packing to look at him. 'Do not gape like melons. Work, work! There is not a moment to lose. Oh!'

The last was a cry of pain, because he had contrived to cut his wrist with the sword. Blood welled, and as the secretaries only gawked uselessly, Chaloner went to his aid, taking the opportunity to disarm him as he did so. Beuningen did not seem to notice losing the weapon, and kept his eyes fixed on the gash.

'The red stuff,' he hissed. 'I am full of it, and it must be drained out.'

Chaloner struggled to prevent him from clawing at the wound with his uninjured hand. 'Stop!' he cried. 'You will make it worse.'

'Everything is worse before it gets better,' whispered Beuningen, trying to wriggle free. 'Just ask the Mongol – the one who will help the devil Heemskerch escape. He will tell you.'

'Beuningen!' came a sharp voice from the door. It was Ambassador van Goch, clad in a baggy waistcoat and an old woollen hat, attire that suggested he had heard his colleague's agitated voice and had hurried to investigate without thought of his dignity. 'Enough! There will be no Mongolian invasion today. Go and lie down until you are rested.'

Astonishingly, Beuningen complied, although he slipped between the sheets with his boots on and retrieved the sword en route. Chaloner took it from him a second time, then wrapped a clean cloth around the gash, wondering what ailed the man.

'You should call a surgeon,' he told van Goch. 'Wiseman is the best.'

'Do it,' van Goch ordered the clerks, who tripped over each other as they vied to be first out through the door. 'Thank you for bringing him home, Chaloner. Where was he this time?'

'We went to a coffee house, where we enjoyed some beans grown in Java,' chirruped Beuningen before Chaloner could reply. 'But the Mongols will give them all to Heemskerch.'

'Go to sleep,' commanded van Goch shortly. 'I shall station a guard outside your door, so do not worry about Mongols. We can talk about them later.'

Obediently, Beuningen closed his eyes and made himself comfortable. Within moments, his breathing turned slow and even. When he was sure his colleague slept, van Goch bundled Chaloner into the corridor and closed the door softly behind them.

'It is good of you to return him to us. However, I do not want it put about that my staff are insane. How much will it cost to keep this matter between ourselves?'

'*Is* he insane?' asked Chaloner, wondering what it was about himself that suggested he was open to bribes. Should he change his tailor?

Van Goch grimaced. 'He has a brilliant mind, but he sometimes suffers from . . . delusions. He will remember nothing about your encounter when you next meet him.'

Thank God for that, thought Chaloner. 'Does it happen often?'

'He can go for months without trouble, then there might be several incidents in a week. They tend to be more frequent when he is under strain.'

'Then are you sure he should be a diplomat? An occupation where one false word can undo months of patient negotiation?'

Van Goch shrugged. 'Perhaps that is why he was sent here – to a place where dialogue is non-existent, so there is nothing to jeopardise. And yet such is his genius that if anyone can broker a treaty, it is Beuningen, so what does de Witt have to lose by deploying him?'

'The Grand Pensionary still hopes for peace?'

'He does, although it is unrealistic in my opinion. But in which coffee house did you find him? The Folly? He is obsessed with that place at the moment, because he thinks one of its patrons is helping Heemskerch to leave the country.'

'Chatelaine's,' lied Chaloner. 'And no one from the Floating Coffee House will help Heemskerch. It is full of sea-officers, who blame him for Vågen.'

A flash of malicious satisfaction crossed van Goch's patrician features, and Chaloner hoped he would pass the claim on to Beuningen. If the diplomat was as clever as everyone claimed, and he contrived to engage Lester, Harman and Cox in conversation, he would guess what they were up to in an instant, and Heemskerch's escape would be compromised.

'Then I shall suggest Beuningen does not waste his time there,' said van Goch smoothly.

Good, thought Chaloner in relief. 'Is he ever violent?'

'He would run Heemskerch through if he ever met him, but so would I – and I have never used a weapon in my life. However, he had nothing to do with Quartermain's death, if that is what you are really asking. No one did. The poor man died of natural causes.'

'Does Beuningen ever go to the Fleece?'

Van Goch blinked. 'He does not! And before you ask, he had nothing to do with the missing courtier, the sunken warship, the gale that blew the tiles from London's roofs, the plague, or your King's decision to skulk in Oxford all summer. Not all bad things can be laid at Dutch doors.'

But Chaloner decided to reserve judgement until he knew more about Beuningen and his clandestine activities – especially those that he later recalled nothing about.

Still thinking about his curious encounter with the diplomat, Chaloner went to Covent Garden, where he began to hunt for the Brouncker family tomb. It was no easy matter when the graveyard was full of fallen trees, and his search involved a lot of undignified clambering. He found it eventually – a garish, marble affair tacked on to the south wall of the altar end of the church.

It had been shaped to resemble a small house with doors of black and gold, and had BROUNCKER emblazoned on the lintel. The lock had been forced, so Chaloner stepped inside, wrinkling his nose at the musty odour. He lit a candle, and saw stairs leading down to an underground vault. They were covered in dry leaves and looked uninviting. He began to descend, hoping Widow Fisher had told the truth about removing the plague victim.

The family crypt itself lay directly beneath the chancel, so one flight of steps followed the line of the church's foundations down, ending in a low, short passage that passed beneath them, while a second, shorter set went up the other side. It was larger than Chaloner had expected, with ceiling-high shelves for caskets. As the tomb, like the church above, was no more than thirty years old, there was only a handful of deceased Brounckers currently in residence.

Widow Fisher had taken over the far end of the vault. She had converted one shelf into a bed, made comfortable by a mattress of newsbooks, while two more held her vegetables, carefully stored to sell later in the year. A fourth held her personal effects – an odd shoe, a broken comb, the stub of a candle and a pile of paper. Chaloner regarded it all sadly, thinking it was not much to represent a life.

He rifled quickly through the documents, assuming she had saved them to augment her mattress. They were almost all rubbish – discarded shopping lists, broadsheets bearing revolutionary songs, copies of sermons from the church, and advertisements for various tonics and cure-alls. There was also a letter. Brief and to the point it read:

Mr Bronker,

There is a matter which you wille not want made publick, soe you wille leave a payment of Seventy Pounds by youre Covent Garden Gate tonight on payne of exposure. I know you will agree to My terms.

Yours humbley,

A friend who means you no harme if you followe these instructions.

Chaloner regarded it thoughtfully. He knew it was one of the papers that Brouncker had lost to the wind a few days before, because he had a vivid recollection of it flying into Widow Fisher's face – the dirty smudges her fingers had left when she had pulled it off were still on it. Later, Brouncker had asked Chaloner if he had retrieved any of his documents, suggesting he had lost one that he deemed to be important.

Did it mean Brouncker had killed Widow Fisher, to prevent her from telling anyone that he was being black-mailed? But she could not read, and was thus unlikely to show the letter to anyone else, so that solution made no sense. Chaloner scanned it again. What had Brouncker done that the sender thought he would want kept quiet? Generally speaking, Brouncker was proud of his scandalous reputation, so it had to be something truly terrible. Or had he laughed off the demand, on the grounds that everyone knew he was a dissolute rogue anyway?

Chaloner supposed he would have to find out.

He took a hackney carriage to Westminster, because one happened to be passing while he was hurrying down St Martin's Lane. Unfortunately, a group of acrobats had decided to perform in Charing Cross, bringing all traffic to a standstill. He leaned out of the window, to ascertain if it would be quicker to get out and walk, and saw with interest that the entertainers were Hall, Gimonde and Clun. All three were masked, but easily identifiable – Gimonde because he was dressed as Pulcinella, Hall because of his loose-limbed gait, and Clun because of his distinctive voice. Chaloner was astonished that they should dare perform so close to the seat of government, and alighted from the hackney to watch.

For a while, the trio did nothing but tumbling tricks, although these served to attract an ever increasing audience. Then, when they adjudged the crowd to be of optimal size, they launched into a satire about the Banqueting House, which was currently being converted into a theatre to celebrate the King's return – at considerable public expense.

'Which drama has the Court chosen to perform for His Majesty while the rest of us mourn his dead father?' asked Clun; he had taken the role of poor, downtrodden Londoner that day. 'One by Shakespeare, perhaps? Or a morality play?'

'*Two Sisters and a Goat*,' squawked 'King' Pulcinella, naming a particularly lewd and infamous comedy written by one of His Majesty's favourites. '*Our* notion of morality.'

He proceeded to belabour the Londoner with his slapstick, although no one laughed, and there were growls of anger as people asked each other if the tale could be true. Unfortunately, a group of reckless young bloods from the palace made themselves known at that point. They surged forward, fists at the ready, vowing to trounce the players for their incautious tattling – which was as good as an admission of guilt as far as the crowd was concerned.

Chaloner braced himself to intervene – courtiers beating Pulcinella to a pulp would spark a riot for certain – but he had reckoned without the players' acrobatic skills. The youths aimed for their quarry, but found themselves snatching at thin air.

'Over here,' taunted Hall from behind them. 'Can you not catch me?'

They tried, but he slithered away with consummate ease, and the audience clapped appreciatively. The courtiers exchanged indignant glances and drew their swords. There was a collective gasp of horror from the onlookers, which turned to laughter as Hall ducked behind one lad and booted him in the rump, sending him sprawling. When Pulcinella laid about another with his slap-stick, the audience cheered wildly.

Then there was a low hiss from a short, hooded figure who stood nearby – Hudson, thought Chaloner – warning of the arrival of Williamson's men in their distinctive buff jerkins and stripy sleeves. But the soldiers were no more adept at catching the agile threesome than the courtiers, and there was much amusement as they dashed this way and that, thwarted at every turn. Hall allowed one to come so close that the crowd bellowed its collective alarm; then it roared its delight when he whipped around and vaulted clean over his startled pursuer's head.

And then they were gone. They ducked behind a cart for a moment, but when the guards ran to surround it, the entertainers had vanished. Chaloner grimaced his exasperation – he had hoped to follow them to their new hideout when they had finished showing off, but there was no hope of that now. With the cheers of the audience ringing in his ears, he continued on to Westminster.

Lester was waiting outside the charnel house when Chaloner arrived, the tails of his sea-coat flapping in the wind. He immediately began to regale the spy with all he had learned from Cox about Merrett's murder, grief and anger vying for dominance on his homely face.

210

'He is sure the culprits are the same men who assaulted them previously,' he confided. 'That the thieves finally realised that he, Merrett and Harman were too strong together, so opted to corner them singly. Cox and Harman are fighting men, but Merrett . . . well, he was a peaceful soul.'

'Has Cox found any witnesses?' asked Chaloner. 'Covent Garden is hardly secluded, and it sounds as though he was killed in broad daylight.'

'He was – a missed appointment means we can fix the time to within an hour of him leaving the Folly on Tuesday – but if anyone did see, they are not talking. Or perhaps the rogues picked a moment when the Piazza really was deserted. The weather was foul that day, and there are not so many folk about as there were before the plague . . .'

As they had half an hour to spare before meeting Wiseman at two o'clock, Chaloner took Lester to a nearby cook-house, where he listened sympathetically and patiently to a detailed list of Merrett's many virtues. While the captain talked, they ordered slices of beef and ale pie, although Chaloner was not sure it was a good idea to eat, given what they would soon have to watch in the charnel house. Eventually, Lester's eulogy ended, and he turned the subject to Heemskerch instead.

'Luck is with you, Tom – *African Sun* sails on Saturday, and her master is Harman's cousin. He has agreed to carry a passenger, although only grudgingly. He is suspicious of the urgency *and* the demand for secrecy, so I am afraid it will be expensive.'

'Saturday?' asked Chaloner unhappily. 'There is nothing sooner?'

'It is only another forty-eight hours, and we are lucky

to find someone who is willing to sail at all – the hyrricano has convinced most captains to stay in port until spring.'

'Where is *African Sun* now?'

'Margate, so we shall arrange passage down to her on a dogger – that is a small fishing boat to you. It will be safer than travelling by road. Incidentally, while I was on the Folly earlier, a man with a scarred nose was asking about leaving England by ship. He claimed it was for himself – that he wants to flee some crushing debts – but he spoke with a foreign accent.'

Beuningen, thought Chaloner. The diplomat had guessed exactly how Heemskerch would escape and aimed to stop him, which meant there was even more reason to hurry. Somewhat uncharitably, he wondered if the delay was deliberate – that Lester *wanted* Heemskerch caught. Then he shook himself. He had been a spy too long! Of course his friend would not stoop to such low antics. Lester was an honourable man.

When Chaloner and Lester arrived at the charnel house at two o'clock prompt, there was an unpleasant surprise waiting for them: of his own volition, Wiseman had obtained the necessary permits to exhume Quartermain. He had overseen the procedure himself, and was standing over the body with an array of sharp knives and a proprietary air.

'Crikey!' gulped Lester, recoiling. 'What happened to his hair?'

'Nothing, because he did not have any,' replied Wiseman. 'He was bald, which explains why he always wore that nasty old wig. I barely recognised him without it.'

212

Chaloner produced the one he had found in Bedford House. 'This one?'

Wiseman took it from him. 'Yes! I would know it anywhere. How did you come by it? No, do not tell me. I shall almost certainly be happier not knowing.'

'What do you make of this?' Chaloner handed over the phial that had been with the hairpiece in the garden of Bedford House.

Wiseman removed the stopper and sniffed. 'It may be empty, but it still reeks of King's Gold – the deadly kind containing poxbane, which Quartermain made before I advised against it. The stench of garlic is unmistakable. Foolish man! I told him to destroy it all.'

'Have you examined him yet?' asked Chaloner, in the hope that the surgeon had been unable to wait, so that he and Lester would be spared the ordeal.

'I have assessed him for external wounds and other suspicious marks. There are none, so now we shall look inside him.'

Fortunately, Wiseman quickly became engrossed in his grisly work, and he did not notice when Chaloner slipped away to Kersey's parlour. Lester held out for a little longer, then followed suit, arriving paler than Chaloner had ever seen him. Ever solicitous, Kersey poured him a glass of wine and encouraged him to sip it. Once some colour had seeped back into the captain's face, the charnel-house keeper turned to business. He handed Chaloner a box.

'The contents of Quartermain's pockets,' he explained. 'Other than the fountain-pen, which Abigail Williams took away with her.'

'I thought you no longer had them,' said Chaloner, surprised.

'We should not have done – we burn all valueless property once a guest is buried. However, it transpires that my assistant Deakin is a hoarder, and has not been very assiduous in that respect. When he heard you were looking into Quartermain's death, he retrieved those for you, in the hope that they may contain something to help.'

Chaloner opened the box. There was no money or jewellery – unsurprisingly, as it was Kersey's right to keep those when no one claimed the body. All that remained was a pot of wig powder, some scissors, a bill from a tailor, a religious pamphlet and an invitation to a special performance by His Majesty's Trumpeters. Disappointed, Chaloner was about to toss it all back into the box when he noticed that the invitation had holes punched in it at irregular intervals.

'What?' asked Lester, seeing him gape in astonishment.

'A cipher key,' explained Chaloner, heart quickening. 'You place it over another message, and it highlights specific words or letters. But it cannot be . . .'

He rummaged in his pocket for the coded missive he had found in Stoakes' house, although he did not imagine for a moment that they would fit together. But they did. It read:

All goes Accdg to plann. Assurance sunk, no Questions asked. Urbann's Men working harde. Money coming from H.B. The Traytor Dutchman wille die soone.

'My God!' breathed Lester, stunned. 'Proof that *Assurance* was sabotaged! I *knew* there was something amiss when she went down.'

Chaloner was bemused. 'Several separate investigations have suddenly become one – this note was sent to Stoakes by whoever sank *Assurance*, and it mentions Urban's satires and the attempted murder of Heemskerch. And if we assume that H.B. refers to Harry Brouncker . . . I found a letter threatening to blackmail him just today.'

'Written by the same person?' asked Lester.

Chaloner produced it and laid the two messages side by side. 'Yes, I think so. Look at the letters *g* and *y* – all have an unusually long tails, while each *T* and *M* is distinctive and identical.'

'The coded message does not mention Olivia, though,' said Lester. 'Ergo, not *all* your enquiries are linked.'

'On the contrary – she is married to *Assurance*'s captain. Moreover, the key is punched out of an invitation to hear trumpets, and I am meant to be looking for one that has been lost . . .'

'Well, well!' murmured Lester. 'The mystery thickens.'

'It will thicken even more when you hear what *I* have to say,' declared Wiseman, striding in with bloodstained hands. He helped himself to Kersey's wine. 'First, Quartermain did not die a natural death, but was poisoned – by his own poxbane-rich King's Gold.'

'By accident?' demanded Chaloner. 'Or did someone force him to drink it?'

'I doubt it was an accident,' averred Wiseman. 'He knew it was dangerous. That leaves murder or suicide. He never seemed self-destructive, so I suggest he was fed it against his will.'

'Fed it where?' asked Chaloner. 'In the gardens of Bedford House?'

'Probably,' replied Wiseman. 'There was mud and

grass under his fingernails, almost certainly deposited when he clawed the ground in his death throes. Do you want to hear my second piece of information? It will confuse you even more.'

'Go on then,' said Chaloner resignedly.

'*Assurance*'s dead sailors were fed poxbane, too,' said Wiseman, smirking at their growing mystification. 'Well, four of them were. I can inspect the rest later, should you deem it necessary, although I imagine they will all be the same. I shall not bore you with details, but the tests I conducted suggest that the poxbane was almost certainly delivered to them via a dose of King's Gold.'

'So your theory is now proven?' Lester asked him. 'They could not jump to safety or call for help because they had been poisoned?'

Wiseman nodded smugly. 'And then they drowned.'

Chaloner struggled to make sense of it. 'Does this mean Quartermain killed them? He must have done, given that we know he tried to murder Heemskerch with toxic King's Gold . . .'

'Unless Heemskerch is lying, and *he* is the culprit,' suggested Lester. 'After all, what Dutchman would not be glad to dispatch twenty English seamen and sink one of our warships, all in one fell swoop?'

Chaloner indicated the coded message. 'This suggests that someone – I assume Quartermain – was trying to kill Heemskerch, not the other way around.'

Lester shook his head. 'Such convoluted treachery! It is—'

He was interrupted by Deakin, who entered the room uneasily, casting sidelong looks at Wiseman. Chaloner recalled that the man should have gone to Chyrurgeons'

Hall after his execution, and was doubtless afraid that the surgeon might still try to claim him.

'Begging your pardon, sirs,' he said, 'but a guest has just come in. A woman, found near the Savoy Wharf. She has a rash on her neck, and you told us to be on the lookout for those. I think she might be the missing Olivia Stoakes.'

Chapter 9

Chaloner was sorry to see Olivia on one of Kersey's tables. She was streaming water and wore the same clothes as when she had gone missing. Her hair formed a fine net over her face, and he pushed it away gently, recalling the intelligent, kindly woman who had liked visiting churches, reading and giving money to the poor.

'How did she die?' he asked Wiseman.

The surgeon stepped forward to find out, knife in his hand, but a sharp voice from behind made him stop.

'No! Leave her be. She has suffered enough.'

Chaloner turned and was startled to see Clun there, Hudson at his side. Moving shadows under the back door told him that more of the troupe were milling about outside. He dropped his hand to his sword, wondering how many he could disable before they surrendered, but Clun saw the move and gave a warning scowl.

'Do not fight us,' he snapped. 'Not with her like this. It would not be decent.'

'It would not,' agreed Kersey, real anger in his voice. 'We respect the dead here, Chaloner, which means we do *not* brawl in their presence. Do you hear?'

'Not even when it may prevent trouble that will see your domain bursting at the seams?' demanded Chaloner archly. 'Because these men have been fomenting rebellion—'

'No, we have not,' interrupted Clun. 'We merely highlight injustices inflicted on the people by a man who is unfit to rule. What they do with the information is not our concern.'

'But you *know* what they will do with it,' argued Chaloner. 'And who will suffer the consequences? Not the King and his courtiers – they will continue to do whatever they please. Not you either, because you will vanish the moment trouble erupts. But the Londoners you have stirred up will die by the dozen.'

'Perhaps,' said Clun. 'Or maybe they will just refuse to pay the taxes that allow these so-called ministers to exploit them. *That* will bring the rogues to the negotiating table fast enough.'

'Besides, what has been started cannot now be stopped,' put in Hudson with a vengeful smirk. 'You may kill us, Chaloner, but it will make no difference in the end.'

'I have no intention of killing you,' said Chaloner, exasperated. 'But what you are doing is dangerous, and will result in harm to the very people you claim to champion.'

'He will not listen to us,' said Hudson irritably to Clun. 'And we have better things to do than debate with him. Ergo, this conversation is a waste of time, so I suggest we end it.'

'I wish we had taken Mrs Stoakes straight to her house, like I suggested,' said Clun bitterly. 'I know this place was closer, but she does not belong here.'

'Then we shall do it now,' determined Hudson, and went to the door to summon his cronies. They filed in

219

silently: Gimonde, unshaven and shabby in his everyday clothes, the sword-swallower, the magician and lithe Hall. The rope-dancer wore a costly brooch from Lady Castlemaine – he accepted her favours with one hand, and publicly mocked her with the other.

'Wait,' ordered Kersey, as they prepared to take Olivia away. 'She died before her time, so the least we can do is find out why. Please let Wiseman look at her first.'

There was a quick exchange of glances, although Chaloner was tempted to point out that the decision was not the troupe's to make. Olivia's generosity at the Fleece did not give a few itinerant players rights over her body.

'He may look,' conceded Hudson eventually. 'But he may not dissect.'

'Dissection will not be necessary,' said Wiseman, pressing on Olivia's chest. 'She drowned. You see that froth? It means air mixed with water in her lungs, so she was breathing when she went into the river. And to think I lectured her on this very subject just a few weeks ago!'

'So you found her body?' asked Chaloner, watching the players intently. They seemed genuinely sorry that she was dead and he wondered why – she was a courtier, and thus represented all they claimed to despise, even if she had given them sixpence apiece.

Hudson nodded. 'We ran down to the river after performing in Charing Cross, where friends were waiting with a boat. We were about to pull away when we saw something lying on the foreshore. I wanted to ignore it, but Clun . . .'

'I recognised her dress from the Fleece,' explained the actor softly. 'And I refused to leave her there like so much rubbish.'

'She lay near the White Hall Stairs,' put in Hudson.

'You wasted a lot of time asking questions in the Fleece, but she was in the palace all along. One of *your* lot killed her.'

'How do you know she was killed?' pounced Chaloner. 'Not all drownings are deliberate. There are accidents and suicides, too.'

'*I* think it was murder,' interjected Wiseman with authority. 'The corpse is cold, but fresh and supple, meaning she was alive a few hours ago. She is unlikely to have hidden herself away all this time, which suggests to me that she has been kept prisoner, and was dispatched today. Or she died trying to escape. Then there is the eruption on her neck – its redness is also indicative of recent death, as it would have faded if she had been in the water for long.'

'My father had a rash like that,' mused Hudson. 'It got worse when he was worried, which tells me that this poor woman suffered much strain before her captors ended her agony.'

'It is worse than when I last saw it,' acknowledged Wiseman. 'However, it is not just strain that causes such afflictions. They also come from substances to which a patient has an aversion. I often see it in customers who use too much face-paint and—'

'So her courtly abductors tired of her,' interrupted Clun, staring down at the body. 'They kept her alive for four days, but then decided to drown her – to prevent her from identifying them and making them pay for what they did. Bastards!'

'You cannot conclude that a courtier killed her, just because she was found near White Hall,' argued Chaloner. 'And why would they want her dead anyway? She was popular.'

221

'They will have their reasons,' said Clun darkly. 'Shall we take her home now, brothers? I do not like her being in here. She deserves better.'

He and his friends lifted the body gently from the table and laid it on a plank, after which they covered it with one of Kersey's blankets. Then they carried it out, although not before each had adjusted his hood or hat to conceal his face.

'No,' said Hudson, putting out his hand to prevent Chaloner from joining the procession. 'We do not want your company, thank you.'

'As you wish,' said Chaloner, deciding to trail them from a distance, because he was determined to observe how Stoakes reacted when presented with the corpse of the wife.

'Should we record her as being a visitor here?' asked Deakin of Kersey, watching them go. 'She was not in our custody for long.'

'Of course,' replied Kersey. 'A guest is a guest, no matter how brief his or her stay.'

'Speaking of guests,' said Chaloner. 'You have one named Widow Fisher. Will you bury her in the Brouncker tomb in Covent Garden?'

Kersey blinked. 'The owners will not mind?'

'Hopefully, they will never know,' replied Chaloner, and handed him a very heavy purse.

'We will do it on Tuesday,' promised Kersey, 'when everyone is busy with the Fast.'

The short winter day was fading to dusk as the sombre procession left the charnel house, and church bells were ringing to announce the four o'clock evensong. Chaloner and Lester stayed well back as they shadowed the players

222

to Stoakes' house. The sight of a body being toted along drew scant attention from Londoners, who had grown used to it during the plague, although Hudson's distinctive physique attracted one or two interested glances. One man called a compliment about the troupe's satires, but received only a curt nod in reply.

'Hudson is a bad-tempered fellow,' remarked Lester, staggering when a blast of wind caught him as they rounded the corner to Charing Cross. 'I think he became a rebel because he does not want *anyone* to be happy – courtier *or* commoner.'

They reached Long Acre, where the dwarf rapped on Stoakes' door. Unfortunately, Chaloner could not see or hear how he broke the news to whoever answered it. Then Hudson and his cronies trooped inside, where they stayed for less than a minute – Chaloner had done no more than trot towards a window to see about eavesdropping before they were out again. Then they scattered like leaves in the wind, each taking a different direction away.

'You had better follow them this time,' said Lester, 'while I see what Stoakes has to say about his dead wife. And about the coded message you found in his bed. Do not worry, Tom, I will prise the truth from him.'

Chaloner was in a quandary. Lester was right: he stood no chance of successfully tracking the players to their hideout. Yet Chaloner dared not entrust such a critical interview to him either – Stoakes may have killed Olivia and tossed her body in the river, so Chaloner *had* to assess for himself how he responded to her being brought home.

'Go after Hudson,' he told Lester, making his decision, although he was far from certain it was the right one. 'He is slower than the others. I will talk to Stoakes.'

'As you wish,' said Lester unhappily. 'But do not get cross if Hudson gives me the slip.'

Chaloner hurried to Stoakes' door, and was surprised when it was opened by Maurice. The coffee-house owner had been at his toilette, and a pair of very dark and determined eyebrows graced his forehead. They arched upwards and made him look startled.

'Emily the cook-maid got herself a new job,' he explained, 'so George, Robert and I have been keeping Stoakes company when we can. We are kin, after all, albeit only by marriage.'

'What about the Folly?'

Maurice winced. 'Closed, because the hyrricano uprooted a tree, which floated into the hull and punctured it.' He lowered his voice. 'But it is a good thing I was here today, because Olivia has just been brought home – as cold and dead as a fish from the Billingsgate market.'

'How terrible,' said Chaloner, trying to sound as if this was news. 'Stoakes must be devastated.'

'He is shocked, but not surprised. Obviously, poor Olivia was kidnapped by criminals who aimed to exchange her for money, but when no demand came . . . well, it was clear to us all that the matter would end badly. We have been expecting the worst for days.'

Chaloner followed him down the hall and into the parlour. Robert and George sat on a bench that was not really big enough for two, while Stoakes graced the only chair. George had removed his false leg, and was giving its toenails a polish. Olivia had been deposited in the room next door, where she would soon become a problem unless someone doused the fire that roared in the hearth next to her. When he saw Chaloner, Stoakes lurched angrily to his feet, but stumbled against George's wooden limb and fell flat on his face.

'Grief renders him clumsy,' explained Maurice charitably, going to help him up.

Stoakes was too heavy for him to manage alone, so Robert went to help, while George retrieved his leg, scowling furiously at a scuff on the calf.

'Look what you have done!' he snapped. 'I told you to lay off the wine.'

'I am upset,' Stoakes snarled back, throwing off the other two brothers and going to a table, where he poured himself a fresh drink with angry defiance. 'My wife's body has just been presented to me.'

'Did Maurice tell you, Chaloner?' bellowed Robert. 'She drowned, poor soul. Some kind people found her washed up by the river, and brought her home.'

'*Kind people?*' echoed Stoakes angrily. 'They were Urban's Men – the scum from the inn where she went missing. *They* took her, and killed her when she proved too feisty a prisoner.'

'Rubbish,' bawled Robert, so vehemently that his teeth popped out, and there was a pause in the conversation while they were retrieved and slipped back in. 'They are too busy performing their seditious little satires. It was other criminals who took Olivia.'

'Yet she would *not* have been a compliant captive,' acknowledged Maurice. 'She was a brave and moral woman, and I am proud to count her among my kin.'

It was a while before Chaloner managed to prise Stoakes away from the Thompsons, and by the time he did, the captain had swallowed the best part of a jug of wine. Chaloner escorted him into the kitchen, and watched him slump at the table with his head in his hands. He could not tell if it was grief or an attempt to stop his wits from spinning.

'So you believe that Urban's Men abducted and killed Olivia,' he began. 'Why?'

Stoakes shrugged. 'Because they were in the Fleece when she vanished, and because I have never liked itinerants. They are thieves and rogues to a man.'

Chaloner pointed out that there had been three hundred others in the tavern that night, all whipped into an angry fervour against courtiers, but Stoakes refused to listen. Eventually, Chaloner gave up and showed him the letter from the mattress, this time with the cipher key. When there was no reaction, he read the decoded message aloud.

'As I told you the last time you asked,' slurred Stoakes, 'I have never seen it before.'

'It reveals that *Assurance* was sunk deliberately. And it has since been proven that your crew was poisoned, probably to prevent them from sounding the alarm as she went down.'

Stoakes blinked stupidly. 'My crew would never take poison! They were sensible men. And as for the ship . . . well, she was a tub, if you want the truth, so it is no surprise that the wind blew her over. I wish I had not put so many of my favourite things aboard – it was a tragic loss.'

'The sailors were a tragic loss,' countered Chaloner shortly. 'Did you know they are still in the charnel house, waiting for someone to pay for their funerals?'

He did not reveal that, true to his word, Lester had left a sizable sum with Kersey to see the decent thing done.

Stoakes shrugged. '*I* cannot afford it, not after losing

the contents of my cabin. My old steward Fowler came to see me last night, accusing me of miserliness, but I said to him what I shall say to you: some do-gooder will oblige, so just be patient.'

Chaloner continued to press him, even going as far as to threaten him with arrest, but it was hopeless: Stoakes was either telling the truth when he claimed to know nothing about Olivia, *Assurance* and the letter, or was he too clever a liar for Chaloner to break.

In the end, Chaloner could stand the self-pitying, self-justifying replies no longer. The encounter left him feeling soiled, and he was sorry for Olivia, married to a man who was more concerned for himself than for what had happened to her.

When Chaloner stepped into the street, it was to find Lester waiting, with the disappointing but not unexpected news that Hudson had given him the slip.

'He must have used magic,' the captain said defensively. 'Because he vanished into thin air before my very eyes. I searched for ages afterwards, and there is no other explanation.'

'When we spoke earlier,' began Chaloner, 'you said you had been on the Folly today. But Maurice just told me that it is closed.'

'It *is* closed,' explained Lester. 'The storm smashed a hole in its keel, so Harman, Cox and I went across to rig a jury-plug. Our repairs will last until he can get it into dry dock – which he will have to do soon, or the barge will sink. Where are we going now?'

'*I* am going to White Hall, to ask more questions about Olivia, given that Urban's Men seem to think her killer is there. You may as well go home, as—'

'I would rather stay with you, Tom,' interrupted Lester. 'You might need me, and it will help to take my mind off poor Merrett. Besides, now we know that the fate of *Assurance* is tied to the brewing rebellion, Heemskerch, Quartermain and all the rest of it, we have no choice but to work together. It would not do to trip over each other as we conduct our enquiries, and I refuse to leave *Assurance* to anyone else. Not even to you.'

But Chaloner did not want Lester as a looming presence at his shoulder while he interviewed courtiers. 'It will be more helpful if you track down *Assurance*'s surviving crew and ask what they think happened to her. And what they know about Stoakes and Olivia.'

'I have already done that. It was a waste of time.'

'Then do it again, Sal. It is amazing how often a second discussion can shake loose answers that were kept hidden during the first.'

Lester did not look convinced, but nodded reluctant assent. When he had gone, Chaloner took a hackney to White Hall; he could have walked, but he was tired, cold and sick of being buffeted by the wind. He was just climbing out when a familiar carriage pulled up next to him. It was the Earl's, so Chaloner went to help him out, lest the combination of wind, slick cobbles and impractical footwear led to a mishap.

'Well?' the Earl demanded, grabbing Chaloner's proffered hand and clinging on for dear life. 'Do you have anything new to report?'

'We found Olivia's body. Wiseman says she has been held prisoner for the last four days. She drowned, so either her captors threw her in the river or she fell in trying to escape.'

'I knew her well,' said the Earl grimly. 'She would not

228

have put herself in physical danger – she would have used her formidable wits to wriggle out of her predicament. Ergo, I think we can assume that her abductors dispatched her. They doubtless hoped her corpse would be washed out to sea with no one any the wiser. Do you know who did this terrible thing?'

'No, but it may be connected to *Assurance*'s fate. Perhaps she saw or heard something she should not have done, and was killed to ensure her silence.'

Just like Widow Fisher had been, Chaloner thought, wondering how many more people would die before he found some answers.

'Well, she *was* married to its captain,' said the Earl. 'What does he have to say about it?'

'Nothing. However, his crew and Quartermain were poisoned with the same toxin, which is another peculiar coincidence. *And* there is a coded message that links my various investigations to the blackmail of a courtier and the brewing unrest. I deciphered it using a key made from a card printed for the King's Trumpeters.'

'Lord!' breathed the Earl, gazing at him through saucer-like eyes. 'How very complicated. Who is being blackmailed? And why?'

'I will find out,' hedged Chaloner, unwilling to tell him it was Brouncker until he knew precisely what the man was supposed to have done.

'Good. However, before you start, find Beale's trumpet. It *must* be played at the Fast. I cannot overemphasise how crucial it is to my plans.'

'Why?' asked Chaloner, not even trying to hide his exasperation. 'I doubt the King will be able to tell whether it is Beale's or someone else's.'

The Earl glared at him. 'It is not for you to question

my orders – just to follow them. Now *go and hunt the wretched thing down!*'

He threw off Chaloner's arm the moment he was on firmer ground, and bustled away, calling angrily for his secretary. Wren hurried after him, but paused to whisper a warning.

'Do what he wants, Tom. Indeed, I think he will be so disappointed if you fail, that he will dismiss you on the spot.'

'Well, then,' sighed Chaloner. 'I had better see what I can do.'

As it happened, Chaloner saw Simon Beale a few moments later. The trumpeter was just entering the Banqueting House – the building that courtiers often used for their japes, as it was the only one large enough to accommodate them all. Chaloner was sure its architect would have been appalled to know his glorious creation was more often the venue for debauched masques than the gracious state occasions for which he had designed it.

It was busy that evening. Carpenters could be heard at work within, while six servants struggled to carry the throne and its trappings to the undercroft. Chaloner recalled Urban's Men's claim – that it was being converted into a theatre at public expense – and suspected he was about to learn that the charge was true.

As he followed Beale inside, Chaloner met Brouncker coming out, a train of pretty prostitutes chattering at his heels. Brouncker looked seedy, rumpled and disreputable – the kind of person who gave White Hall an especially bad name.

'We are preparing for *Two Sisters and a Goat*,' he told

Chaloner, although the spy had not asked. 'Which is how we shall welcome the King home on Tuesday night. Unfortunately, we are behind schedule, so we shall have to scramble if we want the stage ready in time.'

'But Tuesday is the Fast,' Chaloner reminded him, 'when the whole country is expected to spend the day – and the evening – reflecting on the late King's execution.'

Brouncker waved a dismissive hand. 'Commoners can sit around with long faces if they want, but *we* are going to have some fun. The King is looking forward to it.'

'Why not do it on Wednesday instead?' asked Chaloner, exasperated. 'It is—'

'It must be Tuesday, because that is when the King is coming home,' interrupted Brouncker. 'And you can tell your Earl that His Majesty will *not* be going to Covent Garden for the morning miseries. He will go to Westminster Abbey – the Fast organised by my Duke.'

'This is not wise,' said Chaloner worriedly when he saw some of the props that were being toted inside – the kind that would horrify even the most liberal-minded of Londoners.

'*Wise?*' echoed Brouncker in disbelief. 'Who cares about wise? This is White Hall, where we live life to the full and bugger the consequences. If you want staid respectability, go and sit by the fire in Clarendon House with your boring old Earl.'

Chaloner fought down his dislike of the man, noting at the same time that Brouncker looked far from well. There were dark circles under his eyes and his hands shook. Living life to the full was driving him to an early grave – one he would share with Widow Fisher, if Kersey did what he promised. Or was something else depriving him of his usual good health?

'Who is blackmailing you?' he asked bluntly, and when Brouncker began a startled, blustering denial, he showed him the letter he had taken from the tomb.

'That is not mine,' declared Brouncker, glancing around quickly to ensure no one else was within earshot; fortunately for him, his women were more interested in watching the servants struggle with the throne. 'Someone else must have lost it. Tuesday was windy, and all manner of documents must have been blown from their owners' grasp that morning.'

'How do you know when it was lost and how?' pounced Chaloner. 'Enough games, Brouncker. We both know this belongs to you. You even asked me if I had it at one point.'

'Let me see.' Brouncker made a grab for it, but Chaloner kept it at arm's length, knowing he meant to tear it up. 'Oh, *that* message. It is nothing – just a prank played on me by a friend.'

'Are you sure?' Chaloner assumed a sympathetic expression. 'I may be able to help.'

Brouncker hesitated, obviously tempted by the offer, but then forced a feeble grin. 'You cannot help, because there is nothing amiss. It is a jest, no more. Give it to me. I shall consign it to the flames, where it belongs.'

'I shall keep it for now,' said Chaloner, putting it back inside his coat. 'You may contact me if you change your mind.'

'But you just proved that it belongs to me,' Brouncker pointed out quickly and deviously. 'So you cannot keep it – that would be theft.'

Chaloner shrugged. 'Report me then, and let us have the matter out in the open.'

Brouncker regarded him sullenly, but said no more,

leaving Chaloner in no doubt that he did indeed harbour some vile secret. He dreaded to imagine what it entailed, given that Brouncker was proud of his status as brothel-keeper, chess cheat and leading debauchee.

'Widow Fisher was murdered not long after she came into possession of this note,' he said softly. 'You had better hope it did not factor in her death, because if it did, I shall see you swing for it.'

Brouncker glowered back at him. 'If she was in the habit of acquiring documents in an area populated by wealthy and powerful men, then I am not surprised she came to a bad end. But do not point accusing fingers at me, Chaloner. I know nothing about her demise.'

Inside the Banqueting House, Chaloner stood for a moment and looked around him. It was an attractive building, with large windows and a ceiling painted by Rubens. That evening, it was filled with an atmosphere of mischievous excitement, as if everyone knew their antics would cause offence and was delighted by it. All the King's dissolute favourites were there, and had been allocated roles in one capacity or another – if not acting in the play, then erecting scenery, gathering props or preparing costumes.

What would add insult to injury was the fact that, seventeen years ago, the old King had stepped through one of the Banqueting House's windows to the scaffold, where he had been beheaded. Even Chaloner, no admirer of Charles I, felt the King's friends should have used a different venue on the anniversary of his execution.

But it was not for him to chide them, and he had his own problems to solve. He went in search of Beale, eventually tracking him to the gallery, where the trumpeter was preparing to practise the fanfare for the play's finale. He was a short, plump man with yellow curls, who had probably been chosen for his cherubic appearance as much as his talent as a musician. He raised a hand to tell Chaloner to wait, then began to play. It was typical of the Court's idea of humour – a disjointed cacophony that ended in a fart. Needless to say the listening courtiers fell about with infantile laughter, and Beale basked in the ensuing applause.

'Perhaps it is just as well you no longer have your silver trumpet if you use it to make that sort of racket,' said Chaloner coolly, disgusted that Beale should abuse his art in such a way.

Much to his embarrassment, Beale promptly burst into tears. 'I cannot find it anywhere,' he wailed, so loudly that a hush fell over the throng below and everyone looked up at them. 'And I have searched high and low for it.'

'Are you still grieving over that wretched horn, Beale?' called the Duke of Buckingham unsympathetically. 'Forget about it – there are plenty more in the royal collection.'

'Not like this one,' sobbed Beale. 'It is unusually loud – unlike anything you will have heard before. It was unique and I shall never forgive myself for setting it down . . .'

But Buckingham was not interested in the tale of woe, and nor was anyone else. Within moments, they were guffawing at some joke cracked by Brouncker, almost certainly one at the trumpeter's expense.

'Where did you set it down?' asked Chaloner kindly.

'Here, in the Banqueting House,' wept Beale. 'Two weeks ago. You see, Buckingham had sent me a note, inviting me to play the fanfare in *Two Sisters*. It came with an order to attend the planning meeting, along with all the other courtiers involved in the venture.'

'Which other courtiers?'

'*All* of them. Well, all the fun ones – not men like Clarendon, obviously. There were probably two hundred people here, including servants and Brouncker's whores. I have spoken to as many as I can, but no one admits to stealing it.'

'It was stolen?' asked Chaloner. 'Not mislaid?'

'Stolen,' sniffed Beale miserably. 'By a vile, stinking thief. I always knew this place was less than honest, but I never imagined that someone would make off with something so precious and irreplaceable. It was solid silver, so has probably been melted down by now.'

'Clarendon is determined that you will play it at his Fast.'

Beale nodded. 'I know, and he will be disappointed when he learns I cannot do it. But do not suggest substituting it for another – its sound is distinctive and he will know.'

'Damn,' murmured Chaloner, who had been banking on some form of deception to ensure he did not lose his employer's good graces. But there was no more to be learned about the trumpet, so he moved to other matters. He showed Beale the cipher key. The musician took it from him, smiling suddenly at the memories the invitation card stirred.

'My fellow trumpeters and I put together an evening of entertainment a few weeks ago in Oxford. So many people wanted to come that we had to issue tickets – like this one – to prevent overcrowding. But why has someone punched holes in it?'

235

Chaloner explained, but could see from Beale's blank expression that the trumpeter had no idea what he was talking about. 'Was Captain Stoakes in the audience?' he asked eventually.

'No, but his wife was. Poor Olivia! She always brought us wine when we played, which was kind, as no one else thinks of our comfort. And music is hot and thirsty work.'

'How about William Quartermain? Was he there?'

Beale blinked. 'The physician? I do not have the faintest notion. The place was packed, Chaloner – there were well over three hundred seats, while others piled in to stand around the edges. Your Earl came. So did Williamson and his assassin, although *I* did not invite them. They are not my kind of people.'

Beale could tell him no more, so Chaloner returned to the main body of the building, where he began the tortuous business of trying to persuade a lot of selfish, dissolute individuals to stand still long enough to talk to him. Not even the news of Olivia's death made a difference – they professed themselves to be sorry, but not enough to stop enjoying themselves, and he could tell they considered him and his questions a nuisance. As evening turned to night, it became more difficult than ever, as cask after cask of wine disappeared down intemperate throats.

Eventually, he took his leave, tired, disgusted and with the growing conviction that Urban's Men were right to point out all that was wrong with White Hall. Perhaps he should lend his sword to those who aimed to topple the government from power, because he was sure his country would be a lot better off without such a worthless rabble trying to run it.

He stepped into the street, and was immediately aware

of someone watching him. As it was a person wearing a long cloak and a hood that hid his face, Chaloner was instantly suspicious, especially when the figure took to his heels the moment he realised he had been spotted. Chaloner followed him back inside the Banqueting House, and thought he had lost him until a clatter of footsteps told him that his quarry had gone down the stairs to the undercroft.

He took the steps three at a time, and saw the edge of a cloak disappear around a pillar. He hared after it, but when three men materialised in front of him, all armed with rapiers, he realised he had made a very elementary mistake. He whipped around, aiming to make a tactical withdrawal, only to find two more swordsmen blocking his way. He was trapped.

He drew his own weapons – sword in one hand, dagger in the other – although his chances against five opponents were slim, to say the least. As one, they moved in for the kill.

Although Chaloner had never liked firearms, which he considered noisy and unpredictable, he wished he had one that night. The sound of it discharging would have summoned the palace guards and thus saved his life – and he needed help desperately, because he was not going to win the confrontation alone. He yelled at the top of his voice, but the revellers in the hall above were making far too much racket for him to be heard.

He evaded defeat a little longer than he expected, because his attackers were hampered by the fact that they could not see very well with their hats pulled low against recognition. But the inevitable came when one kicked his lame leg, which buckled and sent him sprawling.

Even then he refused to give up, flailing wildly with his rapier, so his assailants were reluctant to close in for the kill. For a while, there was a fraught stalemate, then the leader spoke.

'Surrender,' he ordered hoarsely, breathing hard from his exertions. 'And I will dispatch you quickly. Fight on, and you will suffer a lingering end.'

Chaloner was sure the man was disguising his voice, which meant it was someone who did not want him to recognise it – someone he knew. He struggled to identify him, although he was painfully aware that it would not matter much if he was dead.

'Why do you want me silenced?' he demanded, jabbing with his blade to let him know he would not go down easily. 'What have I learned that so terrifies you?'

'Nothing,' hissed the man. 'But you ask too many questions.' He glanced at his companions. 'Ready? Then *now*!'

But before any of them could oblige, one swordsman reeled away with a howl, clutching his shoulder. A knife protruded from it. Then another shrieked as a blade thudded into his thigh. The others looked around wildly, trying to locate the source of the attack, but when a third dagger flew, the leader decided that discretion was the better part of valour, and raced for the stairs. His men followed, leaving their injured comrades to keep up as best they could. At the same time, a sinister black shape slithered from the shadows: Swaddell.

'We need to follow,' gasped Chaloner, struggling upright. 'Find out who they are.'

He hobbled up the steps, but his lame leg slowed him down, and there was no sign of his attackers by the time he reached the top.

'There is blood,' said Swaddell, pointing at the floor. 'In a trail we can follow.'

But the spots led outside, where it was pitch dark and raining. Swaddell located a few more splatters, but they were being washed away before their eyes, so it was not long before Chaloner was forced to concede that tracking the culprits was impossible.

'Who were they?' he asked.

Swaddell blinked his surprise. 'How should I know? They were fighting you, not me.'

'Someone who did not like my questions,' mused Chaloner. 'I must be getting close to the truth about something, or they would not have bothered – not now, and not in the Fleece on Monday night.'

He reflected on the fracas. His assailants had fought with reasonable skill, so were they professional soldiers, hired by a third party – Olivia's killers, perhaps, or the clean-shoed man who had made Quartermain cry? Or whoever had sunk *Assurance*? They were not Urban's Men, as they would have been a lot more agile. He discounted Stoakes as a culprit, too, but for the opposite reason – he would have been more ponderous. Then was Brouncker responsible, determined that no one else would learn that he was being blackmailed? He had just been in the Banqueting House, after all, so on hand to launch an attack.

'You are welcome, by the way,' said Swaddell, breaking into his thoughts. 'I have nothing better to do than risk my life to save yours.'

'Thank you,' mumbled Chaloner hastily, unwilling to offend such a deadly individual. 'How did you know I was in trouble?'

'Joe and I were just passing the Banqueting House

when we saw two men draw swords and chase after you. I decided to see if you needed help.'

'You happened to be passing?' asked Chaloner, amused that the assassin should ape Robert's way of referring to the Spymaster. He was sure Williamson knew nothing of it, and sincerely doubted Swaddell called him 'Joe' to his face. 'At this time of night?'

'We spent the evening with the Thompson brothers at their James Street house,' Swaddell explained. Then he scowled. 'I was bored rigid – they are dull company, and I have a headache from all Robert's yelling. But we had better report back to Joe – he will be worried about me.'

'Are you sure you noticed nothing to identify those men?' asked Chaloner, falling into step at his side.

'Unfortunately not – they wore disguises. I could not even see their weapons, which might have revealed them as courtier, warrior or common lout.'

A carriage was waiting in King Street, Williamson inside, reading by lamplight. He was so engrossed in his work that he jumped when Swaddell tapped on the window, a reaction that made a lie of the assassin's claim that he would be concerned – he had not even bothered to watch for his safe return, preferring instead to catch up on some paperwork.

'So you let them go?' he demanded, once Swaddell had finished telling him what had happened. 'That was careless. We cannot have armed killers lurking around White Hall!'

Rather than retort that if the Spymaster felt so strongly about it he should have come to help, Chaloner changed the subject. 'How was your raid on Chatelaine's Coffee House?'

'A waste of time,' replied Swaddell, although Chaloner suspected Williamson would have been more economical with the truth, judging by the weary look he shot his henchman. 'It looked promising, with doors and windows closed, and a lot of oddly shaped bundles being toted inside, but when we made our move, we found the patrons innocently parcelling up donated clothing for the poor.'

'Our intelligence was that there would be a "meeting of like-minded activists, who plan to make a difference by placing items where they are most needed",' quoted Williamson angrily. 'So of course we interpreted it as a plot in the making. Who would not?'

Thurloe, thought Chaloner, who would have assessed the situation more carefully before committing himself to an all-out raid.

'All had improper opinions about the King, though,' Swaddell went on. 'One went so far as to call His Majesty a wastrel.'

'Goodness!' said Chaloner, thinking the King had escaped rather lightly, given some of the remarks he had heard of late. 'Did you arrest him or sentence him to summary execution?'

'We considered both,' replied Swaddell, quite seriously. 'But in the end we decided on a third option – to fine them all. They paid up quickly once they learned they would remain in our company until they did as they were told.'

Chaloner did not blame them – he would have done the same. He spent a few moments outlining what had happened in the Fleece while the Spymaster had been persecuting good Samaritans, including his belief that Chatelaine's had been a diversion to ensure that Urban's Men and their audience were left unmolested.

'I might have known!' hissed Williamson furiously. 'Landlord Clifton has always been a bitter malcontent with Parliamentarian sympathies. I shall arrest him tomorrow.'

'If you can find him,' warned Chaloner. 'He went off with Urban's Men.'

'Yes, leaving an empty tavern behind,' said Williamson pointedly. 'And where better for rebels to meet? I want you to monitor it every spare moment you have. Both of you.'

He had no authority to issue Chaloner with orders, but the spy nodded acquiescence anyway. Williamson was right – the Fleece *was* the perfect place for an insurgents' hideout, as it was a large building with multiple exits and plenty of rooms.

'Robert told me about Olivia Stoakes,' Williamson went on. 'It is a damned shame, because I liked her. Well, who would not admire a woman who was kind to moths?'

'I shall relish slitting her killers' throats,' put in Swaddell fiercely, 'and all London will thank me for it.'

Chaloner suspected that 'all London' would not care, although he was certain the first part of the remark was true – Swaddell would enjoy murdering the culprits.

'The Court does seem to be unpopular at the moment,' said Williamson, in something of an understatement. 'And Olivia paid the price.'

'Much damage was done when the King fled the plague without a backward glance,' said Swaddell. 'It exposed him as a man who cares nothing for his subjects, and who is only interested in enjoying himself with his frivolous cronies.'

'Swaddell, please!' snapped Williamson, while Chaloner

gaped to hear such sentiments from a man employed by the Spymaster's office. Was this another instance of the growing rift between the assassin and the man who paid his wages? 'We are outside White Hall, for God's sake – His Majesty's home!'

'It needs to be said,' retorted Swaddell, unrepentant. 'It was selfish, irresponsible and callous, and now we reap the consequences. Even Royalists are beginning to wonder what sort of rogue sits on the throne.'

'Yes, trouble is in the air,' acknowledged Williamson stiffly. 'But it always is, and I do not think this time is any different.'

'I do,' countered Chaloner, 'because so many people feel the same way. Perhaps they will settle down once the King is home and everything returns to normal. But they mourn family and friends dead of the plague, and grief is a powerful force.'

'So is resentment,' said Swaddell, and nodded towards the Banqueting House. 'And it will fester for as long as the Court insists on flaunting its dissolute ways. I predict some very serious trouble at the Fast on Tuesday.'

Chapter 10

The next day was Friday, which meant there were four days left before London erupted into a frenzy of blood and rebellion. Chaloner wondered if anger over Vågen would be a factor in the trouble, and hoped Heemskerch – and Thurloe – would be safely out of the city if it did. So when he rose from his temporary bed in Wiseman's parlour, the first thing he did was hurry to the Floating Coffee House, hoping Lester would be there, so he could ensure there were no last minute hiccups in the plan to spirit the Dutchman away.

'The Folly is still closed, sir,' said Judd apologetically. 'But Captain Lester left a message for you: you are to meet him at the Rainbow at ten o'clock.' He glanced up at the sky to gauge the time. 'Which is about three hours hence.'

Chaloner was irked with himself for not remembering that the barge had been damaged by the hyrricano. He trotted back to the Strand, where he decided to use the intervening time by visiting White Hall, in the hope that some of the acquaintances he had cultivated among the servants might know who had attacked him in the Banqueting House the night before.

He arrived to find the palace just winding down from the previous evening's revels, although one clique of die-hards was still going strong. The Great Court was littered with discarded clothing, broken glass and spilled food, suggesting the occasion had turned very wild after he had left. He entered the Banqueting House warily, noting that some of the scenery for *Two Sisters* had been damaged during the ruckus, which meant it would have to be repaired – no doubt at public expense. He tried talking to the remaining merrymakers he met there, but they barely knew their own names, let alone information pertinent to his enquiries.

He went to the kitchens next, where he learned that most of the servants had gone home by the time he had been attacked, so were unable to help him. He begged a simple but agreeable breakfast of fresh bread and butter, and was on his way out again when he met the Earl, who was often among the first to arrive in the mornings. Clarendon looked tired, and Chaloner saw that the strain of organising his Fast – and hoping that the King would not wound him with a public snub – was taking a heavy toll on his peace of mind.

'Well, Chaloner?' he asked eagerly. 'Do you have the trumpet? My cousin Brodrick tells me that you were still hunting for it when he left the Banqueting House late last night.'

'Most people think it has been melted down, sir, and I cannot bring it to you if it no longer exists. Perhaps you should consider a contingency plan, just in case—'

'You cannot fail!' cried the Earl, distraught at the notion. 'It is important. Well? Do not stand there looking exasperated. Go and find it for me!'

He turned and stamped away, flicking imperious

fingers for his retinue to follow. Secretary Wren was at the end of the procession, his arms full of documents. Chaloner assumed they pertained to weighty legal matters until he read a couple upside down, and saw they were bills for the work being carried out in the Covent Garden church. Both were enormous.

'I shall be glad when Tuesday is over,' muttered Wren unhappily. 'You are not the only one who has been issued with an ultimatum – you should see the miracles he expects from me.'

Chaloner did not doubt it. 'Then let us hope His Majesty keeps his promise to him, or it will all have been for nothing.'

Wren lowered his voice. 'I heard the King swear to grace us with his presence myself, but it would not surprise me if he later denies it. He remembers what he pleases.'

'Regardless, I do not believe the trumpet will be joining us there. Brodrick, Brouncker and the rest are right to think it has already been converted into ingots.'

'Incidentally, I found out why the Earl wants it so badly,' said Wren, and spoke even more softly. 'He has pledged the King a special gift if he comes to our Fast – something unique and priceless. He refused to reveal what, but the King is intrigued, which may be just enough to entice him through our doors. His Majesty loves unusual presents.'

'So the Earl intends to give him the trumpet? Because it is silver and thus valuable?'

'Partly, but mostly because it is the one that played the official fanfare to announce his birth. Of course, the Earl's enemies have stolen the idea, and are offering bribes of their own, so unless ours is better than theirs . . . well, you can see why the trumpet is important.'

246

'But no one else has guessed what the Earl plans to give him?' asked Chaloner. 'Then I suggest you find him something else instead. What about his cradle or baptismal gown?'

'We do not have anything like that – it was all stolen or destroyed during the wars.'

'Then use your imagination. I am sure you can "recover" something suitable.'

Wren gaped at him. 'You mean I should deceive everyone by presenting an object and lying about its provenance?'

'The alternative is disappointing the King, which may damage our employer irreparably. Surely a fib is better than seeing Clarendon driven from Court – or worse?'

'Lord!' muttered Wren, appalled. 'But you are right, of course. I have a chamber pot that the old King is alleged to have used on the eve of his execution. Perhaps that will suffice.'

Chaloner regarded him askance. 'It must be something the King will actually want.'

'I will see what I can do,' sighed Wren unhappily, leaving Chaloner with the sense that the plan would end in disaster, and wishing that he had never suggested it.

As he had time, and it was not far out of his way, Chaloner went to Chancery Lane next, to ensure that Heemskerch was not causing Thurloe any trouble. If he was, the Dutchman would be out of the attic within the hour, and to hell with the intelligence he claimed to possess.

Chaloner arrived at Chamber XIII to find the ex-Spymaster huddled by the fire, having forgone his customary dawn stroll in the garden on account of the

247

weather. The wind was no longer hyrricano-force, but it was still fierce enough to make a tremendous racket as it roared through the trees, and scudding clouds brought sharp, icy showers.

'Well, Tom?' Thurloe spoke softly to avoid being heard by the spy in the room above. 'I hope you are not here to tell me that *African Sun* has delayed her departure because of the gale.'

'As far as I know, she still sails in the morning. Has Heemskerch shown good faith by parting with some of his intelligence?'

'Not so much as a snippet, and I have tried to persuade him, believe me. Williamson says he desperately needs what Heemskerch has, so I pray we do manage to get him away tomorrow. I shall be glad to see him gone; he is not an easy guest.'

'In what way?' Chaloner was sure he could remedy that, given a minute alone with him.

Thurloe smiled. 'Nothing to warrant you running him through or regaling him with threats, Tom; just niggling matters. For example, he demands more food than I can supply without raising eyebrows; he bursts in on me at all hours; and he is a tedious conversationalist – all talk and no discourse, if you know what I mean.'

'I will send you a message if Lester tells me more about *African Sun* today, although I recommend you keep the plan from Heemskerch for as long as possible. I do not trust him.'

Thurloe regarded him lugubriously. 'I was Spymaster General, Thomas. I do not need a lecture on how to manage the likes of Heemskerch, thank you. But tell me about your other work. I heard the Fleece is closed after staging a spectacularly brazen parody of the Court.'

Chaloner told him of his progress to date, embarrassed that there was not very much of it.

'I am sorry about Olivia,' said Thurloe, when he had finished. 'I never met her, but I am told she was an erudite and generous lady.'

'Urban's Men think she was murdered by people from White Hall, and that she was kept there until her captors realised they had bitten off more than they could chew.'

'It is possible, although these players hate the Court, so of course they will accuse it. Do not waste your time searching the palace, though – there will be too many chambers to which you, as the Earl's man, will be denied access, so it would be an exercise in futility. Have you explored the Fleece, to see if she was held there?'

'Of course.'

'Look again – I have never been comfortable with that place.' Thurloe reflected for a moment. 'Have you considered pressing Abigail Williams for more information about Quartermain? She may be more forthcoming now the shock of his death has worn off. She lives in Southwark, next to the Beare tavern.'

'How do you know? And why do you suggest it?'

'Because my contacts inform me that she has already replaced Quartermain with Harry Brouncker, which is suspiciously callous. If she declines to cooperate, threaten to reveal her infidelity to Brouncker's brother. That should loosen her tongue.'

'Lord!' muttered Chaloner, hoping he would not have to resort to that sort of tactic.

'And you could do worse than attend Olivia's funeral, which will be in Covent Garden later today. Perhaps her killer will be in the congregation.'

'It will be difficult to watch everyone. I do not suppose you . . .'

'I wish I could, but I dare not leave Heemskerch unattended. However, if the funeral proves unproductive, try visiting Temperance's brothel tonight.'

Chaloner regarded him intently. 'Why? Who will be there?'

'Olivia's colleagues, who have decided – bizarrely, in my view – that a night there is the best way to honour her memory. They will be drunk, and the inebriated are often indiscreet.'

Chaloner nodded his thanks. 'That should keep me busy for the rest of the day.'

'Incidentally, I heard that there have been several assaults on sea-officers of late, including one late last night. You should be on your guard while you associate with these men on Heemskerch's behalf – thieves will not distinguish between them and you.'

Chaloner did not need to be told.

The Rainbow Coffee House stood near the Temple Bar, the gate where the Strand met Fleet Street. Before the plague, it had been a noisy, frantic, bad-tempered bottle-neck, as coaches, riders and pedestrians waited impatiently to file through. Altercations over precedence were frequent and often violent. It was quiet that day, although Chaloner thought it was busier than it had been the previous week – the King's imminent return was encouraging others to follow suit. Even so, it would be a long time before it regained its former cantankerous bustle.

The Rainbow was Chaloner's favourite coffee house, although he was not sure why. It was cramped, shabby and frequented by men with unpalatable opinions. Its coffee was strong, though, and the owner, James Farr, had a devoted following who claimed they could not start the day without a dose of it inside them.

Chaloner entered with some trepidation, afraid that Farr and his regulars might be dead of the plague, and everything would be changed. But he pushed open the door to be assailed by the same smuggy warmth – a combination of burned beans, wet boots and cheap tobacco. And there they were, as if nothing had ever happened: Stedman the printer, Speed the radical bookseller, and Farr himself, complete with apron and long-spouted pot.

'What news?' called Farr, then glared when he recognised Chaloner. 'We wondered when you would deign to return. Oxford was nice, was it? Safe and bubo-free?'

'There is no news in *The Oxford Gazette*,' sighed Speed before Chaloner could defend himself, which was usually the case in the Rainbow, where customers would far rather talk than listen. 'I have never read such a miserable litany of information in all my life.'

He tossed a copy to Chaloner. It was twice as long as the last edition – four pages, instead of two – and comprised mostly lists of ships damaged by the hyrricano. Chaloner flicked through it, and saw that Speed was right, although there was a brief report from Amsterdam saying that its sea-captains had been paid, but not their crews, which had caused considerable ill feeling. It seemed England was not the only country that treated its sailors badly.

'Have you seen the notice from Hampton Court?' Farr pointed to a paragraph that read:

Upon the continued Decrease of the Sickness,
which (thanks be to God) has this week
reduced the Totall of the Bill to 227 and
the Plague to 56, His Majesty has resolved
as well for the encouragement of his City
of *London*, as for the better conveniency
of his great and weighty Affaires of State,
to remove to-morrow with the Court, to his
Royal Palace of *White Hall*.

'His "great and weighty Affaires of State",' scoffed
Speed. 'He means his pleasures. In other words, he is
bored of Hampton Court, and longs for what only
London can offer.'

'He is coming because it is his duty,' countered
Stedman, the devoted Royalist.

'His duty was to lead us in our hour of need,' countered Speed, 'but I have never seen a cleaner pair of
heels. He is a selfish rogue, and a coward into the bargain.'

'Steady on,' breathed Farr, and nodded at Chaloner.
'We have a courtier in our midst.'

'Chaloner likes honest opinions,' declared Speed,
although the spy never recalled saying so. 'Not like most
White Hall rogues, who would not know the truth if it
bit them on the—'

'The King has timed his return to coincide with the
Fast,' interrupted Farr. 'He wants to be here in person,
to ensure we all reflect on his father's execution.'

'His father's murder, you mean,' interposed Stedman
coolly.

'Have you heard about that Dutch spy – the one
responsible for Vågen?' asked Farr, changing the subject
with an abruptness typical of the Rainbow. 'Well, he has

escaped from his embassy, and is said to be hiding near Chancery Lane. He had better not come *here* for coffee, because I shall not give him any.'

'Who told you that?' asked Chaloner, trying to keep the alarm from his voice. How long would it be before such rumours reached the wrong ears, and someone paid Thurloe a visit?

'I overheard it in the New Exchange,' replied Farr. 'From men I did not recognise, but one was plump with half a nose and a peculiar accent, while the others looked like courtiers.'

Beuningen, thought Chaloner, quizzing the loose tongues of White Hall. Had Heemskerch been followed when he had fled from Bedford House? If so, he must have given whoever it was the slip before he reached Lincoln's Inn, or Thurloe would have been tackled by now. Regardless, the tale told Chaloner that time was running out too fast for comfort.

'On Cheapside last night, Urban's Men performed a very clever satire about the disaster of Vågen,' Speed was saying approvingly. 'They were excellent – even better than they were at the Fleece, when they parodied the King and all his mistresses. Of course, the Fleece is shut now. The landlord abandoned it to his creditors, by all accounts.'

'He abandoned it after a courtier was murdered there by fanatics,' countered Stedman. 'It is no surprise – the place has always been a hotbed of insurrection. Clifton was a radical before the plague, but he grew ten times worse when he lost all his family.'

'How do you know fanatics killed Olivia Stoakes?' asked Chaloner keenly.

'I just do,' came the curt reply, which Chaloner took

to mean that Stedman had just heard about the death and had drawn conclusions to suit himself.

But Speed was regarding Chaloner with dismay. 'The victim was Olivia Stoakes? That is a damned shame! She bought a lot of books from me – she was one of my best customers.'

'So you knew her?' fished Chaloner.

'Not well, but enough to tell you that Stedman is wrong – it will not have been fanatics who killed her, but courtiers, who resented the fact that she was cleverer and nicer than them.'

'They would only resent it if they knew it was true,' countered Farr. 'But they are too stupid to see the truth before their eyes, so I agree with Steadman – radicals dispatched her.'

'Sixteen sixty-six,' announced Speed darkly. 'That is the problem with everything. We all know that three sixes is the Sign of the Beast, and things will now go from bad to worse.'

'It cannot get any worse for Olivia Stoakes,' remarked Farr. 'Or her husband, who lost his wife and his ship within a few days of each other.'

At that point, the door opened and Lester walked in. He indicated that he wanted to speak in private to Chaloner, and was taken aback when it was not just the spy who followed him to one of the little-used booths at the back, but Stedman, Farr, Speed and several others, too.

'It is all right,' Farr assured him. 'We can keep a secret. So what news do you have?'

To his credit, Lester retained his composure. 'That the hyrricano has done terrible damage all over the country. Falmouth, Hull, Dover, Plymouth, Harwich, the Isle of

Wight . . . so many ships lost, just when we need them most.'

'That was all in *The Oxford Gazette*,' said Speed scornfully. 'It is not news.'

'Then allow me to regale you with the latest gossip from White Hall,' suggested Lester. 'Which I had from Harry Brouncker, who is in service to the Duke of York.'

'That Duke is an idiot,' declared Speed uncompromisingly. 'He should have finished the Dutch off after Lowestoft, but he let them escape, just so he could take a nap without the inconvenience of cannonballs bouncing across his hammock.'

'Lord!' breathed Lester, regarding him askance. 'You do not mince words, do you! However, what I was going to say is that there are so many Fasts arranged for Tuesday that the King is at a loss as to which one to attend.'

'I thought it was to be Covent Garden,' said Farr, and pursed his lips to add, 'Where so much money has been spent to beautify the place.'

'Oh, no,' countered Stedman. 'It will be the cathedral, and I shall ring the bells.'

'He will not bother with any of them,' predicted Speed confidently. 'Because they are all in the morning and he never rises before noon.'

Chaloner left them arguing about it, and eased Lester outside, where they could talk without the risk of their conversation being repeated in garbled form to half of London.

'I hope Maurice mends the Folly soon,' remarked Lester fervently, 'because your coffee house is too full of dangerous opinions for me.'

'Speaking of danger, I heard there was another attack on sea-captains last night.'

'Harman and Cox again,' said Lester, 'who were so enraged by Merrett's murder that they fought like lions, aiming to kill the lot of them. Unfortunately, the robbers realised they had bitten off more than they could chew, and fled before Harman and Cox could do more than wound a couple.'

'Wound them seriously?'

'Not seriously enough to prevent them from escaping, more is the pity. But never mind them. I have bad tidings: the dogger we hired to take Heemskerch to Margate was wrecked in the storm. We must find another.'

'How long will that take?' asked Chaloner in dismay. 'And will we miss *African Sun*?'

'Hopefully not. One of Judd's watermen thinks he can help us out; we shall know by tonight. And we cannot postpone Heemskerch's departure, as half the city is baying for his blood, while the diplomat with the damaged nose has been asking questions about him all along the river.'

'Good. It means he considers Heemskerch worth the trouble, which tells us that the information he stole is important. Ergo, we *must* get him away before he is silenced. Will you tell Judd it is a matter of life and death?'

'I will, but I would rather help you look into *Assurance*. She is much more urgent.'

'You will not think so if Heemskerch is killed before he can tell us what he knows, and we lose the next sea-battle.'

Reluctantly, Lester acknowledged that he had a point. 'When I have spoken to Judd, I will start tracking down the robbers who killed Merrett. We cannot allow *that* crime to go unpunished either. And we shall see about *Assurance* together later. Agreed?'

*

256

Chaloner was glad that Lester would not be with him while he worked that day, although he could not have said why. He supposed he was just set in his ways, unable to adapt to having an assistant trailing at his heels. However, when he reached the Fleece, he met someone else who wanted his company: Swaddell.

'Joe ordered us to monitor the place,' the assassin said, emerging from the doorway where he had been lurking. 'So I have been here since dawn, but no one has gone in or come out.'

'I need to search it again,' said Chaloner, 'to see if Olivia was ever held here.'

'Then I shall help,' determined Swaddell, and raised his hand when Chaloner began to object. 'I insist. It will be much quicker with two.'

Unfortunately, there was nothing to find, other than that all the doors bolted from the inside, which meant that Olivia could not have been held captive there unless she had agreed to lock herself in. Amey the tavern maid was still in residence, and had invited some friends to join her, so several chambers were now occupied by squatters. As a result, the inn stank of overflowing slop buckets, dirty clothes and greasy food, and Chaloner wondered if Clifton's creditors would manage to oust them before they did actual damage.

'I suspect the popular gossip is true,' said Swaddell as they left. 'Olivia was kept in White Hall. I would not put such nastiness above some of the King's favourites. But I am ravenous, so come with me to the Rose. I am sure Joe will not object to me putting a nice dinner on expenses, given how hard we have worked on his behalf this morning.'

Chaloner baulked at spending additional time with

Swaddell – and nor had his efforts that day been for the Spymaster's benefit – but he was hungry, too, so he followed the assassin across the Piazza to Angel Alley, where the Rose Inn stood. There, they learned that the cook disapproved of giving his customers choices, so there was only ever one dish on the menu – that day it was stewed trout with jelly. The jelly comprised a wobbly dome of sherry sack, cinnamon, sugar and egg whites, all held together with the gelatinous substance obtained by boiling calves' feet. It and the fish were served on the same platter, prevented from sliding into each other by an intricate barrier of liquorice sticks.

While they ate, Swaddell regaled Chaloner with his predictions for the trouble that would erupt during the Fast. And Urban's Men would be in the thick of it, thought Chaloner, ensuring that no insult inflicted by the King on his people was overlooked.

'There will be strife at Court, too,' Swaddell continued. 'His Majesty declines to say which Fast he plans to attend, which is causing no end of agitation. Your Earl hopes it will be his, but his enemies are doing all they can to prevent it. And even when the King does make a promise, no one can be sure he will keep his word. He is not a trustworthy man.'

'Perhaps *you* should play Pulcinella next time,' said Chaloner drily. 'He has unflattering opinions about His Majesty's character, too.'

'Pulcinella is right to point out his flaws, although I would not say so to anyone else. Not even Joe, if you want the truth. I do not think he appreciates honesty.'

Chaloner almost choked on his jelly. It was a blunt revelation from a man who purported to be the Spymaster's friend, and he was relieved when Swaddell changed the subject by asking after his plans for the rest of the day.

'To see Abigail Williams in Southwark,' replied Chaloner, 'and then to attend Olivia's funeral. After that, I will go to Hercules' Pillars Alley, where Olivia's White Hall colleagues plan to gather, ostensibly to honour her memory.'

'To carouse, more like,' said Swaddell sourly. 'God forbid that they should spend a night mourning. However, you will have to do the funeral first, because it is in half an hour's time. Shall we go together? I dislike such occasions, but your company will make it bearable.'

The Earl had banned lamps from the Covent Garden church until after the Fast, lest smoke stained his new paintwork, but it was an overcast day, so the building was very gloomy inside. Swaddell opted to stand in the darkest part of the church and kept his hat pulled low to hide his face, for which Chaloner was grateful – he did not want to be thought of as the kind of man who hobnobbed with the Spymaster's assassin.

The coffin arrived, although there was a delay in beginning the service, as Stoakes failed to appear. The Thompson brothers were sent to find him, but returned to report that he was not at his home, the Savoy Wharf or his regular coffee house.

'Then we must begin without him,' said the vicar crossly. 'We need the building back for the carpenters.'

The ceremony was a soulless affair, hastily organised by Maurice because Stoakes had declared himself incapable. The charitable blamed grief for Stoakes' conduct, but most put it down to the copious amounts of wine he swallowed now that there was no Olivia to temper his excesses.

The Earl was with soft-hearted Lady Clarendon, who sobbed all the way through the service; she was the only courtier who did. The others shifted restlessly, then began to whisper. From their gestures and nods, it was clear they were discussing whether the Earl's renovations were sufficient to impress a monarch. Then Chiffinch contrived to kick over a pot of paint, which Lady Castlemaine proceeded to track over as many flagstones as she could reach. Their cronies sniggered gleefully at their antics.

Also present were servants, tradesmen and poor clerics – those who had benefited from Olivia's quiet generosity. They included many sailors, and Boatswain Knapp put a restraining hand on Steward Fowler's shoulder when Chiffinch began to chat to his friends in a disrespectfully loud voice. Chaloner thought Fowler was right to be angry, and was tempted to tell Chiffinch that if he did not know how to behave at such occasions, he should refrain from inflicting himself on those who did.

'Someone will cut that sly little Chiffinch's throat one day,' murmured Swaddell, and the way he fingered his dagger suggested that he thought *he* was just the man to do it.

The ceremony over, the vicar led the way outside, where the casket was lowered into a hole that was disconcertingly close to the plague pit. Chaloner was not the only one who kept his distance. After the committal, the courtiers left quickly, unwilling to linger in the biting wind, although others stayed, murmuring to each other about the various kindnesses Olivia had done for them. One was unusually short with a hood pulled low to conceal his face.

'There is Hudson,' said Chaloner to Swaddell. 'And his rebellious friends behind him.'

Swaddell grimaced. 'We had better arrest them then, although it will make Londoners hate us more than ever. You keep them talking, while I fetch help.'

He sped away without waiting to see if Chaloner would oblige, although it did not matter, because the players approached Chaloner. There were a dozen of them, led by Urban himself. Again, Chaloner noticed the peculiar jewellery in the actor's ears, and found himself staring, trying to make out their intricate designs.

'It is a sad day,' announced Hudson pompously. 'Although sadder for decent folk than for courtiers. I saw few tears shed by *them*, God rot their unfeeling hearts.'

'Lady Clarendon wept copiously,' Chaloner pointed out.

'She did,' acknowledged Urban. 'However, the rest came not to pay their respects to the dead, but to spy on the renovations. Compassion and decency are rare virtues in White Hall.'

Chaloner was beginning to dislike Urban's Men for two reasons: their arrogance in thinking that they were qualified to pass judgement on everyone else, and their assumption that all courtiers were the same.

'So why are *you* here?' he asked coolly. 'Surely not because Olivia Stoakes gave you each sixpence?'

Hudson glared at him. 'Yes, as a matter of fact. No one else tipped us, and we were touched by her generosity. We know you suspect us of harming her, but do you really think we would attend the funeral of someone we had murdered?'

'Killers often do,' flashed Chaloner. 'Perhaps they like the challenge. Or they enjoy observing the distress they have caused.'

'How can you think that *we* are in the business of

261

causing distress?' objected Urban, stung. 'On the contrary, we aim to alleviate misery by making people see that they can change their lives for the better.'

'By inciting them to rebellion?' demanded Chaloner archly. 'That will not help.'

'Of course it will!' cried Urban passionately. 'People will see they have rights, and will insist that they are recognised.'

'What will emerge from your agitating is anarchy,' stated Chaloner, 'with all manner of fanatics crawling from their holes to squabble over the spoils. Not to mention the Dutch, who would dearly love us to be in disarray so—'

'No!' snarled Urban, then struggled to regain his composure, so when he spoke again it was more gently. 'You are wrong. All we want is a more benevolent society, where the poor are seen as equals to the rich, just as we are all equals in the eyes of God.'

'Right,' said Chaloner, thinking he had never heard such naive claptrap. 'But—'

'We know you sent for soldiers to arrest us, so we cannot linger,' interrupted Urban. 'However, I have one piece of advice before we leave. Forget us and forget Olivia. Concentrate on more important matters, such as the murders of Widow Fisher and Dr Merrett.'

'Why?' demanded Chaloner. 'What—'

The rest of his question was lost when someone grabbed him from behind – someone who had moved with such stealth that Chaloner had been wholly unaware of him coming. A sack was pulled over his head, and he was given a solid shove that sent him staggering into the wall. By the time he had recovered his balance and ripped the bag away, Urban and his cronies had vanished.

'Gone?' asked Swaddell, when he returned, although only with three soldiers, who would have been unable to take a dozen prisoners anyway. 'What a pity.'

Chaloner regarded him sharply. Was Swaddell one of those who would join in if there was a call to arms on Tuesday – and that by bringing inadequate troops, he had ensured that Urban would be free to lead it? Swaddell did not seem like a closet insurgent, but the King and his Court had earned so many new enemies since the plague, that it was impossible to say who would stay loyal and who thought life might be better under a different ruler. Chaloner supposed he would have to include monitoring Swaddell on his list of tasks, too.

Leaving the assassin to eavesdrop on the remaining mourners, Chaloner hired a hackney to take him to Southwark. The driver declared a dislike for going east of St Paul's Cathedral, and was determined to return to familiar territory as fast as possible, so he tore along at a terrifying lick. After a breakneck race to Fish Street Hill, they descended to London Bridge, where he screeched to a halt, sending Chaloner flying forward violently enough to bang his nose on the front rail.

'What is the matter?' demanded Chaloner crossly, wondering if he should get the man's licence revoked before he killed someone – assuming he did not have a string of victims already, of course.

'I am not taking my horse on that,' said the driver firmly. 'It is too dangerous.'

Chaloner saw what he meant. The buildings on the northern end of the bridge had been destroyed by fire some years before, and although there were plans to rebuild them, none had come to fruition. As a result, there was a long empty stretch, and people were prevented from falling over the edges by wooden fences. The hyrricano had ripped these away, and as the wind was still gusting hard down the river, there was a very real risk of being blown off the bridge and into the raging torrent below.

Chaloner paid him and began to cross on foot, hoping Abigail would be worth the risk he was taking. He glanced over the side as he went, and saw a mat of shattered boats and uprooted trees, all pinned against the arches by the force of the flow. A larger ship was upside down, showing her keel. He staggered on, glad when he was past the open section and into the tunnel-like road that ran between the bridge's houses and shops. Traffic was light, so he had the unusual experience of making the journey without dodging away from thundering carts.

Southwark was a different world from the city across the river – smaller, dirtier, poorer and livelier. Despite the inclement weather, he was instantly besieged by people who wanted to sell him broadsheets, pies, ale, trinkets or their sisters. The air was rich with the scent of the river, a combination of seaweed and salt water. He inhaled deeply, then gagged when a waft of something less pleasant drifted from an alley – sewage and decay. At first he assumed it came from a tannery, but then realised it was just the reek of poverty. Fortunately, it was not far to the Beare, where a grubby urchin pointed out Abigail's house in exchange for a penny.

He rapped on the door, and a maid conducted him to a parlour with views across the river. It had been decorated by someone with more money than taste, and was vibrantly vulgar – rather like its owner, who was dressed in pink frills that were more appropriate for a ten-year-old than a woman in her fifties. Abigail's hair was coiled in the manner of young maidens, and again, she had contrived to conceal her wrinkles with a generous slathering of face-paint. When Chaloner bowed, she simpered at him from behind a fan.

'I remember you from the charnel house,' she cooed. 'A sad day.'

She did not look sad, and he saw why when he saw who was with her: Harry Brouncker, surreptitiously lacing up his breeches. Good, thought Chaloner. Now he could watch how they both reacted to the news he brought about her former lover.

'Quartermain has been exhumed,' he announced baldly. 'He was poisoned.'

Abigail raised the fan so it covered everything but her eyes, which made her expression difficult to read. Chaloner itched to rip the thing away. Unfortunately, he fared no better with Brouncker either, whose attention was fixed on an inconveniently tangled cord.

'Poor Willy,' sighed Abigail eventually. 'I miss him terribly.'

'Of course you do,' said Brouncker briskly. 'But tell Chaloner anything you know that might explain why he was in Bedford House. In return, Chaloner can answer *our* questions.'

'Your questions about what, exactly?' asked Chaloner suspiciously.

'That old woman . . . what was her name? The one who acquired that silly letter my friends wrote as a joke. Have you found her killer?'

'Not yet,' replied Chaloner. 'But perhaps you can help. Where were you on Tuesday?'

'He was here,' interposed Abigail immediately. 'With me.'

'No, Abigail,' said Brouncker haughtily, raising his hand. 'I appreciate your support, my love, but there is no need to lie for me, because I have nothing to hide. I did not kill her, which is what Chaloner is really asking with his so-carefully-phrased questions.'

'Can you prove it?' asked Chaloner, unrepentant.

Brouncker gave a tight smile. 'Yes, I can. *You* saw me leave my house that morning with your own eyes, because we emerged at roughly the same time. After we parted company, I retrieved the papers the wind had torn away, then went directly to White Hall where I remained for the rest of the day. I was working with the Duke – ask him.'

'I shall,' vowed Chaloner, although he doubted he would be granted an audience to do so. 'Did you know that Widow Fisher lived in your family vault?'

Brouncker blinked with such obvious shock that Chaloner crossed it off his list of motives for the old lady's demise. It put him back to his first assumption: that she had been dispatched because she had seen or heard something she should not have done.

'You mean she had moved in with the corpses?' breathed Brouncker, appalled. 'But old Jonas died of the plague!'

And was in the pit with all the other parish victims, thought Chaloner. 'Yes, she told me.'

Brouncker shuddered. 'Poor Jonas. He was a sailor, like me, and we were good friends. But speaking of the navy, why not tell me what you have learned about *that* so far?'

'About what specifically?' asked Chaloner, bemused. 'And why should I anyway?'

Brouncker became serious. 'Because I may be able to

266

help you with answers, but I am loath to waste your time by repeating things that you already know.'

'Then tell me about *Assurance*,' said Chaloner.

'That is the matter you are exploring?' asked Brouncker. He nodded slowly. 'I suppose your Earl would be concerned about her, given that her captain was married to one of his staff. So let me see. I can start by telling you that Stoakes is not as distressed by the loss as I would have been. However, he was at Lowestoft, which was a very bloody business . . .'

Chaloner struggled to grasp what Brouncker was telling him. 'You think *Stoakes* sank her, to avoid taking part in another battle?'

Brouncker raised his hands in a shrug. 'I have no evidence to prove it. Olivia would not have retreated from a fight, but Stoakes . . . well, he is not a valiant soul.'

Chaloner inclined his head in thanks. 'I will bear it in mind when I next speak to him.'

'I could have told you all this at her funeral earlier, had I known you were interested,' Brouncker went on. 'Of course, *he* did not come to see his wife buried. Stoakes really is a disagreeable scoundrel.'

Coming from Brouncker, this was damning indeed. The courtier had no more to add about Stoakes, so Chaloner turned the discussion back to Quartermain.

'Did you know he was hired to kill a clerk in the Dutch embassy?'

'Was he?' blurted Brouncker, stunned. 'He always seemed such a pathetic little mouse. Who would have thought he had it in him? My word!'

Abigail fluttered her eyelashes at Chaloner when he indicated that she should answer his question. 'Willy and

I never discussed such matters. We did *other* things, if you know what I mean.'

She winked, and Chaloner regarded her in distaste, recalling what Thurloe recommended he do should Abigail prove uncooperative – and she was being uncooperative now, because it was patently obvious that she was lying *and* trying to distract him from his purpose.

'Perhaps you mentioned your conversations with Quartermain to Brouncker's brother,' he said coolly. 'He will certainly remember, so I shall ask him when he—'

'All right,' snapped Abigail, the coquettish expression replaced by something cold, hard and nasty. 'Willy *did* confide that he was ordered to make an end of Heemskerch. He did not want to do it, but there was a problem with an early batch of King's Gold – it killed a couple of patients, apparently. Someone threatened to report him to the College of Physicians unless he did as he was told.'

'Which was what?'

'To poison Heemskerch and declare it a natural death. He did his best, but his potion did not work. So the blackmailer told him to try again. *And* again and again. Four times in all.'

'How sordid!' exclaimed Brouncker. 'No wonder you threw Quartermain over for me!'

'The blackmailer being whom, exactly?' asked Chaloner, ignoring him.

'Willy never said. However, on his final visit, the culprit accidentally dropped some messages and a cipher key in Willy's house.' Abigail smirked superiorly. 'Willy did not know what a cipher key was, so I had to show him. I know all about those, because my late husband was a spy during the civil wars.'

'Was he?' asked Brouncker, startled. 'You told me you were too young to remember what happened back in those days.'

'It is a very *early* memory,' said Abigail quickly and turned back to Chaloner before Brouncker could question her further. 'Willy applied the key, and what he read shocked him to the core. He would not let me see what was written, and tossed the letters on the fire, although he kept the key . . .'

'Why?'

Abigail shrugged. 'To translate any future missives he happened across, I suppose. He was appalled by what he had seen, and railed about the blackmailer embroiling him in the filthy world of espionage.'

Chaloner raised his eyebrows. 'Being ordered to murder a clerk from the Dutch embassy had not made that clear already?'

'The blackmailer convinced him that Heemskerch was responsible for bringing the plague to London, although I was sceptical. And that was the last I ever saw of Willy – the Saturday evening, just before he went to Bedford House for his last attempt on Heemskerch's life.'

'What did you do when he failed to reappear? Search for him?'

Abigail blinked. 'How? By going to the embassy and demanding to know what they had done with the man who was sent to dispatch one of them?' The simpering teenager made a brief return as she glanced at Brouncker. 'Besides, by then I had other matters to occupy my mind.'

'Is there anything else I should know?' asked Chaloner coldly. 'Or do I have to ask Brouncker's brother what he—'

'There is no need for that,' interrupted Abigail briskly. 'The only other thing I can tell you is that Willy once saw the blackmailer in the Fleece.'

'Saw him with whom?' demanded Chaloner, hopes rising.

'With no one. Willy said he was on his own.'

'What was he doing?'

'Drinking ale, apparently. When he had finished, he left and Willy followed him, to see where he went in the hope that it would reveal his identity – he thought that might help him to escape from his clutches, you see. Unfortunately, Willy lost him almost at once.'

Chaloner was fairly sure he had prised everything worth knowing from Abigail and her new lover, so he took his leave, wishing the journey had been more fruitful.

Darkness had fallen while Chaloner had been in Abigail's house, and he stepped into a street that was full of skittering shadows. He turned quickly when one materialised behind him. It was Brouncker, who asked if they might walk back to the city together, because there was safety in numbers in these uncertain times. As far as Chaloner was concerned, Brouncker posed a far greater risk than Southwark's felons, although it quickly transpired that all the courtier wanted was an assurance that Chaloner would not expose him to his brother as Abigail's most recent amour – she had not been the only one to blanch when Chaloner had threatened to tell.

They reached the bridge, and Chaloner glanced up at the heads that graced the spikes above, all carefully illuminated by strategically placed lamps. Evidently, they had been more securely impaled than the ones at Westminster Hall, as none had blown down.

'I hate those things,' said Brouncker with a shudder. 'I expect one to fall on me every time I walk beneath them. Moreover, I think I knew a few when they were still alive.'

'You were acquainted with rebels?'

Brouncker shrugged. 'Who was not? And how can *you* ask such a question – you who hails from a clan of regicides and dedicated Parliamentarians?'

'Cromwell's head came down on Wednesday,' said Chaloner, more as a means of diverting the discussion away from his family than to pass on interesting information.

'I heard. Decapitating his corpse was a dreadful thing to do – barbaric and needlessly vengeful. We should be beyond such nastiness.'

Chaloner was surprised to hear him say so. Most courtiers were ghouls, who had been in the front row when the regicides' skeletons had been torn from their graves and 'executed'. Similarly, they loved visiting the Westminster Charnel House or watching Wiseman at work in the Anatomy Theatre.

'We are supposed to be civilised,' Brouncker went on in disgust. 'But here we are, in the second half of the seventeenth century, and still we insist on maiming and mauling each other. It is high time we desisted, and fought our battles through diplomatic channels instead.'

Chaloner shot him a puzzled glance. 'And this from a man who claims he enjoyed the Battle of Lowestoft? Not many days ago, you told me the experience was fun.'

Brouncker shrugged. 'I say what people expect to hear. Oh, it was a magnificent victory, but there was rather a lot of blood. I was standing right next to Boyle, Muskerry and Falmouth when that chain-shot took off their heads. I can still see them rolling across the deck . . .'

The lamplight showed a haunted expression on his face, revealing that he was not the bold and brutal man of war he would have everyone believe. Chaloner liked him better for it. He was about to ask more when Brouncker pulled himself together.

'Ignore me, Chaloner,' he said with a grin that did not touch his eyes. 'Abigail's wine must be stronger than I thought, and I am very tired with all the arrangements for the King's return. Claret and weariness always combine to make me maudlin.'

'Will you be going to a Fast?' asked Chaloner, aware that the courtier was waiting for him to change the subject.

Brouncker yawned, his laconic self once more. 'Not if I can help it. They are all scheduled for the morning, and I am not a peasant who rises with the sun. I am a gentleman, who never shows his face until noon. I am sure you are the same.'

Chaloner thought it was better not to reply to that.

Hercules' Pillars Alley was named for the tavern at its northern end, a noisy, bustling inn famous for serving large portions of meat. The bellman was calling nine o'clock as Chaloner walked down the lane to the house halfway along it. Most businesses had been closed for hours, but the brothel had only just opened. Lights blazed, and expensive carriages were lining up outside it to disgorge their passengers.

Temperance North and her ladies had followed the King to Oxford during the plague, and while they were away, the club had been totally refurbished. Its new décor and upgraded facilities were still a novelty, so London's wealthy elite flocked to enjoy them.

Chaloner expected to be greeted by his old adversary Preacher Hill, a Puritan fanatic who saw nothing wrong with working as a doorman in a bordello by night and ranting against fornication during the day. And a doorman was necessary, as Temperance was particular about who she allowed inside her domain – they had to be Royalists and they had to be able to pay her exorbitant prices.

'He died of the plague,' explained the liveried stranger who stood in Hill's spot. 'He told everyone that the disease would only take sinners, but he was one of the first to go.'

Chaloner was surprised to find himself sorry. He had not liked Hill, but there was something reassuringly predictable about the preacher's constant refusal to let him pass, and he had enjoyed the challenge of besting him, either by stealth, bluff or intimidation. His replacement held open the door with a polite smile, which was no fun at all.

The house smelled of paint and fresh wood. There was also new artwork – portraits by Lely, Cooper and Lanier, and enough sculpture to fill a Grecian temple. There were no rugs or curtains – the patrons spilled wine and set things on fire with their pipes – but the floorboards were a beautiful dark oak, while the window shutters were the best money could buy. Professional musicians played a medley of popular tunes in the main parlour, although as they had been supplied with wine, their timing was off and there were sour notes aplenty.

The atmosphere was already debauched, with a lot of manly laughter and girlish squeals. Most guests were courtiers, although none were doing anything to suggest they were there to honour Olivia. All oozed the kind of

273

smug confidence that came from power and wealth, and were men who denied themselves nothing. They ate Temperance's fine food, drank her exceptional wine, and were vocal about their choice of female companion.

Chaloner was about to retreat to the shadows, to see what he could learn from listening, when he saw a familiar face. It was Wiseman, who, as Temperance's official lover, could usually be found there of an evening. The surgeon grinned an amiable greeting, so Chaloner went to repeat what he had learned about Quartermain.

'I *told* him his poxbane-loaded King's Gold would bring him trouble,' averred Wiseman smugly. 'Naturally, I was right.'

'Who is in a position to threaten him with expulsion from the College of Physicians?'

'Someone with solid evidence, as the College does not heed rumours or groundless accusations about its members. Ergo, Quartermain must have been guilty of these deaths, or he would have shrugged it off. However, King's Gold was expensive, so you can leave paupers off your list of suspects. You must look to the wealthy for answers.'

'I was afraid of that.'

Chaloner eavesdropped until midnight, and spoke to as many guests as would entertain his questions, but he learned nothing about Olivia, *Assurance*, Stoakes, Quartermain, the trumpet, the brewing rebellion or anything else he had been charged to investigate.

'Let the rebels come!' slurred Will Chiffinch, grabbing a poker and waving it like a sword. 'We will show them what is what! Heads will roll.'

His head might, thought Chaloner, hoping the palace

would have plenty of guards on duty for the Fast, because there would be a massacre if courtiers were left to defend themselves. And yet, he thought, as he watched the frolicking, noisy throng, who would miss them?

At that point, the Thompson brothers arrived. They were perfectly happy to talk to him about Olivia, whom they had held in very high regard. However, they could add nothing he did not already know, other than that they had tried to support Stoakes after she had gone missing out of respect for her, not because they liked him.

'Not that he appreciated it,' said Maurice, who had applied especially thick eyebrows to ensure they lasted the night, giving him a rather simian appearance. 'He did not deserve her.'

'He did not even bother to attend her funeral,' bawled Robert. His grimace revealed teeth that had been bleached white for the occasion. 'I assume he is here now, though – he is the one who chose this place, on the grounds that Olivia admired lively women.'

'He is not,' said Chaloner, suspecting that Olivia had been referring to lively minds, rather than lively bodies. 'Should we be concerned for *his* safety now?'

'We should be concerned for the safety of London's wine,' remarked George, sitting down to rest his leg. He swiped fastidiously at a speck of mud on the false one. 'Because he will show it no mercy. Indeed, I do not think he has been sober since *Assurance* went down.'

'We went to collect him on our way here,' said Maurice. 'But he was not at home. Poor Olivia! She was a lovely lady. She had odd ideas about some things – a result of too much reading, probably – but we were so fond of her.'

'We were, and I hope you find her killer, Chaloner,' said George, 'because if anyone deserves justice, it is she.' He glanced around impatiently. 'Have you seen Joe, by the way? We invited him to join us, and I thought he would be here by now.'

Chaloner tried to imagine Williamson enjoying the dissipated atmosphere in the club, but could not do it. Moreover, he suspected the place would empty if the Spymaster did show up.

'He sent me a note begging to be excused,' hollered Robert. 'He said he was tired and needed an early night, although I suspect the real reason for his refusal was Swaddell – *he* wanted to come, too, but he is such a bore! He contributes nothing useful to a conversation, and is wholly ignorant about the Chequered Skipper.'

'A moth,' put in Maurice for Chaloner's benefit.

'Perhaps it is as well that Joe is not coming,' said George to his brothers, 'as it means we can slip away early to watch *Assurance* being weighed. The engineers have been working on her all day, and they predict to have her up by dawn. I want to see it.'

'So do I,' boomed Robert, then gazed around appreciatively. 'Although it would be rude to depart without first sampling the merchandise, and Temperance North's girls are reputed to be the best in the country. Shall we?'

Chaloner left the parlour, weary and ready for bed – preferably his own. However, it was more than his life was worth to go without paying his respects to Temperance, so he went to the back of the house, where she had a small office.

'You survived the plague then,' she said, when Chaloner poked his head around the door.

Despite the frosty greeting, he could tell she was pleased to see him, because her eyes glowed and a smile twitched the corners of her mouth. She had grown fatter since they had last met, yet still none of her friends were brave enough to tell her that the dresses she favoured looked better on slimmer women. Her cheeks were almost as thickly slathered in face-paints as Abigail's, and she wore an ugly but fashionable wig.

'Did you like Oxford?' he asked, sitting opposite and declining her offer of tobacco.

'Not as much as I like London,' she replied, taking her pipe and tamping it expertly. 'It is good to be home. I was sorry to hear about Hannah, by the way. She was a nice lady.'

Chaloner changed the subject abruptly, unsettled as always by the pang of disquiet that speared through him whenever Hannah was mentioned. Temperance leaned forward to pat his hand, but allowed the matter to drop, for which he was grateful.

'Will you go to a Fast?' he asked.

'Yes – Westminster Abbey's, because that is the one the King will attend. I know your Earl thinks he will favour Covent Garden, but His Majesty does not love him any more, and this is a chance to say so publicly. You wait and see.'

Chaloner hoped she was wrong. 'Do you have any other news?'

'Well, I hired some famous entertainers two weeks ago, and it almost ended in disaster. Urban's Men. Have you heard of them?'

Chaloner regarded her in disbelief. 'You invited *them* to perform to your courtiers?'

'I was promised acrobats, fire-eaters, sword-swallowers

and magicians,' she replied defensively. 'And Urban claimed that one of his rope-dancers is Lady Castlemaine's latest beau. Naturally, I assumed that meant they were Royalists . . .'

Chaloner laughed. 'What happened?'

'Nothing at first. My guests, who included the Duke of York, loved the juggling, the magic and so forth. But then Urban launched into a political burlesque. My guests were outraged, and weapons were drawn. Fortunately, the Duke defused the tension by lobbing a syllabub. Others followed suite, and the players fled amidst a hail of flying food.'

'That cannot have pleased them,' said Chaloner, wondering if it had been the catalyst that had provoked the troupe into being more extreme. Regardless, the incident would have done nothing to convince them that courtiers were genteel and responsible human beings.

'They were livid, and Urban was close to tears. But what did they expect? For my patrons to enjoy being mocked? Or to sit and accept censure like naughty children?'

'They are turning people against the government and their supporters, so you should hire additional guards, lest you become a target by association.'

'Already done,' said Temperance. 'Oh, I almost forgot! A man with a scarred nose was in here asking after Mr Thurloe earlier. I informed him that old Parliamentarians tend to avoid places stuffed with Cavaliers, but he was very insistent.'

'Beuningen! Why would he come to the club?'

'Because he had found out that Mr Thurloe was kind to me after my parents died, and concluded that we were friends. I told him the truth – that I have not seen him in months.'

'Did he believe you?'

'I am not sure, because his response was to grab a jug from the table and hit himself over the head with it. He knocked himself quite silly and started blathering about Mongols.'

'Did he say why he wanted Thurloe?'

'Something to do with a missing spy apparently, although it was difficult to be sure when he was reeling around in a daze.'

Chaloner left Hercules' Pillars Alley full of fear for his friend. He went straight to Lincoln's Inn, where Thurloe waved a hand to indicate that he already knew about Beuningen closing in on him.

'He has visited me here twice today,' he said, 'on the pretext of discussing points of law. He has a brilliant mind, so I am not surprised that he has made the connection between Heemskerch and an ex-Spymaster. I do hope Heemskerch will get away tomorrow, as the net is tightening a little too fast for my liking.'

Chaloner hurried to Wych Street and hammered on Lester's door. It was answered by the captain himself, blinking sleep from his eyes, although he was fully dressed.

'Heemskerch,' said Chaloner without preamble. 'The situation has become critical. Have you hired a dogger to take him to Margate or do we go by road?'

'I sent a note to your house,' said Lester, yawning. 'Did you not get it? He will leave on the morning tide. Bring him to the Savoy Wharf at five o'clock sharp.'

'Why so early? The river will not ebb until ten o'clock at least.'

'I know, but we want to put him on the dogger while it is still dark.'

'But it will not be dark,' said Chaloner, feeling his exasperation rise. '*Assurance* is due to be weighed, so the Savoy Wharf will be lit up like a beacon, not to mention bustling with people.'

'Oh,' gulped Lester in horror. 'Lord! I forgot.'

'We will have to use a different pier,' determined Chaloner, running through the options in his mind. 'Preferably one that will be suitably deserted.'

'But it is all arranged!' cried Lester in dismay. 'We cannot start altering things now – it would be begging for something to go wrong. Besides, there is no way to get word to the dogger men about changes of plan, so we will just have to make the best of it.'

'God save me from amateurs!' muttered Chaloner under his breath, deeply unimpressed.

Lester forced a smile and clapped him on the shoulder. 'Do not worry, Tom. I will arrange a diversion. All you will have to do is nod when you want it deployed. You see? Everything is under control.'

Besieged by misgivings, and sincerely hoping that Lester and his friends would prove equal to the challenge, Chaloner raced back to Chancery Lane, told Thurloe to have Heemskerch ready by four – he wanted to leave plenty of time to reach the pier, lest they were obliged to make detours. Then he trudged home, full of worry for what the next day would bring.

Chapter 11

Chaloner snatched a short nap on his makeshift bed in Wiseman's parlour, then rose, knowing he would be busy that day. His first priority was to get Heemskerch to the dogger and take possession of the stolen intelligence. Once the documents were safely in Williamson's hands, he would hold Thurloe to his end of the bargain and make sure he left for Oxfordshire. Only then would he return to his other investigations.

He dashed cold water over his face to sharpen wits that were sluggish from lack of sleep, then donned clothes that were suitable for sneaking around in the dark – black long-coat and breeches, riding boots to keep his feet dry, and a nondescript hat.

He hurried to the kitchen for something to eat, but found two letters propped against the milk jug for him, a place where the servants knew he would find them. He cut himself a slice of pie – mostly carrot with one or two slivers of beef – and ate it while he read them.

The first was from Wren, asking if he thought the articulated skeleton of the King's first dog would serve as an interesting gift from the Earl; he had located where it was buried and Wiseman had offered to wire its bones together. Chaloner dashed off a reply, suggesting that Wren look for something else instead, and left it for the servants to deliver.

The second was from Lester. It was slathered in sealing wax to ensure it did not pop open, which would have told even the most casual of observers that here was a missive with sensitive contents. Chaloner fought his way inside it to discover that Lester had not even attempted to encode the message, but had written out all the details of the escape plan in his bold, confident roundhand. As Chaloner meticulously shredded it into small pieces, he was reminded yet again that his friend was a novice in the world of intelligence.

He exited through the back door, and took the precaution of climbing over the wall into the neighbour's garden before stepping out on to the street, lest Beuningen had deduced that monitoring *him* would be a good way to trace Heemskerch. He waited in the shadows until he was sure no one was watching, then set off towards Chancery Lane.

Thurloe and Heemskerch were waiting, breaking their fast on slivers of bread soaked in milk. It was meagre fare even by Thurloe's abstemious standards, and Chaloner supposed the pair had been on hunger rations ever since Prynne had commented on the ex-Spymaster's sudden increase of appetite. Chaloner pulled his friend aside.

'Have *you* packed?' he demanded. 'You do not want to be here if Beuningen finds out that Heemskerch has been hiding in your attic.'

'I do not,' agreed Thurloe. 'Yet I dislike the notion of running away while the city stands on the edge of a precipice. Perhaps I should stay on and help you—'

'You promised to leave,' interrupted Chaloner firmly. 'And I do not need help. I have Williamson, Swaddell and Lester. So I repeat: have you packed?'

Thurloe smiled thinly. 'Days ago. Now, to business. Heemskerch will hand you the stolen documents as soon as the dogger leaves the quay. It is a compromise: originally, he refused to part with them until he was at sea.'

'They had better be worth it, because if not, Beuningen, the governments of two countries, and the survivors of Vågen will not be the only ones baying for his blood. So will I.'

He glanced at the Dutchman, who had finished the food and was leaning back with his hands clasped over his paunch. He looked so sure of his own importance that Chaloner experienced a surge of dislike for him.

'Put your coat on,' he told him curtly. 'We are leaving now.'

Heemskerch stood, but instead of donning his outdoor clothes, he went to peer out of the window. Exasperated, Chaloner hauled him away before anyone saw him.

'Where is the cart?' demanded Heemskerch. 'I managed to save most of my valuables before being forced to flee Bedford House, and it will take a while to load them up.'

'We will be walking,' said Chaloner. 'Take only what you can carry.'

'But there are too many to carry,' cried Heemskerch in dismay, 'and I am not leaving them behind. You will have to make other arrangements.'

'Then Beuningen will get you,' said Chaloner harshly. 'He is closing in fast, so make a choice: leave now or explain to him why you turned traitor.'

283

'Do not worry about your things, Laurens,' said Thurloe kindly. 'I will look after them until they can be sent after you. Now collect what you need quickly, and let us be gone.'

His face now pale, Heemskerch turned and hared up the stairs. Thurloe waited until his footsteps could be heard thumping frantically across the floor above, then smiled maliciously.

'I cannot imagine he will like Guinea. I understand it is rather bleak.'

'He is lucky to be going anywhere, given the number of people who want him dead. I wish you had turned him away. He is too dangerous to harbour.'

'He served us reliably and regularly for a decade.' Thurloe's tone was reproachful. 'So how could I throw him to the wolves? Besides, Williamson has high hopes for the intelligence he stole, and thinks it may enable us to redeem ourselves after the disaster of Vågen.'

'The intelligence,' said Chaloner. 'Do we collect it en route? He told me he had hidden it somewhere other than here when I asked.'

'A lie,' said Thurloe, 'to ensure we did not take it by force and have him quietly dispatched. It was a sensible precaution, although he had no need to fear such treachery from me. Williamson, on the other hand . . .'

'*You* cannot come to the pier,' said Chaloner quickly, as the ex-Spymaster threw a cloak around his shoulders. 'You must stay here and eliminate all traces of your guest. Destroy whatever he leaves behind – there will be no forwarding of possessions.'

'I know that, Thomas,' said Thurloe irritably. 'But I had to say something, or he would be here arguing still. Very well then, as long as you promise to let me know what happens. Report back to me as soon as you have delivered the parcel to Williamson.'

Chaloner nodded, and turned to watch Heemskerch struggling down the stairs with a sack that was bigger than he was. Chaloner opened it, removed two paintings and a chair, ignoring the resulting squeals of protest, then indicated to Thurloe that they were ready.

'God's speed,' said Thurloe softly. 'Both of you. Now go, before Beuningen arrives.'

'Stay behind me,' Chaloner ordered Heemskerch softly, before they slipped through Lincoln's Inn's back gate to the lane beyond. 'No talking and no dawdling. Do you understand?'

Heemskerch nodded, frightened now he was away from the comfortable familiarity of Thurloe's attic. And so he should be, Chaloner thought acidly, when several sailors emerged from a disreputable tavern called the Pope's Head, and Vågen was a word that was definitely recognisable among the drunken yells.

He led the way at a cracking pace through the dark streets, stopping to hide frequently, until they reached the Strand. Then his stomach lurched when he saw a familiar figure hurrying along it towards them – Beuningen with a sword in his hand. Heemskerch whimpered in terror.

'He will run me through! He is barely sane on occasion, and he is certainly having a peculiar turn now, because why else would he be prancing along one of London's main thoroughfares with a naked blade?'

Beuningen was indeed prancing, swishing the weapon back and forth as he did so. Bemused, Chaloner watched him gyrate towards Bow Street, and thought he could hear him singing. They waited until he was out of sight, then Chaloner indicated that Heemskerch should follow him again, glaring when the Dutchman began to snivel. Heemskerch struggled to control himself, and they hurried in silence to Ivie Lane. Again, Chaloner lurked in the shadows until he was sure no one was watching, before bundling his charge down it to the Savoy Wharf.

'Oh, God,' moaned Heemskerch when he saw it brightly lit and thronged with people. 'I am betrayed! One of your helpmeets blabbed, and everyone is here to kill me.'

'They are here for *Assurance*,' explained Chaloner. 'And crowds are good for us, because we can hide among them. At least, we can if you at least *try* not to look furtive.'

The navy engineers had succeeded in their endeavours, and *Assurance* was afloat once more. Her two weeks in the river had done nothing for her appearance, and seaweed dangled from every mast and spar. Her crewmen were working to remove it, clambering over her with lamps to light their way. Boatswain Knapp and Steward Fowler were among them. The spectators also included a number of familiar faces, despite the unsociably early hour. Chaloner grimaced when he was hailed by one – he had hoped to slip past unnoticed.

'You should have been here, Chaloner,' bellowed Robert, marching towards him with his brothers in tow. The white teeth he had worn at the club had been replaced by an older, browner set, and Chaloner wondered absently if Temperance's cleaners would be in for a surprise when they went to change the bed linen. 'It was a glorious sight to see her surging from the deep.'

'Did Stoakes come to watch?' asked Chaloner, glad

Heemskerch had the sense to keep his face averted. He was aware of the Dutchman's rising agitation, but what else could they do? Hurrying on without exchanging pleasantries would look suspicious.

'No,' replied George, bending to flick imaginary dust from his false leg. 'He would not dare. His crew was buried yesterday, and everyone knows he did not contribute towards the cost.'

'He is probably skulking in a tavern,' hollered Robert. 'Too ashamed to show his face.'

'He should have attended the funerals, though,' put in Maurice, whose eyebrows had been rubbed off during the night, so that Chaloner had visions of one of Temperance's ladies waking up to find them transferred on to her. 'And I confess I am concerned. I last saw him on Thursday, when Olivia was brought home. It is a long time for a drinking spree, even for him.'

'I will ask Judd and his friends to track him down,' yelled Robert. 'They know the taverns better than we do, and they have nothing else to do now that the Folly is closed for repairs.'

'Will *you* keep an eye out for him, too, Chaloner?' asked Maurice.

Chaloner promised he would. Aware that Heemskerch was growing increasingly unsettled by the delay, he hurried on before the Dutchman could give himself away.

The far end of the quay was empty, and it was there that the dogger was moored, identifiable by the nets and winches used for catching fish. It was a rough little craft. The name painted on its stern was so battered as to be unreadable, and Chaloner would not have trusted its foremast in a gentle breeze, let alone the kind of wind it was likely to meet on the way to Margate. It rocked sluggishly, suggesting that it either carried a very heavy cargo or it leaked. Two men were aboard, skidding about on its slippery decks.

'Is this him?' came a low voice.

Chaloner turned to see Harman, who had contrived to make himself appear patently suspicious in a dark coat with a hood. Irritably, Chaloner wondered if he had done it on purpose, to attract attention so that Heemskerch would be caught. Or was he just like Lester – a novice in such matters? Fortunately, their end of the pier was poorly lit, unlike the bright halo around *Assurance*, so hopefully no one would notice what was happening there.

'Is everything ready?' he asked softly.

'It is,' replied Harman, 'although I am afraid this wretched little vessel is the best we could manage after the hyrricano. We have named it *Vågen*.'

He shot Heemskerch a sour look, which the Dutchman returned in full. Chaloner stifled a sigh, thinking it was no time for such pettiness.

'Where is Lester?' he demanded. 'I expected him to be here.'

Harman nodded to the spectators. 'Over there with Cox, waiting to deploy the diversion we have arranged for when your spy boards the dogger. Of course, such precautions are not really necessary, as everyone is more interested in *Assurance* than in us.'

Chaloner winced at the reckless overconfidence, especially from a man who had been attacked several times by robbers, so was clearly not very good at identifying imminent danger. Harman seemed to read his mind.

'We have learned from those experiences,' he said shortly. 'Why do you think we have donned these disguises? It is to ensure that we do not invite another assault – one that might interfere with the spy's escape.'

'I see,' said Chaloner, wishing the whole escapade was over.

'Of course, it will not matter after today,' Harman went on, 'as *Royal Charles* is ready for sea at last. We ride to Deptford as soon as we have finished here, where we shall oversee a few minor adjustments before sailing on Wednesday.'

'Is she seaworthy?' asked Heemskerch, edging forward to hear what they were saying.

'*Royal Charles?*' asked Harman. 'She had better be! She has been in the dockyard for months, and if so much as a spar is out of place, I shall—'

'Not her,' interrupted Heemskerch, and stabbed a finger at the dogger. 'That thing.'

'She does not have to be seaworthy,' replied Harman, regarding him with undisguised contempt. 'She just needs to reach Margate. Then you will be on your way to Guinea.'

'*Guinea?*' squawked Heemskerch in horror. 'I am not going to Guinea! I expected Spain, Portugal or Greece. Somewhere warm and nice.'

'Guinea is warm, believe me,' said Harman drily. 'And once there, you can buy passage to anywhere you choose. Even Amsterdam.'

'I do not think that would be a very good idea,' pouted Heemskerch, removing a fat package of papers from inside his coat. 'Not once I have put these in English hands.'

Chaloner moved towards them, but Heemskerch skittered away and held them over the river, threatening to drop them in. 'Oh, no! You know the agreement. You may have them when the dogger pushes off and not a moment before.'

'I hope for your sake that they are as important as you claim,' said Harman coldly. 'Because if you have betrayed us, I will hunt you to the ends of the Earth, and the defeat of Vågen will be avenged tenfold – on your person.'

Heemskerch was unable to prevent a shiver of fear. 'You will be pleased, I promise,' he averred. 'Now are you going to gossip like fishwives all morning, or may I climb aboard?'

Chaloner had been watching the spectators around *Assurance* and decided it would be safer to load Heemskerch on the dogger without whatever diversion the three seamen had concocted. But before he could say so, Harman signalled to Lester, and the plan swung into action. It entailed Lester casually strolling up to a navy clerk and shoving him off the pier.

'Man overboard!' roared Cox, while Lester gazed heavenwards in a grotesque parody of innocence. 'Deploy ropes before he drowns!'

'Lord!' muttered Chaloner, thinking the resulting furore was more like a scene from one of Urban's satires than the serious business of saving a life. He dragged his attention away from the kerfuffle, and addressed the Dutchman. 'Go, quickly! I will be back for the documents when the dogger leaves. Meanwhile, stay out of sight.'

He and Harman grabbed Heemskerch's limp, sweaty hands and swung him aboard, although Harman contrived to withdraw his support at a critical moment, so the Dutchman landed on all fours. The crew quickly bundled their passenger below, at which point Chaloner recognised one as Scull, the man who had ferried him to the Floating Coffee House on two different occasions. The other was younger and smaller, and looked to be his son.

'They had better know how to sail that thing,' he informed Harman worriedly. 'I have only ever seen them row.'

'They will manage,' said Harman, fastidiously wiping the fingers that Heemskerch had touched on his handkerchief. 'And we are lucky they agreed to help us, as that hyrricano did a lot of damage to small craft. I was beginning to think we might have to take him to Margate by road, which would have been much more dangerous, But Scull came through.'

'I hope he did not steal this boat,' said Chaloner, thinking that if so, it had been an unnecessary risk.

Harman raised his hands defensively. 'Ask no questions, hear no lies. However, it was not cheap, so I hope you have plenty of money with you.'

He named the enormous sum he had negotiated, which Chaloner had no choice but to pay. Scull's eyes gleamed greedily as the heavy purse was tossed down to him. Again, Chaloner hoped Heemskerch's documents would be worth it.

As he did not want to draw attention to *Vågen* by hovering over her while they waited for the tide to turn, Chaloner went to the other end of the pier, aiming to hide among the crowd. Harman joined him, and they watched Cox and Lester haul a wet, shivering and frightened clerk from the river, then take the credit for having saved him.

'I was sorry to hear about Merrett,' said Chaloner to Harman, feeling obliged to make a stab at polite conversation. 'He was a good man.'

291

'He was,' agreed Harman, his habitually supercilious expression softening briefly. 'But I will avenge him. The next time those damned robbers show their faces, they are dead men.'

Chaloner could see he meant it. He nodded towards *Assurance*, thinking it would be a less contentious subject. 'Will she ever be seaworthy again?'

'Oh, yes,' replied Harman. 'The damage is mostly superficial. It was touch and go for a while as to whether we could bring her up, but we managed in the end. Of course, we had to remove her guns and ammunition first. She was too heavy with all her ordnance on board.'

Chaloner glanced to where he pointed, and saw a row of cannon, barrels pointing across the river. They were squat, ugly things on sturdy carriages with thick wheels. He frowned.

'I thought *Assurance* was a thirty-two gun frigate.'

'She is,' replied Harman, 'although there are plans to augment her to forty. We shall need all the firepower we can get with the Dutch snapping at our heels.'

'Then why are there only twenty-eight cannon here? Where are the other four?'

Harman whipped around and counted them for himself. Then he did it again, the blood draining from his face.

'Cox!' he roared. 'Cox? Where are you?'

'Here,' replied the portly sailing master, hurrying over. Lester joined him, both absurd in the cloaks that they thought made them anonymous, especially given that Harman had just bawled Cox's name loud enough to be heard in White Hall. 'What is the matter?'

'Who was detailed to guard the guns last night?' demanded Harman.

'*Dragon*'s crew,' replied Cox. 'It was a poor choice actually, because they were told yesterday that they would never get their back pay. Not surprisingly, they avenged themselves by abandoning their duties as the first opportunity. Why?'

'The treacherous rogues!' exploded Harman. 'I see what they have done – they have stolen four of our cannon with the aim of selling them back to us.'

Lester raised his eyebrows. 'Well, we shall certainly have to pay, because we cannot afford to lose guns. Personally, I take my hat off to their ingenuity.'

But Chaloner had a bad feeling that disgruntled sailors had nothing to do with the theft. 'Check the ammunition,' he suggested. 'If none is missing, then perhaps the guns *have* been kidnapped. However, if powder and balls have also gone . . .'

'It means that someone took them with the intention of shooting at something,' finished Lester in alarm. 'And there is a lot of resentment against the government at the moment . . .'

Harman and Cox exchanged glances of horror, then dashed to a stack of wooden crates. While they embarked on a frantic stock-check, Lester went to the clerk he had almost drowned, and demanded an inventory. It did not take them long to put the information together.

'So fanatics have made off with four of our finest cannon and plenty of ammunition to deploy them,' whispered Harman, aghast. 'From right under our noses, thanks to the Dragons.'

'No, thanks to the government,' corrected Cox bitterly. 'Which told the Dragons that they would never be paid and expected them not to mind. Of course they declined to work for free and decanted to a tavern instead! That clerk is an ass for choosing them as guards. We should have let him drown.'

'So which of London's many lunatics has these weapons?' Lester demanded of Chaloner. 'And how do we get them back?'

'I do not know,' replied Chaloner soberly. 'However, I strongly suspect that the culprits aim to deploy them during the Fast.' Then he sagged in relief as a thought occurred to him. 'But they will fail! The powder will be sodden after two weeks in the river, and will not ignite.'

The three sailors regarded him pityingly.

'That gunpowder was going to sea, Tom,' said Lester. 'A place that is always wet, so we have learned to store it in watertight barrels. It will ignite, believe me.'

There was a short, tense silence, then Harman began to issue orders.

'Report the situation to the Navy Office,' he told Lester. 'They will know what to do. Cox, stay here in case common sense prevails and the rebels hand them back. Chaloner and I will try to identify potential culprits. Understood? Good – now go!'

Chaloner rubbed his eyes. The Navy Office clerks were no more likely to know what to do than the sea-officers, while the chances of the thieves suddenly turning honest was improbable to say the least. The cannon were almost certainly now in very dangerous hands, and the trouble expected in less than three days had suddenly taken on a far more deadly turn.

As Chaloner dared not leave the quay as long as Heemskerch and his documents were there, he put the time to use by questioning onlookers about the theft of the guns, although to no avail. All their attention had been on *Assurance* rising from the deep, and the pile of munitions at the far end of the pier had held scant interest by comparison.

He glanced at Harman, who had stuck to him like glue all the while, growing more disconsolate with every empty reply. Now his shoulders were hunched and his face was grim. Chaloner was unsympathetic. Harman was an officer in His Majesty's navy and had been on the pier all night: he should have been more vigilant.

'So tell me,' Chaloner said, eventually turning his mind to another of his enquiries, 'why did *Assurance* sink?'

Harman shrugged. 'The engineers will let us know soon – they can board her now the water has been pumped out. Then we can put these foolish rumours about sabotage to rest.'

'May I go with them? Stoakes has been bemoaning the loss of his belongings, and I want to look in his quarters to see if his distress is justified.'

'If you insist. I will signal Cox to keep a discreet eye on the dogger, while you and I reconnoitre *Assurance* together.'

Chaloner did not want Harman's company while he explored the ship, but it transpired that he had no choice – the Navy Board had decreed that no civilian was allowed aboard without an official escort. Thus Chaloner had no alternative but to follow Harman up the gangway.

Assurance reeked from her time underwater, and her open deck was treacherously slick. Harman strode to the ladder that led below, and was down it with the agility of a monkey. Chaloner followed more cautiously. The rungs were cold, wet and slippery, and he was glad when he reached the bottom. The main deck was lit by lanterns, and was busy with carpenters, navy officials and crew.

Among the last were Fowler and Knapp, who had finished pulling seaweed from the masts and had come to scrub the floors.

'Do *you* two know what happened to those four missing guns?' Harman asked, when they came to touch their hats to him.

'We were not looking at the ordnance, sir,' said Knapp apologetically. 'We were watching the ship, as it was where our mates died – mates who would still be in the charnel house, were it not for Captain Lester.'

'But not Stoakes,' growled Fowler, while Knapp poked him in the back, warning him to silence; the steward ignored him. 'The moment his wife disappeared, he "forgot" his promise to pay for their graves. God rot his filthy soul!'

Chaloner regarded him intently. 'His *soul*? Do you think he is dead then? His kinsmen have not seen him since Thursday and—'

'He is not dead,' interrupted Knapp hastily. 'And the moment he appears, we will let you know. We are watching his house, see, as we still hope that he will go to the Navy Board for us, and ask for our wages.'

'Come, Chaloner,' ordered Harman impatiently. 'The tide will turn soon, and we do not want *Vågen* to sail off with that parcel of papers. Do what you must and let us be off.'

He led the way to the stern, where Stoakes had occupied three handsome cabins. The largest was a dining room for the captain and his officers, while the two smaller ones were crammed to the gills with furniture, books, paintings, sculpture, clocks and clothing. No wonder his house was bare, thought Chaloner, gazing around in astonishment. All lay under a layer of silt and were swollen and pulpy with water. He doubted much could be salvaged, and Stoakes had been telling the truth about the extent of his loss.

'Good heavens!' muttered Harman, also amazed. 'I would never take this much clutter to sea with me. Where will it all go when he gives the order to clear for action? The stern chasers have to be fired from in here.'

'Stoakes would never risk his possessions being damaged in a battle,' said Chaloner. 'So I suspect he had another destination in mind – one that did not entail joining the fleet.'

Harman regarded him blankly. 'What destination?'

Chaloner explained the direction his thoughts had taken. 'It looks to me as if he aimed to sail *Assurance* to a place where he could begin a new life. No wonder he was dismayed when she sank! It was not just the loss of his most precious belongings, but the end of all his carefully laid plans to leave England behind for good.'

'Gracious!' breathed Harman, round-eyed. 'That is a wild conclusion to draw from the fact that a fellow likes to be surrounded by a few creature comforts.'

But Chaloner knew he was right. He began to search, and almost immediately found a drawer full of small phials. The ink had run on most of the labels, but a couple were still legible, telling him that the bottles had contained King's Gold. All were empty, but a faint scent of garlic lingered in one. He stared at it. Did this mean Stoakes had poisoned his own crew? Then his attention was taken by Harman, who was also poking around.

'Look at this!' the captain exclaimed, holding up a decanter of wine. 'Remarkable! It is stoppered tightly enough to have survived its time under water. Shall we try some?'

'No, thank you!' replied Chaloner, not liking to imagine what might have bobbed against it while it lay in the sewage-choked Thames.

'It must be from the supply that Stoakes bought for the dinner he planned to host,' Harman went on. 'A lot of us were invited, including the Duke of York and seven admirals. Unfortunately, the Duke wanted to see some show at the Hercules' Pillars Alley brothel, so Stoakes cancelled. I was affronted, as it implied that he considers the rest of us unworthy of—'

'When was this dinner exactly?' interrupted Chaloner urgently, recalling suddenly that Stoakes had also mentioned his intention to host a banquet – it was why *Assurance* had been moored in the city, rather than at a naval dockyard. 'Not two Saturdays ago?'

'It was, actually – the same night that *Assurance* sank. It was a pity, because if we had been aboard, we might have been able to save her.'

'Or you might have joined the twenty seamen in their graves. Give me the wine.'

It took both of them to remove the stopper, but when they did, Chaloner immediately detected a powerful stench of garlic. He supposed it would have been served later in the meal, when the distinguished guests were less discerning. He explained its significance to Harman, who gaped his horror.

'So Stoakes aimed to murder the cream of the English navy? But that would have been catastrophic for the war! And if you are right about that, then you are also right about him planning to sail off to a new life elsewhere – he would have had no choice, not after a crime of that magnitude.'

'If you look around, there is nothing of Olivia's here.

I think he intended to leave her behind, to face the consequences of his actions alone.'

'What a rogue!' cried Harman. 'Thank God for the Hercules' Pillars Alley brothel and the Duke's penchant for acrobats and jugglers!' He turned as Boatswain Knapp appeared in the doorway. 'Yes? What is it?'

'The engineers just found out why she went down, sir,' said Knapp, his face dark with anger. 'So I came to tell you: her keel was hacked through with axes.'

'No!' breathed Harman, flabbergasted anew. 'So the rumours about sabotage were right? Who would have thought it?'

'It would have made a tremendous racket,' Knapp went on bitterly, 'so I cannot imagine why the boys never heard.'

'Because they were incapacitated with poison.' Chaloner stared thoughtfully at the decanter in his hand. 'But not deliberately. I suspect they stole some of this when they heard that Stoakes' banquet was cancelled. They probably thought he would not miss a bit, and they would not have minded its garlicky flavour. They were dead or dying when the saboteur came with his axe.'

'Yet this still does not make sense,' said Harman, as he led the way back to the pier. 'You have shown that Stoakes invited us sea-officers here for the express purpose of killing us. And that the crew stole his wine and died for it. But who sank *Assurance*? Not Stoakes – not if he planned to steal her and sail her away with all his favourite belongings.'

'He was sent a coded message,' mused Chaloner, 'in which he was informed that *Assurance* had been sunk with no questions asked. He denied knowing about the letter, despite the fact that it was hidden under his bed. Clearly, he did not wield the axe himself, or he would not have needed to be told about *Assurance*'s fate.'

'I wonder if Olivia guessed what was going on and was killed for it,' said Harman. 'She was clever – much more so than him.'

'It seems likely,' said Chaloner.

Chaloner was glad to leave the reeking ship. He stepped on to the quay, where a keen wind scythed. He glanced down at the river and saw the water was almost at a standstill; it would not be long until it began to turn. Scull and his son were already busy with lines and ropes, although he thought neither appeared to be particularly competent. Still, Margate was not far, and the river was fairly placid that day. They should make the rendezvous with *African Sun* safely.

Lester had returned from the Navy Office, and was standing nearby with Cox, both leaning over the pier to assess the water with expert eyes.

'There!' said Lester, stabbing his finger. 'The ebb begins. Tom, get the documents from the traitor while I distract everyone.'

'How will you do that?' asked Chaloner uneasily, hoping he did not intend to push another clerk into the water, as someone would smell a rat for certain.

'By discussing what happened to *Assurance*,' replied Lester. 'People will want to hear the opinions of three naval men, so we shall start speculating the moment you reach the dogger.'

'Do not speculate about Stoakes,' Chaloner warned Harman, unwilling for their discoveries to be brayed across half of London. 'It will warn him that—'

'Just go,' ordered Harman testily. 'We have wasted

enough time on this spy, and my duties now lie with *Royal Charles* in Deptford. Are you ready? Good. We shall start as soon as you are in position.'

Full of disquiet, Chaloner walked to the dogger. The moment he reached her, Lester began to speak in a stentorian bellow that caused all heads to turn towards him. It was out of character, and Chaloner suspected it would not be long before someone guessed he was doing it for a reason.

'Heemskerch,' Chaloner called softly. 'It is time to give me what you promised.'

There was a moment when he thought he might have to jump down and take the documents by force, but then Heemskerch's head poked through the hatch. The Dutchman shoved a package at Scull, and ducked back inside again without a word. Scull tossed the bundle up to Chaloner, and told him to untie the mooring ropes.

Chaloner obliged, then turned his attention to the parcel, wanting to make sure that Heemskerch had kept his side of the bargain before it was too late to do anything about it. He ripped off the outer wrappings and scanned the papers within. They comprised a dozen letters from Grand Pensionary de Witt to Ambassador van Goch, and an equal number of missives in code.

'Wait!' he hissed urgently. 'We cannot decipher—'

'*A Few Sighs from Hell*,' came Heemskerch's muffled reply. 'By John Bunyan. I sent a copy to Williamson, and it contains the key. When he applies it, you will have all manner of vital intelligence. You will see.'

Chaloner hoped he was telling the truth, and that Williamson had not taken one look at what sounded to be a very deadly piece of prose and tossed it away. He watched *Vågen* ease away from the quay, slowly at first,

301

but then more quickly as the current caught her. Seeing the craft under way, Harman, Lester and Cox abandoned their discussion with suspicious abruptness, and came to stand next to him to watch her go.

The dogger turned her bow into the wind, at which point the sails began to flap in a way that even Chaloner knew was wrong. Scull and his son struggled to remedy the situation, and were so preoccupied that they did not seem to notice that they were drifting directly into the path of a lumbering coal barge. The barge crew hollered at them.

'Lord!' muttered Harman. 'They assured me that they could manage the thing.'

'Perhaps they should *row* to Margate,' said Chaloner acidly, as Scull appeared to realise they were in imminent danger, and began to howl a stream of conflicting commands at his boy. 'It might be safer.'

Vågen disappeared behind the barge and Chaloner listened for the rasping crunch that would tell him that the two vessels had collided. He saw the tip of the dogger's mast jolt slightly, and then she was past, emerging behind the barge unscathed, although her sails still flapped uselessly.

'Thank God they are not in the navy,' declared Lester. 'I would never allow—'

The rest of his sentence was lost as *Vågen* erupted in a ball of flames. Then a boom reverberated all down the river, and everyone cried out in alarm as the pier trembled under their feet. When the sound faded, all that remained of *Vågen* was a mat of floating wreckage, all of it in very small pieces.

Chapter 12

For several moments, Chaloner stood in stunned immobility on the pier. He stared at the spot where the dogger had been, sure he could see body parts among the bobbing flotsam. He looked away, appalled. It was bad enough that Heemskerch should die after being promised safe passage, but Scull and his son had done nothing to deserve such a fate.

Lester, Harman and Cox were at his side, although none seemed particularly disturbed by what they saw. Was it because they had been in sea-battles, so exploding boats were nothing new to them? Yet surely they should feel something for the hapless watermen – guilt for hiring them, or sorrow for two people they had known? Or had they *expected* the dogger to blow up, and it was revenge for Vågen? Chaloner heartily wished he had never involved them.

'Who else did you tell about Heemskerch?' he demanded tersely.

'No one.' Lester sounded offended that Chaloner should ask. 'You requested discretion.'

'Besides,' put in Cox sourly, 'that bastard was responsible for the most humiliating naval defeat in living memory. We do not *want* anyone else to know that we played a role in organising his escape. Our colleagues would never forgive us.'

'You told Scull and his boy,' Chaloner pointed out. 'And the owner of the boat you aimed to use before the hyrricano smashed her. Not to mention the master of *African Sun*.'

'We did no such thing,' objected Harman indignantly. 'What do you take us for? Fools? They were informed that Heemskerch was a wealthy foreign prince running away from a despotic uncle. They have no idea of his real identity.'

But it would have been easy to guess it, thought Chaloner in disgust, given that the story they had invented was far too outlandish to be true. Moreover, Lester had written everything down in a letter. Had it been intercepted? The seal had appeared to be intact, but Chaloner could open missives with no one any the wiser and so could many others.

'I should not have embroiled you in this insalubrious affair,' Lester told his friends apologetically. 'It was unfair of me to ask for your help.'

'Nonsense,' said Cox, clapping him reassuringly on the shoulder. 'Besides, it is over now. We can go back to being sailors, and leave the sordid business of espionage to those who enjoy it.'

He gave Chaloner a glance that was none too complimentary.

'Sordid indeed,' agreed Lester. 'And three people dead. I cannot grieve for Heemskerch, but Scull and his boy . . .'

'They knew it was dangerous,' shrugged Harman dispassionately. 'It is why they demanded so much money.

They were greedy, and I would not have used them if there had been another choice. It was unfortunate that the hyrricano came when it did, thus depriving us of options. But what is done is done, and we cannot change it.'

While they talked, Chaloner surveyed the wreckage again, thoughts tumbling as he tried to work out what had happened. Was Beuningen responsible? The diplomat had been hunting Heemskerch, and was certainly clever enough to guess what Lester and his friends aimed to do.

He glanced behind him, at the spectators crowding around to gawk at the bobbing mat of flotsam. His eyes narrowed suddenly. Was that Beuningen near the back? He began to weave towards him, but by the time he reached the spot, the Dutchman was nowhere to be seen. Had he imagined it? Regardless, he decided to visit Bedford House later, and see what van Goch's staff had to say about the blast. He walked back to Lester, Harman and Cox, supposing he had better make his farewells before going to report the sorry news to Thurloe.

'There you are,' growled Harman, regarding him coolly. 'We thought you had skulked away without a word of thanks, which would have been churlish. You cannot—'

'We were just saying that you had better deliver those documents to Williamson at once,' interrupted Cox, clearly used to preventing his captain from making remarks he might later regret. 'We did not go to all this trouble just for you to lose them.'

'I will not lose them,' said Chaloner between gritted teeth, itching to point out that *he* was not the incompetent one here.

'But do not waste your time investigating what

happened to the traitor,' ordered Harman. 'You have far more pressing matters to concern you. Namely asking Stoakes why he aimed to murder all the navy's senior officers and finding out who took an axe to *Assurance*.'

'Heemskerch was a traitor,' acknowledged Chaloner. 'But Scull and his son were not, and they deserve—'

'They were not honourable men either,' Harman cut in harshly. 'They almost certainly stole that dogger from some poor fisherman, and then they demanded an exorbitant fee for their services. They were rogues and "deserve" nothing from us.'

'Besides, you cannot avenge every Londoner who suffers an untimely end,' put in Lester more kindly. 'Like the old woman whose death upset you so. You will drive yourself mad.'

'If you must hunt murderers, then look for the robbers who killed Merrett,' suggested Cox. 'He was a *good* man, who shared his pay with *Royal Charles*'s crew. *He* is the one who deserves vengeance, not the venal trio on *Vågen*.'

'Now there is a thought,' pounced Chaloner. 'Perhaps Heemskerch was not the target at all – perhaps *you* were. There have been several attempts on your lives of late, so maybe someone hoped it would be *you* sailing down the river towards Margate on the dogger you hired.'

'What an absurd notion!' scoffed Cox. 'Those attackers were after our purses, which they would never get if we were blown to pieces. Of course we were not the target.'

'You always claim robbery as a motive for these assaults, but how do you *know*?' pressed Chaloner. 'Why do thieves consistently pick on you when there must be easier prey available?'

'Who knows what goes through the minds of criminals?' shrugged Cox, beginning to be irked with him.

'They are not rational beings. I know this for a fact, because half our crew hails from prisons.'

'So what will you do first, Tom?' asked Lester amiably, although Chaloner would have been quite happy to quiz Cox and Harman further about the assaults they had suffered.

'Take the papers to Williamson,' he replied shortly, 'given that Cox seems to think I might mislay them otherwise. What about you?'

'Cox and I will leave for Deptford as soon as we can hire horses,' sniffed Harman. 'I cannot wait to be at sea again, away from the slippery affairs of landsmen.'

'I wish *Swiftsure* was ready,' sighed Lester. 'Because I should like to feel the roll of waves beneath my feet, too. But she is not, so I shall stay here and help Tom instead. Anything for King and country.'

The explosion had attracted much attention, and people gathered to stare at *Vågen*'s wreckage not just on the Savoy Wharf, but from the nearby piers and the buildings overlooking the river, too. As he eased through them, Lester at his heels, Chaloner heard the start of many false rumours – the blast was the work of Catholics, the Dutch, fermenting vegetables, or fanatics. One tale even held the Court responsible, to attract attention away from the bawdy play that was being prepared in the Banqueting House.

'There are the Thompsons,' murmured Lester, pointing. 'Maybe they saw someone putting gunpowder on *Vågen*. I know for a fact that they were here for at least part of the night, because they watched *Assurance* being weighed.'

'We did notice a dogger arrive at about two o'clock

307

this morning,' said Maurice, when Chaloner approached and put the question. 'We thought it was odd that Scull – a waterman – should have charge of a sailboat, but we were not curious enough to go and quiz him about it. Now I wish we had.'

'Well, I am glad we did not,' averred George. 'Or it might have exploded while we were chatting to him, depriving Robert of more teeth, me of a second leg, and you of . . . well, not another eyebrow, as you have none left. Your moustache, perhaps.'

'I understand the dogger collided with a coal barge shortly before she blew up,' bellowed Robert. 'So what happened is obvious: the resulting jolt caused some deadly cargo to ignite and . . .' He raised his hands to indicate a blast.

'I disagree,' countered George. 'I think Catholic priests were aboard, so God made her explode because He does not like those. He told me so Himself, when I was in the Covent Garden church with the Earl of Clarendon the other day.'

'Told you how?' asked Chaloner warily.

'I was gazing at the Popish altar screen that Clarendon has seen fit to renovate, when a bird flew through the open door and left a deposit on my favourite hat. The meaning of the incident is perfectly clear to me now.'

'Is it indeed?' murmured Chaloner, thinking it was no surprise that London was always in turmoil when people interpreted the most mundane of happenings to suit their own purposes.

'What about *Assurance*'s guns?' asked Lester, once George had finished explaining the 'obvious' link between bird droppings and Catholic-inspired artwork. 'You must have noticed *something* to help us find them. You were here for several hours. I saw you.'

'Then the same applies to you,' retorted George. 'Did *you* spot anyone trundling cannons away surreptitiously? No? They how can you expect us to?'

'Wishful thinking,' sighed Lester. 'It is vitally important to recover them, because while we may not know *who* took the things, we definitely know *why* – rebellion.' He lowered his voice for the last word, as if even speaking it aloud might bring it about.

'Really?' asked Maurice, alarmed. 'Are you sure? Because there is no point in me spending a fortune to repair the Floating Coffee House if London is going to be blasted to smithereens. What evidence do you have to suggest that an uprising is in the offing?'

'How can you even ask such a question, when the very air we breathe reeks of treachery and insurrection?' demanded Lester, growing frustrated.

The brothers exchanged bemused glances.

'Does it?' asked George. 'I cannot say I have noticed.'

'Well, it does,' stated Lester. 'So I recommend you hold off the renovations until after the Fast. We should know where we stand by then.'

'I saw a cart,' hollered Robert suddenly. 'It was very heavily laden, and rumbled up Ivie Lane to the Strand, where it turned right. As this was about an hour after that dogger arrived, I assumed the craft had just offloaded its cargo. But with hindsight, now I wonder . . .'

'Then I saw it, too!' exclaimed George. 'Lord! You mean it was full of stolen cannon?'

Chaloner looked to where the remaining guns stood, thinking it would have been simplicity itself to filch some. The front row had been illuminated by lamps, but the back ones had been in darkness, while everyone had been intent on watching *Assurance* rising from the riverbed – the perfect diversion.

Although Chaloner knew he should deliver Heemskerch's letters to Westminster at once, not to mention reporting Heemskerch's death to Thurloe, he lingered at the quay for two reasons. First, because it would be impossible to trace some of the explosion's eye-witnesses once he left; and second, because he predicted that Williamson would come to the pier anyway – investigating an explosion in a city on the verge of serious civil unrest was something no Spymaster worth his salt would delegate to an underling.

Meanwhile, he and Lester learned what they could – the captain by begging answers of anyone who would talk to him and Chaloner by eavesdropping. Neither approach yielded answers, and when their paths crossed half an hour later, neither had anything new to report to the other.

'There is Brouncker,' said Lester. 'Shall we see if he noticed anything?'

'No, no and no,' snapped Brouncker in reply to Lester's desperate barrage of questions. 'I was *not* here when *Assurance* was raised; I do *not* know who blew up the fishing boat; and I have *not* seen Stoakes since he was in White Hall on Thursday morning.'

'So why are you here then?' demanded Lester, nettled by the curt response. 'To gawp?'

'To look for Harman and Cox. I have a message to give them from the Duke, and someone told me they would be here. Have you seen them?'

'You are too late,' replied Lester with gleeful spite. He

was not usually vindictive, and Chaloner saw he had taken a dislike to Brouncker. 'They will be on their way to Deptford by now. *Royal Charles* is ready at last, and they aim to sail in a few days.'

'Her refit is complete?' asked Brouncker, smiling suddenly. 'That is good news!'

'Not for you,' retorted Lester. 'Because you will not be aboard when she goes. They told me last night that you will never be invited to set foot on her again.'

Brouncker shrugged his indifference, although indignation flashed in his eyes. 'I have better things to do anyway. I am leaving London tomorrow myself, so I am far too busy for idle jaunts.'

'To go where?' asked Lester archly. 'Somewhere with Abigail before your brother reclaims her? I heard at the Navy Office that he is due back from Portsmouth today, and he will certainly want to know why you have poached his mistress.'

'Just to Chelsey,' replied Brouncker stiffly. 'Alone. On a personal errand for the Duke.'

'What personal errand?' demanded Lester, while Chaloner listened in silence, all admiration for his friend's brazen persistence.

'A *private* one,' replied Brouncker archly. 'He told me in White Hall just now that it requires the utmost discretion, so I cannot indulge your prurient curiosity, I am afraid.'

'It will be to do with procuring prostitutes,' predicted Lester disapprovingly, watching Brouncker strut away. 'His master is bored with the current batch, so that fellow is going to recruit new ones. Is there no end to the profligacy of this regime?'

'There will be if you holler that sort of thing in

crowded places,' remarked Chaloner drily. 'You will achieve in moments what Urban and his helpmeets have been trying to do for the last two weeks.'

'Would that be so terrible?' asked Lester, although he did lower his voice. 'To spend money on sailors' pay, rather than on sending courtiers to Chelsey in search of whores?'

Chaloner thought it wiser not to reply.

Shortly afterwards, Williamson arrived, Swaddell gliding at his heels like an oil slick. Within moments, the crowd began to melt away, either to return to their daily business or to find some other vantage point – the supercilious Spymaster and his deadly assassin were not company most people were eager to keep. The exceptions were the Thompson brothers, who hailed the pair cheerfully.

'I shall leave Williamson and his creature to you, Tom,' muttered Lester, edging away. 'It is time to move the hunt for answers about *Vågen* and *Assurance* to the nearby taverns. We shall reconvene in an hour, to compare notes about all we have learned and deduced.'

'We will cover more ground separately,' said Chaloner, deciding in that instant to work alone until his investigations were complete. He would not meet Lester in an hour, and nor would they 'compare notes' – it would be safer for everyone that way. Moreover, he needed to see Thurloe safely out of the city, and he did not want company while he did it.

Lester nodded reluctant agreement. 'Then unless one of us solves these crimes in the interim I shall see you at the Fleece at seven o'clock tomorrow morning.'

'The Fleece is closed,' said Chaloner briskly. 'And this business grows more deadly by the day. Perhaps you should go to Deptford with Harman and Cox—'

312

'I am not a coward, to run away at the first sign of a storm,' objected Lester indignantly. 'So tell me where you want to meet.'

'There is no need,' insisted Chaloner. 'If you learn anything new, just send me a message.'

Lester winced. 'I have a bad feeling that the last time I wrote you a letter, it was intercepted.'

Chaloner frowned. 'What are you—'

'What other explanation is there?' blurted Lester, a stricken expression suffusing his bluff features. 'Harman, Cox and I told no one else about the arrangements for Heemskerch, and I am sure you did not, so there is only one solution left – that someone read the letter I sent outlining our arrangements. I see now that I should have taken it to your house myself.'

'You mean you gave it to someone else to deliver?' Chaloner was stunned to learn that Lester had entrusted such a sensitive communication to a third party. 'Who? One of your sailors?'

'Some fellow who was keen to earn a penny. He did not look like the kind of man who would open it, but spies are sly, so perhaps I should have been more careful . . .'

'Perhaps you should,' agreed Chaloner, struggling to conceal his disgust – not at Lester, but at himself, for assuming that his friend would know how to take basic precautions. 'But what is done is done, so let us say no more about it.'

'Good.' Lester's sheepishness lifted, and he grinned, his cheerful self once more. 'We shall meet at the New Exchange tomorrow morning then. Seven o'clock. Do not be late.'

But the letter incident served to reinforce further still

313

Chaloner's conviction that he would fare better alone. 'There is no need for you to—' he began.

'It is the least I can do. I am not sorry Heemskerch is dead, but I *am* sorry he perished on the dogger that I organised. Therefore, we shall work together to bring the culprits to justice.'

He strode away purposefully before Chaloner could beg him to keep his distance.

When Lester had gone, Chaloner headed for Williamson, who stood staring moodily at the river. The tide had carried most of the wreckage away, although a few fragments had washed up on the shore below. The Thompsons had just taken their leave, and Swaddell was glaring at their retreating backs. Robert seemed to sense it, because he rubbed his nape, as if it burned. Had he glanced around, he would have seen one of the most malignant scowls ever produced, and Chaloner hoped the assassin would never look at *him* like that.

'You have them?' blurted Williamson, as Chaloner pulled the documents from his coat. 'Thank God! I assumed Heemskerch was killed before he could hand them over.'

'A few minutes later and he would have been,' said Chaloner, watching the Spymaster leaf through them. 'He told me that the cipher key you will need is in a religious pamphlet he sent you. I hope he was telling the truth.'

'*A Few Sighs from Hell?*' asked Williamson in surprise. 'I assumed he was being ironic, so I put it aside to tear up as bedding for my hawk-moths, but it is easily retrieved. What of these letters in Dutch? Do they contain anything vital? I assume you have read them.'

314

'A glance,' confessed Chaloner, unimpressed that the Spymaster had not examined more closely something passed to him by a valued spy. 'They appear to be routine correspondence between de Witt and van Goch, but hopefully the key will prove otherwise.'

'I shall apply it and see,' said Williamson, slipping the bundle into his pocket. 'So what happened here? Did the Dutch kill Heemskerch? Or was it someone angry over Vågen?'

'I have been trying to find out, but no one is talking. Officially, only four people knew he was to be a passenger on that dogger – me and three sea-officers.'

Chaloner was not about to remind him of Thurloe's involvement.

Williamson's eyes widened in alarm. 'I hope you do not intend to accuse *them* of murder. We need such men for the war.'

'The killer may have learned about the plan from an intercepted letter,' Chaloner went on. 'Or he could have seen through the story these officers invented to explain why a dogger was needed – a silly tale of rich foreign princes and bullying uncles. Scull and his son may have repeated it, and its absurdity reached the wrong ears.'

'God save us from amateurs!' spat Williamson. 'But I cannot spare anyone to investigate the matter. All my resources are needed to learn what manner of trouble will erupt at Tuesday's Fast – trouble that I am now informed may involve four stolen cannon.'

Chaloner glanced at him. The combined strain of war and rebellion was taking a heavy toll on a man who prided himself on his cool detachment. Williamson was pale and there were dark rings under his eyes, although he still struggled to be elegantly aloof.

'What have *you* found out about the guns, Tom?' asked Swaddell hopefully.

'Just that they were taken by people who aim to use them,' replied Chaloner, and explained his theory regarding the ammunition.

Williamson blanched even further. 'At who or what will they be fired?'

'The government,' said Swaddell promptly, before Chaloner could speculate. 'Because of their selfish and irresponsible behaviour during the plague. Or because of their shabby antics over sailors' wages. Or because of the cost of the King's debaucheries. Or because—'

'All right, there is no need to belabour the point,' interrupted Williamson irritably. 'What else can you tell us about the theft, Chaloner? Did the rogues leave clues?'

Chaloner went to the guns, now guarded by the Spymaster's men, and examined the spot where the missing ones had stood. Tracks in the mud showed where they had been wheeled away, while hoofmarks and foot-prints revealed how.

'There were at least six men,' he explained. 'They pushed the cannon to the lane, where they were hoisted on to a wagon – a large one, with an integral winch, drawn by four horses.'

'So?' demanded Williamson crossly. 'How does knowing these details help us?'

'It reveals that the culprits are resourceful – they knew where to borrow or steal such a vehicle. Or, more likely, where to hire it, which means they have money. And it suggests meticulous organisation and a lot of audacity. Of course, it was no secret that *Assurance* was to be weighed this morning, so they have had plenty of time to plan.'

'And anyone with a modicum of intelligence knows that

316

ordnance always comes off first whenever a vessel is weighed,' put in Swaddell. 'They must have waited until all the guns were up, then casually wheeled four away when everyone was watching the engineers tackle the ship. Of course, they and Heemskerch's killers are one and the same.'

Chaloner frowned. 'What makes you think so?'

'It cannot be coincidence that the dogger was blown up just after a lot of gunpowder was stacked nearby. It is not easy to come by – you cannot just purchase it from your local grocer. Moreover, it is unlikely that two separate sets of criminals were at work here last night.'

Chaloner was thoughtful. 'So the thieves began to plan their crime when the Navy Board announced that *Assurance* would be weighed. Naturally, they would watch the pier like hawks the whole time . . .'

'And what would they see?' continued Swaddell. 'A dogger sailed by a man who usually rows, who likely went to a tavern and bragged that he was going to earn a fortune by ferrying a foreign prince downriver. In other words, the theft was premeditated, but Heemskerch's murder was an unlooked-for bonus.'

'It would have been easy to smuggle a keg of *Assurance*'s powder on the dogger,' said Chaloner. 'Especially if Scull did visit a tavern, and so left her unattended. Then a fuse was set, timed to ignite once *Vågen* was under way. It would not need a genius to predict when that would be, as most river traffic is dictated by the tides.'

'It makes sense to me,' said Williamson wearily. 'The only question is why? *Why* would gun-stealing rebels kill a spy who had already told us everything he knows?'

He patted the documents in his pocket to emphasise the point.

'Perhaps the dogger exploded later than intended,'

suggested Swaddell. 'Maybe she was meant to go up while she was still at the pier, killing Heemskerch, destroying his letters and helpmeets, and demolishing the wharf in the process, thus concealing the fact that four guns are missing.'

'Lord!' breathed Williamson, appalled. 'But how could they be sure the powder was be good? It has been in the river for days. Would it not be soaking wet?'

'Watertight barrels,' explained Chaloner. 'Which means it will ignite on Tuesday, too.'

Williamson grimaced, but then became businesslike. 'I shall work on decoding these documents, while you find the guns and the men who stole them.'

'Both of us?' asked Swaddell.

'Of course both of you,' snapped Williamson. 'You must visit every informant you have and bring me answers as soon as possible. Well? What are you waiting for?'

Chaloner strode away purposefully, aiming to give Williamson the impression that he had dozens of informants eager to shower him with details about the stolen cannon. But the moment he was out of sight, he turned east. It was time to report to Thurloe.

He took more care than usual to ensure he was not followed, and arrived at Lincoln's Inn half an hour later. As he crossed Dial Court, he thought of all that had happened in the eight or nine hours since he had sneaked Heemskerch away that morning. Now the Dutchman was dead, his intelligence was in the hands of the government, the navy knew that *Assurance* had been sabotaged, and dedicated insurgents had possession of four cannon.

Thurloe was ready to leave. He wore a thick travelling cloak, and his carriage was waiting by the gate, loaded with chests. He had hired six burly soldiers to go with him – men who had performed such a service before, and whom he knew he could trust.

'I assume you heard what happened?' said Chaloner grimly.

'To Heemskerch, yes, but not his documents. Did you manage to get them to Williamson? Yes? Good! So who killed our Dutch friend? One of your three sea-officers?'

'Perhaps. Or one of them let something slip by mistake – their covert skills are dismal. It is even possible that Scull put two and two together and sold the answer to one of Heemskerch's enemies. God knows, he had enough of them.'

'It is rare that a spy is hated by everyone,' mused Thurloe. 'Usually one side considers him a boon. But Heemskerch achieved a level of antipathy that I have never seen before.'

'Swaddell thinks that whoever killed him also took the guns.'

Thurloe was thoughtful. 'He is probably right, given that both crimes occurred in the same place within hours of each other. Incidentally, I found this while I was eliminating all traces of my guest from the attic.'

He handed Chaloner a folded piece of paper. It was a message addressed to Heemskerch:

The Physitian who tendes youre ague is in the paye of One who Means you Harme. Drink no more of his medicine as hee has been Told to Kill you with hayste, but Levinge no Trayce of Foule Murther. And Putt not youre Fayth in the Governement's Spyes, as you will be Betrayed.

From A Friende.

'It explains why Heemskerch insisted on staying with you,' said Chaloner, putting it in his pocket. 'He knew the accusation against Quartermain was true, so assumed this 'Friende' was right about Williamson and his people as well. Was he? *Would* they have betrayed him?'

Thurloe looked troubled. 'A few weeks ago, I would have said the allegation was just the usual sowing of distrust among rival spies – the sender aiming to turn Heemskerch against Williamson and deprive him of a valuable asset. But there have been incidents involving the Westminster office . . .'

'What kind of incidents?'

'Leaks – serious ones. The most recent concerns a report by Sir William Brouncker, who returned from Portsmouth today with a full account of our fleet. A copy is already in Dutch hands, which is an impressive feat of espionage by any standard. De Witt will know our naval strengths and weaknesses before most of our own admirals.'

Chaloner was appalled, but not surprised. 'Williamson pays his clerks a pittance and he is not someone who inspires respect. It is inevitable that some will sell his secrets.'

'I do not believe his clerks are the problem. I have a feeling the rot goes higher.'

'How high?' asked Chaloner uneasily. 'A member of ruling elite in White Hall?'

'That would be my guess.'

'I assume Williamson is aware of your concerns. What is he doing about them?'

'He has initiated an internal review, and all I hope is that he is equal to ending the problem discreetly. There can be no public accusations – if it emerges that a courtier or a senior minister is betraying us to the Dutch, Londoners will overthrow the government for certain.'

Chaloner grimaced. 'So we lost *our* spy in the Dutch nest, but de Witt still has his in ours – and will continue to have him until Williamson rousts him out?'

'*If* he rousts him out,' said Thurloe unhappily. 'I can tell you from experience that it will not be easy. The culprit will not only be shielded by his rank, but will have all manner of cunning safeguards in place to protect himself.'

'Should I go to Bedford House and try to steal the navy's report back again?'

'It is too late; copies have already been made and dispatched towards enemy hands.' Thurloe sighed. 'Are you *sure* the blame for Heemskerch's death lies with your captains' ill-conceived escape plan?'

'Not really. Why? Do you have another solution?'

'Beuningen – he is clever and determined, and I am fairly sure he knows that Heemskerch was hiding with me, which is why I am prepared to honour my promise to you and travel to Oxfordshire today. Of course, I would much rather stay and help you prevent—'

'You have done enough already,' interrupted Chaloner. 'You must go, as we agreed.'

'Very well. But I shall leave you with two pieces of advice. First, you could do worse than begin your enquiries into the explosion with Beuningen. Not tonight, though – give him a few hours to think he has bested us, which may encourage him to lower his guard. Of course, it will be dangerous to ask the sort of question that might produce useful answers, so take your friend Swaddell with you.'

'Swaddell is *not* my friend,' said Chaloner firmly.

'But he wants to be, and you should not offend such a lethal man by shunning him: it would be a serious mistake. And yet there are other, even more, deadly and unfathomable forces at work in this business, which leads me to my second piece of advice.'

'Which is?'

'Trust no one, no matter how loyal or honest they appear. Smile and be amiable, but rely only on yourself.'

Chaloner did not need to be told.

Chapter 13

As Thurloe was loath to leave Lincoln's Inn in daylight, Chaloner waited with him until dusk, glad when his coach finally clattered away. As soon as he had gone, Chaloner went to Stoakes' mansion on Long Acre, but was not surprised to find no one at home – the captain would have to be insane to linger once *Assurance* was weighed, thus exposing his plot to poison the navy's most senior commanders. As no one had seen Stoakes since Thursday, Chaloner could only assume he had made his escape then, cunningly leaving everyone to assume he was drowning his sorrows in a tavern. He considered breaking in, but what was the point? It was the man he wanted, not another opportunity to search the house.

He spent the rest of the evening in the taverns near the Savoy Wharf, hoping to learn something about the explosion or the stolen guns, but conceded defeat at ten o'clock, when most patrons were too drunk to answer questions. He went home, where he fell into an exhausted sleep, although not for long – he was up and dressed by five, his mind too full of his enquiries to let him lie around in bed.

It was Sunday, and he was acutely aware that time was running out. In forty-eight hours, the country was expected to mourn the death of the old King, but most Londoners would almost certainly respond by showing they were not sorry at all. Even if Urban's Men performed no more provocative satires, people still itched to right the injustices heaped on them by a morally bankrupt Court. The King would arrive to find defiance in place of sorrow, which he was unlikely to ignore. And what were his asinine friends doing? Adding insult to injury by staging an obscene drama!

Chaloner left his temporary bedroom in Wiseman's parlour and walked to Long Acre, where the hairs he had placed on the handles of Stoakes' front and back doors were still in place – no one had been in or out since he had put them there the previous evening. He decided to ask Williamson to issue a port alert: Stoakes may have fled the city, but he might still be intercepted before he could slip out of the country.

Next, he went to Bedford House. It was far too early for visitors, but Chaloner did not care. After all, it was not as if bad manners would spark a diplomatic incident – not if relations between England and the United Provinces were already deemed irreparable.

The embassy had been pelted with rotten vegetables during the night, and its elegant façade was pasted in stinking slime. Worse, the front door bore signs of having suffered an assault by cudgels, while someone had been at the nearest window with an axe, slashing the shutter and shattering the glass. Iron bars on the inside had thwarted the would-be invaders, although it was only a matter of time before the culprits found another way in.

He hammered on the door with his fist, and while he

waited for someone to answer, he saw three familiar figures reeling past. It was the Thompson brothers. Maurice held a lamp, but not carefully enough for George, who was complaining bitterly about having stepped in something disgusting with his false foot.

'From a dog,' he cried in revulsion. 'Or a person. And you know how difficult *that* is to scour from wood. I shall be living with the reek for days. It is—'

'What are you doing out so late, Chaloner?' called Maurice cheerfully, cutting across the tirade. His eyebrows had rubbed off completely, and his face was flushed red from the amount of wine he had swallowed. 'Good night, was it?'

'Ours was,' bellowed Robert tipsily, before Chaloner could inform them that he was up early, not out late. 'We went to Hercules' Pillars Alley again, and had a *lovely* time.'

'We were not really in the mood the night before,' confided Maurice. 'Not after Olivia's funeral. But we popped in yesterday evening, to ask if Temperance had found Robert's best white teeth – he thinks he must have dropped them there – and she persuaded us to stay. What a place! Those ladies know how to amuse a man!'

'They do,' agreed George with a happy grin. 'They have only just let us out, and look at the state of my leg! They had the stocking off it before I could—'

'Have you seen Stoakes?' interrupted Chaloner, more interested in his enquiries than what Temperance's employees could do with a wooden limb.

'No,' bawled Robert with a scowl of disapproval. 'And we have decided to wash our hands of him. It was one thing to beg us to arrange Olivia's burial on his behalf, but another altogether to expect us to pay for it – and then not even bother to attend! He is no gentleman.'

'Now Olivia is dead, we can renounce our kinship with him,' slurred Maurice. 'It was her we liked, not her selfish sot of a husband. It is a pity her father forced her to marry him, because she deserved better.'

'She should have wed Joe,' hollered Robert, loudly enough to rattle windows. '*He* would have made her happy. It is a pity we did not know him before Stoakes came along.'

Personally, Chaloner thought Olivia had had a very narrow escape, even if it was into the arms of the unpal-atable Stoakes.

'I have some good news,' Maurice declared, when Chaloner made no reply. 'I have decided to reopen the Folly on Tuesday with a spectacle that will thrill all London. It is the day of the Fast, as you know, so we shall offer a lively alternative to all the doom and gloom.'

'Are you sure that is wise?' asked Chaloner, certain it was not. 'There is a lot of bad feeling over the wealthy organising frivolous entertainment when London is supposed to be mourning the old King. Moreover, Lester told me that the repairs he made to your hull are temporary, and can only be properly mended in dry-dock.'

'Nonsense,' argued Maurice with a careless wave of his hand. 'Navy men are too particular by half, which is why their shipyards are always full. Most of their boats are perfectly seaworthy, but the captains will accept nothing short of perfection.'

Chaloner was inclined to trust Lester's opinion more, and made a mental note to decline any invitations to the Floating Coffee House until he could be sure it was safe.

'Are you after a chat with the Dutch?' asked Maurice, suddenly noticing on which door Chaloner had been knocking . 'If so, you are out of luck, because they have gone. I saw them yesterday evening at about six o'clock, when I was hurrying home to reapply my eyebrows. Robert was with me. Tell him, Rob.'

'The Dutchmen jumped into coaches and raced away as if the devil was on their tail,' shouted Robert. 'And not a minute too soon, because a mob arrived shortly afterwards, and laid siege to the place.'

'I think one might have stayed behind, though,' Maurice went on. 'At least, he darted back inside and did not reappear. They called him "Bone Again", but when he shouted that he would rather fight Mongols, they left without him.'

Chaloner was unimpressed with van Goch: it was hardly charitable to abandon a deranged colleague in a hostile city.

At the back of Bedford House a few moments later, Chaloner scaled the wall for the second time in three days. He scrambled down the other side and made his way through a garden that still bore signs of the recent bad weather – trees torn up, branches blocking paths, and rotting leaves from the last autumn blown into great soggy piles.

He reached the house, which was in total darkness. All the window shutters were closed, although the back door was not only unlocked but ajar. He stepped inside cautiously, lit a lamp and saw evidence of a very hasty departure. Papers littered the floors, while several of the chests he had noticed on his previous visit had been opened and their more valuable items removed. Several hearths were piled high with ashes, where sensitive documents had been incinerated.

He searched the house quickly, which was no mean

task when every room was in chaos, with abandoned clothes, papers and books scattered in confused jumbles. Only Heemskerch's quarters were untouched – the Dutch had gone through those with a fine-tooth comb when the traitor had fled, so had seen no need to bother with them again.

Van Goch's suite was relatively neat, perhaps because he had had servants to help him pack, but Beuningen's looked as though it had been hit by a cannonball, and was by far the messiest in the house. Chaloner was momentarily daunted. But he was a professional, and years of experience meant he knew exactly where people concealed their secrets in the expectation that no one would ever find them. Despite his formidable reputation for cleverness, Beuningen was no different, and within half an hour, Chaloner had found a hollowed-out space behind a skirting board. It contained mostly letters in code, which Chaloner pocketed to study later, but one was in plain English. It was addressed to the diplomat, and read:

What you Seeke and What you Want is at the Savoye Wharfe, but you must Acte in the Deepe of the Night.

Chaloner stared thoughtfully at it. Did it refer to Heemskerch's escape, and the writer was advising Beuningen to make his move quickly? Or did it refer to the fact that a veritable arsenal had sat on the pier unguarded, because *Dragon*'s crew had elected to abandon their posts? Or was it both – the sender knew that Beuningen *sought* Heemskerch but *wanted* cannon? Either way, Chaloner needed to talk to the diplomat without delay.

He aimed for the back door, wracking his mind for

places where Beuningen might be, but stopped abruptly when he heard singing coming from a pantry. He drew a dagger and crept towards it. Beuningen was there, humming to himself as he brushed his ceremonial hat – a glorious affair with a large brim and feathers. Chaloner watched him just long enough to ensure he was unarmed, then entered.

'God in heaven!' blurted Beuningen, one hand to his chest to indicate that Chaloner had given him a serious fright. 'How did you get in? There are no servants to open the door.'

He had donned his courtly finery that day, and looked every inch a representative of his government. He was also calm, with no hint of the manic speech he had used the last time Chaloner had broken into Bedford House. Indeed, the spy might have been forgiven for thinking he had imagined the whole incident, were it not for Beuningen's bandaged wrist.

'It was open,' explained Chaloner. 'But why are *you* here? The rest of van Goch's entourage has fled. Wisely so, given the unfriendly mood of the city.'

'I shall follow in a day or two,' replied Beuningen, turning his attention back to his hat when he saw Chaloner meant him no harm. 'But there are a few loose ends to tie up before we abandon England entirely. Van Goch thinks we should leave them flapping, but *I* am not a man to shirk my responsibilities.'

'Do you mean loose ends like killing Heemskerch and stealing guns?'

Beuningen laughed, and Chaloner marvelled at the difference between the man who had tried to drain himself of unwanted blood, and the poised, self-confident envoy who was willing to risk his life to serve his country.

'I know nothing of stealing guns, and as for Heemskerch . . . well, suffice to say he had his just deserts. I did not blow him up, though. I would have preferred to take him alive.'

'How do *you* know Heemskerch was blown up?' pounced Chaloner. 'It is not common knowledge that he was on the exploding dogger.'

Beuningen smiled enigmatically. 'We have our informants, just as you have yours.'

'I saw you on the quay yesterday, watching what was happening.'

'Yes, I was there,' acknowledged Beuningen. 'Van Goch sent me when we learned that Heemskerch was one of the casualties. But all I did was look – as did half of London.'

'Do you remember Quartermain, the physician you denied knowing?' asked Chaloner. 'Well, I have a witness who will swear that you hired him to poison Heemskerch.'

It was untrue, but Beuningen was not to know it.

'Then your witness will perjure himself,' shrugged Beuningen, blowing a speck of dust from the hat. 'I have already told you: I did not wish Heemskerch dead – I wanted him to stand trial in The Hague, where his fate would serve as a warning to others who might consider taking the traitors' *gulden*.'

'Then who did kill him?' demanded Chaloner, not sure what to believe.

'Someone who blames him for Vågen, I suppose. Justifiably, as it happens. He knew it was a trap designed by de Witt to humiliate your navy, but he did not care. He just wanted to be paid. Did he tell you afterwards that all he did was provide information, and the responsibility for interpreting it was your government's?'

'I would not know,' fibbed Chaloner, not about to admit that he had spoken to Heemskerch himself.

'Well, ask your Spymaster: you will find I am right. Heemskerch was greedy and unprincipled. He knew we were closing in on him, and that his days of secret-selling were numbered, so he aimed to make as much money as he could before he was forced to abandon his lucrative but disgusting profession.'

'Was it Vågen that allowed you to name *him* as the traitor?' asked Chaloner curiously. 'The misinformation had two objectives – exposing the spy and inflicting an embarrassing defeat on the enemy?'

'We *hoped* it would let us catch him,' confessed Beuningen, 'but he was too clever for us. It pains me to admit it, but we only knew Heemskerch was the culprit once he had vanished. Personally, my money was on van Goch's secretary, a man I have never liked.'

'So which loose ends do you want to tie up today?' asked Chaloner, supposing Beuningen was telling the truth, although it was difficult to tell when he was in full diplomatic mode.

'Details pertaining to prisoner exchange, along with agreements relating to the return of seized property and establishing maritime exclusion zones. All may save lives, so it is my duty to ensure they are in place before I slink after my colleagues.'

'You do know you are in danger here, all alone?'

'It is the nature of the work, and I understood the risks when I accepted the post.'

'You were . . . unwell the last time I saw you. You cut yourself.'

Beuningen stared at his bandaged wrist. 'I did this in my sleep. God knows how. I am told a surgeon came, although I have no recollection of it – I dozed through the entire procedure. I had stayed up late the previous night, you see, reading about the travels of Marco Polo.'

Chaloner supposed that explained his peculiar obsession with Mongols. He showed him the letter he had taken from his room. 'How do you explain this?'

Beuningen raised one eyebrow. 'You searched my quarters, did you? Well, I suppose such liberties are inevitable now the guards have gone. However, all I can tell you is that the message was shoved under the front door late last night – hours after Heemskerch was killed. Now, is there anything else? I do not want to be late.'

'Late for what?'

'An appointment with the Duke of York about my loose ends. Will you escort me to White Hall? As you say, it is dangerous for me to go out alone, yet I cannot ignore a summons from the heir to the throne.'

Chaloner did accompany Beuningen to the palace, not because he felt any obligation to protect him, but to see if he was telling the truth about meeting the Duke. As no hackney carriage was willing to pick up fares outside the Dutch embassy, they walked, Beuningen talking eloquently and passionately all the way about his hopes for peace. Not for the first time, Chaloner thought it was a pity that van Goch, and not Beuningen, had been appointed ambassador.

As they passed the New Exchange a bulky figure emerged from the shadows and fell into step at their side. It was Lester. Chaloner had forgotten that the captain had suggested meeting there that morning, and cursed himself for it. It would be difficult to ditch him now – at least, not without hurting his feelings, which he had no wish to do.

'You are early, Tom,' said Lester brightly. 'Good! Time is running out. Where are we going first?'

'White Hall,' replied Beuningen amiably, although the question had not been directed at him. 'To meet the Duke of York.'

'No!' blurted Lester, so vehemently that Beuningen and Chaloner regarded him askance. 'He will be too busy with important navy business. We *cannot* disturb him!'

'Will he?' fished Beuningen nosily. 'What kind of navy business?'

'He will be carousing with his friends,' countered Chaloner quickly, in case Lester was aware of a military campaign in the planning, and inadvertently let something slip.

'Even more reason not to interrupt then,' averred Lester firmly. 'He will not like it.'

'But he told me to come at seven,' argued Beuningen. 'And I cannot offend him by failing to appear. Shall we hurry? He might take umbrage if I am late.'

He strode on before Lester could object further, and it was not long before they arrived. The palace thronged with people, just as it had done before the plague had sent its occupants scurrying for safety. The Banqueting House was busiest, with courtiers hurrying in and out as preparations continued apace for *Two Sisters*. Lester's mouth tightened in disapproval at the sight – and at the sounds of a noisy party emanating from Lady Castlemaine's apartments.

'Is that the rope-dancer from the Fleece?' he asked, stopping suddenly to stare up at her window. She had curtains, but rarely remembered to deploy them. 'What is he *doing*?'

'Best not look,' advised Chaloner, taking his arm and pulling him on. Lester was inclined to be prudish, and would be shocked by what Jacob Hall was up to with the Lady, once he had worked out which legs belonged to whom.

'We should not be here,' grumbled Lester unhappily. 'It is no place for decent men. Come away, Tom. I am sure this gentleman can find his own way now.'

Chaloner ignored him, and conducted Beuningen right to the Duke's quarters, a sumptuous range of rooms overlooking the river. He informed the doorman that Beuningen was there for a scheduled appointment, expecting the diplomat to 'remember' all of a sudden that he had been mistaken about the time or the day, which would prove him a liar. But the servant smiled politely and opened the door.

'He is expecting you, sir.'

Even then, Chaloner was not entirely convinced, and followed him inside, Lester at his heels. The Duke was not cavorting with whores or in conference with the Navy Board, but sitting in a chair by the fire. Minions scurried around him, removing his travel-stained coat and boots, and offering him refreshments. He regarded his visitors with haughty disdain.

'Have you seen Brouncker?' he demanded. 'I need him.'

'I am afraid not,' replied Beuningen, while Chaloner supposed the Duke had forgotten that his henchman had been sent to recruit new ladies of pleasure from Chelsey. 'But you look weary, Your Grace. Have you ridden far?'

'From Deptford, in the dark,' growled the Duke. 'I

334

have been living on *Royal Charles* for the past week, assessing whether she is finally ready to trounce your fleet. She is, so you might want to advise Grand Pensionary de Witt to surrender while he can.'

'All her guns are in working order?' probed Beuningen slyly.

The Duke laughed as he came to his feet. 'All eighty of them, so you can report that as well. Now let us see about these rules that you want to impose on us, although mercy to captives seems a perverse notion in the midst of war, if you ask me.'

He walked to the door, shoved Lester out through it and slammed it in his startled face – Chaloner had escaped the same insult only because he had backed away the moment he realised what was about to happen. It was needlessly offensive, especially to one of his own officers. Perhaps the King had been wise to save himself from the plague after all, thought Chaloner sourly, because his odious brother was clearly unfit to take his place on the throne.

'I have something to confess, Tom,' whispered Lester, as they walked across the Great Court a few minutes later. He was careful to keep looking straight ahead, so he would not be obliged to witness the revelries around him. 'But I did not want to say anything in front of that Dutchman.'

'Something about the guns?'

'About Heemskerch. Last night, I located the fellow who delivered my letter to your house – the one in which I outlined all our plans. The rogue *did* let someone else read it. He denied it at first, but relented when I told him that honesty was vital to national security.'

'And?' asked Chaloner, struggling not to show his

disgust that Lester should have entrusted such a sensitive missive to a man he did not know.

'He could not tell me the person's name, but he was able to describe him. How many people do you know who dress completely in black, other than a clean white falling band?'

'Swaddell?' blurted Chaloner, astonished. '*He* killed Heemskerch?'

'It makes sense to me. After all, once Heemskerch had passed his secret documents to you, he became worthless to the intelligence services.'

'I thought they would have more pressing matters to attend than dispatching spent spies.'

'Swaddell murders people for a living. Perhaps he could not help himself.'

Chaloner was unsettled. Had Swaddell intercepted his correspondence on other occasions, too, or was Lester's letter the first? Williamson had never trusted Chaloner, so may well have designated him a 'person of interest' to the intelligence services. Perhaps *that* was why Swaddell kept trying to make friends – to worm himself into his confidence and thus make the task of monitoring him easier.

'Shall we go to the Fleece and confront him about it?' asked Lester, when Chaloner made no reply. 'Demand an explanation?'

'He will not be at the Fleece. It is closed.'

Lester gave him a superior glance. 'It is *meant* to be closed, but it is still being used – I witnessed all manner of comings and goings last night. And Swaddell was in the shadows like a spectre, watching it all.'

Chaloner's thoughts tumbled in confusion. *Had* Swaddell killed Heemskerch? Since learning that Beuningen had been telling the truth about meeting the Duke, he had crossed the diplomat off his list of suspects. First, Beuningen had a good point about making a spy stand trial in the United Provinces, as it would indeed send a stronger message to other would-be traitors than explosions on distant rivers. And second, Beuningen was shrewd: he would be more likely to use Heemskerch to inflict more damage on England than arrange a brutal execution.

But Swaddell loved nothing more than state-sanctioned murder. Had he planted the explosives, either on his own or with Williamson's connivance? Or was it the work of the high-ranking traitor, who knew about Heemskerch's planned escape because Swaddell or Williamson had told him in all innocence? Regardless, Thurloe had been right to recommend trusting no one. Chaloner glanced at Lester. Including him.

'Why did you try to stop me from seeing the Duke, Sal?' he asked softly. 'What were you afraid that an encounter with him would reveal?'

Lester shot him a stricken glance. 'What nonsense is this?' he blustered unconvincingly.

'Is it something to do with the attacks on Merrett, Harman and Cox? You have learned that they were not random robberies, but something more sinister?'

Lester gaped at him. 'How did you guess . . .' He recovered himself quickly. 'No! No, you are quite wrong. There is nothing—'

'The assaults make no sense, because petty thieves do not persist with victims they fail to best the first time. And the culprits cannot be discontented sailors, as Harman, Cox and Merrett are popular. However, all three served on *Royal Charles*—'

'What of it?' demanded Lester, his voice rising in alarm. 'That means nothing.'

'—and *Royal Charles* is the Duke's flagship. Did something happen on her? Something involving him, which only Merrett, Harman and Cox know? What was it? An incident that occurred when they were last at sea? At the Battle of Lowestoft, perhaps?'

There was a moment when Chaloner thought Lester would continue to deny it, but the fight suddenly went out of him and he slumped wearily on the bench that surrounded the Great Court's central fountain. It was too cold for sitting around on stone seats, but Chaloner perched next to him anyway, patiently waiting for answers. Lester put his head in his hands, his expression anguished.

'I promised never to tell,' he said in a low, guilt-wracked voice. 'Late last night, when we finally worked out what it all meant. I gave my word.'

'Then you must break it,' said Chaloner firmly. 'Because I will find out anyway. Or would you rather I asked the Duke?'

'*No!*' gulped Lester. 'He must *never* know of your suspicions. It is more than our lives are worth. Well, more than yours anyway – as our commanding officer, he can silence Harman, Cox and me by sending us away to sea for years on end. But he has no such control over you, and that will make him uneasy . . .'

'Just tell me, Sal,' said Chaloner tiredly. 'Before any more harm is done.'

There was another lengthy silence as Lester agonised over what to do, but eventually he spoke again. 'Do you remember after Lowestoft, when we were waiting for the order to pursue the Dutch fleet and finish it once and for all?'

'Yes – the order came, but within the hour, it was retracted.'

Lester nodded. 'We were told to shorten sail, which allowed the enemy to escape . . .'

'It was a massive tactical blunder. True, we were able to rescue far more drowning sailors, but not nearly as many as will die now that the war is set to continue. We were appalled that the Duke should have made such a stupid decision.'

'And there is the nub of the matter, Tom,' said Lester wretchedly. 'The Duke did *not* make the decision. He had gone to his cabin to rest, and not long afterwards, one of his courtiers appeared with a verbal message to call off the chase. Harman did not believe it, so sent the man back down below to check. The fellow returned a few moments later with a "confirmation".'

'Are you saying this courtier *fabricated* the command to shorten sail?'

Lester nodded. 'Because he is a coward who could not face another battle. Now he is ashamed and frightened, and wants to make sure that no one ever learns that *he* was responsible for preventing us from ending the war that day. Two other men were on deck when he passed Harman this false order . . .'

'Cox and Merrett,' predicted Chaloner.

'Exactly! The recent attacks on them were not robbers after purses, but this courtier aiming to kill them to ensure their silence. Not that he needed to worry – the Duke swore them to secrecy, and they are men of their word. They would not even tell *me* his name, despite the fact that they regard him as the lowest of scum.'

'Oh, but I think we can guess it,' said Chaloner heavily. 'A man who boasts about his valour that day, but who is privately haunted by the experience, especially of his courtly cronies being decapitated by the single chain-shot.'

'But they *all* boast about their valour,' cried Lester, exasperated. 'Some even claim to have *laughed* at the heads bouncing across the deck. I have no idea who the culprit might be.'

'Brouncker,' said Chaloner softly. 'Cox said he was seasick while *Royal Charles* was still in port, so I doubt he was trusted with any important duties during the battle. Ergo, all he did was stand there. How can that be construed as courageous?'

Lester reflected. 'It might be him, I suppose. Merrett did once let slip that he had to give Brouncker calming potions to stop him from shaking – before, during *and* after the fighting.'

Chaloner was bemused. 'So why does the Duke protect Brouncker? He must know that everyone thinks the blunder is *his* fault. Why take the blame for something he did not do?'

'Because Brouncker claims he acted on behalf of the Duchess – that *she* made him promise to keep her husband safe. And when some admiral quipped that the following day's fight would be bloodier than the one we had just finished . . . well, the rogue maintains that his vow to her obliged him to prevent another skirmish at all costs.'

Chaloner raised his eyebrows. 'And the Duke believes him?'

'I am not sure. However, the King later informed the Court that *he* was glad there had been no second battle, and congratulated the Duke on his "wise" decision to withdraw. So the Duke's hands are now tied – if he accuses Brouncker of giving false orders in his name, he will expose the King as an idiot and his wife as a meddler in naval affairs.'

'I see,' said Chaloner, feeling it might be worth it, if it meant Brouncker was held to account for his cowardly actions.

'And *that* is why I tried to keep you away from the Duke today,' Lester went on. 'Lest you inadvertently said something to make him think the story was out of its box.'

'How could I?' asked Chaloner. 'I had no idea about any of it until the last few minutes.'

'But *I* did not know that,' said Lester miserably. 'You are not very good at sharing information, so I had no idea what you might have learned or guessed during the course of your enquiries. I was afraid for you . . .'

Still bemused by the tale, Chaloner turned the discussion back to the Duke. 'Why does he believe this nonsense about an oath to the Duchess? Surely he can see that Brouncker's real motive for countermanding the original order was to spare himself further horrors? Moreover, he must have guessed that it is Brouncker who has been attacking his sea-officers – and thus Brouncker who murdered Merrett.'

'I am afraid the Duke is not the sharpest sword in the armoury,' sighed Lester, 'and Brouncker is a convincing dissembler. I seriously doubt he has put two and two together.'

Chaloner considered the assaults on the three *Royal Charles* officers. 'Merrett was easy to dispatch, but Brouncker bit off more than he could chew with Harman and Cox. They know how to fight. And so do I.'

Lester frowned. 'He attacked you as well?'

'Twice – once in the Fleece and once in the Banqueting House – because I told him I was investigating "a navy matter". Wracked by guilt and fear, he instantly assumed that meant Lowestoft. Once he learned it was only *Assurance*, he left me alone. Of course, the danger is over for him now – he aims to flee London today.'

'Only to Chelsey. On a personal errand for the Duke, or so he said yesterday.'

'Another lie. We just heard from his own lips that the Duke has been in Deptford all week, so how could he have spoken to Brouncker in White Hall yesterday?'

Lester was silent yet again, mulling over what they had reasoned. 'He murdered your old lady, you know,' he said eventually. 'Widow Fisher.'

Chaloner blinked. 'What?'

'Merrett was killed on the Piazza, and I thought it remarkable at the time that no one saw what had happened. Now I suspect that someone did. Both the crone and Merrett were dispatched by blows to the head, and Brouncker lives nearby. He probably met Merrett there by chance, and seized the opportunity to be rid of him. But his crime was observed . . .'

Chaloner closed his eyes. Lester was right, of course, and Widow Fisher had told him herself that nothing happened on the Piazza without her seeing. Merrett's friends had ascertained that he had been killed within an hour after leaving the Folly, which meant that Brouncker must have happened across the physician near his Covent Garden home, and seized the opportunity to rid himself of one of the men who knew his unsavoury secret while he could. But his crime was witnessed, so Widow Fisher had had to go, too.

'His own false tongue will hang him,' he said softly. 'He claimed he was working with the Duke in White Hall on the day she was murdered, but we now know that the Duke has been in Deptford all week. He doubtless expected that poor Widow Fisher would be forgotten by the time the Duke came home, so no one would bother to check his alibi.'

'So we know he killed Merrett and Widow Fisher, but we cannot accuse him of it,' said Lester bitterly. 'If we try, he will threaten to reveal the truth about Lowestoft, after which the King, the Duke and his Duchess will crush us like worms. He is untouchable.'

Chaloner considered the dilemma briefly, then gave a grim smile. 'Come with me.'

A few moments later, in the nearest coffee house, Chaloner borrowed writing materials, and dashed off a note to Sir William Brouncker. He told Lester to deliver it at once.

'But he is in Portsmouth,' objected Lester. 'Inspecting the fleet.'

'He came home last night,' replied Chaloner, recalling Thurloe's disgust that the Navy Commissioner's top-secret report was already in Dutch hands. 'So hand him the letter, make sure he reads it, and then this is what I want you to do.'

Lester listened carefully before hurrying away. Chaloner waited in the coffee house for exactly an hour, then went to Brouncker's house, where he let himself in through the back door, taking care to leave it unlocked behind him. The servants were out – at their Sunday devotions, probably – and the place was so quiet that he thought he might be mistaken about how his quarry would spend his last few hours in the city. Then he heard voices upstairs. He crept towards them, although Brouncker and Abigail were too engrossed in each other to pay heed to any sounds he might have made as he approached their bedchamber.

'Are you sure?' Abigail was asking, as she divested herself of the last of her clothes and slipped between the covers. 'I should not like him to catch us.'

'He will not come here today,' said Brouncker confidently, leaping in beside her, clad only in stockings and an earring. 'There has been a security breach, so he is at the Navy Office, trying to contain the damage. And I hate to think of you all alone in this great big house. It would be a terrible waste.'

Then Chaloner heard the sound he had been waiting for – Lester's low whistle on the stairs to say he had arrived. It was time to make his move. Abigail was giggling at something her lover had said, but the laughter froze in her throat when Chaloner flung open the door and stalked in. She opened her mouth to scream.

'No shrieking, please,' he ordered curtly, resting his hand on the hilt of his sword to show he meant business. 'Just lie there quietly while I talk to your beau.'

'Not my beau,' she gulped, while Chaloner wondered why the Brouncker brothers were so enamoured of her; her face was slathered so thickly in powders that it was a different colour from the rest of her body, and made it look as though she was wearing someone else's head. 'Harry and I are just discussing the party we shall organise to welcome Sir William home.'

'And it is necessary for you both to be naked for this conversation?' asked Chaloner archly.

Abigail opened her mouth to answer, but could think of no convincing explanation, so she turned to Brouncker instead.

'You will have to kill him,' she said matter-of-factly. 'William will toss me out without a penny if he learns what we have been doing. And *you* cannot afford to lose his good opinion – you are his heir, due to get both his title and his wealth when he dies.'

'Violence will not be necessary,' gulped Brouncker, looking Chaloner up and down and deciding that trying to dispatch him would be much too risky for his person. 'I will explain everything to William when I reach . . . Chelsey.'

'You mean France,' said Chaloner coldly. 'Because you are a vicious murderer and you aim to escape justice by fleeing there.'

Abigail's response to this claim was to pull a blanket over her head and lie still, as if she expected them to forget she was there once they could no longer see her. She remained that way for the rest of the discussion, which made Chaloner wonder about her sanity, not to mention her intelligence.

'I suppose you mean Merrett,' said Brouncker without a flicker of remorse. 'Did the crone tell you? I thought I had silenced her before she could gossip. But if she blabbed to you about Merrett, why have you waited nearly a week before accusing me? To assess what I will pay for your discretion? Well, go on then: name your price.'

'I want nothing from you,' said Chaloner in distaste.

Brouncker's mystified frown turned into a sneer of understanding. 'You think you will arrest me! What a fool you are! The lives I took are of no consequence, and a high-ranking courtier like me will never face charges for them.'

'What about the lives of two sea-officers?' asked Chaloner, tempted to run him through there and then, and inform him that *his* life was of no consequence either. 'Do you think the Duke will look the other way when he learns about your assaults on Harman and Cox?'

Brouncker laughed mockingly. 'You will never prove it was me and my bravos who tried to make an end of them. We were careful to leave no evidence.'

'You attacked me, too.' Chaloner stepped forward threateningly as Brouncker reached for his breeches with the clear intention of getting dressed and walking away. 'Twice.'

Brouncker withdrew his hand hastily and shot Chaloner a sour look. 'That trick with the water in the Fleece was low – my hirelings hated being drenched. And when the Spymaster's assassin joined the skirmish in the Banqueting House . . . well, it was fortunate that I learned I could leave you be, because they would not have fought you a third time.'

'And all because you are a coward,' said Chaloner in disgust. 'You were terrified at Lowestoft, and decided you wanted no more of it. You gave the order to abandon the chase, and if that were not craven enough, you claimed the Duchess told you to do it.'

For the first time, a flicker of unease crossed the arrogant face. 'It will be Harman's word against mine, and I am the Duke's favourite. No one will believe Harman, especially once I put it about that calling off the chase was *his* idea.'

'Cox and Merrett heard you, too.'

'But everyone knows that Cox is Harman's creature, so *his* testimony will hold no weight. And Merrett is dead.'

'But they are not the only ones who know the truth, are they? What about the blackmailer – the one who sent you that letter? How much more will you pay him for his silence?'

Brouncker scowled. 'He had better hope I never discover his identity, because if I do, I will brain *him* with a stone. But do not stand there all bristling menace, Chaloner. We both know you cannot touch me. I did the right thing.'

'Killing navy physicians and helpless old women is right?'

'I mean Lowestoft. It was my duty to protect the Duke's life, which could only be achieved by preventing another sea-battle.'

'And is it your duty to steal my woman, too?' came a low, angry voice from the door. 'Not content with bringing our family into disrepute with your lies, treachery, cowardice and corruption, you must also steal my Abigail?'

Brouncker's jaw dropped in horror when he realised that his brother had been listening to the entire discussion from the corridor outside. From under the blanket came an agitated whimper. Then Brouncker tried to smile.

'You cannot believe anything you just heard, William,' he blustered. 'Chaloner threatened me with violence unless I repeated what he told me to say. Look – he has a sword.'

William stalked across the room and yanked away the blanket, causing Abigail to screech her alarm. 'That does not explain why you are stark naked with my mistress. In *my* bed.'

'Be reasonable, William,' said Brouncker testily, as if it was his brother who was at fault. 'Abigail was lonely, so I was doing you a favour by stepping in and—'

He broke off when William tried to slap him. Rashly, he smirked when the swipe missed, which was a serious mistake, as William's next blow was a punch that landed squarely on his mouth. He howled as teeth shattered, and tried to duck away, but the next clout caught him

347

on the ear and the one after that on the nose, which began to bleed copiously. He rolled into a ball and begged for mercy as blow after blow rained down on him.

'Should we drag him off?' asked Lester, entering in William's wake, and wincing when a soggy crunch suggested Brouncker's nose had been broken. 'He might kill him otherwise.'

'Let *them* do it,' said Chaloner, nodding to the navy clerks, who he had told Lester to bring as witnesses. They were staring in astonishment, stunned by the sight of their staid and respectable master trouncing his dissolute younger brother. 'Our business here is finished.'

Brouncker was still shrieking as they walked down the stairs and into the street, although Abigail was silent. Chaloner supposed she had crept back under the blanket, in the hope that William would overlook her transgressions if she was not immediately visible.

'Is that it then?' asked Lester, once they were outside. 'We let Sir William decide what to do with the rogue? You know the affair will be hushed up – that he will never answer for Merrett and Widow Fisher, or for his faint-heartedness at Lowestoft?'

'I disagree. The truth will come out now that Sir William, the blackmailer, Harman, Cox, you, those clerks *and* I know what he did. Not today, perhaps, but soon. And then Brouncker will pay. Until then, smashed teeth, a broken nose and black eyes will have to suffice.'

'I would have run him through, personally,' said Lester, uncharacteristically vicious. 'But I concede your solution has its merits. For a start, Harman and Cox will be glad that others now know what Brouncker did – keeping such a filthy secret was not easy for decent men. Of course, they will be livid when they learn he will never answer for Merrett.'

'He will not answer *yet*,' corrected Chaloner. 'But it will all come out eventually. Will you ride to Deptford and tell Harman and Cox? They will want to know.'

'I shall write,' determined Lester, 'which will leave me free to help you solve your other mysteries. I shall always be grateful to you for exposing Merrett's killer, and one good turn deserves another.'

'That is not necessary,' said Chaloner hastily. 'I am—'

'No arguments,' interrupted Lester, and gave a wolfish grin. 'I have made up my mind.'

Chapter 14

As it was Sunday, Chaloner was obliged to put in an appearance at his parish church, lest his absence was noted and he was branded a nonconformist. The matins bell was chiming across the Piazza for the noonday service, so he made his way there, Lester at his heels.

'Lord, it feels uneasy in here,' breathed Lester, stopping inside the door and looking around uncomfortably. 'Can you sense the anger in the air?'

Chaloner could, because it was an almost tangible thing, and oozed from the congregation like a miasma. The Earl and his elegant retinue had claimed the best places at the front, which was causing considerable resentment among those who had been ousted to make room for them. In revenge, they contrived to scratch the polish on the new pews, and leaned against the freshly painted walls in the hope of leaving greasy stains. Vergers monitored the doors, and those who had deliberately tracked through the muddiest parts of the churchyard were denied access until their boots were clean. Trouble was brewing there, too.

Despite the locals' attempts at petty sabotage, the

church looked splendid. The gilt on the walls and ceiling glittered in the pale winter sunshine, windows sparkled with clean glass, and the altarpiece had been restored to its original blaze of colour. The wooden gallery had been repaired, too, although more arguments broke out when the regulars were denied access to it. The choir had been practising, and was singing an anthem by Tallis. Impressed, Chaloner stopped to listen, realising that he had not played his viol in days.

At that moment, the Earl decided it was time for the service to start. He flicked imperious fingers at the vicar, who signalled the choir to stop singing. They ignored him, obliging him to shout across them. They faltered indignantly, and the congregation exchanged even more outraged glances. The vicar cleared his throat and began to bellow an official edict from the government – the one that would be read aloud at every church in the country that day.

'I announce the proclamation before Almighty God for observation of the thirtieth day of January,' he intoned, 'as a day of Fast and Humiliation in the most devout and solemn manner, according to the late Act of Parliament for that purpose.'

The Earl nodded approvingly as the vicar droned on, but he was the only one. His people were uneasy among a horde that did not want them there, while the parishioners responded to the announcement with hisses, muttering and the occasional catcall.

When he saw a clerk glance at him and write his name in a ledger, Chaloner was free to go. It was easy to escape unnoticed, as the vergers were struggling to evict a defiant apprentice, who had scrawled 'Long live Adam Urban' on the wall with a piece of charcoal.

'What first?' asked Lester, once they were outside. 'A dish of coffee to sharpen our wits? The Folly is closed, so I suppose you will suggest the Rainbow.'

The disapproving tone of his voice revealed what he thought of that establishment and its opinionated patrons.

'We do not have time. I need to speak to Swaddell now, to see if he has any information to share – and to quiz him about interfering with my correspondence.'

'Very well. And when we have finished with him, we will tackle Stoakes about the poisoned wine. Harman told me what he tried to do. It was despicable, and the sooner he is charged with his crime, the better.'

'And that is another thing I need to discuss with Swaddell,' muttered Chaloner. 'Getting a watch put on all ports to make sure Stoakes does not leave the country. Assuming he has not already done it, of course.'

'I recommend we break into his house later, to see if he left any hint as to where he might have gone. Where will Swaddell be at this time of day? Not in a church, I warrant – he does not strike me as a godly man.'

'You suggested the Fleece earlier,' said Chaloner. 'We are almost on its doorstep, so let us try there first.'

He hurried across the Piazza, although there was a delay while Lester bought some quince-cake from a passing baker. He pressed some on Chaloner, on the grounds that no man should meet an assassin on an empty stomach. He was right, but Chaloner chafed at the delay anyway, and to take his mind off his rising agitation, he told Lester all he had learned about Heemskerch, Stoakes, Olivia, *Assurance* and the brewing rebellion. He also confided Thurloe's suspicion that a high-ranking courtier or member of government was responsible for several damaging leaks from Williamson's office. He did it against his better judgement, and not because he expected Lester to have any valuable insights, but because if the captain was going to help, it was safer to have him fully informed than ignorant.

'Then you already have answers to most of your enquiries,' remarked Lester, once Chaloner had finished. 'You can prove that Stoakes tried to poison our admirals, and that *Assurance* was scuppered the same night. He probably murdered his wife, too, for finding out and trying to stop him.'

'But Stoakes did not sink his ship – not with all his precious belongings aboard. I still have no idea who did that.'

'You have solved Heemskerch's murder and the theft of the guns, too,' Lester went on. 'It was the Dutch, and the letter you found in the embassy proves it.'

'Not if Beuningen is telling the truth – that it was delivered *after* the dogger exploded. And I do not see the Dutch stealing artillery anyway.'

'I do, Tom. It means four fewer cannon to be deployed against their fellow countrymen.'

'If so, they took a massive risk for very little gain.'

'That leaves the bubbling rebellion,' said Lester, apparently of the opinion that Chaloner was splitting hairs. 'How can we stop it?'

'I do not think we can. Unless we can persuade Urban to help. People will listen to him.'

'They will. Unfortunately, he *wants* London in flames.'

'Does he? Or will he settle for reform? Perhaps we can encourage him to request peaceful negotiations instead – to present his grievances to the government, and see what can be done to remedy them. White Hall will not listen, of course, but it will avert a crisis now.'

Lester regarded him doubtfully. 'I doubt he will agree. Why would he, when he has the upper hand?'

'Because a rebellion will hurt the very people he is trying to protect. Hopefully, he is intelligent enough to know it.'

'If you say so, but how will we find him? He is in hiding.'

'He will not be hiding today, not when there are dozens of ready-made audiences sitting in churches. He will—'

'Cheapside!' exclaimed Lester. 'He and his friends like to perform there. I will go and look for him, while you deal with Swaddell. A fair division of labour. Well, fair for me, at least. I confess I do not envy *you* your task.'

Chaloner arrived at the Fleece to find Lester was right – it was indeed the centre of 'all manner of comings and goings'. However, it was not being used as a tavern or a meeting place for rebels, but as a tenement for London's poor, who had moved into the empty building en masse. In charge of them was Amey, Clifton's serving lass. As usual, her hair was scraped under a turban-like scarf, exposing the terrible scars on her neck. Chaloner could only suppose she considered them badges of honour – her proof that she had survived the disease.

'You cannot oust us,' she informed Chaloner challengingly, as at least twenty men came to stand in a threatening semicircle at her back. '*We* live here now. Clifton's creditors can whine all they like, but we are not leaving. It is our home.'

'I do not want to oust you,' said Chaloner, although he suspected the creditors would, and there would be nothing Amey could do to stop them. 'I want to speak to Adam Urban. Have you seen him today?'

'He will be out telling folk that they do not have to cower while the King tramples them like rubbish,' she declared loftily. 'That they are entitled to a home, food and warmth just as much as the wastrels at Court.'

'More,' growled one of her helpmeets. 'Because *we* work. We cut logs and dig coal, we spin cloth and make plates, and we grow and sell vegetables. *We* are useful. But what do they do? Squander good money on performing some filthy play for the King to cackle at. Well, we have had enough. Things are going to change.'

There was a growl of agreement from the others, after which someone else stepped forward to say his piece. Then Amey spoke again, and Chaloner took the opportunity to slip away, aware that the mood of the listeners was growing darker and more defiant with every word that was brayed. Was this what Urban's Men intended? To light the fires of discontent at key places and then leave them to burn unchecked? Regardless, Chaloner was sure that if trouble did erupt, Amey and her friends would be in the thick of it.

He went to the doorway that Swaddell liked to use for spying, and was pleased to find him there. The assassin was disgruntled, and immediately launched into a diatribe about Robert Thompson, who had visited Williamson that morning, and squandered precious time in a long conversation about moths.

'I do not understand why Joe likes him,' he muttered venomously. 'Even if he does know a lot about the Grey Scalloped Bar. But never mind him. Have you learned any more about the trouble that is set to happen at the Fast?'

'No,' replied Chaloner, acutely aware that anything he told the assassin might end up relayed to the wrong ears. 'But it is possible that Stoakes is involved, and he appears to have fled the city. Will you alert the ports to be on the lookout for him?'

It was an abridged version of the truth, but it served its purpose.

'Consider it done. Did he kill his wife as well? They were an ill-matched couple, and she would not have stood by mutely if she suspected him of something unsavoury.'

'It is possible.' Chaloner looked the assassin right in his black, beady eyes. 'Why did you open the letter that Lester sent me on Friday?'

He expected a vehement denial, but Swaddell had the grace to blush.

'Because I thought it might be urgent, and you had not been home all day,' he replied. 'If it had been important, I would have hastened to find you at once and hand it over. But it was not – it was just about your plans to get Heemskerch out of our lives.'

'Right,' said Chaloner flatly. 'Now tell me why you really did it.'

Swaddell grimaced. 'There is no pulling the wool over your eyes, is there? Very well. I did it because we are desperate for answers and I hoped the message might contain some. It did not, so I sealed it up again in the hope that you would never know. How did you?'

'Did you tell anyone else what was in it?'

'Just Williamson . . . I mean Joe.' Swaddell knew exactly why the question had been put. 'But you cannot accuse *us* of killing Heemskerch. All we cared about were his documents. Once they were in our hands, it did not matter to us what happened to him.'

'Williamson was the only one you confided in? No one else?'

'Well, I mentioned it to the clerks who deal with expenses. I had to – I was putting in a claim for the sealing wax I used to close it back up again. However, I did not tell them what I had read. I repeat: the explosion cannot be laid at our door.'

With an unnerving sense that events were marching relentlessly forward while he raced around uselessly like a rat in a barrel, Chaloner spent the rest of the day in a frantic search for Urban's Men or anyone who might have witnessed the guns being stolen, explosives being planted on *Vågen*, or Stoakes' unsavoury antics. He came close to Urban several times, running to the place where he was said to be performing, only to learn that he had departed just minutes before.

'He and his friends are everywhere today,' beamed one satisfied customer, who then informed Chaloner that *she* would not attend a Fast on Tuesday, but would make her objections to the Court known by standing outside White Hall and spouting a few home truths.

'That would be dangerous,' warned Chaloner. 'The palace guards—'

'Will cower inside once they see how many of us have come to express our opinions,' interrupted the woman firmly. 'Mr Urban said so, which means it must be true.'

Chaloner continued his hunt with a rising sense of urgency. His stomach hurt, which he attributed to hunger, but the beef pastry he bought on Fleet Street made him feel worse. He considered stopping at the Rainbow for a restorative dish of coffee, but decided he did not have time. Besides, Farr's brew was unlikely to make him feel better, given that it made his heart pound when he was not gripped with agitation. He hurried on past it, his sense of impending doom inten-sifying when he heard a bellman call the hour – seven o'clock already, and he had virtually nothing to show for all his efforts that day.

'Tom!' called a familiar voice, and he turned to see Lester emerging from Rainbow. 'I knew I would catch you if I sat there long enough. Of course, I was starting to think I was going to be there all night, as well as all afternoon. Where have you been?'

'Racing all over the city,' replied Chaloner, unable to keep the bitter frustration from his voice. 'What about you? Did you manage to waylay Urban on Cheapside?'

'He had gone by the time I got there, although I did learn that he and his troupe have split into twos and threes, so as to perform to as many people as possible. They are winning friends hand over fist, while the King and his friends lose them – everyone is outraged that White Hall will stage a lewd play while the rest of us are expected to mourn the beheaded King.'

'Their own worst enemies,' agreed Chaloner, leaning against a wall and feeling his lame leg throb from fatigue. 'So you have nothing useful to report?'

'I do, actually – news about Stoakes. I ran into *Assurance*'s purser earlier. He met Stoakes on Thursday morning, and is convinced that he had no intention of going anywhere. He believes he is still here – at home, working his way through the contents of his wine cellar.'

'I think someone would have noticed if that were the case.'

'Why? His wife is dead, the cook-maid has left, the Thompsons have washed their hands of him, he has alienated his crew, and I doubt his White Hall cronies are the type to stick by a man in a crisis. The man is a sot, so it is entirely possible that he *is* at home in a stupor, too inebriated to answer the door.'

'Did you go to find out?'

'I thought we should do it together,' said Lester, then grimaced. 'Although, to be honest, I did try, but there was no answer to my knock, and I have no idea how to break into houses. I am no burglar, I am afraid.'

Chaloner suspected that even Stoakes would struggle to stay drunk and avoid all company for three days straight, but went with Lester to Long Acre anyway. He picked the lock on the back door, aware of Lester watching intently, presumably so as to know what to do the next time he wanted to invade someone else's home. Then he searched downstairs, while Lester took the upstairs. He had just finished in the kitchen and was about to check the parlour when Lester summoned him with an urgent shout.

'Under the bed,' he said tightly, as Chaloner entered the room at a run.

Chaloner dropped to all fours and saw a man lying flat on his back with his hands folded across his chest; blood had pooled in a dark halo around his head. He leaned forward, took a handful of coat, and hauled the body out.

'Stoakes!' exclaimed Lester. 'Battered to death by the looks of it. So the purser was right – Stoakes did not flee, but was here all the time. When did he die, Tom? Can you tell?'

'The blood is dry, which suggests it has been a while. Perhaps even since Thursday, which seems to be the last time anyone saw him.'

'So who did it? The same rogue who took an axe to *Assurance*? You did say that Stoakes would not have

359

scuppered her himself as long as all his belongings were aboard.'

Chaloner had no answers to give him.

Stoakes' house was soon a flurry of activity, as the murder of one of His Majesty's sea-captains was a matter of concern for any number of official bodies. Navy Commissioner Sir William Brouncker was among the first to arrive; his coat was splattered with blood and the knuckles on both hands were split. Then came bureaucrats from Trinity House, White Hall and Westminster. Such a hubbub attracted attention, and a crowd gathered in the street outside. Boatswain Knapp and Steward Fowler were among the curious onlookers, along with a dozen of their crewmates.

Given that Stoakes was implicated in so many suspicious matters, Chaloner expected Williamson to put in an appearance – or at least send Swaddell. Instead, one of his aides appeared, a sour-faced man named Edward Riggs, who stamped around barking unnecessary and self-important orders at a pair of harried clerks. Sir William objected to his noisy presence and the situation quickly degenerated into a mean-spirited struggle for jurisdiction.

Chaloner wanted to leave, but Riggs decreed that he and Lester were to remain in the house until he had taken their statements in person. Chaloner tried to explain that their time would be better spent elsewhere, to which Riggs responded by informing him that he had been in Stoakes' home illegally, and would be arrested for burglary unless he and Lester did as they were told. Thus they had no choice but to wait until he deigned to see them.

To take their minds off the wasted minutes, they conducted their own search of the house, although not with much hope of finding anything useful. Thus Chaloner was astonished when Lester made a discovery.

'It was inside the harpsichord,' the captain whispered, glancing around to make sure no one was watching before handing over a tightly rolled piece of paper. 'Between the strings.'

Chaloner unrolled it carefully. It was a receipt from Quartermain, acknowledging payment by Stoakes for twenty bottles of 'Fortifyed King's Golde for the Purpose of killing Ratts'. It was dated the day before Stoakes had expected to entertain the Duke and his senior officers aboard *Assurance*.

'Why would Stoakes keep such an incriminating item?' murmured Lester, shaking his head in mystification. 'I would have thrown it on the fire.'

Chaloner was about to shrug his own bemusement when he recalled Swaddell's insistence on recording every item of expenditure. Understanding came in a flash and he pointed at the enormous sum written at the bottom.

'Because Quartermain charged him a fortune, and I think he aimed to be reimbursed.'

Lester gaped his disbelief. 'You mean he was going to claim *expenses* for murdering the cream of the navy? Lord! Landsmen never cease to amaze me!'

'Which means he was not acting on his own,' Chaloner went on, 'but for someone who must have promised to pay him enough to begin a new life elsewhere.'

Lester took the receipt and stared at it. 'But why would Stoakes agree to such a despicable act? The loss of so many senior officers would have seriously damaged us at a time when we need every available man for the war.'

'Greed,' replied Chaloner. 'And we have three other examples of it with him: refusing to bear the cost of his crew's funerals; declining to pay his men's wages out of his own pocket, as you have done; and mourning his lost belongings more than his dead seamen. He was not motivated by grand principles or ideals, but the desire to win an easy fortune.'

'Without Olivia,' surmised Lester. 'He arranged for her to be abducted, perhaps in the hope of persuading her over to his point of view, and when she refused, he killed her. And then his paymaster bashed *his* brains out when he was no longer of any use.'

Chaloner disagreed. 'The mass poisoning was carefully planned, but Stoakes' murder was not – his wounds suggest that he was bludgeoned in a fit of rage. I suspect the encounter between him and his killer began innocently enough, but then he did or said something that resulted in an explosion of tempers.'

Lester nodded slowly. 'The damage to his head did suggest a couple of very wrathful blows, perhaps inflicted before the culprit really knew what he was doing . . .'

'*Assurance*'s crew is angry,' said Chaloner, glancing out of the window, where several of them could be seen outside, their faces illuminated by the bobbing torches.

'No!' said Lester firmly. 'Sailors know better than to attack their officers.'

'Stoakes treated them abominably,' Chaloner went on. 'He not only refused to help them get their back pay, but he failed to bury their shipmates – shipmates who were still in the charnel house on Thursday, when Stoakes was last seen alive. I imagine their friends came again to beg him to do the decent thing, but he was almost certainly drunk—'

'I refuse to listen to this,' interrupted Lester tightly. 'You are mistaken.'

'Then look at Fowler now.' Chaloner nodded to where the steward could be seen wringing his ham-sized hands in agitation. 'I sincerely doubt his distress can be attributed to grief. That is guilt you see before you.'

'It might be grief,' argued Lester stubbornly. 'You cannot be sure it is not.'

'On *Assurance* yesterday, Fowler virtually told me that Stoakes was dead. How would he know, unless he had had a hand in it? Moreover, hiding a body under a bed is hardly sensible. It smacks of panic, and now he is terrified because his crime is discovered. He does not even have the wits to know that the best course of action would be to make himself scarce.'

'He is not the cleverest of men,' acknowledged Lester. 'And he does have a short temper, but to brain his captain . . .'

'Then shall we go and see what he has to say for himself?'

'We cannot,' hedged Lester. 'Riggs ordered us to stay in the house.'

'He will not mind us stepping outside for a moment – not if we tell him we are following a lead for Stoakes' murder. Come. Or would you rather I did it alone?'

'No,' said Lester. 'Well, yes. But no.'

Lester dragged his feet as he and Chaloner approached the crew, and his unease intensified when they regarded him with such frightened resignation that their guilt was obvious.

'So it is true,' he said heavily. 'You *did* murder Stoakes.'

'Not intentionally, Captain Lester, sir,' replied Fowler

wretchedly, wringing his hands so hard that his knuckles cracked. 'It just happened.'

'What did you do? Come to discuss your dead shipmates again?'

Fowler nodded miserably. 'On Thursday, not long after his wife's body was brought home. We thought that if we visited him at a time when he was thinking about burying someone *he* loved, he might be more sympathetic to our feelings.'

'But he told us that all funerals are a waste of money,' put in Knapp. 'So I asked about our pay instead, and mentioned our children, crying for lack of food . . .'

'He told us to drown them,' said another man harshly, 'to put them out of their misery.'

'Then he laughed,' whispered Fowler, a stricken expression on his face. 'And he drew a pistol, saying he would shoot Knapp, to show what happened to crew who kept pestering him with stupid demands. So I hit him with my cudgel . . . I did not mean to kill him, sir! Before I knew it, he was lying on the floor and there was blood . . .'

'It is not fair,' said Knapp, tears of impotent rage starting in his eyes. 'He was an evil, selfish bastard who was on the verge of shooting me dead in cold blood. But now it is us who will hang, even though it was all his own fault.'

'Yet *he* would not have hanged for Knapp,' put in Fowler bitterly. 'Urban is right: there is one set of rules for the rich, and another for us. And we are always the losers.'

'No one will hang for Stoakes,' determined Lester, which was news to Chaloner. 'You will all go to Deptford and sign on with *Royal Charles*. Tell Harman I sent you.'

Knapp's eyes narrowed in suspicion. 'You are letting us off?'

'No,' said Lester sharply. 'You will pay for your crime, but not on the scaffold. You will do it by serving your country in her war against the Dutch. Well? Do not stand there gaping like halfwits! Go, before I change my mind.'

'Are you sure that was wise?' asked Chaloner, when the sailors had hurried away in a considerably lighter frame of mind. 'They may decide that Harman is not to their liking either, and then where will the navy be?'

'Harman can keep the likes of them in line,' said Lester impatiently. 'It is only courtiers like Stoakes and Brouncker who allow this sort of thing to happen. You agree with me, or you would have said something when I made my decision.'

'In front of a dozen belligerent seamen, who would have bludgeoned *me* if I had objected?' asked Chaloner archly. 'All I can say is that I hope you are right about them.'

'I am. Will you tell Riggs that the case is solved?'

'Only if you are willing to explain how.'

Lester considered. 'Then we shall leave him to ponder. You can invent some credible tale to hoodwink the Spymaster later.'

They went back inside, where Riggs indicated that he was now ready to take their sworn testimony. It took but a moment to relate the tale while his clerks wrote it down. When they had finished, Riggs indicated that Chaloner and Lester were of no further use to him by turning on his heel and stalking away without another word.

'Well, I am glad we wasted so much time hanging around for *that*,' said Lester irritably. 'In the navy, we have a name for men like him, but it is not one I shall use in polite company.'

'It was not a waste of time,' said Chaloner. 'We solved Stoakes' murder, and you are not the only one who uncovered a useful clue. I found these, caught in a fold of his coat.'

Lester recoiled in revulsion when he saw what Chaloner held. 'Are those *teeth*?'

'Robert's – his best white ones, which I saw him wearing in Hercules' Pillars Alley the evening after Olivia's funeral. As they were on *top* of the body, it means he lost them while he was looming over it. In other words, he has known for days that Stoakes lay here bludgeoned to death, but has not seen fit to mention it.'

'Why would he do that?'

'Why indeed? I suggest we go and find out.'

James Street was only around the corner, so Chaloner and Lester arrived there within moments. The brothers' home was in darkness, and while Lester knocked on the front door, quietly at first, but then with increasing urgency, Chaloner went to the back and smashed a window – time was too precious to waste in picking locks.

He climbed inside, but knew immediately that the house was abandoned. There was a cold, stale smell, and when he lit a candle, he saw the kitchen had been stripped bare. He ran along the corridor – now devoid of the exquisite artwork he had admired just the week before – to open the front door for Lester.

'Search the downstairs,' he ordered briskly. 'I will check the bedrooms.'

But there was nothing to find. The building had been emptied with impressive diligence, and had also been thoroughly cleaned – not so much as a scrap of paper or a dropped coin had been left behind. He hurried back to Lester, who was waiting in the hall. The captain had been doing some thinking.

'So the Thompsons are behind all this nastiness,' he surmised. '*They* persuaded Stoakes to murder all our leading seamen. It all makes perfect sense to me now.'

'Does it?' asked Chaloner, struggling to see how.

'Of course! All three brothers fought for Parliament during the wars, and they only *pretended* to become Royalists at the Restoration. Now they let their true colours show.'

Chaloner was not so sure. 'The government does not consider them radicals, or George would not hold a Court appointment and Williamson would not be friends with Robert.'

Lester was dismissive. 'Williamson would befriend anyone who smiles at him – he is a deeply lonely man – while George was granted his post because he has lots of money and the government wants some of it.'

'I hardly think—'

'Their money!' interrupted Lester, slapping his forehead in understanding. 'Of course! Stoakes would not have sold his soul cheaply, so only a very rich person could have made committing such a terrible crime worth his while.'

'True,' acknowledged Chaloner. 'But—'

'The only way to prove our suspicions is by putting these questions to our suspects directly,' determined Lester, all brisk business. 'So I suggest we visit the Folly at once.'

'It is closed.'

'Closed to customers, but not its owners. Maurice,

Robert and George are probably on board, safe in the knowledge that no one will think to look for them there.'

'You have.'

Lester ignored him, and began to stride towards the Savoy Wharf. Chaloner fell into step beside him. He did not expect for a moment that the Thompsons would be on the Folly, but there was no harm in checking. He had neglected to search Stoakes' house when it should have been clear that something was amiss, and he was not about to make the same mistake twice.

As they hurried through the dark streets, Chaloner thought London was oddly quiet. Was it because so many people had died in the plague? Because the survivors did not have the money to squander on noisy evenings out? Or because they were biding their time for the trouble that would strike the day after tomorrow?

He and Lester reached the Savoy pier, both reflecting on how different it was from the last time they had been there, when it had thronged with people after the weighing of *Assurance*. Now it was pitch black, silent and unsettling.

'The Folly has gone!' cried Lester, stopping abruptly and peering across the water. A ship happened to passing, blazing lights, so the coffee house's part of the river was briefly illuminated. 'They must have taken it to dry-dock for repairs.'

'Unlikely. Maurice told me this morning that it will reopen on Tuesday – for the Fast.'

'Not unless he wants to drown along with his patrons. Our jury-plug will keep it afloat for a day or two more, but after that . . .'

'Are you sure it will not last longer?' Chaloner recalled

the words Maurice had used about sea-officers and their ships. 'You are not being overly particular?'

Lester eyed him lugubriously. 'There is a great hole in its keel, Tom, so no, I am not. The wadding we used will lose its water-resistance, and the hold will flood. Assuming the plug does not pop out first, of course. Either way, disaster will quickly follow.'

Chaloner gazed across the dark waters. 'Are you sure that has not happened already? Maybe the Folly is sitting on the bottom of the river as we speak.'

'Our plug will last today and tomorrow, but after that the wadding will begin to fail for certain. If you say Maurice has not taken the barge for repairs, then the only other explanation is that he has sailed it downriver to the sea.'

'To escape?'

Lester nodded. 'It would not be my first choice of getaway vehicles, but after what happened to Heemskerch, perhaps they were leery of buying passage on anything else.'

'We have to find them,' said Chaloner urgently. 'Perhaps you are right, and they did hire Stoakes to poison the admirals. Regardless, we need to talk to them – to accuse them or eliminate them as suspects. Will you search for the Folly downriver, then come back and tell me where it is? It cannot have gone very far yet.'

'What will you be doing?'

'Continuing the hunt for the guns; looking for Urban's Men; trying to find out exactly what mischief is planned for the Fast. I will also speak to Williamson.'

Lester regarded him worriedly. 'Are you sure that is wise, given that his assassin has already confessed to opening your personal correspondence?'

369

'Williamson is Robert's friend – he may know where he has gone. I will also find out how often Robert visited his office, and if those visits coincided with certain leaks of information.'

Lester gaped at him. 'You mean the traitor who has been feeding our secrets to the Dutch is not some high-ranking courtier or member of government, but the Spymaster's new bosom crony, who helps himself to classified documents whenever he drops in for a chat?'

Chaloner shrugged. 'It is possible. Williamson does leave sensitive papers on his desk, because my report on the Dutch fleet was there.'

Lester shook his head slowly. 'I know I was the one who mooted Maurice, Robert and George as Stoakes' paymasters, yet all this is very difficult to believe. The brothers are wealthy, and have good lives here.'

'Why does anyone turn traitor? However, the note I found hidden in Stoakes' bed ties together the sinking of *Assurance*, Heemskerch's murder and the unrest fomented by Urban. All these, along with poisoning the admirals, do one thing: harm England. And a weakened England will be very good news for our enemies overseas.'

Lester blanched. 'You think all this is about facilitating a Dutch invasion?'

'Maybe not an invasion,' said Chaloner. 'But a defeat, forcing us to sue for peace on unfavourable terms.'

Determination filled Lester's face. 'I will find the Folly, Tom, never fear. And then those treacherous Thompsons will learn what happens to those who betray my country.'

Chapter 15

Chaloner was exhausted. He had gone directly to Westminster on leaving Lester, only to be told that neither Williamson nor Swaddell were there. He had then hurried to the Spymaster's fine mansion in Hatton Gardens, but the servant who answered the door did not know where his master might be, and only said that Williamson rarely slept in his own bed these days. Chaloner had spent the rest of the night in a frantic hunt for him, Swaddell, the guns, Urban's Men and the Thompson brothers. He found none of them.

He did learn, however, that many Londoners planned to make the King aware of their antipathy towards him when he arrived home on Tuesday. Opinions varied as to how best to do it. Some aimed to stand outside White Hall and bellow their grievances, which sounded innocuous enough, but Chaloner knew how quickly such demonstrations could turn violent. Others aimed to disrupt the various Fasts, either by making a racket outside the churches, or by menacing those who aimed to take part.

As Monday's dawn lit the eastern sky, Chaloner hurried

371

to the Rainbow, where he had agreed to meet Lester. The captain was waiting for him, so forbidding in his tense agitation that the regulars had given him a wide berth. As he listened to Lester's report, Chaloner gulped down a dish of Farr's powerful coffee and a stale venison pastry, hoping they would revive his flagging energies.

'Nothing,' spat Lester. 'I went all the way to Wapping, hammering on doors and storming into taverns, but no one admitted to seeing the Folly. Perhaps they are all part of it – *everyone* wants the Thompsons to set London aflame, to repay the King for abandoning them to the plague.'

'No,' said Chaloner tiredly. 'There would be at least one dissenter among so many, and if the barge had passed by – and it is distinctive and thus memorable – you would have been told. You say it will not have sunk, we know it has not gone downstream, so there is only one other possibility left: Maurice took it *up*river.'

'Impossible! It has no sails, so cannot move against the tide, and it is too heavy to tow far. But you are wrong to say that taking it upriver is the sole remaining option: there is another – namely that the Folly is still here, hidden in some abandoned quay – and the Thompsons with it, biding their time before launching their vile plot.'

'We do not know for certain that they are the culprits,' warned Chaloner. He struggled to force his tired mind to think. 'Perhaps Judd will help us. Where does he live?'

'Judd!' exclaimed Lester. 'Of course! The Folly is his livelihood, so of course he will be acquainted with Maurice's plans for it.'

He led the way at a rapid clip to the Liberty of the Savoy, an area where the forces of law and order dared not tread, and where thieves and cut-throats ruled.

Chaloner was acutely aware of unseen eyes watching them as they hurried through its dark and dirty alleys, and his unease intensified when he realised that they were running down one lane for the second time.

'We have been this way before. Are you lost?'

'No,' replied Lester unconvincingly. 'Just a little further.'

It was more than 'a little', and Chaloner was on the verge of suggesting they asked for directions when Lester stopped outside a dingy tenement. They were spared from entering its reeking interior because Judd was sitting on the doorstep outside, smoking his pipe. He was surrounded by his friends, all idle now the Folly was closed.

'We heard you got Fowler and his mates away, sir,' he said to Lester with a conspiratorial wink. 'We should have thought of that – sending them to sea, where they will be safe.'

'The Floating Coffee House,' said Lester shortly, not looking at Chaloner. 'Where is it?'

'At a dockyard near Chatham,' replied Judd. 'Mr Maurice says she will be there for three months, which is a hard blow for us. We cannot earn a living until she comes back.'

Chaloner watched them intently, thinking they did not seem unduly distressed by the notion. Why? Because they had enough tips put by to see them through? Or because they were lying?

'Did you see it leave?' he demanded. 'No one else did.'

'Then everyone else is blind,' shrugged Judd. 'We waved her off last night.'

'Were Maurice, Robert and George on board?'

Judd glanced at his cronies, all of whom wore suspiciously blank expressions. 'Maybe. It was dark, so we could not see very well. They did not sail her themselves, obviously. They are not qualified, and it will take a rare pilot to shoot the London Bridge in her.'

Chaloner was not even sure it was possible – the unwieldy barge would be a monster to manoeuvre through such narrow openings. 'Maurice told me that he would not repair it until after the Fast – lest London burned and it proved to be a waste of money.'

'That was probably before he took *me* over there,' replied Judd, who seemed to have an answer for everything. 'I told him the plug was failing earlier than expected, and he did not want to lose her, so he made some hasty arrangements with a shipwright.'

Chaloner would have asked more, but Lester nodded his thanks and began to walk back to the Strand. It was now fully light. Shops and businesses were open, and the streets were busy. There was a distinct atmosphere of anger and excitement, which boded ill for the following day.

'The King and his monkeys are about to reap what they have sown,' predicted Lester grimly. 'We have four cannon and three dangerous traitors ready to provide the spark that will see the monarchy topple once and for all. But what can we do to stop it?'

'You can go to Chatham, to see if Maurice really did take the Folly there. I will continue to ask questions here. Someone will have answers. It is just a case of being persistent.'

'But we *have* been persistent,' snapped Lester irritably. 'It is not working. Besides, I cannot leave you to thwart a rebellion alone – and you *are* alone, because who else is helping? Not Williamson and Swaddell, who are suddenly nowhere to be found. How do you know they are not involved in the mischief – that Williamson did not *give* Robert our country's secrets?'

'I hardly think—'

'He is greedy and ambitious, and Robert may have convinced him that he will fare better under a new regime.'

Chaloner shook his head stubbornly. 'Williamson is many things, but not a traitor.'

'Then prove it,' challenged Lester. 'Go to Westminster and if he has deigned to show up for work, demand to know everything about his dubious friendship with Robert.'

Chaloner doubted that approach would work, but agreed that another attempt to confer with the Spymaster was in order. Unfortunately, they arrived to learn that both Williamson and Swaddell were out, and the staff had no idea how to contact either. Chaloner was aware of Lester looking at him meaningfully.

'Their absence is a nuisance,' sighed Riggs. 'Because I need to ask their advice about the Stoakes case. I have no suspects, but the Navy Board still clamours for answers.'

'Welcome to the world of intelligencing,' muttered Chaloner.

Chaloner and Lester returned to the Savoy Wharf, where they asked questions of anyone willing to talk to them. More time ticked past, and Chaloner noted that there were a lot more people inside the taverns and coffee houses than outside, and that very little work was being done. The atmosphere seemed to grow darker and more deadly with every establishment they entered.

'How much longer must we persist with this futile

venture?' burst out Lester eventually. 'We have been at it for hours and learned nothing. The Thompsons are too clever for us. Perhaps we should just acknowledge it and concede defeat.'

'And sit back while London burns?' asked Chaloner archly. 'I do not think so!'

'Then at least let us stop for a pie. I could eat a horse.'

Suspecting they might get horse in their pies if they visited the Maypole, which was where Lester was heading, Chaloner made for the Golden Lion instead. They ate standing, taking the opportunity to quiz the landlord at the same time. Much to their surprise, the man was more forthcoming than anyone else had been.

'Urban's Men? Yes, Gimonde and the dwarf were here earlier, but I refused to let them perform their nasty little satire in my yard. I am a Royalist, and I want none of their incendiary nonsense on *my* property.'

'How long ago?' demanded Chaloner.

'Oh, ages – just after daybreak. I asked why they wanted to see our city in flames, and they had the audacity to claim that no Londoner's blood would be spilled in tomorrow's nonsense. That it will be a day of peace and rejoicing. Pah!'

'They said that?' pressed Chaloner. 'In those words?'

'Those exact words, yes. I told them there would be no rejoicing here, because we will be observing the Fast. Gimonde said I was entitled to do as I pleased, but the dwarf called me foul names. I tossed the little bugger out by the scruff of his neck.'

'"No Londoner's blood",' repeated Chaloner to Lester when they were outside again. 'The King is not a Londoner . . .'

'Shall we go to the Fleece again?' asked Lester tiredly.

'That is where all this started, and I have never been happy with its role in the affair.'

It was as good a suggestion as any, so Chaloner began to trot there, aware of every muscle burning with exhaustion and a dull ache between his eyes from lack of sleep. But how could he rest when some foul plot was in the making?

They reached Covent Garden, arriving at the same time as a deputation from Clarendon House, which had come to inspect the church for the last time before the Fast.

'The Earl!' exclaimed Chaloner with sudden hope. 'He will not want His Majesty to come to harm, so *he* can help us thwart whatever is in the offing.'

'I doubt his assistance will count for much,' grumbled Lester disparagingly. 'He is more interested in winning the King's favour than saving his life.'

Chaloner ran towards the church, but one of the Earl's sentries moved forward to prevent him from entering. The man toted a musket to show he meant business, but gave a sigh of relief when he recognised Chaloner.

'I thought you were another local, bent on mischief,' he said, which told Chaloner that all the hours spent trawling taverns had taken their toll on his appearance. 'You should have seen what they did here yesterday – tracked mud all over the floor, scrawled slogans on the walls, and left dirty marks wherever they could put their grubby fingers.'

Chaloner shoved past him and hurried to the Earl, who was informing the vicar that he needed to find a better wig if he expected to take part in the following day's ceremony. Lester hung back, close enough to hear, but not to join in.

'The King will be here,' the Earl was informing the cleric grandly. 'And he will not be impressed if you appear looking like a sheep. Everything must be perfect. *Everything*. Ah, Chaloner. Where is that trumpet? I assume you are here to hand it over, although you are cutting it rather fine.'

'Trouble is brewing all over the city, sir,' reported Chaloner urgently, 'and I fear the King will be in danger if he attends a Fast. Will you persuade him to stay in White Hall? Or better yet, remain at Hampton Court?'

'No,' replied the Earl shortly. 'I cannot.'

'Please, sir,' begged Chaloner. 'It is a—'

'I cannot,' repeated the Earl, and a pained expression filled his plump face. 'Which is not the same as *I will not*. I cannot, because he refuses to listen to me. He will come to London tomorrow, regardless of any advice I try to give.'

'Even if you tell him his life may be at risk?'

'He will not believe it. He thinks his subjects will be delighted to have him home, and refuses to heed the few of us who warn him that may not be the case. It is his sycophants' fault – they assure him that he is popular, because it is what he wants to hear.'

'But *you* know I am right, because you have also heard the rumbles of discontent.'

'What sane man has not? However, I can protect him if he comes here. I will flood Covent Garden with loyal palace guards. No mischief-maker will get anywhere near him.'

'Lord!' muttered Chaloner, hoping his employer had delegated such critical arrangements to someone efficient. If he had done it himself, His Majesty would be in trouble indeed. 'Are you sure he will come here? He has not changed his mind?'

'He gave me his word.' The Earl looked away. 'Yet I do fear he may snub me.'

'Then perhaps you should tell him that your Fast will not only be the best in the capital, but that it comes with added security.'

The Earl gave a short, humourless laugh. 'He would interpret that as a sly ruse on my part to ensure his presence. He knows how important tomorrow is to me – to my standing at Court – and will assume it is desperation speaking.'

'Better his poor opinion than his blood spilled.'

'It will be *my* blood spilled if I lose his good graces,' said the Earl bitterly. 'My enemies will strike if there is even the slightest indication that I no longer have his protection. Of course, I do have one advantage over them: the trumpet. He knows I have a very special gift for him, which alone may be enough to entice him through my doors.'

'But I cannot find it, sir,' said Chaloner in despair. 'And the general consensus is that it has been melted down. I cannot bring you what no longer exists.'

The Earl put his hands over his face. 'Then I am finished! I do not know what will be worse – for him to go elsewhere, or for him to come here and then be told that the promised surprise will not be forthcoming.'

Chaloner thought fast. 'You could give him the flag that flew when his father won the Battle of Cropredy Bridge. Would that suffice?'

He heard Lester make a strangled sound at the back of his throat, although the Earl's bleak expression lifted. Chaloner was sorry for Lester, but he was out of options, and sacrifices had to be made if they wanted the King safe and the country stopped from sliding into anarchy.

'It would,' nodded the Earl eagerly. 'But how do we lay our hands on such a prize?'

Chaloner indicated Lester. 'My friend will sell it to you if the price is right.'

'It will be,' promised the Earl, surging forward to grip Lester's hand in gratitude. 'Because I will pay whatever you ask. Thank God! Wren has been telling me that I might have to present His Majesty with his mother's dwarf instead.'

'Jeffrey Hudson?' asked Chaloner sharply. 'You have him standing by?'

'Yes – Wren promised to send word to the Fleece, should he be required. However, I am glad he will not, because I remember Hudson very well indeed. He was amusing as a child, but then he developed opinions, and turned into a most unpleasant young man.'

'Now he is an unpleasant older man,' muttered Lester.

'He came to Oxford a couple of months ago, expecting to be welcomed back at Court, but Chiffinch and Brouncker sent him packing. They were right to do so. He is a malcontent, who thinks the world owes him something. The King will not want *him* as a Fast Day gift.'

'No,' agreed Chaloner. 'So did Wren discover him here in London, or did Hudson visit Clarendon House?'

'He came to us, but it was Wren's idea to offer him to the King in lieu of the trumpet. Hudson said he would be delighted to oblige us with a display of his unique talents.'

'I am sure he did,' said Chaloner, 'but I doubt the King will appreciate the kind of entertainment he likes to offer these days.'

*

'That was unkind, Tom,' said Lester angrily, as they left the church. 'You know that flag is my most cherished possession.'

'It may prevent the King from being assassinated,' retorted Chaloner, unrepentant, 'which should mean something to an officer in His Majesty's navy.'

Lester shot him a foul look. 'You push me too far. It is—'

'Wren!' exclaimed Chaloner, as the secretary hurried towards them, brandishing something victoriously and grinning all over his face. 'Is that what I think it is?'

'Beale's lost trumpet,' crowed Wren. 'It was not melted down after all.'

'Thank God,' breathed Lester in relief. 'You no longer need my banner.'

'Oh, he will take that as well,' said Wren, after Chaloner had explained what had happened. 'Just in case His Majesty does not like the bugle – which I doubt he will, because it is horribly shrill. Listen.'

He played a scale, and Chaloner cringed. It was an appalling sound: brassy, strident and very, very loud. Had it been made of a lesser metal, he was sure it would have been destroyed years ago, and he wondered if Beale had 'lost' it deliberately.

'You can tell your Earl that I want fifty pounds for my flag,' Lester told the secretary sullenly. 'I doubt he will agree to such a vast sum, but if he does, you may leave it with my steward when you collect the banner from my house. And if he asks why it is so expensive, you may say that I am raising funds to help wounded sailors.'

'In that case, I shall tell him the price is a hundred,' said Wren, and smiled when Lester's jaw dropped. 'He can afford it, and no cost is too high where His Majesty is concerned. You will never guess who brought the trumpet to me. Not in a million years.'

'Lady Castlemaine?' suggested Chaloner, knowing she would sooner die than do anything to benefit the Earl. Of course, so would many others. 'Buckingham? Chiffinch? Arlington? Thomas Clifford? Bristol? Ashley Cooper? The Earl of—'

Wren raised a hand to stop him, aware that the list would run for some time. 'Adam Urban! I met him on King Street just now, where he had been lying in wait for me. He said a White Hall servant had offered it to him cheap. Apparently, the fellow thought that Urban could sell it back to its rightful owner at a profit – a profit that could then be used to fund his rebellion.'

'Which White Hall servant?' demanded Chaloner.

'Urban did not know his name, but I imagine it was one of those forced to stay here during the plague, when their more popular colleagues were whisked away to safety. The insult still rankles, and I am not surprised that one has decided to have his revenge.'

'The King should never have left the city to save his own skin,' declared Lester. 'Thank God he is not in the navy, or the Dutch would have defeated us without a shot being fired.'

'So why did Urban not take the trumpet to Beale?' asked Chaloner of Wren.

'He did,' replied the secretary, 'but Beale has no money, so recommended that Urban approach me instead, knowing we are keen to lay hold of it.'

Chaloner narrowed his eyes. 'So Urban offered to sell you stolen goods, the proceeds of which will be ploughed into overthrowing the monarchy? And you obliged him?'

Wren became flustered. 'It was not like that! The *servant*

told Urban to use the money for rebellion, but *Urban* promised that it would be put towards helping London's downtrodden poor. He sounded sincere, so I believed him.'

'He is a professional actor!' snapped Chaloner, exasperated. 'Ergo, he can sound however he chooses. You should have arrested him, not given him money to fund more mischief.'

'I did what was best for my Earl,' retorted Wren tightly. 'His future without this trumpet was looking bleak, but at least now he has a chance of keeping the King's favour. I am not sorry for my actions.'

'You will be if there is an uprising, and Urban makes it known that it was made possible by a donation from Clarendon House. The Earl will lose his head for certain!'

Wren had no answer.

'How did this thieving servant find Urban, anyway?' asked Lester, after a short and uncomfortable silence. 'We have been hunting him high and low for hours with no joy.'

'He waylaid him when he performed outside the palace,' said Wren sullenly. 'Lots of our servants went to listen, especially the disgruntled ones. He urged them to mark the Fast in a city church, well away from the "evil stink of corruption" around White Hall and Westminster. When the guards tried to arrest him, the crowd surged forward to help him escape.'

Chaloner was appalled by what Wren had done, but there was no point berating him further, so he nodded a curt farewell and headed for White Hall, hoping that Urban might still be in the area. If so, he would beg his help in preventing trouble, which, if he really did care about the "downtrodden poor", he would willingly give.

If he refused, Chaloner would know the assurances he had given Wren were a pack of lies, and his real aim was to ignite trouble.

He and Lester arrived at the palace, but there was no sign of Urban or anyone else from the troupe. Lester looked around in frustration.

'I feel as though I am in one of their satires,' he muttered. 'The one where clever Pulcinella dances circles around his stupid, lumbering opponents. Now what?'

'Back to the Fleece,' said Chaloner. 'To tell Hudson that his offer is accepted and that he should report to Clarendon House immediately. Once we have him, we will force him to take us to Urban on pain of—'

He stopped at a sudden roar of anger from the crowd that had assembled further down King Street. Every year, on the eve of Charles I's execution, a number of particularly devoted Royalists gathered at the spot where the scaffold had been erected. There they knelt quietly and prayed for his soul. That day, however, the racket emanating from within the Banqueting House was so loud that one man had hoisted a child up on his shoulders, so the lad could look through the windows and explain what was going on.

'Sacrilege!' howled an old lady, torn between distress and rage when she heard what the boy had seen. 'How *dare* they make frivolous use of the place where that saint spent his final moments! Today, of all days!'

'Hardly a saint,' murmured Lester to Chaloner. 'He was—'

He stopped as a carriage rattled past with Lady Castlemaine inside. There was a second howl of outrage – the King's mistress had long been seen as one of the worst offenders in the depravity department. The mob

384

began to pelt the coach with stones, forcing the driver to urge his horses into a gallop. Chaloner glanced back at the Banqueting House, and saw the child egging the stone-lobbers on.

'That is no boy!' he hissed. 'That is Hudson! After him, quick!

But his legs were stiff from so many hours trailing around taverns, while Lester was not built for speed. They did their best to lay hold of the man, but Hudson and his companion had too great a lead. They soon vanished into the maze of alleys around Westminster.

Weary and disheartened, Chaloner and Lester trudged back to the Fleece, hoping Hudson would have returned there, but if not, to leave a message with Amey telling him to report to Clarendon House as soon as possible. As they went, Chaloner thought Lester was right to say he felt as though he was in one of Urban's satires. His lame leg throbbed unpleasantly, and he wondered how much longer he would be obliged to race all over the city. Until it was in flames and his efforts no longer mattered?

They arrived to find the tavern crammed to the gills with paupers. Some were genuinely homeless and grateful for a roof over their heads, but most were just there for the spoils. They were in the process of stealing the remaining furniture, and ripping out doors and windows to use as firewood. Many were drunk, and the once-gracious public rooms were full of loudly belligerent voices. Chaloner and Lester separated to hunt for Hudson and Amey, but no one they cornered had seen the acrobat or anyone else from the troupe that day.

'I wish Hudson *was* here,' sighed a chimney sweep ruefully. 'He makes me laugh. Of course, once off the

385

stage he is a surly brute – angry, vicious-tongued and bitter.'

'He *hates* courtiers,' added a tanner, and looked Chaloner up and down. 'So if you are one, you might want to tell him you are something else if you happen across him. I heard him declare that he will not be happy until every last one of them is dead.'

'Does he say that sort of thing in his satires?' probed Chaloner.

'*He* does, but Urban does not,' replied the sweep. 'Urban just explains why we should be irked with the government. He says we should express ourselves peacefully, and never raise a finger against our oppressors, because the King will listen to us if we are nice.'

'Urban is a good man, but a damned fool,' growled the tanner. 'Hudson's approach is the one that will work – kill the courtiers to get the King's attention, *then* negotiate.'

So the troupe no longer spoke with one voice, thought Chaloner. Regardless, he was beginning to realise that no one could defuse the situation now. Londoners might begin by expressing their grievances peacefully, but they would quickly move to anger when they were ignored – and he had seen nothing to convince him that the King and his government were ready to acknowledge their mistakes.

'Are you here to look for the spy?' asked the sweep, dragging Chaloner's thoughts away from his concerns.

'What spy?'

'Williamson's – the evil creature who dresses in black and hides in doorways, where he thinks no one can see him. But we *can* see him, as clear as day. Someone else saw him, too, because they came along and bundled him into a carriage, much against his will.'

'What sort of carriage?' asked Chaloner uneasily.

'A hackney. He fought like a lion, but they overpowered him in the end. He dropped his knife when they put a hood over his head. Do you want it? You can have it for a shilling.'

The sweep produced a blade that was unmistakably Swaddell's – black and very sharp. Chaloner handed over the coin and took it from him.

'Can you remember anything else about his abductors?' he asked.

'There were six in all. Two distracted him by pretending to drop some money, and while he watched them scrabble for the coins, the other four pounced on him.'

'Can you describe them?'

'No, because their hats were pulled down to hide their faces. They were probably courtiers, doing it for a joke. It is the kind of prank those arses think is funny.'

Chaloner went in search of Lester, and found him with Amey. The scars on her neck looked worse than they had the last time, and he wondered if they were infected. She was scowling at Lester, who had just ordered her to tell Hudson to report to Clarendon House immediately.

'I am no slave, to be taking messages hither and thither,' she bristled indignantly. 'Besides, what makes you think *I* will see him?'

Lester ignored that. 'Just tell him that the Earl wants to accept the offer he made.'

'Offer?' she demanded suspiciously. 'What offer?'

'And if you see Urban and Gimonde,' Lester went on, 'beg them to stop these dangerous satires. They think they are helping Londoners, but they are not. The city will explode into violence if they continue, and it will not be the wealthy who suffer.'

'The city will do no such thing,' she spat contemptuously. 'And you cannot accuse them of inciting rebellion – not when all they do is point out the injustices of the current system. If the King has an ounce of sense and compassion, he will make amends at once.'

'Hudson was not pointing out injustices outside the Banqueting House just now,' retorted Chaloner. 'He deliberately turned a peaceful crowd into a baying mob.'

'You are mistaken,' argued Amey. 'He would never do such a thing.'

She turned on her heel and flounced away. Chaloner walked outside and hurried to the doorway where Swaddell liked to lurk. The assassin was no fool, so it would have had to have been a very convincing display of coin-dropping to have deceived him. He was also dangerous, so any abductors would need lightning-quick reactions to best such a deadly opponent. Could Urban's Men be responsible – professional actors staging the diversion, while the acrobats overpowered him by virtue of being too agile for his blades?

'We need to visit Williamson again,' he told Lester. 'We will tell him about Swaddell's capture and ask about his friendship with the Thompson brothers at the same time.'

'We can try,' muttered Lester. 'But it is my guess that he is sitting in a coffee house somewhere, waiting for the trouble to start so he can take advantage of it.'

Westminster Palace was oddly deserted when they arrived, as if its lawyers and clerks had made themselves scarce lest they were accused of being complicit in the crimes perpetrated by an inept and corrupt government. Chaloner hurried to the Spymaster's building and led the way upstairs, aware of Lester's unease – even honest men disliked being in such a place. This time, the door to the office was open, revealing Williamson sitting at his desk.

Chaloner was shocked by the change in him. A few weeks ago, he might have been considered handsome, but now he looked old, pale and haggard.

'Ah, Chaloner,' he said, effecting nonchalance, although his voice was hoarse with fatigue. 'Riggs mentioned that you had been asking after me.'

'Where have you been?' demanded Chaloner – recklessly, given that the Spymaster did not answer to him. 'It is not a good time to disappear without telling anyone how to find you.'

Williamson raised his eyebrows indignantly. 'You of all people should know that disappearing is sometimes necessary. It goes with being Spymaster General.'

'Your absence did not involve Robert Thompson, did it?' asked Lester bluntly.

Williamson regarded him askance. 'If you must know, I have been closeted in White Hall with the Duke of York and a Dutch diplomat, discreetly hammering out an agreement pertaining to the eventual exchange of prisoners.'

'You mean Beuningen,' said Lester flatly. 'I *see*.'

Williamson frowned, but evidently decided he was not interested in deciphering Lester's obtuse remarks, because he looked back at Chaloner.

'I have just received a disturbing piece of news,' he said, picking up a letter from his desk with unsteady hands. 'It informs me that Swaddell has been kidnapped, and will die unless I pay a ransom of one hundred pounds by midnight.'

'What will you do?' asked Lester.

'Pay it, of course,' replied Williamson irritably. 'Unfortunately, I can only raise fifty-two pounds at such short notice. I do not suppose you two . . .'

'He was taken from the Fleece,' said Chaloner, and repeated what he had been told. 'I suspect Urban's Men are responsible, because they have continued to use that tavern as a base for their operations, and Swaddell's monitoring of it would have been a nuisance.'

'He did that on *your* recommendation,' said Williamson accusingly. 'You were the one who said it staged a treasonous satire while we were raiding Chatelaine's Coffee House.'

'It did,' said Chaloner. 'And I suspect he witnessed something else significant, so they abducted him to make sure he could not tell you about it. The ransom is an afterthought.'

Williamson stared at him as he digested the information. 'Does it mean he is dead?'

'No, no,' said Chaloner reassuringly. 'It would have been much safer to kill him there and then, rather than subdue him and drag him away by force. I imagine he will be returned unscathed eventually – as long as you pay what they ask.'

Meanwhile, Lester had been staring at the documents on the desk, trying to read them upside down. 'Are any of these the secrets we got from Heemskerch? We risked our lives and reputations to lay hold of them, so I hope they were worthwhile.'

Williamson winced. 'Unfortunately, they were not. They told us nothing we did not already know, and Heemskerch was lying when he claimed they were important. It is a bitter disappointment – and deeply vexing to know he deceived us all.'

Lester gaped at him. 'You mean it was all for nothing?'

'Blame Thurloe,' said Williamson harshly. 'Heemskerch was *his* informant, not mine.'

But it was Williamson who had declared the intelligence worth the trouble, thought Chaloner angrily. Thurloe had never expressed an opinion one way or another, almost certainly because he had harboured reservations but was too politic to say so.

He was about to defend his old friend when Lester launched into a denunciation of Robert. Chaloner stifled a sigh. He was still working out the implications of their discoveries regarding the Thompsons, and wished Lester had let him handle the discussion.

'Robert is not the friend you think,' Lester began. 'His dentures were found on top of Stoakes' body, Maurice's coffee house has mysteriously vanished, and the brothers have moved out of their James Street home.'

'What are you blathering about?' demanded Williamson impatiently. 'Robert has *not* moved house – I am to attend a soirée there tomorrow evening. Here is the invitation.'

'Oh, Lord!' groaned Chaloner, as he took the proffered page and saw the handwriting with its distinctive lettering. 'He wrote this himself?'

'Yes,' replied Williamson warily. 'Why?'

Chaloner felt in his pockets for the various communiqués he had been carrying around for the past few days – the one from Stoakes' mattress, the one blackmailing Brouncker, the one warning Heemskerch about Quartermain, and the one he had found behind Beuningen's skirting board. He laid them side by side, along with Robert's invitation and the note about Swaddell's kidnapping. Four were in the same hand. Only the warning to Heemskerch and the note to Beuningen were different.

'Robert communicated with Stoakes in code,' said Lester, after Chaloner had explained what each meant and where it had been discovered. He watched Chaloner place the cipher key over the document from Stoakes' mattress. 'There! Read the message now, Mr Williamson. Robert mentions a plan that involves sinking *Assurance*, Urban's Men fomenting revolt, blackmail, and Heemskerch's murder.'

Williamson said nothing for a long time, a silence that neither Chaloner nor Lester was brave enough to break. It seemed like an age before the Spymaster eventually spoke.

'I did wonder about Robert's sudden and inexplicable desire for friendship,' he said. 'It began with a musical evening featuring trumpets.' He indicated the cipher key. 'That event, in fact – the special performance organised by Beale and his friends. Not long after, we discovered a shared interest in moths.'

'It was not Robert who forced Quartermain to poison Heemskerch, though,' said Chaloner. 'That was George.'

'How do you know?' Williamson spoke as if nothing had the power to shock him any longer.

'Clean shoes. It was the one thing the neighbour recalled about the heavily disguised man who visited Quartermain four times and made him weep. George takes good care of his false leg, and hates anything marking it.'

'But why would they do these terrible things?' asked Williamson in a low, flat voice.

'Because they are Dutch spies,' stated Lester with authority. 'Why else would they want to poison the Duke of York and his leading admirals and captains?'

Williamson blanched when he heard what they had reasoned about *Assurance*.

'So Lester is right about the brothers being in the pay of the Dutch,' finished Chaloner. 'Why else would they want Heemskerch dead? And they succeeded in the end, thanks to us: Lester wrote details of the escape plan in a letter that Swaddell read; Swaddell doubtless passed the information to you, where it was seen by Robert when he called in on you.'

'Robert does visit me here,' acknowledged Williamson, while Chaloner struggled to keep the disgust from his face; he did not like to imagine what other secrets the spy had learned while he listened to Williamson prattle about Grey Scalloped Bars. 'However, he did not write *all* these letters. The warning to Heemskerch is in a different hand—'

'The warning that tells him not to trust *you*, Mr Williamson,' put in Lester ruthlessly. 'And rightly so, given who had access to all your most sensitive intelligence.'

'Nor did Robert send the one telling Beuningen to go to the pier,' Williamson went on.

'The author of those is *not* someone who sides with the Dutch,' agreed Chaloner, 'but someone who aimed to save Heemskerch's life and have Beuningen blamed for the exploding dogger and the stolen guns. Someone who is part of the same plot, but who pulls in a different direction to Robert and his brothers.'

Williamson picked up the ransom note. 'So Urban's Men abducted Swaddell on *Robert's* orders?' He swallowed hard. 'Robert often said that having an assassin on my payroll was unsavoury. He loathes Swaddell, and urged me several times to send him overseas, where he could do no harm. I thought it was simple jealousy speaking . . .'

'In that case, I am afraid it is unlikely that Swaddell

will be released alive,' said Chaloner, surprised to find himself sorry. 'Not if he has been abducted out of spite and envy.'

'So do not pay the ransom,' advised Lester. 'It will be tantamount to disbursing them for taking his life.'

'Yes,' said Williamson tightly. 'I had worked that out for myself, thank you.'

'Did Swaddell send you any reports before he was taken?' asked Chaloner.

'Just a transcript of a sly and urgent discussion between some men who aim to overwhelm the King in Deptford. But the King has no plans to go there, so I did not consider it a priority.'

'Overwhelm,' mused Chaloner, thinking it a curious choice of phrase. 'Are you sure they did not mean overwhelm *Royal Charles* – the ship? She is in Deptford.'

'And they could do it,' gulped Lester. 'There are thousands of unpaid sailors who would love to strike a blow at the government by throwing in their lot with rebels. Harman and Cox will be powerless to fight them all off.'

'Harman and Cox,' murmured Chaloner to himself. He had never been entirely happy with their role in the affair. Could they be traitors, too?

'And then what?' Williamson was asking warily. 'These traitors sail a warship up the Thames and turn her against the city?'

'Why not?' asked Lester. 'Such a show of force would certainly encourage others to join the fight against a dishonest and callous regime – along with the guns stolen from *Assurance*.'

'Well, Swaddell's report did mention promise of a spectacle that would thrill all London,' said Williamson uneasily. 'Which that would certainly do.'

Chaloner stared at him. 'Those are the exact words Maurice used when he described what would happen when the Folly reopened tomorrow. They must be significant.'

Williamson stood suddenly, anger taking the place of dull bewilderment. The colour was back in his cheeks, his hands were steady, and he had regained his customary haughty demeanour. He began to make decisions.

'You two must ride to Deptford and warn Harman. I will muster troops and follow.'

'We cannot leave the city,' objected Chaloner, alarmed by the notion. 'We have to find the missing guns and stop Hudson from—'

'We have been struggling to do that for hours, Tom,' interrupted Lester soberly. 'And we have failed. Williamson is right: our duty lies in Deptford. If we can stop the rebels from taking *Royal Charles*, the trouble here will fizzle out.'

Chaloner was unconvinced. 'You two go. I will stay here and—'

'I need you there,' interrupted Williamson shortly. 'I shall require an accurate report when I arrive, and to be frank, you are the only one I trust now that Swaddell is . . . unavailable. Now go. Take torches – it will be dark soon.'

Chapter 16

'I hope you are right about this,' muttered Chaloner. He and Lester were clattering along the Strand on a pair of lively stallions from the Spymaster's stable. 'Because if you are wrong . . .'

'I am right,' Lester assured him. 'I know you are worried about what might happen while we are gone, but the situation will be much worse if *Royal Charles* sails up the Thames with all her guns blazing. Besides, Harman and Cox are my friends. I must warn them.'

'They should be able to repel invaders without our help,' grumbled Chaloner. 'If they cannot, they should not have command of her.'

'They will not expect an attack in home waters,' argued Lester. 'And most of her crew will be ashore, enjoying their last few hours of freedom before sailing away to war. She will be seriously undermanned – which Robert and his helpmeets will know, of course.'

'Williamson should not need us both to go,' Chaloner went on unhappily, wishing he could talk to Thurloe about it. 'Moreover, I should be on hand to deploy the Earl's guards around Covent Garden. He will lose his head for certain if the King dies at the Fast *he* organised.'

'We will be home long before the Fast,' said Lester soothingly. 'All we have to do is warn Harman and assess the situation for Williamson. It is the work of moments.'

Chaloner kicked his horse into a gallop. 'Then we should hurry.'

It was not easy to ride fast. The streets were busier than they had been earlier, and although it was dusk, people were emerging from houses and shops, rather than retreating inside for the evening. There was no particular sense of anger, just a quiet expectation that things were about to change for the better. Chaloner wondered how soon the peaceful mood would be manipulated by the rabble-rousers into something dark and ugly.

They reached the bridge, which teemed with pedestrians, most heading into the city. Chaloner heard more than a few mentions of Urban's fine performance in the Beare Garden – an arena used for bloodsports, which could accommodate several hundred people at a time. Again, there was an air of hopeful anticipation, which he knew would evaporate if – when – the promised improvements failed to materialise.

Unfortunately, he and Lester encountered a problem the moment they were south of the river and turned east: the direct route via Rotherhithe was closed by floods, meaning they would have to take the longer way along the Dover road. Feeling as though fate was conspiring against them at every turn, they hurried on, cantering for as long as they could make out the track in front of them, and slowing to a walk when darkness fell.

Even so, they made reasonable time until they reached the first of the two major bridges they had to cross. It spanned the Neckinger River, a sluggish stream that drained St George's Fields to the south. It had been damaged in the hyrricano, and workmen were there to ensure they crossed one at a time. The structure certainly felt unstable, and Chaloner felt it judder as he led his horse over.

After the Neckinger bridge, they lit torches in an effort to travel faster, but the recent rains had turned the road into a morass. They were forced to dismount again, struggling through mud that was calf deep in places.

'We should leave the horses here,' gasped Chaloner when they reached a roadside inn. 'We will make better time without them.'

They laboured along on foot, Chaloner aware of a deep, burning ache in his leg that was becoming increasingly difficult to ignore. He let Lester lead the way for a while, but the captain was even slower than he was. He forged past him, feeling sweat course down his back with the effort, although he had been chilled to the bone when they had started out.

'I know Harman and Cox are your friends,' he gasped, glancing back at Lester, 'but when we arrive in Deptford . . . well, we should reconnoitre before boarding *Royal Charles*.'

'Your suspicions are offensive, Tom,' declared Lester stiffly. 'There are no more loyal men than those two. I would stake my life on it.'

'Good,' said Chaloner shortly, 'because that is exactly what we will be doing.'

At that moment they reached the second crossing – a trio of wooden bridges over the wide but shallow Deptford Creek. It was angry that evening, a frothing torrent of brown draining from the rain-swollen marshes.

These bridges had also suffered during the hyrricano, and a team of labourers was working on them by lamplight. One came to tell Chaloner and Lester that they would have to make a detour, as none of the structures were safe.

'We cannot – it will take too long,' said Chaloner in alarm. 'We must cross now.'

'It is too dangerous,' said the man apologetically. 'This route is closed.'

Lester removed a coin from his pocket. 'Are you sure it is not open to us?'

The man grabbed the money quickly, then looked around to make sure no one was watching. 'Very well, but do not come crying to me if you drown.'

Chaloner set off before he could change his mind, aware of an ominous creak as the first bridge took his weight. He ignored the agitated shouts of the workmen beneath it, and hurried to the next, relieved to find it much less wobbly.

'Do you think they will bear Williamson and his troops?' wheezed Lester. 'There will be a lot more of them, and he will have a horse – I cannot see *him* racing along on foot.'

'The men might make it,' replied Chaloner tersely. 'The horse will not.'

The third bridge was also sound, and then it was not far to the Deptford yards. Chaloner was limping badly, although he was still more fleet-footed than Lester, who lumbered along with all the grace of an elephant.

'There!' said Lester, stabbing his finger to where a tall, proud ship was tethered to a pier. '*Royal Charles*. Thank God! And Harman is still in command.'

'How can you tell?'

Lester shrugged. 'If she was in enemy hands, she would already be tacking upriver.'

Chaloner hoped he was right.

Although all his instincts clamoured at him to race to the ship, warn Harman and tear back to London as fast as he could, Chaloner forced himself to heed the warning he had given Lester. He approached *Royal Charles* cautiously, stopping frequently to look and listen, and scowling at Lester for sighing in agitation.

'We did not half-kill ourselves rushing here so you could loiter around in the shadows,' the captain snapped eventually, his voice fraught with strain. 'We *must* hurry.'

Every fibre in his body alert for trouble, Chaloner continued to ease towards the ship. One or two lamps were lit, but it was mostly dark and silent. He indicated that Lester was to go first up the aft gangway, on the grounds that he was more familiar with it. Lester obliged, but lost his footing almost at once, yelping sharply as he scrabbled for balance.

'For God's sake, Sal!' hissed Chaloner. 'Anyone would think you *wanted* these insurgents to catch us. What is wrong with you?'

'Nerves,' came the terse reply. 'I cannot abide sneakery.'

He steadied himself and scrambled up the last few feet. Chaloner followed, then froze in shock when there was a sudden flood of light and the collective sound of pistols being cocked, muskets aimed and cutlasses drawn.

'Harman?' called Lester, squinting into the brightness. 'Is that you? What are you doing?'

'Repelling two uninvited guests,' replied Harman shortly, although he lowered his gun and indicated that his crew were to stand down. 'What do you mean by

400

creeping on to one of His Majesty's warships in the dead of night?'

Chaloner glanced around and saw there were at least thirty sailors on deck, with others posted in the rigging and near the hatches. All were heavily armed. Cox commanded a similar detail at the forward gangway, which included Fowler and Knapp.

'We thought you might be overrun by rebels,' explained Lester, removing his hat and wiping sweat from his face. 'The Spymaster has intelligence to suggest that some aim to try.'

'Then they will fail,' growled Harman. 'After what happened to Heemskerch's dogger, we doubled the guard, not just on *Royal Charles*, but on every ship. One can never be too careful in these uncertain times.'

Lester turned to Chaloner with a happy grin. 'We did it! There will be no violent revolution aided by one of His Majesty's warships, and when Robert and his help-meets appear, we shall we waiting to greet them with a show of force. I imagine they were foiled by those broken bridges. At least some good came from the gale!'

'Did you come through Rotherhithe then?' asked Cox, who had come to join them. 'We were told it was impass-able, due to floods.'

'It still is, so we used the Dover road,' explained Lester. 'The bridges over the Neckinger River and the Deptford Creek are under repair, because the hyrricano rendered them unstable.'

Harman frowned. 'They were sound when Cox and I rode over them last night – and that was *after* the storm. Are you sure you are not mistaken?'

Chaloner slumped against a rail as the truth dawned. 'There was never any plan to take *Royal Charles*!' he groaned. 'It was a trick – a ploy to get Williamson and his men away from London for tomorrow.'

Lester shook his head. 'But Swaddell overheard a conversation that—'

'A conversation he was *meant* to overhear and report – one designed to draw attention away from the real plot.'

'Which is what?' asked Harman warily.

'An attack on the city with *Assurance*'s guns, which will spark a rebellion against the King and his government. Williamson will not be in a position to stop it, and now neither will we. I *knew* we should not have come. I should have listened to my instincts.'

'What do you mean?' asked Lester, puzzled. 'Of course we can stop it. We will just slog back the way we came, and when we meet Williamson, we will tell him to turn around.'

'We cannot, because the bridges *will* be down by the time we reach them,' said Chaloner bitterly. 'And Williamson will be trapped between the two sets, unable to retreat or advance. It was not workmen repairing the things, but saboteurs. That is why we were allowed over the first, but challenged at the second.'

'If you are right, we would still be there,' argued Lester. 'But we were allowed across.'

'Only because the guard wanted the money you offered him. He probably told himself that two men on foot posed no threat to the grand plan. And he is right.'

'I am not very impressed with you,' said Harman, looking from one to the other in disgust. 'Or with Williamson, for that matter. It sounds as though you have all been very easily duped. Of course, I have never trusted that Spymaster General. Perhaps *he* is in the pay of these rogues, in exchange for a seat in the new government they aim to install.'

'Well, he is a friend of Robert's,' said Lester, and told him all that had happened since they had last met, while Chaloner fretted impotently as time ticked past.

When he had finished Harman's face was grim. 'We did not risk our lives at Lowestoft to see Dutch spies wreak havoc in our own capital. They led you to believe that they planned to steal *Royal Charles* and sail her upriver, so that is what we shall do. Then we will attack *them*.'

'It will not be easy,' hedged Lester. 'The tide will be against us most of the way.'

'The wind is in our favour though,' countered Cox, frowning as a series of complex nautical calculations flashed through his mind. 'It will be hard work, but the drill will be good training for our new crewmen. I think we can do it.'

Harman laughed in sudden glee. 'Hah! The appearance of His Majesty's biggest and best warship will make these traitors think twice about what they are doing!'

It was an agonising journey for Chaloner, who could not escape the conviction that he had been browbeaten into making *two* bad decisions that day – to go to Deptford in the first place, and then agreeing to remain on board while *Royal Charles* sailed for London. All the while, he kept thinking that the Thompsons would be amazed by how easy it had been to implement their plot, and imagined they would be delighted by the credulity of those they aimed to defeat.

He glanced at Lester, who possessed the mariner's ability to sleep anywhere – he was curled up on a pile

403

of sailcloth, oblivious to the bitter wind that scythed across the deck. Cox was at the wheel, Harman at his side. The pair had said little once the journey had started, perhaps because they were absorbed in zigzagging the ship upriver, pitting sail and wind against tide at every bend and turn.

Yet there was something about the two mariners that had unsettled Chaloner from the first. They were unhappy about the government's treatment of their crew, so what was not to say that they thought the King had been given a fair crack of the whip, and it was now time for a different form of leadership? In which case, Chaloner would be responsible for presenting the rebels with a warship to further their cause.

And how long was the journey going to take? He was sure he could have gone miles inland to find alternative crossings over the Neckinger River and the Deptford Creek, and still been in London quicker than *Royal Charles*. He paced anxiously, then forced himself to sit and rest his leg. He also ate some of the salted beef that Fowler brought him. He did not want it, and it was not easy to force down, but he knew he needed to keep his strength up if he was to be of any use later. Assuming they ever arrived, of course.

He had not meant to sleep, so was disorientated when he started awake some hours later. It was still dark, but the stars were beginning to fade. He was frozen to the bone, despite the boat-cloak that someone had thoughtfully draped over him. He sat up blinking, acutely aware that it was Tuesday – the day of the Fast and very possibly the last dawn before civil war broke out again.

'Why have we stopped?' he asked, struggling to his feet. His muscles had stiffened during the night, and he hoped he would not be obliged to run anywhere, not sure he would manage it.

'Something is in the way,' replied Lester, and nodded toward to where the London Bridge loomed out of the early-morning mist. 'Obviously, we cannot sail underneath it with our masts, so Cox is going ashore in a tender, to see about getting the drawbridge raised.'

'We need to be near the royal palaces if we are to defend them,' added Harman. 'Being all the way down here is no good to man nor beast.'

But raising the drawbridge was a time-consuming operation, and Chaloner doubted the right people would be on duty at such an hour. He decided to go ashore with the tender, feeling that at least then he would have control over his own movements, as opposed to being stuck on a ship that was on the wrong side of the bridge. He clambered awkwardly into the little boat, where he was joined by Cox and Lester. Knapp and Fowler were at the oars.

'Do not worry, Tom,' said Lester kindly, sensing his agitation. 'The navy is here.'

'Then let us hope it will be in time,' said Chaloner, not much comforted. 'Because the last time I saw this drawbridge raised, the process took hours.'

'I will order them to hurry,' promised Cox. 'And if they drag their heels . . . well, our cannon are very good at removing unwanted obstacles.'

'Lord!' muttered Chaloner, sure London would erupt into rebellion for certain if one of His Majesty's warships opened fire on the city's only crossing over the Thames.

They alighted on the Southwark side, where Chaloner aimed for the bridge's entrance, leaving the sailors to see about getting the drawbridge raised. He was a little surprised to find himself accompanied by Lester, Knapp and Fowler.

'You may need us,' explained Lester. 'And Cox can manage alone. He has a pistol.'

Chaloner was not sure why that was supposed to make him feel better, but he said nothing, and forced his weary legs into a trot, hoping exercise would drive the chill from them.

Dawn was still some way off, but although trading had been banned for the Fast, there were plenty of people up and about. Like the night before, Chaloner detected no obvious anger in the massing crowds, just eager anticipation. There was something about them that reminded him of lambs to the slaughter, and he wondered if that was what the Thompsons had in mind.

He flagged down a hackney when he reached Fish Street Hill, and the four of them piled into it. The driver was one of the garrulous types, and began regaling them with his opinions as they rattled along.

'Did you see any of Urban's wonderful satires?' he asked, after informing them that very few courtiers would have time to mark the Fast, because they would be in the Banqueting House rehearsing their lewd drama. 'He is a great man, and will make a far better ruler than that miserable, selfish old King.'

'Does Urban intend to put himself forward for the post then?' asked Lester.

'He has not offered, but we all know that life will be better for us with *him* in White Hall, just as it was better when Cromwell was there. We had no plagues when the Lord Protector was watching over us. He would not have allowed it to happen, see.'

There was no point telling him that not even Cromwell could have prevented an epidemic, and Chaloner was glad when they reached the New Exchange, where they alighted.

'Tom!' hissed Lester, staring down an alley towards the river. 'The Floating Coffee House. It is back!'

He was right – the low, square shape was unmistakable. It was lit by lanterns from within, and there was a moment when Chaloner thought Maurice might be hosting a party, because the rumble of early-morning traffic was all but drowned out by the sound of loud music, shrieks and raucous laughter. Then he realised that the rumpus was coming from the Banqueting House, which was impressive, given that the palace was some distance away.

Knapp pursed his lips. 'They expect *us* to be solemn today, but hark at them! You can tell just by listening that they are not painting scenery. They are having fun.'

'They are fools,' declared Lester angrily. 'They must know the mood of the people is against them, so why do they provoke it? Surely they can control themselves for one day?'

'They can,' growled Fowler. 'But they choose not to, because they do not care what we think. We are nothing to them, and that racket proves it.'

Chaloner suspected he was right, and marvelled that there was not one courtier among the merry rabble sensible enough to advise discretion. Not for the first time, he found himself wondering if he should just find a quiet spot and let events take their course. And if the Court debauchees met with an angry mob, they only had themselves to blame.

'I wonder where it has been,' said Lester, tearing his attention away from the racket and nodding towards the

Folly. 'Not for repairs, as there has not been enough time to mend a hull breach of that size.'

'To a secluded pier, where it was loaded with *Assurance*'s cannon,' predicted Chaloner. 'Maurice bought that barge for one purpose and one purpose only – and it has nothing to do with coffee. He and his brothers must have been planning this for months.'

'Well, the barge will provide a perfect platform for discharging artillery,' said Lester, surveying it with a professional eye. 'It is flat, low in the water, and will raise no eyebrows in the interim, because everyone is used to seeing it there. But how could they know that *Assurance* would provide them with cannon at the salient time?'

'That was lucky chance,' surmised Chaloner. 'I imagine they planned to steal some from elsewhere, but *Assurance* saved them the bother.'

'All this explains why Maurice's so-called improvements were superficial,' mused Lester. 'A lick of paint inside, but the outside left to rot. He knew it would not be needed for very long. So what do they intend? To aim a cannonball at the King?'

'And at White Hall and Westminster – the seats of government. Most ministers and officials will gather there today, because they will want to be on hand to greet the King as he enters his city for the first time since the plague. The rebels may not kill all of them, but there will be enough casualties to throw the country into disarray.'

'Which will give the Dutch a chance to deliver a decisive blow,' finished Lester. 'Should we inform Williamson?'

'How? He will be trapped on the Dover Road.'

Lester became businesslike. 'I shall return to the bridge and tell Harman to forget *Royal Charles* and fight from the shore. You go to Clarendon House – your Earl *must* order the King to stay at Hampton Court. Knapp will run to Westminster, just in case Williamson left a deputy who may be able to help. And Fowler can warn the debauchees in White Hall.'

'Knapp can go to Clarendon House after he has been to Westminster,' said Chaloner. 'I will row over to the Folly and disable the guns. It is the only sure way to prevent them from being deployed on some unsuspecting target.'

'I will *not* go to White Hall,' declared Fowler firmly. 'It is their fault that there is no money to pay us sailors, so I hope they *are* blown up.' He nodded at Chaloner. 'But I will go to the Folly with him to fight Dutch spies.'

'Very well,' said Lester, capitulating rather easily, while Chaloner baulked at the notion of having a self-confessed killer as his sole assistant. 'Knapp can stop off at White Hall when he has finished at Westminster and Clarendon House. If he has time. Agreed?'

'Agreed,' chorused Knapp and Fowler, although Chaloner was silent, his sense that he was powerless to prevent what had been set in motion intensifying with every passing moment.

It was light by the time Fowler had stolen a boat from the Savoy Wharf and was rowing Chaloner towards the Floating Coffee House. As they approached, Chaloner saw armed sentries at each corner of the vessel, which made him all the more certain that the guns were indeed aboard. Unfortunately, it meant that he and Fowler could not launch a surprise attack.

'It is Scull!' exclaimed Fowler, squinting at the guards in astonishment. 'And his boy! Can you see them, on the starboard side? They are not blown up after all!'

'No,' sighed Chaloner, recalling the coal barge that had cut across the dogger's path just before it had exploded, apparently by accident. He had seen the tip of *Vågen*'s mast judder – now he realised the movement had not been from a collision, but from when the Sculls had jumped to safety, leaving Heemskerch to his fate. 'The blast was perfectly timed – Scull must have lit the fuse himself.'

'So he is part of this, too?' asked Fowler. 'I am not surprised. Did you know he has kin in Holland? I always wondered if that was why he never joined the navy.'

Chaloner tried to think of a ruse to distract the guards so he could sneak on to the Folly unseen, but his mind was blank. Could he swim there? Unfortunately, that would involve holding his breath underwater for longer than he thought he could manage, not to mention the fact that the river was cold enough to render him immobile with the shock of it.

'I can get you aboard, sir,' said Fowler, reading his mind. 'But you have to promise something: if I drown, you get my pay and take it to my young ones. They live by the Beare Garden. Do you swear?'

'Yes,' said Chaloner. 'But before you do anything rash, I want to know what—'

'Lie in the bottom of the boat and put my cloak over you,' interrupted Fowler. 'Then climb aboard when everyone is looking the other way. Ready?'

'No, wait!' hissed Chaloner. 'Tell me what you—'

But Fowler began to row towards the barge, singing at the top of his voice. Alarmed, Chaloner ducked under the cloak, aware of the sentries' guns swinging towards them. The steward was going to get them both killed, and then there would be no one to stand between the Thompson brothers and their nefarious plans.

'Fowler, stop!' he whispered frantically, a sentiment with which Scull agreed, because he was yelling the same thing. 'This is not the way—'

'Scull!' bawled Fowler, and Chaloner winced at the unconvincing display of drunkenness; the conspirators would see through it in an instant. 'You owe me money. Pay up!'

'No, I do not,' cried Scull indignantly. 'Now back off, Fowler, unless you want a musket ball in your stupid head.'

'How about a drink instead?' slurred Fowler. The boat rocked precariously as he stood up. 'With an old ship-mate.'

'We were never shipmates,' snapped Scull. 'Now piss off!'

There was a jolt as the boat bumped into the barge and grated along its side. It was followed by a great splash and the sound of Fowler bawling for help.

'Toss him a rope,' ordered Scull in exasperation. 'The stupid, clumsy oaf.'

Chaloner lifted a corner of the cloak to see what was happening. Three of the sentries were leaning over the side to stare at the flailing Fowler, while Scull's son prepared to lob a lifeline. None were looking his way, so Chaloner used his hands to propel his boat to the far side of the Folly. When he was out of sight, he scrambled aboard. His boat bobbed away, clunking into three others, which were tethered to the stern ready for the conspir-ators to escape once their deadly work was done. Chaloner cut them loose and watched them float away. That would put the cat among the pigeons. Of course, it meant that he was now trapped as well . . .

'Where is he?' Scull was shouting. 'Fowler! I cannot see you.'

'Swept off by the undertow,' came a voice that Chaloner recognised by its volume: Robert's. 'Forget him and return to your posts. You should not have let him get so close.'

Chaloner looked at the water and shivered. All he hoped was that if he was not in a position to fulfil the promise he had made to Fowler, Lester would think to do it.

There were two ways to enter the coffee house from the outside deck: through the main entrance on the port side, or via a service door at the back. As Robert had just used the former, Chaloner aimed for the latter. It opened into a little vestibule, which contained a second door giving access to the main room, and a ladder leading down to the hold. Chaloner closed the outside door behind him, and peered cautiously around the inner one to see what was happening within.

The long table at which Maurice had served coffee to his guests had been shoved to one side, clearing the way for the guns. All four were mounted on their carriages, with a box of ammunition sitting ready next to each. The two in the bow were pointed at White Hall and Westminster, while the others were aimed at the Savoy Palace and Covent Garden beyond.

Maurice stood by one, eyebrows freshly applied for the occasion. He was briefing a score of men – all the disenchanted sailors whom Judd had hired to ferry passengers to and from the Folly. Maurice was outlining his plan, which entailed nothing more complex than firing when he said so. The seamen had already divided themselves into crews, with designated captains, loaders and spongers.

George and Robert were there, too. They stood with Hudson, and held handguns that were trained on Urban, Gimonde, Hall and Clun. Hudson wore a spiteful grin, while his fellow players stood in a huddle, their faces white with fear and confusion. Absently, Chaloner noticed the curious rings in Urban's ears, so at odds with the rest of his attire.

'*Everything* was a lie?' Gimonde was asking Hudson in a shocked whisper. 'You did not join us because you think Londoners were treated badly during the plague, but because the King snubbed you when you asked to rejoin his Court?'

'I should have been showered with honours for the loyal service I gave his mother,' Hudson replied icily, 'but instead I was tossed out like so much rubbish. Well, no one insults *me* and gets away with it. Today he pays for his ingratitude.'

'When a courtier told me that you had been preaching sedition, I did not believe him,' said Urban, in a voice that was high with strain. 'But it was true.'

'Please,' begged Hall. 'Fire on White Hall and Westminster by all means – they deserve it – but not Covent Garden. There are good people living in the Fleece now.'

'Paupers and beggars,' spat Hudson contemptuously. 'Who cares about those?'

'*We* do,' insisted Urban tearfully. 'We agreed that no Londoners would be hurt. We did not encourage them to the city to be killed, but so that when we destroy the palaces, they will be on hand to decide what manner of government they would like to—'

'A people's democracy indeed!' scoffed Hudson. 'You are fools to think that would work, and fools to think I

413

would help you install such a ridiculous regime. I want one thing and one thing only: the King and all his lick-spittles dead.'

'I do, too,' said Clun with a sickly smile. 'I never cared about social justice like these three. Let me help you, Hudson. I—'

'No,' snarled Hudson, as the actor took a step towards him. 'Stay back. I do not want your company when I forge a new life for myself abroad. You will— I *said* stay back!'

But Clun kept advancing, hands held out in supplication. 'I can be of use to you, Hudson. I am a—'

There was a flash and a bang, and Clun dropped to the floor. Urban screamed his shock, while Hall and Gimonde cowered, whimpering in terror.

'He was going to rush me,' explained George, reloading. 'I could see it in his eyes. He thought my missing leg would make me an easy target and he aimed to grab my gun. Well, he will not make *that* mistake again.'

'Why are you doing this?' asked Urban in a small voice. He seemed diminished, and there was no sign of the impassioned orator now. 'What will you gain by turning on us?'

'Do you really need to be told?' bawled Robert, removing his teeth and putting them in his pocket for safekeeping.

'Oblige them,' shrugged Maurice. 'It will pass the time until the King arrives in Covent Garden, and we begin the spectacle that will thrill all London.'

'Which will not be long now,' said George, glancing out of the window to gauge the hour.

'Very well,' hollered Robert, and turned to address the prisoners. 'When the King first took his throne, we had high hopes. But he is just like his father – lazy, selfish, unreliable and greedy. He kept none of the promises he made at his Restoration, so we opted to serve a better master instead.'

'One who pays us very well,' put in George smugly.

'But you already have money,' cried Urban, bewildered. 'You are wealthy men, and *you*, George, were given a Court post because the government hopes to get some of it.'

George laughed. 'It was fun watching them fawn over me. However, one *never* has enough money, especially if one aims to leave England and settle in the United Provinces.'

'Is that what this is about?' Urban was stunned. 'You are Dutch spies? Traitors?'

'We prefer to think of ourselves as ex-patriots,' said George smugly. 'Of course, this was a very expensive venture – it cost us a lot, but the rewards will be considerable.'

'We shall be richer still when Brouncker pays up,' put in Maurice, all gloating satisfaction as he grinned at George. 'It was excellent luck that you heard him and the Duke of York discussing a certain error of judgement.'

While they talked, Chaloner opened the outer door and peered downriver. There was no sign of rescue from *Royal Charles*, Lester or anyone else. Would there be, or was Harman even now preparing to add his firepower to that of the Folly? Heart pounding in agitation, Chaloner returned to his eavesdropping, frantically trying to come up with a way to thwart the rebels. Could he release the anchor that held the barge midstream, so the Folly would drift to a place where it would be useless?

But that would involve sawing through chains, which the rebels would hear the moment he started. Then could he unbolt the chains from their moorings? He grimaced. Unfortunately, that would be a noisy operation, too.

'So it was you who killed Heemskerch?' Hall was asking fearfully.

'At Grand Pensionary de Witt's request,' replied George. 'The villain had been betraying his country for a decade. We had hoped to do it less dramatically, using a physician who was willing to oblige once we threatened to expose a batch of poisonous medicine . . .'

'But someone warned Heemskerch, so we had to make other arrangements,' bellowed Robert. 'Our explosion came too late to stop him from passing one final batch of intelligence to the enemy, but it could not be helped.'

Urban had flinched at Robert's mention of the warning, a reaction that did not go unnoticed by George.

'It was *you*!' George cried furiously. '*You* alerted Heemskerch to the danger we posed. You stupid little—'

'Killing was not part of the plan,' bleated Urban, frightened but defiant. 'We agreed to rid the country of corrupt leaders, not murder anyone we do not like.'

'I suppose it was you who tried to get the Dutch blamed for killing Heemskerch and stealing the guns, too,' sneered George, 'by delivering that ridiculous note to the embassy. Well, it did not work. Beuningen declared his innocence and was believed. He told me so when I happened across him in White Hall yesterday.'

'The *Assurance* debacle was not part of the plan either,' added Gimonde softly. 'We agreed to the elimination of courtier-captains, whose incompetence at sea endangers common sailors. We did *not* agree to dispatching every admiral and senior captain in the navy. Nor should we have had to be the ones to take an axe to the thing, to clear up the mess you made of the whole affair.'

Maurice sneered. 'You cleared up nothing! You merely delayed the truth coming out. Besides, it was your fault that the Duke cancelled at the last minute. We would not be having this discussion if *you* had not elected to perform in Hercules' Pillars Alley that night.'

'You should have stopped them from doing it,' George told Hudson sourly.

The dwarf shrugged. 'I would have done, had I known what they intended. But they did not mention it until after the event. I was livid. All that planning with Stoakes – sending out invitations, the cunningly poisoned wine. For nothing!'

'Stoakes!' spat Maurice. 'It made my skin crawl to work with him – a greedy, unscrupulous drunkard. I am glad he is dead.'

'And Quartermain?' asked Urban in a small, defeated voice. 'Did you kill him, too?'

George grimaced. 'No one did: it was suicide. I accidentally dropped some messages and a cipher key in his house once. His mistress showed him how to apply one to the other, at which point he realised he was in the pay of the Dutch. Full of self-recrimination, he killed himself in Bedford House, in the hope that a corpse there would see the ambassador investigated – his pathetic, last-ditch attempt to make up for inadvertently serving the enemy. Originally, I told him I wanted Heemskerch dead because he gave London the plague, and he believed it until he decoded my letters.'

'But he went in a pauper's grave with no one any the wiser,' smirked Maurice. 'And now he no longer matters, and nor do you.'

417

Gimonde and Hall whimpered, while Chaloner looked again for something to use against the brothers, aware of a growing sense of helplessness. There was still no sign of Lester or Harman, and he was beginning to think that even if they did come, they would be too late. Then his eye lit on the ladder, and he recalled the jury-plug. Maybe he could knock it out.

He descended the stairs quickly, and saw that Maurice had been monitoring the repair, because a lamp was lit next to it. His heart jumped. It would be better still to set the barge alight! But the planking was too damp to catch alight, and even if it did, the rebels would smell smoke and douse the flames long before they did any meaningful harm. Sabotaging the plug was his only hope.

He eased forward and saw a mess of cordage holding a sturdy brace in position. He drew a knife and hacked at one rope, astonished when it parted with ease. He realised he was using Swaddell's blade, which had been sharpened to within an inch of its life. Within moments, he had chopped through all the lines. A kick dislodged the brace, and the river immediately began to fountain in. He ran for the ladder, water frothing around his ankles.

He put his foot on the lowest rung and stopped. Someone was lying in the shadows beyond. He held the lantern aloft to reveal Swaddell. There was blood on the assassin's white falling band and in a viscous puddle around him.

Chaloner eased forward and touched his hand to the assassin's neck. There was a life-beat, so he gripped his shoulder and shook it. Swaddell's eyes flickered open, but there was no recognition in them and they were soon closed again. Chaloner's brief surge of hope that he would have a helpmeet faded. He was still on his own.

Chapter 17

The sound of water gushing into the hold suddenly grew much louder. Galvanised into action, Chaloner grabbed Swaddell and hoisted him over his shoulder. They had been colleagues of a sort, and he was loath to leave him to drown. He left him on the deck outside, aware that in the city, bells had started to ring to mark the start of the Fast. He returned to the coffee-room door, and what he saw filled him with horror.

The brothers had also heard the bells, and their gun crews were in position. The ammunition boxes were open, and with despair, he counted six balls in the closest one alone. They would blast London to pieces, and the Folly would sink too late to make a difference! Maurice and Robert loomed over one cannon, while George guarded their erstwhile accomplices, although the hand that held the pistol shook with tension.

'Are you sure you can hit Covent Garden?' Maurice was demanding of Scull.

'Yes,' replied Scull tersely. 'Can we start? I am tired of waiting.'

'Not until the signal,' yelled Robert.

George smirked at the prisoners. 'For which we have you to thank.'

'What do you mean?' demanded Gimonde uneasily. 'What do we have to do with it?'

'When the King enters the church, a fanfare will be played on an especially loud trumpet,' explained George. 'The one Hall stole from the Banqueting House, to keep safe until it was needed. When Judd hears it, he will send a runner, who will wave to us from the Savoy Wharf.'

'But that plan was to *protect* the King, not to kill him,' objected Urban wretchedly. 'To inform us when he arrived in Covent Garden, so we could open fire on White Hall. Please do not harm him, George. He will rule wisely once free of bad influences. I know he will.'

George expressed his contempt for such artlessness by turning his back on him. Urban seized his chance. He hurtled forward and gave George an almighty shove that sent him sprawling. Hall vaulted over the cannon and punched Maurice, while Gimonde managed to jump on to Robert's back. Alarmed, the gun crews surged to the brothers' assistance.

The odds were terrible – the brothers and a pack of sailors against the three entertainers – but Chaloner did not hesitate. He exploded among them, flailing with his sword and feeling the blade bite with every swipe. He was aware of Robert taking aim at him, but no shot came, because Gimonde bit off his ear; Robert dropped his gun in screeching agony. Maurice was back on his feet, pistol in his hand, but Hall snatched it from him in one easy, fluid movement. He tossed it to Urban, and advanced on Hudson, who had drawn a dagger.

'Put up your weapons!' shrieked Urban, brandishing the dag. 'Refuse, and I will shoot Maurice. I mean it.'

Unfortunately, the Thompsons knew he did not have the courage to kill in cold blood. So did the sailors, who turned as one to deal with Chaloner.

'Kill them and get back to your stations,' roared Robert. Blood streamed down the side of his face, and he was still struggling to dislodge Gimonde from his back. 'You must—'

He faltered when Urban swung the gun away from Maurice and aimed at one of the boxes of ammunition instead. It was the crate next to George, whose false leg had come off during the tussle, which meant he could not clamber away.

'Do not be stupid,' snarled George, pale with horror. 'We will all die if you shoot at that.'

'Not all of us,' said Urban resolutely. 'But *you* will. Now surrender!'

'Come back!' Robert screamed at the sailors, who were scrambling towards the door, unwilling to be aboard if Urban carried out his threat. Hudson tried to follow, but Hall felled him with a punch. 'Return to—'

There was a sharp report, followed by a hot blast that hurled everyone from their feet and blew out all the windows. Chaloner was saved from serious harm by a pillar, which bore the brunt of the explosion. He opened his eyes to swirling smoke, and for a few moments, everything sounded as though it was underwater. Coughing, the sailors picked themselves up and staggered towards the door again, although several of their comrades lay in unmoving, bloody heaps. George was also still, his body on one side of the room, and his last leg on the other.

'Scull!' bellowed Robert furiously at the fleeing seaman. 'Come back! I *order* you to come back!'

He had managed to fling Gimonde off and was trying to lay hold of him, but the actor slithered away from every angry lunge, just as Pulcinella had done on stage. Then water began to bubble up through the floorboards. It fountained into Hudson's face, reviving him abruptly.

'Help!' he cried, staggering dazedly to his feet. 'We are sinking!'

Chaloner also clambered upright and glanced through one of the shattered windows. Hudson was right: the Folly was definitely lower in the water.

'Kill them!' howled Maurice, tearing agonised eyes away from George's mangled corpse. 'Kill them all! A guinea to the man who brings me the head of Chaloner, Hall, Gimonde—'

'*Two* guineas,' roared Hudson. 'And *ten* for the man who fires his cannon at the church.'

Most of the sailors immediately turned back – it was a fortune for a few minutes' work. Chaloner prepared to fight again, although he had lost the element of surprise and was now seriously outnumbered. He prepared to sell his life dearly, but there was a sudden dull thud and one of the seamen gaped in horror at the knife protruding from his chest. A second thud followed and another man died. It was Swaddell, unsteady on his feet, but as deadly as ever. His arm went back a third time, and then Robert staggered backwards with a blade in his throat.

'That will teach you to betray Joe,' Chaloner heard him mutter.

'But I *killed* you,' cried Maurice in disbelief. 'You cannot be—'

He did not finish, because Gimonde struck him a terrible blow on the head with the pan used for roasting coffee beans. Seeing the last brother down, the seamen

422

aimed for the door again. Hudson joined them. They ran for the boats, and there were wails of horror when it was discovered that they had gone.

'Is that my knife, Tom?' asked Swaddell hoarsely. 'Give it to me. We should cut a few throats now, lest these bastards regain their wits and try to overwhelm us.'

'No time,' said Chaloner, glad of it. They were ankle-deep in water, and the barge's bow was beginning to inch skywards. 'It—'

'We can still do it,' shouted Urban frantically. He was gazing out of a window, where a lone seaman was waving from the pier: the signal that the King was in the Covent Garden church. 'We can still rid London of White Hall's carrion.'

'It is over,' said Chaloner tiredly. 'Give yourselves up.'

'Give up?' demanded Urban, and Chaloner saw he had acquired another gun. 'After all we have been through? We certainly will not! And *you* will not stop us – not unless you want to suffer the same fate as George.'

Once again, it was money that convinced the surviving sailors to stay. They ran to their guns, while Chaloner watched helplessly. Gimonde and Hall had also found dags, and while Chaloner might have rushed one, he could not manage three, especially after they had disarmed him. Swaddell collapsed on a bench, his face so pale that Chaloner feared he was dying. Urban hopped on to the table to avoid the rising water, and Chaloner wondered how long it would be before the cannon were submerged and useless. He grimaced. Not long enough.

'Stop this,' he urged. 'The moment you fire, everyone will know the attack came from here. There is no way to escape and you will be caught.'

The sailors hesitated, aware that the fortune they had been promised would be no use if they were hanged.

'We have arranged for boats to come and rescue us,' lied Urban. 'Now aim at the Banqueting House. Hurry!'

'No!' begged Chaloner desperately. 'You will murder servants as well as courtiers – innocents, who do not deserve to die.'

'The servants will be at Fasts in the city.' Urban rubbed a spot on his neck that had been injured during the skirmish. 'I told them to get away from the palaces myself – during a performance outside the Great Gate, in full view of their corrupt masters.'

'I did likewise, every time I visited Lady Castlemaine,' put in Hall, and smirked. 'She did not suspect me for a moment.'

'But most servants will not be allowed to leave,' argued Chaloner. 'Their duties will keep them in the palace all day. And do not say you will only hit the Banqueting House, because you cannot rely on the accuracy of these guns or their crews.'

'Nonsense,' countered Urban. 'The only casualties will be those involved in *Two Sisters*. And anyone associated with *that* filth deserves whatever they get.'

'Hurry up, Scull,' urged Hall tautly, joining Urban on the table. 'Please!'

'Yes, do,' agreed Gimonde, who alone seemed oblivious to the icy water surging around his calves. 'Or we will sink before we fire. And we have worked our whole lives for this . . .'

'*You* certainly have,' muttered Chaloner. 'I saw you in Bologna, whipping the local populace into a frenzy with your radical politics.'

'Pulcinella tells folk what they need to hear,' said Gimonde in his squeaky voice. It was disquieting, and the sailors shot him wary glances. 'Only then can they improve their lot.'

'Scull!' shouted Hall in agitation. 'Why the delay? I thought you were ready.'

'We were,' Scull snapped, 'but we have to adjust for the barge being lower in the water.'

The river was almost up to the windows now, at which point the Folly would sink fast, because none had glass to keep it out – it had all been shattered in the explosion. The water would rush in, and Chaloner wondered if he would be able to escape through one when the time came. Or would the torrent keep him inside to drown with everyone else? He glanced at Swaddell, whose eyes were closed. And what about him?

'Gimonde,' came an oily voice from the door. It was Hudson, all false smiles and forced bonhomie. 'You and I have been friends for ages now, and you know I am on your side. What you heard with the brothers just now was a ploy, so that I could save you from—'

He did not finish, because Gimonde picked him up and lobbed him through a window. There was a plop followed by a lot of frantic splashing and pleas for help. When it became clear that none was going to be forthcoming, the voice turned vengeful.

'Robert put gunpowder in the Covent Garden church, lest the cannon failed to hit it. It will explode within the hour and your King will die. Londoners will never follow regicides again, so the Thompsons and I have won after all – we have given England to the Dutch . . .'

There was more, but it was too faint to hear, and then it faded altogether.

'He is lying,' said Urban, raising his free hand to claw his neck again. 'Ignore him.'

As he scratched, Chaloner had a sudden, sharp memory of someone else doing the same thing, and noticed a rash beneath the collar. He gazed at it, answers tumbling so fast into his mind that he barely knew where to begin working out what they meant.

'You are Olivia Stoakes!' he breathed.

As Chaloner stared at "Urban" he realised he was looking into Olivia's eyes – steady, intelligent and determined. He was appalled that he had allowed himself to be deceived when answers had been in front of him all along. With disgust, he recalled the Christmas revels, when she had amazed everyone with her ability to mimic courtiers.

'What gave me away?' she asked curiously, then glanced at the fountaining water. 'Not that it matters now.'

'The rash,' Chaloner explained, more calmly than he felt. 'Wiseman told me that it might be caused by some substance that irritated the skin – probably the face paints you wear when you become Urban.'

She smiled briefly. 'I meant to investigate alternatives, but there has been no time.'

'It probably got worse when you pasted scars on your neck to become Amey, too,' he went on. 'The hideous ones, which make people avert their eyes. That is why "Urban" wears those peculiar earrings, of course – items that draw attention away from your face.'

'The oldest trick in the book,' breathed Swaddell weakly. Chaloner was glad he was still alive. 'And you fell for it?'

'*Three* times,' said Chaloner bitterly. 'Emily the cook-maid had a running sore on her face. That was Olivia, too, trailing me around her house to make sure I found nothing incriminating.'

'Urban has been everywhere,' whispered Swaddell. 'He was not just Olivia . . .'

The assassin was right, of course. Urban was just an old man with white whiskers and striking earrings – any of the troupe could have donned that disguise, which explained why 'he' had managed to make so many appearances over the last few days.

'Scull!' shouted Hall. The water was up to Chaloner's knees now, and icy cold. 'For God's sake! The powder will get wet if you take much longer.'

'We are going as fast as we can,' snapped the boatman. 'Two more minutes.'

'*We* were easy to deceive,' rasped Swaddell, struggling to sit up straighter, 'but how did you fool Wiseman and Kersey? They know a corpse when they see one.'

'She prepared,' replied Chaloner, when Olivia did not. 'Wiseman told me that she had quizzed him about drowning, so she knew what he would look for. She was wet and cold, and her mouth was full of foam, which she allowed to dribble out when he pushed on her chest.'

And, he thought in disgust, who had taken her to the charnel house and then stood guard to ensure Wiseman did nothing more invasive? Her accomplices, who had then whisked her home, where dry clothes had doubtless been waiting. He recalled noticing that her bier had been placed in a room with a fire, and cursed his own stupidity. Everyone knew corpses and warm places did not mix, and he should have been suspicious at once.

'Risky,' murmured Swaddell. 'Wiseman loves dissection. Why chance it?'

'To stop *him* from looking for me,' snapped Olivia, jabbing her gun in Chaloner's direction. 'I told all manner of people that I liked visiting churches in the hope of being quietly forgotten, but he refused to accept it, even when faithful "Emily" urged him not to bother.'

'So the Thompson brothers knew what you—' began Swaddell.

'Of course they did,' spat Olivia, 'although I kept wondering why they did not invent some tale that would make Chaloner leave me alone. But now I understand: we were not comrades in the fight against injustice. They were using me for their own ends.'

'They were,' agreed Chaloner. 'So why not put down the gun and—'

'But even after seeing my body and attending my funeral, you *still* would not leave me be,' Olivia continued bitterly. 'You just turned your attention to finding my "killer". I lost two perfectly good hideouts because of your irritating persistence – my home and the Fleece.'

'But why disappear at all?' asked Chaloner, glancing agitatedly to where Scull was struggling to elevate the barrel of the biggest gun. 'Why not just pretend to be ill or indisposed? No one would have questioned it, and you would not have needed to burn all your bridges.'

'It was a mistake,' she admitted. 'I did not expect to be missed when I went off to become Urban for a few days. But before I knew it, everything was out of control – you were hunting me, there were rumours of abduction and murder, and my husband did not help . . .'

A distant part of Chaloner's numb mind wondered what *Royal Charles* would do when Scull blew the

Banqueting House to pieces. Or was she still stuck on the wrong side of the bridge, so not in a position to fight for either side?

'Stoakes was a liability,' spat Gimonde. 'He could have invented a plausible excuse for your disappearance, but all he did was sit and drink, so eyebrows were raised.'

'Did you drag him into this business?' asked Chaloner, although it hardly mattered now and he was not sure why he persisted with questions. 'Or did he drag you?'

'We dragged each other,' replied Olivia. 'Although in different directions, apparently. I had no idea he was in the pay of the Dutch or that he intended to sail off and leave me behind. I thought all our best possessions were still in storage after our stay in Oxford – I was shocked to discover most were stowed on his ship, ready to begin a new life without me.'

'Speaking of treacherous kin,' began Chaloner, 'are you really related to the Thompsons?'

'No – it was just a convenient way to explain our association. But *you* could join our cause. You care about the downtrodden and lowly – you and Lester emptied your purses for poor, abandoned Amey, while your distress over Widow Fisher was genuine. I could tell.'

'No!' snapped Hall. He was more agitated than the others, and the gun he held wavered dangerously. 'I do not want him as an associate, and your chatter is driving me to distraction. Scull! For God's sake, just point that thing and shoot!'

'Please do,' begged Gimonde. 'Or we will sink before—'

'You will die if you do, Scull,' Chaloner warned. 'There is no escape plan, not now the boats have gone. You will all drown when the—'

He flinched in alarm as Olivia took aim at the ammunition box near his feet and pulled the trigger. Her gun flashed in the pan, so she hurled it away and made a grab for Hall's dag instead. At the same time, Scull put his flame to the touchhole and the gun crew jumped back. There was a tremendous bang and the ball was away. Moments later, there was an answering boom from outside, followed by a whistle and the sound of something heavy skipping past the Folly's bow.

Hall ran to a window. 'Christ God! It is a warship!'

'*Royal Charles*,' said Chaloner. 'It was a warning shot, telling you to surrender. Refuse, and she will blow you to pieces.'

Later, Chaloner would have no clear recollection of exactly what happened next. Olivia screamed at Scull to reload, knowing she had nothing to lose. He hesitated, so Gimonde fired at the ammunition box she had missed, although nothing happened, as the powder was wet. Scull and his cronies promptly abandoned their posts and rushed for the door. With only spent pistols left, Olivia, Gimonde and Hall were powerless to stop them.

'Help me, Gimonde!' Olivia shouted, wading towards the cannon. 'We can get one more shot away, and God will guide it to the Banqueting House. Come on!'

Gimonde grabbed a ball from the box and began to ram it home, while Hall hunted for dry powder and Olivia adjusted the sights. Chaloner left them to it. He slung Swaddell over his shoulder and tottered outside, struggling to move quickly in water that was now thigh-deep. He was about to jump overboard when he saw three boats rowing towards them. Lester's was in the lead.

'Back!' Chaloner yelled frantically. 'Go back!'

Two of the craft faltered, but Lester's continued and soon bumped alongside the Folly. Chaloner leapt in, Swaddell flopping limply across him.

'Go!' he screamed. 'Get away from the barge. *Now!*'

'Do it!' roared Lester at his crew, and Chaloner was glad he was a man of action, not one who demanded explanations first.

Obediently, his men began to haul on their oars for all they were worth. Chaloner opened his mouth to tell him what had happened, but there was a deep boom from inside the Folly, which demolished its port side. It listed sharply, then slid under the surface faster than he would have believed possible.

'Lord!' breathed Lester. 'What . . .'

'They neglected to sponge out the cannon before reloading,' said Chaloner tiredly. His leg gave a monstrous throb, reminding him of the last time he had seen a ball rammed home while there was still burning debris inside the barrel.

'Go and check for survivors,' Lester shouted to the other two boats; he glanced at Chaloner, who was looking sceptical. 'You never know.'

'The shot they managed to get off.' Chaloner stood to see where it had landed, but his knees were wobbly, so he sat back down before he toppled overboard. 'Did it hit White Hall?'

'Not even close. Incidentally, we fished that dwarf out of the river a few moments ago. He claims there is yet *another* plot to blow up Covent Garden – something about the dead having their revenge on a callous King. What does he mean?'

Chaloner's mind was a blank for a moment, then the brothers' back-up plan became horribly clear. 'The tombs! They must have put gunpowder in one of them. And if the blast opens the plague pit and scatters its contents . . . We have to stop it!'

Lester bellowed more orders, and within seconds, their boat was skimming towards the Savoy Wharf. His men hissed and groaned with the effort, but it was still too slow for Chaloner.

'We will be too late,' he whispered in despair. 'The ceremony must be almost over by now, and fuses will have been lit . . .'

It felt like an age before they reached the pier. Chaloner left Swaddell with the sailors, charging them to deliver him to Wiseman with all possible speed. Then he struggled up the steps, feeling every muscle burn with fatigue. He hurried up Ivie Lane, Lester at his heels.

The Strand was disconcertingly empty, and he wondered where everyone had gone. To church? Or were they outside the palaces, where other dangerous fanatics would almost certainly be waiting to capitalise on the trouble that Urban's Men had started?

Eventually, he and Lester reached the Piazza, breathing hard. It, too, was deserted, although the choir was singing a final, triumphantly processional piece by Tallis. In moments, the ceremony would be over and the congregation would leave. Obviously, the explosion to deprive the country of its monarch would happen before then . . .

'Maybe the King decided not to come,' panted Lester, looking around hopefully. 'I know he told your Earl he would, but we all know how fickle he can be.'

'He is here,' gasped Chaloner, nodding towards the distinctive gilded carriage that waited nearby. 'He must have wanted the gifts he was promised.'

'My Cropredy Bridge flag!' cried Lester, horrified anew. 'Blowing up the King is bad enough, but that banner is irreplaceable!'

'There!' barked Chaloner, stabbing his finger towards the Brouncker tomb. One of its doors was open and he recalled that the vault itself lay directly beneath the chancel – the perfect place for a bomb, as it would likely bring down the whole building. 'Wait around the corner, Sal. This does not need both of us.'

'It might,' countered Lester grimly. 'Lead on.'

Chaloner hobbled towards the mausoleum, cursing legs that did not move as quickly as he wanted. Then the choir stopped singing. There was a brief pause, followed by a fanfare played on a trumpet that was unusually loud, brassy and shrill. It was unquestionably Beale's, and Chaloner knew instinctively that it was the rebels' second signal – the one that would tell a fellow conspirator to ignite a fuse, should the first part of the plan fail.

He descended the steps as fast as he could, noting that there was a lamp burning at the bottom. At least he would not lose vital moments fiddling with a tinderbox. Then he saw the first of the powder kegs. It was stamped with the name of the ship it had come from: *Assurance*.

The fanfare ended. The service was over.

'We are too late,' whispered Lester hoarsely. 'Damn it, Tom! We have failed!'

Heart pounding, Chaloner reached the bottom, crossed the little landing and started up the stairs to the vault itself.

And stared in astonishment at the last three people on Earth he would have expected to see there together: Williamson, Kersey and Assistant Charnel-House Keeper Deakin.

'Good God!' cried Lester, shoving past him to gaze around in horror. 'There is enough powder in here to destroy half of Covent Garden.'

'But not today,' said Deakin quietly. He held up a fuse, its blackened end showing where it had been set alight and then pinched out.

'What . . .' began Chaloner, but so many questions surged into his mind that he did not know which to ask first.

'Deakin and I found these barrels when we came to bury Widow Fisher just after dawn,' explained Kersey. 'You asked us to put her down here, if you recall.'

'Yes,' acknowledged Chaloner. 'I did.'

'So I ran to fetch Mr Williamson,' Kersey went on, 'while Deakin stayed here, to monitor the situation. By the time I returned, he had taken a would-be regicide into custody.'

'Clifton,' said Deakin with a grin of pride. 'Former landlord of the Fleece. He was supposed to wait for some signal before lighting the fuse, but he was impatient – he set it going and bolted for the door. I stopped him, and he is now on his way to the Tower.'

'Deakin saved hundreds of lives today,' averred Kersey, clapping his assistant affectionately on the back. 'He is a hero.'

Chaloner turned to Williamson. 'How is it that you are here? I thought you would be trapped between the sabotaged bridges on the Dover Road.'

Williamson smiled thinly. 'After you had gone yesterday, I decided you were right – I *did* need to stay in the city to monitor the situation. I sent Riggs to Deptford instead.'

'And thank God you did,' muttered Kersey fervently. 'Because I doubt any of your minions would have taken

434

charge as you did. You knew exactly what to do with Clifton.'

Williamson gave a small bow to acknowledge the praise, then turned to indicate the barrels. 'The three of us were just trying to decide how best to dispose of these,' he told Chaloner and Lester. 'We cannot transport them openly through London. At least, not today. We do not want some other fanatic chancing his hand.'

'Leave that to the navy,' said Lester promptly. 'They are our property, after all.'

Chaloner felt his legs turn to jelly as he finally accepted that the danger was over. He sat heavily on a Brouncker coffin.

'It is fortunate that Deakin happens to be an expert with gunpowder,' said Kersey, beaming proudly at his assistant. '*I* would not have known how to prevent a massacre, but he did. It is because of *him* that Covent Garden is saved.'

Deakin blushed modestly. 'Well, we could not have a guest blown to kingdom come, could we? Poor Widow Fisher! It would not have been right.'

Lester laughed suddenly. 'So Widow Fisher is inadvertently responsible for saving the King's life? Hah! She would have been delighted!'

Chaloner seriously doubted she would.

Epilogue

A full month had passed since rebels and malcontents had tried to relieve the country of its King and his favourite debauchees. Blithely oblivious, His Majesty had moved back in to White Hall, and celebrated his return by enjoying not one performance of *Two Sisters and a Goat* but three, one after the other, all accompanied by plenty of wine and raucous laughter. At dawn, he retired to bed with one of the actresses, slept until mid-afternoon, and woke demanding to know what fun was next on the agenda.

His antics were reported with tight-lipped disapproval in taverns and coffee houses, and two questions were on everyone's lips: where were Urban and Pulcinella, and why had nothing happened at the Fast to improve the lot of Londoners? Resentment festered fiercely for several days, but it gradually faded, leaving everyone with a sense of anticlimax and disappointment.

Chaloner had not been there to see it – the Earl had sent him to Dover the next day with dispatches for van Goch. As the ambassador had already sailed, Chaloner followed him to the United Provinces. Such dedication was not really necessary, but he had experienced a sudden yearning to be away from England and its tribulations, just for a little while. He had arrived home the previous afternoon, and had spent the evening with Wiseman and Lester, being appraised of all that had happened after he had left.

Three sailors had been fished alive from the river after the barge had exploded, but the rest had been killed. Their bodies, along with those of Robert, Maurice, George, Scull and his son, Clun and poor, brave Fowler had washed ashore during the following days. Stoakes, Quartermain and what remained of Heemskerch had been quietly buried, while Widow Fisher occupied the best niche that the Brouncker tomb had to offer.

By some miracle, Olivia and Gimonde had survived the explosion, and were with Hudson, Clifton and the rest of Urban's Men in the Tower. Hudson brayed his innocence to all who would listen, but Clifton had discovered a sudden and unexpected loyalty to the Crown, and was telling Williamson everything about the plotters in return for a commuted sentence. The Spymaster listened to him during the day, and spent his evenings with Swaddell who, contrary to all expectation, was recovering well.

'Because you insisted that *I* tend him,' Wiseman informed Chaloner. 'All the other surgeons declared him to be a lost cause, but I saved his life. Do you want to know how?'

Chaloner did not, and what followed was grisly in the extreme, but he supposed Wiseman deserved to bask in the glory of his success. He found himself glad that the assassin was still in the world of the living, although he was not sure why.

The next morning he donned his best clothes and set off for Piccadilly, to tell the Earl that his dispatches had been safely delivered into van Goch's hands. He glanced around as he walked, noting that there were more private carriages on the roads than there had been before he had left – the wealthy elite returning now that the King was back. Shops and market stalls were open, and the city rang with noise, although there was still a long way to go before it would reach pre-plague levels. And when an old woman sneezed, those nearby gave her a very wide berth.

He heard snippets of conversation as he went: the Queen had recently miscarried again, and the Royal Society had enjoyed a lecture on felt-making. Lent would begin the following Wednesday, and the newsbooks had printed a statement from the King, who urged his subjects to observe it with fasting and prayer. Most Londoners declared that they would rather follow *his* example, which meant the weeks leading up to Easter would be a lot less gloomy than usual.

Chaloner arrived at Clarendon House, where Wren greeted him with a friendly smile.

'I am glad to see you home, Tom,' the secretary said, gripping his hand warmly. 'You were missed. We kept fearing some terrible crime would be committed, and one of us would be ordered to solve it. Now the responsibility will be yours again, thank God.'

Chaloner supposed that plying his skills as an investigator was one way to make himself popular with his colleagues. He entered My Lord's Lobby to find the Earl in a very good mood.

'The King remains delighted with that flag you found,' he said happily. 'And he touched my head in a *most* affectionate manner yesterday. I do not suppose you know of anything else I can give him, do you? It is an excellent way of staying in his good graces, although a hundred pounds *was* rather steep.'

'No,' replied Chaloner shortly, aware that Lester had given the money to Fowler's family – six tearful children, who sobbed that they would rather have their father back.

'Pity. Of course, you failed miserably in the other tasks I set you. You never did learn who killed Olivia, why Quartermain died, or how *Assurance* sank. You also neglected to protect Heemskerch from assassins, and the rebellion you predicted did not come to pass.'

Williamson had decided that no one should ever know how close rebels had come to bombarding White Hall and killing the King with stolen cannon, lest it encouraged others to try. Thus the Earl had been given a very watered-down version of the truth. However, Chaloner was unwilling for the Earl to think him completely inept. He settled for a compromise.

'Actually, sir, I do have answers. Olivia's fate came about because she fell in with the wrong crowd; Quartermain died from drinking his own King's Gold; and *Assurance* sank because its captain was incompetent, greedy and unscrupulous.'

'I suppose those explanations are acceptable,' conceded the Earl. 'And Heemskerch?'

'He offered secrets in return for safe passage, but he reneged – the papers he gave us were worthless. He got exactly what he paid for.'

'Well, that is one way of looking at it. Which leaves the rebellion that never was. I was on tenterhooks all day at the Fast, but nothing happened. People muttered and grumbled, but they always do. This time was no different from all the others.'

And it was that sort of complacency which would let it happen all over again, thought Chaloner acidly. The King and his wastrels were making no attempt to moderate their behaviour, so it would not be long before someone else told Londoners that they deserved better.

The Earl was silent for a while, then grinned vengefully. 'I have just had some good news about one of my enemies – Harry Brouncker. It has emerged that *he* gave the order for the fleet to abandon the chase after the Battle of Lowestoft. There is solid testimony from a Dr Merrett, who witnessed the whole affair.'

'Unfortunately, Merrett is dead. Murdered by Brouncker, in fact.'

'Yes, but before Brouncker got him, Merrett wrote a letter to his sister, and she has made it public. It reveals that Brouncker gave the order out of cowardice, not to protect the Duke. Moreover, Brouncker's brother and several navy clerks claim they heard him confess as much to a third party. In light of such damning evidence, Brouncker has been exiled.'

Chaloner smiled to himself. It had not been easy to persuade Merrett's sister that the letter was genuine. He had mimicked the doctor's handwriting perfectly, but it had been a lot harder to capture his individual turn of phrase. She had been deeply suspicious when he had delivered it to her on his way to the United Provinces, and he had left her house thinking his plan would fail. He was glad it had not.

'Incidentally, I do not think I ever thanked you for finding that trumpet,' said the Earl, 'even if you did cut it rather fine. Wren told me that it was because of your efforts that he was able to present it to me in the end.'

Chaloner started to deny it, knowing that Wren had told the lie because he had been unsettled by the notion that 'Urban' might use the money for rebellion, and aimed to distance himself from his error of judgement. But Urban was safely in gaol, so why not take the credit for something that had pleased the Earl? Especially as the Earl was less than impressed with the results of his other investigations.

'Was the King pleased with it?' he asked.

The Earl winced. 'Nor really. He told me it sounded like a donkey in labour, so thank God I had the Cropredy Bridge flag in reserve. He took the trumpet anyway, because it was silver. It is already melted down, and he is turning it into a necklace for Lady Castlemaine.'

The news made Chaloner glad he had spent so little time looking for the thing.

Londoners had been sorry to lose their iconic Floating Coffee House to an exploding barrel of lamp oil, and had petitioned for a replacement. A barge had been purchased and a hut built on top of it, almost identical to its predecessor. No one knew who owned it, but it was Deakin who greeted customers with a long-spouted jug. Chaloner went to visit it when he left Clarendon House, and laughed when he saw the ex-charnel-house keeper's assistant's green face.

'He will become accustomed to the movement in time,' said Swaddell, as Chaloner sat next to him. One of the assassin's arms was in a sling and he had still not lost his deathly pallor.

'But will his patrons? Lester tells me that sea-officers are reluctant to come here now, so Deakin's customers will be landsmen, who may not appreciate having their coffee slopping into their laps.'

'Fortunately, his victory over the hangman has made him famous, so people are willing to endure the inconvenience to hear how he did it.' Swaddell smirked. 'And he has promised to keep us appraised of any seditious talk.'

'Oh, I see,' said Chaloner heavily. '*Williamson* owns this place, and he offered Deakin a choice: work for him or be returned to the executioner as the convicted felon he is.'

'Not so! The coffee house is a reward for saving the King's life.'

'Yes, there is no doubt that Deakin is a hero. It is Williamson's motives that I question. Or would you rather I referred to him as Joe?'

Swaddell winced. 'Please do not. It reminds me of that villainous Robert.' He glanced around quickly to ensure that no one was within earshot and lowered his voice. 'I broke them out of the Tower two nights ago, by the way – Olivia, Gimonde and the rest of their troupe. We cannot execute them for wanting the King's wastrels dispatched, not when most Londoners feel the same way.'

Chaloner gaped at him. 'But what if they try it again?'

'They promised to leave the country and never return. I believe them. A trusted henchman escorted them to the coast, and I doubt we shall ever see them again.'

Chaloner continued to stare. 'You were not even tempted to cut their throats?'

'Of course I was tempted! Who would not be, when

each was alone in a cell and the guards were in my pay? But that would make me a hypocrite, so I opted for mercy instead. Williamson does not know my role in their escape, naturally.'

Chaloner was not surprised that Swaddell had chosen to keep his antics to himself, sure the Spymaster would be livid if he ever found out. 'What about Hudson and Clifton?'

'Now they *are* dead, and good riddance. But Olivia and her friends should be in the United Provinces by now, where Urban and Pulcinella will make regular and frequent appearances in all the major cities.'

'Clever,' acknowledged Chaloner grudgingly. 'I imagine they were delighted by this unexpected chance to continue their work with the downtrodden poor?'

'They were, and if they cause Grand Pensionary de Witt half as much trouble as they caused us, I shall be well pleased.'

'What about the three sailors who survived the blast? Not to mention the ones who were stationed on shore, waiting for the Thompsons' signals and orders?'

'The navy is desperate for trained seamen, and Harman and Cox know how to manage malcontents. *Royal Charles* sailed with a full complement of crew. You did the same for Fowler and his cronies, so do not look at me askance.'

'Fowler was not an insurgent.'

'No, but he murdered his captain, which is just as bad.'

They were silent for a while, Chaloner sipping his coffee and thinking it was a lot better than the Rainbow's. However, he would not be transferring his allegiance any time soon. The Folly held too many unpleasant memories, and taking a boat back and forth was hardly convenient.

Moreover, it would be reckless to frequent a place that was owned by the Spymaster General, particularly for someone in his line of work.

'I am in your debt,' said Swaddell eventually. 'You saved my life.'

'You exaggerate. It was not a—'

'We now share an even deeper bond,' Swaddell went on, and grinned wolfishly. 'And I told Williamson that you were a valuable asset. He agreed, so we shall be partners again the next time England is threatened by dangerous radicals.'

'Will we?' gulped Chaloner. 'Crikey!'

Williamson sat in his office and stared through the window at the heads outside Westminster Hall. Their hair undulated in the breeze, and their teeth shone brown-white in their pitch-blackened faces. He had been shocked to learn that some of the last lot were made of wax, and had hastened to replace them with real ones. It would not do for Londoners to think that traitors were given a decent burial.

His eye lit on the three skulls in the middle, and he could not resist a smile. It would be his private joke for as long as they remained there – Robert, Maurice and George, who had gone headless into their graves. He had not, for one moment, been deceived by their trans-parent protestations of friendship, even if Robert had been able to converse intelligently on moths. He had guessed at once that they were Dutch spies, and had used them accordingly, leaving false intelligence for Robert to pass to de Witt. None of the brothers had suspected a thing.

Unfortunately, he could not tell anyone else how

cunning he had been, because some of the leaked information was still working its magic in The Hague. He hated being thought of as sad and gullible, but it could not be helped, and the truth would emerge eventually. Then everyone would be forced to acknowledge his superior talents.

He dragged his gaze away from the skulls and looked instead at the documents from Heemskerch's final parcel. He was mortified that they had transpired to be useless, especially as Thurloe had warned him that might be the case. The key in Bunyan's pamphlet had worked on none of the coded letters, except one, which read: *Spymaster Williamson is a credulous ass who believes every stupid word I feed him*. The clerk who had decoded it was dead, and no one else would ever see the message.

Luckily, the documents that Chaloner had stolen from behind Beuningen's skirting board had proved to be far more valuable, so Williamson had simply claimed that *these* were from Heemskerch. It was better than having everyone think that he had been played for a fool. Chaloner and Lester knew the truth, confessed when he had been near the end of his tether with anxiety and overwork, but they could be trusted not to contradict him – Chaloner, because he was an experienced intelligencer used to keeping secrets, and Lester because the whole affair disgusted him so much that he had vowed never to speak of it again.

But despite the Heemskerch debacle, Williamson was generally satisfied with the way things had turned out. A man skilled in explosives, like Deakin, would be useful to him in the future, especially as Deakin knew his lucrative coffee house could be taken away just as easily as it had been given. Deakin offered a viable alternative to

445

Swaddell, whom he sensed was drifting away from him. Of course, that was Chaloner's fault: the assassin had never questioned orders before they had started working together. And as for Swaddell's recent insistence on honesty . . . well, that was downright perverse.

Perhaps Deakin could eliminate them both – Chaloner for being an irritating nuisance who knew too many awkward truths, and Swaddell because he was far too dangerous a man to have as an enemy.

But not yet. He would wait a while, and see what the future held.

Historical Note

Intrigue in Covent Garden is based on several true events. In 1666, England was at war with the United Provinces, which was bad news for a country still reeling from the devastating impact of the plague. The King and his Court had fled the city the previous summer, but returned to White Hall after Christmas, timing their arrival to coincide with the 'Fast and Humiliation' of 30 January, when all churches held services to mark the anniversary of Charles I's execution. Records reveal that there were many complaints about the rambunctious revels that were enjoyed in White Hall that evening.

His Majesty and his followers were not received very warmly when they returned from their self-imposed exile, and there was considerable resentment about them high-tailing it to safety at the first sign of a bubo. The criticism was not unreasonable, as the government had left the city with no proper plans for coping with the crisis, let alone bringing it to an end, and no means of dealing with the mounting piles of dead.

There was a tremendous gale around 22/23 January. Samuel Pepys records it in his diary as 'the Great Storm', and the following week, *The Oxford Gazette* was full of news from coastal towns, telling of all the ships that had been lost or driven aground. And there was an embarrassing naval defeat at Vågen, Bergen's port, in August 1665, when the English fleet tried to attack a convoy of Dutch merchantmen. The King of Denmark had secretly sanctioned the action, but official orders failed to arrive, so the resident Norwegians elected to side with the Dutch. A month later, Denmark declared war on England.

In June 1665, shortly before Vågen, the Battle of Lowestoft was fought. It has been noted that the English could have delivered a decisive and final blow to the Dutch had the pursuit not been called off early. Nothing much was said about it at the time, but scandal broke in 1667, when it emerged that Henry (Harry) Brouncker was the courtier responsible for giving the order. The Duke of York, Admiral of the Fleet and heir to the throne, was said to have been asleep at the time, and Brouncker convinced Captain Sir John Harman and sailing master John Cox to shorten sail. All this happened on the Duke's flagship, *Royal Charles*.

The full truth about Lowestoft will never be known, although it seems peculiar that York should have dozed off after what must have been a fraught and desperate day. It was rumoured that Brouncker was acting on the orders of York's wife Anne (the Earl of Clarendon's daughter), who hoped to be Queen one day and so wanted her husband to stay alive. Brouncker was impeached by Parliament, after which he fled to France. He was later pardoned, and became Cofferer to the Household in 1679.

Brouncker was an unattractive character. According to Pepys, he was 'a pestilential rogue [and] an Atheist'.

He ran a brothel and pimped for the Duke of York, and about the only positive thing written about him was that he played a good game of chess. His brother Sir William was a Navy Commissioner, who kept a mistress named Abigail Williams.

Other people in the book were also real. Captain John Stoakes died in 1665. He was master of *Assurance*, which was lost to a 'gust of wind'. He was not on board at the time, and it transpired that the ship had not been properly secured to the pier. Twenty sailors were drowned, although it was the loss of his clothes and money that Pepys later heard Stoakes bemoaning. The sinking actually occurred in Woolwich, not London, some years before. She was weighed within a few days.

Captain Lester was master of *Swiftsure* in the 1660s.

Michiel van Goch and Coenraad van Beuningen were Dutch diplomats active in the mid-1660s. Beuningen was highly talented, and thought to be bipolar. Poor van Goch was not talented at all, and is generally considered to have been well out of his depth in London while the two countries were at war.

Simon Beale was Trumpeter in Ordinary to the King. He was appointed in 1660, and did indeed lose a valuable silver instrument, although not until 1676. He was described as State Trumpeter during the interregnum, and played at Cromwell's funeral.

Dr Christopher Merrett was a physician and a member of the Royal Society, who did not die until 1695. Richard Wiseman was Surgeon to the Person, and owned a house in James Street, Covent Garden, in the mid-1660s. He had been Master of the Company of Barber-Surgeons the previous year, and was famous for making surgeons more respectable. His colleague William Quartermain was physician to both the King and Clarendon. Quartermain died in 1667.

Matthew Wren was Clarendon's secretary in 1665; he was the son of the bishop of the same name, and a cousin of Christopher Wren the architect.

William Clifton was the proprietor of the Fleece from about 1651 until at least 1676. He had a servant named Amey Watts.

Pietro Gimonde was an Italian puppeteer, whom Pepys saw perform in 1662. It is thought that Gimonde had an early version of what grew into the popular Punch and Judy Show. His character was Pulcinella, character-ised by a long nose and squeaky voice, considered to be a subversive maverick. Other entertainers of the time were Jacob Hall, a 'rope-dancer', who is said to have had an affair with Lady Castlemaine, the King's mistress; and Walter Clun, an actor who was murdered in 1664.

Jeffrey Hudson, the 'Queen's Dwarf', was a favourite of Henrietta Maria, queen consort of Charles I. He was clever and ambitious, and soon tired of being a Court pet. His prickly temper led him to challenge another courtier to a duel, during which he fatally shot his oppon-ent in the head. He was exiled and spent the next thirty-eight years in relative obscurity.

There were actually four Thompson brothers – Colonel George, Major Robert, Maurice and Sir William. George lost a leg during the civil wars, and was suspected of disaffection at the Restoration, but made his peace and was later appointed to the committee that looked into the finances for the Dutch war. Maurice and Robert were accused of spying for the Dutch in 1665. William was an alderman, Member of Parliament and successful merchant. All four were reputed to have made vast fortunes during the Commonwealth, from dealing with lands seized from the bishops.

Joseph Williamson was in charge of the intelligence services in 1665, and although an able man, his character led him to make few friends. He was prickly, aloof, arrogant and ambitious, and was not trusted by his contemporaries. Despite his flaws, he was considered to be an accomplished civil servant, who survived the uncertain world of Restoration politics until the Popish Plot of 1678–1681. He had a secretary named John Swaddell.

The Chaloner Series

THE BARTHOLOMEW SERIES

TWENTIETH ANNIVERSARY EDITION
SUSANNA GREGORY
A PLAGUE ON BOTH YOUR HOUSES
THE FIRST CHRONICLE OF MATTHEW BARTHOLOMEW

TWENTIETH ANNIVERSARY EDITION
SUSANNA GREGORY
AN UNHOLY ALLIANCE
THE SECOND CHRONICLE OF MATTHEW BARTHOLOMEW

TWENTIETH ANNIVERSARY EDITION
SUSANNA GREGORY
A BONE OF CONTENTION
THE THIRD CHRONICLE OF MATTHEW BARTHOLOMEW

SUSANNA GREGORY
A DEADLY BREW
THE FOURTH CHRONICLE OF MATTHEW BARTHOLOMEW

SUSANNA GREGORY
A WICKED DEED
THE FIFTH CHRONICLE OF MATTHEW BARTHOLOMEW

SUSANNA GREGORY
A MASTERLY MURDER
THE SIXTH CHRONICLE OF MATTHEW BARTHOLOMEW

SUSANNA GREGORY
AN ORDER FOR DEATH
THE SEVENTH CHRONICLE OF MATTHEW BARTHOLOMEW

SUSANNA GREGORY
A SUMMER OF DISCONTENT
THE EIGHTH CHRONICLE OF MATTHEW BARTHOLOMEW

SUSANNA GREGORY
A KILLER IN WINTER
THE NINTH CHRONICLE OF MATTHEW BARTHOLOMEW

SUSANNA GREGORY
THE HAND OF JUSTICE
THE TENTH CHRONICLE OF MATTHEW BARTHOLOMEW

SUSANNA GREGORY
THE MARK OF A MURDERER
THE ELEVENTH CHRONICLE OF MATTHEW BARTHOLOMEW

SUSANNA GREGORY
THE TARNISHED CHALICE
THE TWELFTH CHRONICLE OF MATTHEW BARTHOLOMEW

SUSANNA GREGORY
TO KILL OR CURE
THE THIRTEENTH CHRONICLE OF MATTHEW BARTHOLOMEW

SUSANNA GREGORY
THE DEVIL'S DISCIPLES
THE FOURTEENTH CHRONICLE OF MATTHEW BARTHOLOMEW

SUSANNA GREGORY
A VEIN OF DECEIT
THE FIFTEENTH CHRONICLE OF MATTHEW BARTHOLOMEW

SUSANNA GREGORY
THE KILLER OF PILGRIMS
THE SIXTEENTH CHRONICLE OF MATTHEW BARTHOLOMEW

SUSANNA GREGORY
MYSTERY IN THE MINSTER
THE SEVENTEENTH CHRONICLE OF MATTHEW BARTHOLOMEW

SUSANNA GREGORY
MURDER BY THE BOOK
THE EIGHTEENTH CHRONICLE OF MATTHEW BARTHOLOMEW

SUSANNA GREGORY
THE LOST ABBOT
THE NINETEENTH CHRONICLE OF MATTHEW BARTHOLOMEW

SUSANNA GREGORY
DEATH OF A SCHOLAR
THE TWENTIETH CHRONICLE OF MATTHEW BARTHOLOMEW

SUSANNA GREGORY
A POISONOUS PLOT
THE TWENTY-FIRST CHRONICLE OF MATTHEW BARTHOLOMEW

SUSANNA GREGORY
A GRAVE CONCERN
THE TWENTY-SECOND CHRONICLE OF MATTHEW BARTHOLOMEW

SUSANNA GREGORY
THE HABIT OF MURDER
THE TWENTY-THIRD CHRONICLE OF MATTHEW BARTHOLOMEW

SUSANNA GREGORY
THE SANCTUARY MURDERS
THE TWENTY-FOURTH CHRONICLE OF MATTHEW BARTHOLOMEW